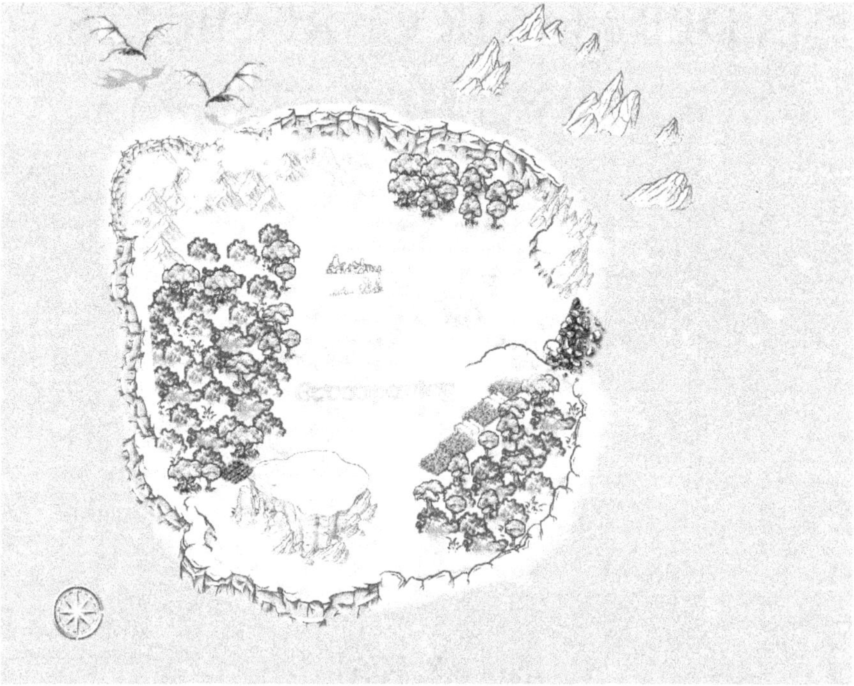

ELDER MAGIK CHRONICLES DESCENDANTS

Ruby M. Knight

To my beautiful daughter who inspired me to keep pursuing my dream of publishing my work. My sister who was always there for me. Thank you. This is for you both.

Elder Magik Chronicles Descendants
Elder Magik Chronicles Darkness rising
Elder Magik Chronicles Finale
Elder Magik chronicles Descendants, Darkness rising and
Finale

Copyright November 2023.
Published by Lulu Publishing.
Printed in the USA

ISBN paperback 979-8-89660-870-7

Cover art created by Ruby M. Knight
Map created by Ruby M. Knight

Sometimes someone isn't ready to see the brightside.
Sometimes they need to sit with the shadow first.
So be a friend and sit with them.
Make the darkness beautiful.

Victoria Erickson

Dante

"Are you going to sit here watching the graveyard all night? I thought we were here for closure." Shadow stated as I shook my head watching the cemetery. Feeling tired I looked up at him over my shoulder.

"I am making sure none of my father's men are here before I walk in."

"I sense nothing." Shifting his feet he nosed my shoulder to visit my father's grave. Sighing heavily I nodded walking into the graveyard keeping my senses wide open. The grass was fairly springy telling me it had rained just recently. The air was heavy with moisture as well. That made this feel all that much more foreboding. Kneeling down in front of the stone it felt real that he was gone. That he would never again whip me to a bloody pulp or give an order to kill.

"You deserved death. You should never have worked for the master at the rank you were. Mom and Gabby deserved better than you. We all deserved better than you. All I wanted was for you to be proud of me. Like you were Matt. In the end that just was never going to happen. You despised me. I never understood why. You will turn over in that grave when I tell you that I am seeking out the council. I am turning against you. Good bye."

"*Dante. You're surrounded.*" Shadow's voice told me as the hair on the back of my neck stood up. Slowly I stood at full height my muscles tensing as I looked up at the men around me. Holding my hands in the air showing I would not fight them.

1

"Dante. Where have you been?" My sword instructor, and father's second in command Theo asked slowly walking closer to where I stood. His face showing concern though his thoughts expressed none. That was the bitch of my powers. I could choose to know a person's thoughts. Most of the time I despised it. But it had proven useful when push came to shove. I had to choose my words carefully as I kept my peripheral vision open.

"Traveling. I wanted to explore the world after being confined to training most of my life. Why? Is something wrong?" Theo stepped closer leaning over to talk so we were not overheard.

"The Master thought that maybe you had ran out on him. You are the rightful leader of the Syracuse branch with your father gone. You need to stay and take your place." Glancing to my sides the rest of the men had began moving in closer. They knew what I had in mind. I had to keep them talking until I could figure a way out.

"Shadow. They don't know you can shift. Any kind of big cat would be helpful. Attack when you feel the time is right. I'm going to try to stall them."

"I know what to do." He responded back causing my muscles to tense further yet. The men began moving closer slowly.

"Dante. We are not here to hurt you." Theo was trying his best to keep his voice calm. But this was one of few times I could feel how desperately I needed to leave. Laughing drily I stepped back.

"Right. There are ten to fifteen of you surrounding me. Yet you are not here to hurt me. Sorry. But I am not too convinced." My muscles tensed like coil ready to spring at any given second. Come on Shadow. Anytime.

"Dante. Stop moving." Theo growled causing me to look at him scowling.

"Theo. I am not going to stay. Even if I did. You and I both know I could not lead my father's men."

"They respect you." I scoffed angrily.

"No. They respected my father. They have none for me and you know it. I'm sure my brother would be more than happy. Ask him." Theo huffed impatiently.

"Dammit Dante." He grabbed my arm hard at the elbow pulling me up to face him. Theo's face was turning red with anger. His patience had never been great. "You are next in line. You will lead them. I also know your brother does not make split second decisions as well as you do. In the year you have been gone he has shown us that." Angrily I pushed him away adjusting myself once I was free. Theo shook his head scowling as he did the same.

"Maybe not. But at least my father was proud of him. He never had to beat on Matt like he did me."

"Matt is not a leader Dante. He was trained by your father to kill and that was all." Shaking my head I backed away slowly.

"No. I will not lead. I want no part of this. He's gone. Everything he worked for is gone with him. Just let it go. I am. I'm starting over somewhere new." Sighing Theo shook his head looking disappointed.

"Sorry. I cannot allow that to happen." Twisting around I drew Guardian fighting the men attempting to grab me to take me prisoner. A loud roar caught my attention as Shadow burst into the fray as a panther tearing everyone he touched to shreds.

"Run!" Shadow yelled as I broke free from the fight running as hard as I could. Next to me Shadow appeared as we both ran. In a flash he was back to a horse stopping long enough to mount up running away together.

For days we ran as far away from home as we could manage. Our only saving grace was the fact we had already survived over a year this way. We had learned years ago how to stay dry when it was torrential rainfall, high winds, and cool when it was terribly hot. While traveling the first night I had called for Izabella to no avail to let her know I had run. She had tried to convince me to leave for years but I never could do it. Hell. I should not have ran away now. I should have just let them kill me.

"Dante. Be easy on yourself." Shadow told me sternly as he stood over my shoulder. I had set up a camp when we passed the last town in Texas. I was sitting on a large log near the fire I had built when we made camp. The fire crackled nicely as the sun was setting with it the air grew colder.

"I should never have ran. They will just come looking for me and kill me anyways." Snorting angrily he pushed on my shoulder as I shook my head dismally.

"You have never had it in you to be like them. If we could find Izabella and tell her"

"Tell her what exactly?" I asked him angrily. "That I need to be protected from my father's army because I ran away? I have been calling for her since I left Shadow. She has not answered or showed up."

"You really need to learn to be more patient." Rolling my eyes irritably I nodded in agreement.

"I'm horribly aware."

"Maybe she is actually busy. You know time on the island where she lives works differently. What feels like days here is only minutes there."

"Fair enough. We'll just keep going east. Maybe we will bump into someone eventually."

"Someone? Or Izabella is who you are hoping for?" Glancing up to where he rested I frowned.

"What is that supposed to mean?" Snorting he stepped closer.

"What I mean is we have lived freely for the past year. You did not have to deal with taking commands or going places you have no desire to go. Are you sure you are ready to help the council?"

"Yes. I sure as hell don't want The Master and his followers running the world." Snorting he nodded his head before glancing up.

"I will remember you said that for a later time." Confused I turned to look at him.

"Why?"

"You have a hard time letting go of old habits my friend." Growing aggravated I sat up turning to look at him.

"What are you getting at? I think you have been around Izabella far too much. You're beginning to sound like her." He tossed his head before staring at me.

"Once you begin to help them. You cannot withhold information from them. You cannot pick and choose what you tell them or they will just think you are there to spy on them." Sighing I knew he was right.

"A few more days. I think we need to keep heading east. If this war is heading where I think it is the council will be sending recruiters everywhere to retrieve anyone they can left with power." Tossing his head in response we both settled down for the night. Shadow turned into a panther laying by the fire curling up around me protectively. I laid wide awake looking up at the stars. They were shining so very bright tonight.

"Rest Dante. You are going to need it." Nodding in agreement I turned in my sleeping bag quickly falling asleep.

Maylee

I was opening the door to my truck so that my sister and I could leave the fairgrounds. Carl, a member of the board for the show grounds along with the judge of our lovely horse show walked up in front of me.

"Maylee. I'm sorry. But after that stunt your sister pulled the board has decided to ban you both from competing here." My anger flared immediately knowing the reason they were actually banning us.

"Are you kidding me! The stunt my sister pulled? What about the girls that were surrounding her? They were threatening her and her horse!" Pausing I calmed momentarily to indicate him. "But I am so sure you didn't see that. Now did you?" Keep your temper in check I told myself. There are still kids here. Carl stood there looking dumbfounded stuttering his response to the best of his abilities or lack there of.

"Um, well. No, I guess we did not see that" Knowing he did not know what to say to that I cut him off.

"Of course not. I did not think so. Now what? You banned us. Congratulations on that. But you listen. They will not be happy with just that. They want us gone for good. Well that is just too damn bad! We are sticking around. If those girls would actually get off of their asses and practice half as hard as we do. Than they would be able to compete with us without trying to get rid of us." I turned to leave seething when the judge walked up to the two of us with a bemused look on his face.

6

"I know it is not my place to voice my opinion, but she is right. I have watched them compete all day. They work hard. And from what I have saw today, all of the work. Their trainer is not here riding for them between classes, shouting instruction from the rail or here at all." I looked at him over my sunglasses. Impressive. He had noticed all that in a few hours of competing. Smirking slightly I looked over to Carl.

"And why did you not think of that yourself?" I sneered at him before looking back to the judge. "Thank you for defending us when no one else would. But. We can handle ourselves."

"I can tell." Turning he smirked at Carl before walking back to the pen to finish judging the show. With one final contemptuous look at Carl I stepped into the truck heading for home.

This had certainly been a day from hell. And I do not mean the town my sister and I hail from. Annabelle and I show horses. Today we were at a local competition that the grounds finally had the funding to put on. I had sat at meetings pulling for them to have this show because the closest place other than this one was fifty miles away. When they finally did decide to have it. The showground's board asked that my sister and I did not make an appearance. So I argued. And won. After all that's what I do best. Fight and win. I will explain why they did not want us there in the first place.

My sister and I have shown on the Quarter Horse Circuit for five years now. We have a lot of points. Not that big of a deal. We just want to hang out with our friends and have fun. I was the leader of a local 4-H club. Most of our horses were registered with the Quarter Horse Association. The only one who is not is grandpa Charles's horse Drake. He is actually double registered, with Quarter Horse and Paint Horse

Association. All those shows meant to us was good friends, tough competitors, and amazing horses.

Anyway. Back to today. We are on our way to the local fairgrounds that was holding the show that I fought to have. This is what happens when we pull in and park the trailer. Dirty looks in our direction along with people talking as we walked by. And of course the original trash talk behind our backs. This was going to be a long day. Glancing over at Annabelle I could sense her anger building almost a mirror of my own.

"Do you want to go home?" Scowling she looked over at me.

"No! That is what they want us to do. And it's not going to happen. I'm not leaving until I want to." Smirking I nodded. I had to admire her courage as she was seventeen years old. She had only turned seventeen a week ago. Smirking at her response she was much like myself four years ago.

"It sure is a beautiful day to show." Keeping my voice light I glanced to my sister. She smiled wide shaking her head. It was true. The weather could not have been more perfect. Seventy degrees with no wind, some cloud cover and no humidity. Unheard of this early in April.

The only people that were not treating us like garbage were the people in my 4-H club. Quite a few of them had turned up to attend the show. Out of twenty kids at least twelve were here. We all had the most fun when we went for trail rides, and an occasional weekender. Annabelle always had to take our project horse Delilah instead of her show horse Oscerr. He was just too freaked out outside the arena. Trail rides were always relaxing. I could use one about now with all this going on around us. We had sailed through most of the day without anything too horrible happening other than dirty looks.

I was leaving the show pen from Hunter Hack which was my favorite class. Hunter hack is where you jump two consecutive jumps, usually straight bars only eighteen to twenty four inches high. After everyone has a turn you ride one direction around the pen. The jumps they had today were like loping poles for my horse. That is because he is so tall. My horse's name is Rocki. He is jet black, sixteen two hands tall with only a sunburst looking star on his forehead.

For those of you who do not know what a hand is. It is how you measure a horse's height at their withers. The withers is the bony bump between the neck and back. A hand is four inches. So at sixteen hands two inches, Rocki is five foot six at the withers. Not fun when he bucks you off which has only happened once. Thank god. He can actually jump over five feet, but only hunter hack at this show.

As I am walking out the exit gate I notice that Annabelle is surrounded by a group of mean looking girls. Uh Oh. This could turn ugly real quick. Now. Annabelle did not look worried. I certainly was not worried about her. More for the girls surrounding them. My sister and Oscerr could defend themselves well enough. You see. Oscerr is a world class kicker. Only when he wants to be of course. And right now he was angry as his ears were pinned flat with his nose wrinkled up.

I overheard the girls telling Annabelle if she did not scratch her next class they would hurt Oscerr. As if, I said to myself almost laughing as I watched everything unfold. That was not the most intelligent thing to say when a horse understands plain english very well. Oscerr flattened his ears to his head again wrinkling his nose baring his teeth as to say bring it! One girl kicked her horse toward Annabelle raising her crop whip she had used for hunter hack. Shifting her weight pulling her reins back queued Oscerr to unleash a couple good kicks. She had unintentionally taught him this trick years ago.

Oscerr is also a big boy at sixteen hands even. That makes him five foot four at the withers. He is sorrel. Or reddish brown I should say, with a crescent moon shaped star and a white sock that extends up to his knee on his front right leg. He is very muscular, and broad making it a terrible idea to make him angry.

I would know. He kicked me last summer because I walked behind him at a show. I did not scare him. He knew I was there. He looked to see where I was aiming to kick. I stayed by the gate as I watched Oscerr kick at the girl who had raised the whip at him. He missed. Which actually infuriated him further yet as he hopped up with his front end shaking his head. The group scattered. The girl screamed and Annabelle looked at her angrily.

"Than stay away from me! Do not threaten my horse because next time he will not miss. And I will let him bite too."

Needless to say they left her alone after that. There were angry outbursts from parents about Annabelle's horse kicking at their children's horses. And missed I might add. Walking Oscerr over to the practice pen Annabelle kept him away from the crowded make up pen. The make up pen is where everyone groups together to wait for their class to go into the show pen.

Keeping an eye on them I followed still riding Rocki. She looked up to see who it was relaxing when it was me.

"Did you see that? They will not leave me alone or back off! Did you see what they were going to do?" It was frustrating that we had to constantly defend ourselves like this. Sighing I nodded glancing to the make up pen.

"Yes, I saw. Maybe you should have let him actually hit the target though." I smiled continuing. "Maybe it would have taught them a valuable lesson in the fact horses can still do what they want when they want." The anger on my sister's face flickered away like a burning out light bulb as she looked down at Oscerr.

She was checking to make sure they had not hurt him. Even I would have came unglued if they had actually hurt him. I looked down at him too. He was watching the girl who had raised the whip at him very intently. That gleam in his eye was one that I recognized all too well. Years ago I had a horse that only I could ride. Not all that common with most horses. This one would throw everyone else and I mean anyone besides me. He had even attempted to throw my sister, but I ran to him grabbing his bridle before he could do it.

His name was Danny. He was the same height as Rocki, only a bay. A bay is a reddish brown color with a black mane, tail, legs from knees and hocks down, and points of their face. He was really strong. For example; five years ago at a local show three girls boxed me in. Until that day I did not know horses could have such a temper. Danny wrung his tail, pinned his ears, wrinkled his nose and ground the bit with his teeth. The whole time I was in that class I could actually feel how tense he was through my saddle. That could be a terrible feeling when the horse under you is angry.

These girls thought they had a good plan. Make one of your toughest competitors look bad so that they could win the class. Well, that was not a good move. At least not with Danny. By the end of the class I was wondering if the bit was going to break. We left the ring from that class which had been hunt seat equitation. Equitation is based on the rider as far as how they handle their horse, how well they sit in the saddle and the ability to present their horse to the judge. Danny kept watching something but I did not pay any attention to it as I kept him moving around. Entering our next class it was hunt seat pleasure. Pleasure classes are based on the horse's movement at each gait such as walk, trot and canter for Hunt seat. And their ability to transition to each gait as asked.

"Trot please trot" Came the announcer's voice. Danny began trotting when I asked but I could tell he was holding back some power. Now that is not a good feeling. It's almost as bad as when you're riding a horse that wants to explode but you don't know when, what they will do or how hard they will do it. So, as we go around the pen I realized with a jolt that all three riders were directly in front of me. Oh great! In my head I kept repeating the same thing. Please don't ask. Please don't ask. Of course they had to ask.

"Extend the trot please, extend the trot" I almost lost my balance as Danny powered forward to catch up to the first rider. Now Danny's extended trot is like watching the grand prix dressage horses. That boy could sit back onto his rear and flip his front feet out like it was nobody's business. So we trot up beside the first horse. Looking for the judge she turned away from where we were. Danny cut off the horse beside us and wham! The brakes hit hard making me fly forward a little onto his neck. He tilted his head back at the horse like what now? As suddenly as he stopped he powered off again repeating the process to the other two riders that had boxed us in our previous class. Here was the greatest part. The judge never caught me doing anything but caught all three of them stopped.

After the class was over we left the ring. The same three riders walked up to me.

"That was not fair! You cut us off and did not even get caught!" I stared back at them. With a scowl on my face sitting back in my saddle crossing my arms over my chest.

"Well, maybe next time you will know better than to box me in." They were not happy with that answer, but what could I do? He had grabbed the bit and I had no control over what he did. Oh well. I led him back to his stall to untack him. Holy shit! The bit had huge gauges from where he had chomped his teeth from being so angry. I had to replace it before I could ride hunt seat again. Unfortunately I no longer had him. He had to be euthanized over three years ago. It was devastating to say the least as it had been so sudden. Somehow his back had broken. Not even the top vets could tell me why after the autopsy was done. The vets at the university said his back had been healthy and they just could not explain it. I had Rocki at the time too. Luckily I had just bought him that spring for a project. Needless to say he ended up being my new ride. He was a lot like Danny minus the bad attitude.

As I looked at Oscerr I knew what he was going to do. He was going to pull a Danny. I had to bite back a smile. This is what caused us trouble.

"Annabelle go in your next class."

"No"

"Annabelle Paige! Go. Now!" I raised my voice.

"Fine!" She snapped back finally entering the ring at a trot. Instantly his head shot straight up looking for the girl who had attempted to hit him. She was a few horses ahead of them. Grabbing the bit Annabelle's face told the story. No control. Oscerr lengthened his stride catching up to the girl slamming her horse into the rail two, three, four times total. Hard too. And just when you thought he was done, he cut her off stopping dead backing up to kick. Annabelle managed to kick him forward after saying something to the girl.

I could read lips very well. I'd taken a sign language class my junior year of high school. So I laughed when I saw it. The announcer asked the class to line up in the middle. Annabelle dismounted to walk out of the ring when the judge stopped her to talk. While he spoke she began to smile. Even Oscerr looked proud of himself. No one could hear what he was telling her but when he walked away he was laughing. She walked out motioning for me to follow.

"What did he tell you?" I asked. Annabelle was laughing so hard she was crying.

"He said. He said even though that was a really dangerous stunt my horse pulled. He was glad I got back at that girl for threatening my horse. Even though it could have ended badly."

I watched as he spoke to the rest of the line up. A few of them looked toward us. That could not be a good sign.

"Maylee. That wasn't the best part." I looked at her with a feeling of foreboding

"What do you mean?"

"He's still going to place me." Oh no. There will be protests for that one. Guaranteed.

"We better leave." The faces of the other girls as they announced the results of the class were murderous. As were the looks from their parents. Annabelle seen their reactions.

"You're right. Let's go!"

I dismounted Rocki leading the boys back to the trailer, untacked, loaded up and changed into our street clothes. As we were leaving we were stopped. And well. It wasn't pretty.

Once home we unloaded the boys. That was what we had come to call Oscerr and Rocki because they were so much alike. We put them in their stalls giving them extra hay for the work they had done for the day. Annabelle gave Oscerr a couple treats telling him "Good boy" for what he had done for her in the show pen.

Grandpa Charles came into the barn leading his fifteen year old reliable horse Drake. Drake is also a sorrel, darker red with a blaze down his face, four tall white socks and a small splash of white on one side. Which is what made him registered as a paint

14

but still a quarter horse. He is only fifteen hands tall at the withers, making him five foot even.

"What are you doing back so early?" He asked as I gave him a dark look. He let Drake go into his stall before he began brushing him.

"They decided to ban us from showing there ever again. It is all because of the brats in Annabelle's class." Looking up at me from brushing he frowned.

"What did they do?" I proceeded to tell him exactly what they did to Annabelle and Oscerr prior to their second hunt seat class. Followed by what Oscerr did in the class. Thinking it over he shook his head letting Drake loose in his stall. "What did you tell Carl when he told you they had banned you guys?" He asked looking amused by the fact.

"I told him that if those girls would get off of their asses and work half as hard as we do than they would be able to compete with us without trying to get rid of us." Grandpa smiled wide at me.

"You kept your temper in check than?" I gave him half a grin.

"No, not really. When he stopped me from getting into the truck it flared instantly."

"Other than that?" I shook my head with a shit eating grin.

"No. The judge was backing us up. Which by the way was pretty amusing. I just told him we did not need his help and he said he could tell and walked away. Yeah, you should have seen everyone's faces when Annabelle still placed in the class." Annabelle just looked up from brushing Delilah. Who as I said is our project horse.

Delilah is only fourteen two, technically fifty eight inches, and literally a pony compared to the boys. She is a palomino or a golden colored coat with a white mane and tail, not bleached.

She was the best trail horse we had with only basic pleasure horse training.

"I could ride Delilah and they still would not want me there. You were too easy on him." It was a statement as she continued brushing.

"I know. But our club was there so I had to behave." Grandpa closed the door to Drake's stall before he gave us each a hug walking up to the house. "You are right by the way. You could take her and they still would be stupid about it. Everyone in our club knows we work hard, and that Delilah would stumble through the entire class like it was a foreign language to her." Annabelle laughed. "We better get going. I personally don't want to be around when he tells grandma about our being banned." Nodding in agreement we scurried out to my truck to go home. Our real home. Grandma's house was my second home, especially when mom and I were not getting along. Which was quite a bit. I actually had my own room in the upstairs of the house.

As I parked the truck in the driveway, it was definitely not home sweet home. Our mother was standing on the porch with her arms crossed over her chest looking every part of angry. My mom had high cheek bones, dark brown perfect beach day hair, and almond shaped blue eyes. Nothing about her was ugly except her attitude towards me. She had been this way since I was thirteen. The woman was in great shape as she went to spin class three days a week. Sighing heavily with what I knew would come I shut off the engine.

"Just go to your room." I told Annabelle resignedly as we stepped out walking towards the porch feeling like we were walking to the gallows.

"How many times do I have to tell you to stay away from those stupid rinky dink shows?" Our mother's voice was full of

16

spite. I bit back my anger as it was rising very quickly with her words.

"Annabelle and I just happen to like going to those shows because they are fun. We love our friends, but we are sick of the big shows."

"And just how much *fun* did you have today? Hmm? You were banned from the closest fairgrounds to us because your sister could not control her undisciplined horse." Okay. I officially skipped angry straight to pissed off.

"It was *not* the fact that she could not control him! He did it to get back at someone who was going to hit him with a whip." Check it. Check it now! Came a voice in my head as my anger began to roll out in massive waves. Times like this I was only too appreciative I did not have powers of any kind. Hilarious coincidence that would be.

"How would he know? They don't know when someone is trying to hurt them if they have not done it yet. He is just a stupid horse after all." My nails dug into the palm of my hand as I reminded myself to calm down. Her eyes were like daggers as she yelled making her point.

"Yeah. Keep talking like you would know what they were actually like. Especially when they are just an object to you. Just play toys. Yes, they are animals. But they are just as smart as that stupid thing you call a dog that runs around here. Oscerr hates whips to begin with and I don't blame him for going after the bitch." I walked away before I lost all control. Mom reached out grabbing my upper arm yanking me around to face her. Stopping I yanked my arm away from her.

"Grab me like that again. And I will knock you on your ass! It does not matter what you are to me."

"I was not finished with you yet!" She yelled at me.

17

"Well I am. Good night." Walking into the house with finality straight to my room. God I could not wait to have my own damn place. Picking up my music player I turned it to one of my favorite hard rock songs turning it up as loud as I could stand it. After that I chose a few more songs to follow that were more screamo than rock.

Walking by my study desk I picked up one of the thickest books I owned. It was about fictional characters with magical powers who battled evil. Ironic right? I loved those kind of books. I loved imagining myself fighting evil with awesome powers and fighting skills. My sister and I read the same kinds of books. Fantasy, mystery, or paranormal and the same kind of music. We also disagreed ninety five percent of the time with our mother when it came to the horses.

***

Have you ever felt like you were being closely watched? I had had that feeling since we left the show yesterday following us all the way home. Shaking it off I turned on the TV watching as crews were still cleaning up wreckage of a freak hurricane that had hit New Orleans a week ago. The news anchor was receiving a new report as I watched.

"Just in. There has been another seven point earthquake. This occurred in Brazil. This is following the seven point in Haiti three days ago and the six point four in Chile."

Interesting I thought. As if people were not freaked out enough by the freak hurricane and two huge earthquakes let's have another. Not to mention California was having more frequent trembles causing it to break at the fault line in several spots. Mount Saint Helens had become active again blowing up as it had done so many years ago destroying lives and wilderness alike. The geyser at Yellowstone park had started spewing lava instead of hot water causing great alarm to its visitors. The only saving grace was that it did not blow up into a super volcano as everyone had been predicting.

Could all this be connected? I asked myself. There was no way. Experts would have told us by now if it was. They were always itching to be right about something. Letting out a deep sigh I looked at the clock going through the motions of readying myself for work.

I worked in a big office building. A corporate mess. Never in my wildest dreams did I think I would end up in a place like that. It was owned by some big shot in Syracuse Texas, named Paul Farraro. I did not complain though. I made good money filing folders, papers, making copies, and doing whatever my friend, co-worker, and the one I was assistant to Roxanne needed. Walking up to my room I pulled on my black with grey pinstriped pant suit with a lilac colored button up to go under my jacket. Standing in front of my full length mirror I sighed as I pulled my hair into a high ponytail. Closing my eyes I breathed in and out evenly before opening them looking to the corner where I had kept an inspirational quote to keep me motivated. Ready at last I walked out the door to my truck.

As I was driving along the highway something strange ran out in front of me. I hit the brakes hard looking at it. Looking into the rearview mirror I wanted to make sure no one had been close enough to rear end me. When I looked back whatever it was, was gone.

"Okay." I told myself. "I have to be seeing things. Stress. Yep that's it. I'm just stressed." Great, now I was talking to myself too. As long as I did not answer back I guess I'm okay. Right?

As I walked into the building everything was the same as it always was. It was one of the normalcy's that I loved about the place. Roxy looked up at me from her desk as I walked through the door to run her morning errands. Roxanne was thirty years old has dark red hair that tightly curled around her light colored face. She has bright green eyes that always sparkled with life. I loved that she was always so positive.

"Maylee. Hold up before you run off." Swearing under my breath I stopped in my tracks turning back pivoting on my heel.

"Is there something else you need me to do instead?" Frowning she stood walking around from behind her desk.

"You seem frazzled this morning. Is something wrong?" Making a face at her I relaxed resting a hand on my hip.

"I'm fine." Not looking too convinced she walked up in front of me taking the errands.

"You should go prep the meeting room. For a change of pace." Confused I glanced out to the hallway. There was much more movement in the office today than usual.

"I thought that was Marcy's job every morning."

"Ethan wants you to do it instead. He said you have a better eye for detail than Marcy. So go. Impress the boss." Smirking I rolled my eyes. She knew I could not stand our boss. Ethan was not that old either at thirty three. He had black hair that was shoulder length pulled back into a ponytail. It was obvious he did not know how to care for it as it was always so oily. With a round face and dark eyes he always creeped me out when he watched me walking around the office.

"I do not want to impress him Rox. I can barely stand to be in the same room." Nodding knowingly she pointed to the door.

"Just go. Please?" Rolling my eyes once again I walked to the meeting room to begin preparations for the meeting. As I was just finishing up laying the binders in their places I overheard Ethan yelling at someone. Glancing up just enough I could see he was right outside the door. The only feature of this room I truly appreciated was the fact that it was all glass. Hence you could see everything from everywhere.

"She's in our meeting room." I heard him talking into the phone in his hand. Turning to see what I was doing he repeated into the phone. Frowning I thought this was strange. Standing straight I walked out of the room.

"Maylee, hold on." It was difficult for me to not cringe at Ethan's voice as it was slightly higher pitched than usual.

"Is there anything else you need done?" He looked nervous and sweaty. Gross. He was oily enough. All I wanted to do was put some serious distance between us.

"Well. Our boss from corporate will be in on this meeting. I just wanted to be sure everything was in perfect order."

"I guarantee it is, sir." Inside my head I was screaming to get away from him. He always gave me bad vibes along with being oily and gross.

"Okay. Thank you for your sharp eye." With a single nod I left that room in a hurry. What was that all about? Shaking it off I continued my day.

When I arrived home from work I found that my sister Annabelle had saw the same creature in the same day. That I found to be strange. Not the worst that's ever happened to us but odd none the less. Shrugging it off I proceeded to drive over to my grandparent's place to work with the horses.

Upon arriving I walked out to the barn up to Rocki's stall as he was waiting for me at the gate for his brushing and workout. He was not being worked hard today as it is lunging day. Lunging is where you make the horse go through his or her commands on a line fifty to eighty feet out in a circle around you.

We usually lunged anywhere from fifteen minutes to an hour depending on the horse's condition and energy level. Rocki and Oscerr were first, followed by Drake and Delilah. My sister and I cleaned the four stalls that our horses occupied followed by the three boarder's stalls.

"Why don't we practice?" Annabelle asked picking up a long stick she used as a fake sword. Her eyes twinkled as she knew I needed to relieve stress from the last couple days. Her and I were similar in facial features apart from eye color hers were hazel. Mine were bright blue.

"Okay, hand me the other one." We liked to practice sword fighting, nothing too serious. Just to teach ourselves defense moves. You just never know when it could come in handy. We never hurt or hit each other. It was just to practice the steps. Similar to fencing without all the equipment or instruction. We also liked to practice with a long stick throwing it like a Javelin. Suddenly I had the feeling that I was being watched looking around I walked out of the barn. There was nothing anywhere.

All I could see was the neighbor lady weeding her garden. Could not blame her as our grandma was doing the same out front. Shrugging it off I walked back into the barn continuing to spar until I accidentally scratched Annabelle's nose. For some reason we were being more aggressive with each other than usual. After that we decided to stop for the night to feed the horses. It was now eight o'clock and still light out. This is what I loved about spring, longer days.

My sister and I decided to go home for the day. At least this time we did not have an angry mother waiting on the porch to greet us. Walking into the house dad was watching the news looking up from watching the TV pointing to it for us to pay attention. Stopping I turned to look at it. A tsunami had taken out almost half of Japan.

"Wow!" I heard Annabelle murmur. "That is insane."

"They think it has to do with what is supposed to happen December twenty first." My dad replied to her. I did not think that it had anything to do with it. That was too far away yet. They had been predicting this since the Mayan calendar supposedly ended years ago. Yeah. It never happened.

"Just trying to get a story." I responded turning to go to my room.

The next morning when I woke I was startled to say the least at the dreams I had that night. I was sparring with a real sword against someone I apparently knew and was flirting with. The odd part was I never saw his face nor did I hear what was being said. Shaking my head I stood walking downstairs turning the TV on. There had been a category four hurricane that developed overnight hitting Florida full force. No warning, casualties were high. I did not have to work deciding to wait for Annabelle to get around for school. Her alarm blared out at six thirty. She made her way down the hall glancing up to see me in the recliner chair.

I watched her walk toward the living area, her medium length black hair straightened so that the layers showed. Her eyes were hazel in color, which would cloud up to look grey when she was angry. Her complexion is fair, but with all the work we do outside she was tan. Standing five foot five in height and in good shape. Not a model but she was thin. Thinner than myself at least. Annabelle is a size six or smaller depending on how much she worked out. As for me. I'm a size ten. Which was huge by any horse showing standard. My sister finished buckling her belt noticing that I was watching her.

"What?" She asked noticing that I was watching the news.

"There was a category four hurricane that hit Florida last night with no warning. It just appeared out of no where." Watching the TV for a minute before she turned to get her backpack walking out the door. She poked her head back in for a moment.

"They are too busy worrying about all the other countries when our own needs the help." Hesitantly she paused looking worried. "Hey, Maylee?" Looking up at her from the TV I raised my eyebrows at the look on her face.

"Yeah" Turning to face me she rested against the door.

"Have you had any nightmares lately? I mean. I know you told me nothing happened but"

"I'm fine Anna. And one day I will tell you. I promise. Just trust me when I tell you I plan on staying single for a while. And for damn good reason." She nodded worriedly walking out the door to go catch the bus. Intellectually Annabelle was more mature than most seventeen year old girls. Sighing I had scraped by that conversation. It was one I knew I had to have with her. Especially since she was present when I received that call two years ago about my ex boyfriend.

After my sister had left for school I called one of the parents in my 4-H club arranging for us to go for a trail ride later on in the day. Trail riding always helped me to relax. Annabelle said that it helped her too. And after the show two days ago we needed that. I drove to my grandparents' to pack our equipment into the trailer. Bridles, saddles, saddle pads, combination boots, and rope halters. Annabelle's combo boots were bright pink, mine were neon orange. We used them religiously for riding and lunging. Combination boots support tendons and ligaments in the horse's legs when they are wrapped properly.

Double checking to make sure I had everything we would need I drove back home to pick up my sister. She walked through the door straight to her room re-emerging several minutes later in barn clothes. We left driving to our grandparents' but something was still bothering me. The creature we had saw, it had looked straight at me like it was looking for me. Suddenly as I thought about it. There it was in the road directly in front of us. No one else besides the two of us could see it. At least that is what I figured out when cars behind me whipped around my truck honking because I had slammed the brakes for no apparent reason.

"You alright?" I asked Annabelle who nodded looking as panicked as I felt.

"What the hell is that thing?" Shaking my head I had no idea as it ran off the side of the road.

"I have no clue. But it's gone for now." Nodding in agreement she looked where it had disappeared as we drove by.

Pulling into our grandparent's driveway I informed Annabelle we were going trail riding at Susan's house. They had over a hundred acres of wood and non wood trails. Annabelle gave me a hard measuring look her jaw jumping with stress.

"After that thing jumped out in front of us. You want to go for a trail ride?" Getting out of the truck I turned in her direction.

"Yes, it's not like it will actually attack us while we are riding. And if it does I pity it because Rocki and Delilah will stomp it into the ground." Annabelle looked leery but agreed to go anyways.

Our grandpa had already loaded the three horses we would be taking with us on the trails. Annabelle had to take Delilah because like I said earlier, Oscerr was an idiot on the trails. There were several times we tried to ride him through one trail without a problem. Summed up in one word, impossible. In fact the last time we tried he bolted running top speed all the way back to the trailer. Some how Annabelle managed to cling on.

We drove for twenty minutes pulling into Susan's driveway. It was absolutely gorgeous outside today. Unloading the horses

Delilah was last in, first out. Followed by Rocki and finally Drake. We tacked up heading out to the trails for a well deserved vacation type ride.

Three hours had passed when we stopped at the river for the horses to take a drink. Annabelle held our two while I wandered toward the edge of the woods. A tree I found had a couple of good strong branches that were like the sticks we used at home, but longer. Something further out moved causing me to freeze where I stood. Grabbing a branch I snapped it off and a second one for my sister. She looked at me questioningly.

"This is not a time to practice our sword skills." Taking another look around it was still there moving closer to us. Glancing up at her I tossed one of the branches at her.

"They are not for practice. I'm afraid we may need them soon." I took Rocki's reins back as the whole group remounted to continue on.

"Since this is a long ride. Why don't we have that conversation you avoided this morning?" Sighing as I glanced to my right I nodded defeatedly.

"Alright. This is a conversation we need to have. And I know it is long overdue. The problem Anna is I had to really wrap my head around what all happened the entire time." She nodded knowingly as the others were pulling away from us.

"He hurt you. A lot. And I was angry you stayed with him as long as you did. But. I was also there when you told him to pack up and go. I was so proud of you for that. I could not tell you because then you would know I was there. But I am Maylee. I am proud of how you handled that situation." I smirked at her.

"Thank you. It was not easy for me. We had been together for so long. I was just fed up. But then" Taking a deep breath I continued. "He killed himself because of me. At least that was what his mom told me." Annabelle scowled angrily.

26

"That's bullshit Maylee. Caleb had been abusing you for over two years. Him driving into that semi was not your fault. He chose to end his life. Not you." I nodded immediately frowning stopping my horse turning to her.

"I never told any of you how he died." Suddenly my senses were alerting me that the creature close by. But when would it actually attack? How bad? As suddenly as it was following us, it was gone. I felt Rocki tense. His head shot straight into the air wide eyed snorting loudly.

"Easy." I told him patting his neck. "We will finish this later." Annabelle nodded looking around as well. That was strange. Could Rocki sense it too? My answer came fairly quick as it jumped out in front of us causing Rocki to jump sideways and backwards snorting louder. Delilah never even flinched. Hell she couldn't see it! Not a good indicator if this creature attacked us.

The creature was the size of a large Rottweiler looking similar too. There were quite a few differences. Such as scales instead of hair, a small set of wings, long fangs in place of teeth and some really nasty looking claws. It damn near looked to be a hell hound.

"What. The. Hell. Is. That?" Annabelle asked between breaths looking to me horrified. I shrugged shaking my head tensed to fight.

"I have no clue." Raising our sticks up we watched the creature. Almost as if that had been its cue the creature began running straight for us, growling with white foam dripping from its mouth as if it had rabies. My sister met it first but Delilah would hardly move. It almost had her ankle when I jabbed it hard on the head. Unlike Delilah, Rocki could see exactly what was in front of us.

He moved where I needed him when I needed him to move. Annabelle hit it even harder over the head dazing it just enough. I jumped off Rocki taking out my jackknife stabbing it in the rib cage. I must have hit the right area because it burst into black flames disappearing. Looking up at my sister I told her.

"I think we need to keep these handy until we leave." For once we were glad our trail ride was over. I was on edge after that creature attacked us jumping with every slight sound. Nothing happened after that. We un-tacked the horses loading up to go home. No one had noticed we had dropped back from the rest of the group or that we were carrying long heavy branches across our saddles. This was only the beginning of the attacks. More happened over the next week.

The peculiar part was that we could both see the creatures. But they would only attack when we were together. As I had suspected Oscerr could also see the monsters like the two of us and Rocki. I could not figure out exactly why the two of them could see the creatures but neither of the other horses could. Maybe it was because we felt connected to them? Or they reacted the way we did feeling our bodies tensing as the creatures drew near.

These creatures and their attacks on my sister and I were not the only oddities that week. My third day of work that week I was given a promotion. It would ensure that Ethan, our floor manager would be keeping a closer eye on me. This also meant that Roxy and I were now co workers and not boss and employee. That day after work she insisted we go to the bar to celebrate my sudden promotion. I went as far as to ask her if she had known. With complete honesty she replied she had not. I did not press her more about it though I was sure something was going on. No one even knew the bosses had been looking to fill the position I was just given. Shaking my head at my thinking I chose to celebrate for once.

The next day my sister and I were attacked by another creature. This one was the size of my co-worker Roxy's small four door hatchback. And took us much longer to battle. It was nearly an hour before I was able to get close enough to stab it with my jackknife.

We sat on the ground against the barn exhausted from fighting. Looking over at my sister she looked how I felt. Man, talk about a second job! I thought my regular one was enough. My co-workers had nothing on these monsters. Five minutes passed in silence looking to my sister I smirked as we sat resting up.

"If only my co-workers knew what I did when I was not working." She scowled looking up at me as sweat rolled down her face.

"Why? Are you worried that they would think you're nuts?"

"No, I would love for them to know I could kick their asses like no tomorrow if I wanted to." Laughing she knew the kind of slime ball boss I had after rehashing what had happened at the bar the night before. Ethan had full on hit on me. Going as far as to take my elbow to escort me to a different location so that we could have a more private area. No. Thanks. He did not act too upset when I yanked away storming right out into the street taking a cab to my truck in the parking lot at work.

"So. How long do we have before the next one attacks?" Annabelle asked as we sat resting. As the horses grazed out in their pastures I watched them thinking about how much time had passed between each attack.

"Well, each time we kill one it takes at least two days before the next one shows its ugly face." I was hoping it would give us enough time to re arm ourselves. We had broke our sticks we used to fake sword fight to fight these creatures for real. The sun started setting making the sky absolutely stunning. The air was cooling fast now.

"We better head for home. It's getting late." Annabelle stared at Oscerr for a moment before speaking.

"We might want to soak in the hot tub before we go to bed tonight." I nodded in agreement as that sounded like a good idea indeed. My body was rather sore from all the fighting we had been doing this week. I was feeling muscles I never knew existed even when I went to boot camp with my horse.

We stood up off the ground to go do our chores shutting the door when we finished. As I turned to walk up to the house a tall figure wearing a long black, must have been a cloak. With the hood over his or her face approached. This was private property except for the three boarders we had and they never came this late. Or let anyone else ride their horses for that matter. The figure stopped in front of us throwing back the hood of the cloak.

The figure was female. She could not be a day over twenty years old, pale skin, bright green eyes with long silvery blonde hair that was pulled back into a half pony. She was model thin, but did not look weak in any way shape or form. First she looked at my sister than to me before looking to the arena where we had fought the creature. You could plainly see the area where it had went up in black flames after I had killed it.

"The Dileroz have been after you?" She asked in a soft almost reassuring type of voice. The two of us looked at each other confused as hell. Annabelle spoke up first.

"You can see where it was?" The girl nodded vaguely.

"What did you call them? And who the hell are you?" I asked as she acted like she knew what was going on. The woman walked in between us to where the creature had disappeared kneeling down to inspect the burn marks.

"I called it a Dileroz. They take on many sizes and shapes. The only way to kill them is to stab it in the heart. They are created by those who have powers of dark sorcery." Standing she walked back over to where we were rooted in shock. "As for who I am? I am Izabella." Bowing to us slightly she stood upright again crossing her arms as if assessing us. "I will be your guide, discoverer, trainer take your pick on what you want to call it."

"Okay. But why did you need to find us? How did you find us?" Shifting her feet Izabella looked around behind her.

"Why will take some time to explain as for the how would take even longer." This woman is nuts I told myself. Maybe brain damaged or something. Too many fictional books. I better lay off in case they begin to make me that way. "What was the size of the last Dileroz?"

"The size of a small car." My sister answered looking every bit serious. Izabella's eyes widened as she looked toward the setting sun. Moments passed before she looked back to us.

"You need to pack your belongings and come with me right away. You are in danger." Yeah right I said to myself rolling my eyes as I thought it.

"It is almost pitch black out. It's late. Cold and not to mention we are exhausted from fighting that thing. We are going home. And not packing." She stared at me as if I were talking nonsense. Making a sound of impatience I felt compelled to explain. "Look. We have two days before it attacks again. We will be ready to kill it. Again. And we will go on with our lives." In the back of my mind if the next one was any bigger I knew that we would need help.

"Go if you wish. You have two days before the next attack. But I warn you, it will not be a Dileroz. The force that is after you will send something more viscous. You will not be able to fight it by yourselves." Annabelle looked at me worriedly as we had barely killed the last one. If anything worse came along what would we do? Why were they after us to begin with? Izabella turned to leave. I wanted answers.

"Wait." Stopping she turned around looking calm. "Why are they after us? You owe us that much of an explanation. You seem to know what's happening." Looking around to make sure there was no one there she walked back to where we were standing. If anyone was there they would have figured we should all be in a mental institution.

"You know or have learned of the ancient gods no doubt?" I looked at her totally dumbfounded.

"Don't try telling us they currently exist." I stated knowing now that she must be insane. There was no way they still existed if they ever did. I mean we had read books that explored the idea, but they were fictional. She gave a small smile.

"Not now. No. But at one time. Yes, they did. They disappeared thousands of years ago. Fading away because no one believed in them anymore. There were also many magikal beings. Including two individuals you need to know about. An evil sorcerer Vladimir and the sorceress Sarita. Sarita was not evil. Though they had two children together and there were others too." Annabelle looked at me like okay let's go now! I thought it over as she explained.

"What does that have to do with us?" Looking at us smirking she pulled her bag around pulling out a map. It was of our home state Michigan. As she rolled it out there were three glowing dots over the one that was our city. The dots were a swirl of two colors, teal and red. There was a third I assumed Izabella's that was a swirl of pink and dark red.

"These two dots represent the two of you." Pointing to the two teal and red dots. I had kind of figured that out already.

"What do the colors mean? And why are they swirled and not mixed together?" As she unfolded the map more we caught a glimpse of a map key. I could only see three of them.

Blue= Poseidon Yellow= Zeus Black= Hades

"Each color represents a different god or magikal being."

"Whoa! Hold it! You are trying to tell us that we are somehow related to the greek gods?" Frowning she looked between myself and my sister to get a feel on what we were thinking at this point.

"Yes. Though not demigods or the direct result. They have been gone too long for that. You are descendants which means at least three or more generations after them. You two are descendants of the god of war Ares." Annabelle broke in laughing.

"That explains Maylee's infamous temper and why things tend to happen when she gets angry. Like objects move that should not." Izabella continued like she had never stopped.

"Has anything happened that you could not explain?" I thought back a few years.

"My locker sprang open once, and it was a combination lock. Sometimes when I was looking for something it would appear where I had already looked."

"I remember the locker. That was really creepy." Annabelle told us looking afraid of what came next.

"That is because you are also descendants of the sorceress Sarita." Pausing she allowed us to swallow that information.

"So because we are descended from Sarita. You or whoever sent you is assuming that we will have powers. Right?" Izabella nodded glancing to my sister who did not look amused now. If anything she looked irritated. That was odd.

"Yes. With training you would be able to use them at will." Scowling I shook my head at her.

"I do not have any powers. Trust me. If I did I would not be working where I do." It was growing colder out as silence prevailed. I could tell Izabella was choosing her words carefully.

"Go home. Pack for a long trip. I must take you to the island of Ettoupaviog to begin your training for what is to come." It took a moment for me to find my bearings as I shook my head once again.

"No. We are not going anywhere with you." I turned walking to my truck. "Come on Annabelle. It's late. And I'm tired." With one last look at Izabella Annabelle ran to my truck shooting me a look after shutting the door.

"Maylee. I don't like this." Her eyes were storm clouds indicating her true anger for the situation. Nodding in agreement I started the truck leaving our grandparents place before responding.

"Neither do I."

***

The next morning I was sore from our battle with the monster. Barely able to move I called in at work waiting for my sister to get up and around for school. As I waited for her I tried to remember the dream I had that night. It was the same as before. I was sword fighting with someone. Obviously male since I appeared to be flirting. I wish I could see what he looked like or hear the voices. Dammit. At six thirty Annabelle wandered out grabbing an apple for breakfast glancing over in my direction as she walked by.

"I'm taking you to school this morning." I informed her. Shrugging her shoulders she sat back in the recliner eating her apple. A few minutes later she stood up throwing the core away in the trash can. Leaning against the back of the chair she had been sitting in she looked at me.

"Have you thought anymore about Izabella's warning last night?" Truth was I had not thought about it because I hoped it had all been a terrible yet vivid dream. Knowing what she had told us was not a lie or a prank. Izabella could see the creatures when no one else could.

"I've considered it. That's as far as it has went."

"Well, it does explain your temper. And why things happen around us." Why did she sound so sure? Like she actually believed in what Izabella was telling us?

"Are you going to follow her advice? Just pack up leaving everything and everyone we know behind?" My temper was flaring again. Lately I was having a difficult time keeping it in check. Sighing she shook her head defeatedly.

"Not until we have to. We should be okay until tomorrow." Looking up at the wall clock she checked the time. "If we don't leave soon I will be late for first period." I drove her to school dropping her off at the door. For nearly fifteen minutes I sat in my truck in the parking lot thinking about what was going on. All scenarios playing through my head one right after the other. If we left anytime soon we would need money for travel expenses.

I drove to the bank withdrawing all of my money from my savings account leaving enough for my bills in my checking account. There was enough there to pay for at least six months if anything happened to me. With my money in tow I drove back home packing all my money into Ziploc bags for safekeeping hiding them in my dresser. Logging into my computer I hit the internet first checking my e-mail arranging for all my monthly payments to be made automatically. At least we had the truck when the time came knowing it would be the fastest way of travel.

Something in my gut told me it would be soon. The result of that feeling I decided to pack up some necessities for my sister and I into a couple of hiking packs. Three changes of clothes, notebooks, pens, rain coats, sunscreen, phone chargers, bottles of water, granola bars, a box of toaster pastries which I dumped into the bags instead of leaving in the box, and of course all hygiene essentials.

I packed my computer into its case with the hotspot for internet. As I packed up the power cord I saw a picture of myself with Danny. Picking it up I looked it over, it was one of my favorite pictures. We had just mastered jumping the five foot fences. This was the two of us in mid air. Taking it out of the frame I shoved it in with my computer. I double checked both packs for everything we would need just in case. Looking at the clock it was already two thirty. I made my way over to the school to pick my sister up.

Half way there I noticed a large shadow hovering over my truck. Looking up I could not see what it was. No freaking way I thought. Not now. We were literally defenseless. No weapons at all except for my jackknife. What use would that be against something that big? Pulling up to the doors I waited for her to walk out. Not even a minute passed as she walked out opening the passenger side door.

"We're going straight to grandma's." Scowling she looked at me to say something before she saw the shadow pass over.

"Let's go than! We don't have anything to fight with!" Great. Now she panics while I'm driving to get us the hell out of there. While on the highway the shadow creature swiped at us. I nearly lost control multiple times swerving hard almost turning into a roll once.

Only a mile away from our grandparents' house the creature's claws gripped the cab of my truck picking us up off the road. Annabelle was having a full blown panic attack. Admittedly I did not feel much better. The shadow seemed to be made of black smoke. How could it cause that kind of damage? Suddenly it released my truck right over the river! Screaming to my sister I told her to brace herself as we free fell. The truck hit the ground shattering the windows instantly. It was really lucky for us that this river was not deep. We rolled several times our seatbelts held us in place along with the air bags. Again we were lucky as it stopped right side up. Breathing hard from the impact I forced myself to shut off the engine. As I looked around I noticed a small opening in the front where the window had been that we might be able to squeeze through out. Reaching over to my sister to check on her she was out cold.

"Annabelle? You okay?" No response. A moment later she began moving and I felt I could breathe at ease. "Are you okay?" I asked again when she looked up her eyes were glazed over. She most likely had a concussion, another problem to deal with. How was I going to explain this to the insurance company? A loud thunderous screech sounded overhead telling me the shadow creature was still very close.

The seatbelts would not unhook. Of course. Pulling out my jackknife I began cutting through the seatbelts. Grabbing a jacket from behind the seat I placed it along the window to keep it from cutting us as we slid out.

"I will go first." Annabelle nodded looking as if she wanted to puke her guts out. It was a tight squeeze but I made it through the space. Looking in a shard of broken mirror I noticed a gash to my face from the flying glass. Signaling to my sister she climbed out with ease as she was smaller than I was after all.

Resting for only a moment we set off to walk the remaining mile to our grandparents' house.

No phone reception. Go figure. Staying under the cover of trees we made our way along the fence line to where the horses were out grazing. Luckily all our stuff was in the barn. Sticks to fight with and all. Keeping an eye out for the creature we walked slowly through the pasture sliding into the barn through the door. Grabbing the longer sticks I had sharpened two of them to a point at one end.

The double doors of the barn opened on their own. Standing in the entrance was the shadow creature. As we were able to actually look at it, it looked like a dragon. This could get real ugly quick. Smoke swirled around it engulfing it so we could not see what it was doing. When the smoke cleared there were five cloaked and hooded figures standing where the creature had been. The figure closest spoke up.

"Surrender now and we will spare you your lives." I glanced over at my sister. She looked determined as she swung her stick around ready to fight. I followed suit smirking.

"We won't attack you if you leave us alone." We both took a step forward.

"I'm afraid we cannot do that. You are descendants and we can use fighters like you two on our side."

"What side would that be?"

"It does not matter right now. Our rightful leader has yet to be ready to fight."

"Well your leader must be the evil asshole we have heard so much about."

"He is not evil. But he is very powerful. True. He senses the end of your world coming."

"Only because he's the one causing it. Your answer is no. We will not join you." With that fighting ensued. They had swords too. Dammit. We just could not catch a break. Yeah, I said swords. Like swords from medieval times except much fancier and these guys were cutting our sticks to pieces. Out of no where Izabella appeared drawing out a sword of her own fighting them along with us. Looking at her sword it was a light silver metal, the center was frosted over with something etched into it. Not even in the movies had I seen a blade like it. Similar, but not quite. Her sword moved through two of the figures making them dissolve in a puff of black smoke.

The leader was locked in one on one with Izabella while Annabelle and I battled the remaining two. Pulling out my jackknife I swiped at the figure in front of me hitting my target he disappeared. Just two left, one battling Annabelle the other still with Izabella. Walking to where Annabelle she was still trying to push the figure back with a stick I stabbed him in the side without him knowing I was even there. Annabelle looked at me wide eyed in shock. Nodding to Izabella as she fought the only one remaining. They were locked sword to sword. She pushed him backwards her sword slicing through as he walked back toward her. He merely looked at her disappearing in a haze, not smoke like the others did.

Sheathing her sword she walked toward us signaling for us to follow her into the barn.

"We have only bought a few minutes before they reform. You two already look like you have been through a small battle. Save the story for later. Where is your truck?" Without realizing it I was barely breathing all the while my ribcage hurt.

"I don't have it. That's why we look like hell. It's in the river a mile up the road." Rubbing my aching ribs I checked to make sure I had not been struck by a sword.

"That shadow thing attacked us while we were on our way here." Annabelle told her as she held her head like it was going to split in two. Izabella looked around the barn at each of our horses.

"We can go by horseback. Saddle up your two for yourselves. I will need one and that small one there we can use for packing." We set to work saddling the boys using our brow band style bridles so they could not shake them off. Taking out the protective boots we placed them on their front legs.

Running into the house I went to the tack room grabbing four rope halters, my triage kit with other odds and ends. The halters had lead ropes attached to them that they could be attached to our saddles as we rode. Sliding them on under the bridles for when we took breaks or stopped for the night to picket them with. After those two were done we set to work preparing Drake and Delilah with the same type of equipment. Handing Izabella the reins for Drake she nodded for us to leave. As we walked out of the barn Izabella stopped just outside the door looking around frowning.

Turning to the woods she made an eerie whistle like the one I used to use to call Danny. I turned to see what she was doing before I saw him. Danny came walking out of the woods like he had never left. He stopped just outside the wood line. Watching him there I had tears in my eyes feeling my muscles protest.

"How. How is he here?" I choked out my voice quivering at the sight. He was the only horse I had ever felt fully attached to.

"You know him?" Nodding I watched him in the distance as he pawed the ground nervously tossing his head.

"He was mine. Before he" My throat constricted too much before I could say it. Looking amazed she smiled shaking her head incredulously.

"That is why the Dileroz have not been able to seriously injure you. He has been protecting you all this time. What is his name?"

"Danny, his name was Danny."

"Danny has been protecting you this entire time." Thanks I told him in my mind. As if he actually would hear me. "He has been stuck in purgatory since he died." Izabella informed me. "He was supposed to move on, but he wanted to watch over you." I walked toward him wanting to touch him so bad as he walked up to where we stood. My hand moved through him like a ghost that looked solid.

"Why did he become visible when you whistled?" Figuring that was a legit question.

"So that I could tell you he wanted to reveal himself to us. To let us know he was here when we needed him, and later on we may." Snapping her fingers he disappeared into the wind as if he had never been there. As we walked the boys out of the barn to follow her out she stopped me to inspect Rocki. A minute later she did the same with Oscerr. I found this strange frowning as I looked to Annabelle who shrugged indifferently. After she had inspected them both closely she took a step back.

"This is impossible." Mumbling her face registered disbelief amazed that we owned the two horses.

"What?" I finally asked. "Is something wrong?"

"No. There is nothing wrong. Not a problem at all." A screech from the sky brought her back to her senses. "Come on, mount up. We need to go. We can take back ways and trails to where we are going. Where are your packs?"

"I left them at home. At least they were not in the truck when we went into the river. I know the back way to our house from here. I'll lead." Urging my horse on we all loped across the road through the field into the woods.

41

The shadow creature was following us. Watching and waiting for its chance to attack. Luckily we had gone on trail rides in between the houses and knew exactly where we were. There was one trail we had discovered that led right up to the back of our house.

It only took half an hour to arrive loping the horses the whole way. When we stopped Drake and Delilah were sweating looking tired already. Rocki and Oscerr were not even warm barely breathing harder than normal. Dismounting I sprinted into the house up to my room to grab the bags I had packed earlier in the day.

Opening the front of my pack I shoved all my money into it I had withdrawn from the bank. Annabelle met me in the hall throwing her pack to her.

"Thanks" She said looking through it for what was in it. Out in the kitchen we grabbed a sports drink to replenish ourselves from the whole eventful day. Turning we both jumped a mile. Izabella was standing right behind us.

"What are you doing?" I asked as she began walking around the house.

"Looking for items of power. There are some in this house. I can sense them. If I am able to find them all they will help you later on." She walked around the entire house taking nearly half an hour giving the horses a chance to catch their breath.

I followed her up into my room where she picked up a jar of seashells I had gathered when we went on a camping trip to Lake Michigan. She handed them to me walking further she picked up a small round blue stone I had bought at a local craft show years ago handing that to me as well.

"Hold on to these. They will be of great assistance later on." This was too weird as I scowled at her.

"Explain" Was the only word I could manage as she frowned back.

"Later." Next was Annabelle's room. Izabella repeated the process walking out with three items. A flat blue stone, a spring assisted knife, and a bling belt. She handed them over to Annabelle walking to the living area where the front door was. Stopping short of grabbing the handle to the door she walked over to the computer desk. As she looked it over she reached into one of the small compartments pulling out a box of stones my grandparents had bought while they were in Germany.

Handing the box over to me signaling to pack them up as well. Taking the box I managed to stuff it into my now overly packed backpack. We were walking toward the door when I remembered something running to the kitchen instead. Izabella and Annabelle waited while I rummaged around the cabinet taking out a first aid kit, a good sized bottle of Motrin, because you never know. An ace bandage and two rolls of vet wrap. I made room in my backpack shoving it all into a different compartments. Finally we walked out the front door running from we did not really know what. Nor did we actually know where we were going.

Running to where the horses were standing restlessly we remounted pointing them south through the trails we knew and some we did not. Occasionally we could hear the creature near. Occasionally we would be blasted by black flames. Around dark we stopped to make camp in a clearing. Where the hell were we now? I asked myself looking around. Shaking my head I knew we had work to do.

Unsaddling the horses we let them rest tied up to some small trees. The boys acted like they could have kept right on going. They shifted their entire bodies around nervously, snorting loudly as they looked around the camp. Annabelle and I walked to where Izabella had made a campfire.

"Are we safe?" Looking up at me calmly she nodded before indicating she wanted us to sit by the crackling fire.

"Take out the items I gave you at the house." Turning we each grabbed our backpacks digging out the items she had handed over. We both held them in our hands. Why did we need these? Was the question that kept going through my mind. Izabella reached over taking Annabelle's items looking at the charm bracelet she was wearing. Sitting back down on the cold ground she began examining each item closely. First was the spring assisted knife. When she was done she tossed back to my sister

"What am I supposed to do with it? Use it? It's too small." Izabella shook her head before explaining.

"Open it up and give it a name. It will reveal its true form." My sister looked at Izabella like she was crazy but opened it up anyways.

"Fury." A minute passed before it glowed in a blue shimmering light revealing a sword. A real silver sword with a double sided blade, hand and a half sword. It had a silver hilt with a blue crescent moon on each side. "Wow." Annabelle said looking at it in amazement. I just stared in total disbelief. This was real magic. This was just way too ironic. My sister swung the sword around testing the balance. The scabbard appeared a moment later. Annabelle picked it up looking at it. It was made of brown leather inscribed in another language I could not recognize. Moving on Izabella picked up another item. The flat blue stone.

"This can only be used once, it will turn into a blade that will cut through anything. Be wise when it comes to using it."

She handed it back and Annabelle put it in her front jeans pocket. The belt was next, it transformed into a rope.

"This will hold any creature you need to capture no matter the size or strength." Lastly was her charm bracelet. There was only a single charm that resided there. A crescent moon.

"This bracelet is what helps you to communicate with your horse. He is one of the last descendants of the moon god's horses which is why he is marked with a star the shape of a crescent moon."

Annabelle looked at me completely stunned, it explained a lot. The reason he would only work properly for her and no one else. Notice though I said *properly* not just for her and dump everyone else the way Danny did. Izabella turned to me now.

"Your items please." I handed over what she had given to me at the house. "Your jackknife too." Stunned I handed it to her, but it dawned on me that it must have been my sword this whole time. That is why I was able to actually kill the Dileroz when they attacked.

"My knife is my sword. Isn't it?" Izabella looked up at me in slight disbelief.

"How did you figure that out?"

"When we were fighting those creatures my knife was the only thing that would kill them." Nodding she handed it back to me looking weary.

"You are very observant. Yes, it is. Open it up and give it a name." Opening it I had a few different names lined up in case the first one did not work. Looking at it I pictured what it may look like.

"Star burst." I said out loud. It grew and lengthened to two feet long, it was a steely dark silver nearly black that glinted silver in the light. There were golden stars going down the center, double sided blade with a black grip with silver winding down to the hilt. The hilt was silver with a golden sunburst on each side. The scabbard appeared with the strange language, it was black leather. Izabella looked at my sword wearily as well.

"It should not have formed that way." I looked it over swinging it around a few times, it was nice and balanced. Taking the scabbard I belted it on sheathing my sword. The only part of the process that was unnerving me was the way Izabella kept looking at me. It made me uneasy. Like she was expecting me to be evil or something. My blue stone was next. Handing it over she squeezed it in her palm which glowed a whitish blue reappearing as a silver flask. Very much like the kind hunters use to keep whiskey in.

"This is filled with a liquid that will heal you instantly, but only take a single swallow. More than that will kill you from poisoning." Taking it I placed it in the front pocket of my backpack.

Taking the jar of seashells Izabella dumped them all out arranging them into piles of others like them.

"This thin spiral shell will bring you water from where ever you are. The flat spread out ones will allow you passage in any water you need access to. The last three here are called conch horns. They can only be used once because it will shatter after the call is complete. You can use them to call reinforcements." Taking the jar back I dumped the shells back in placing it between some clothes in my backpack.

"Your necklace. Let me see it please." Reaching up I unhooked the leather corded necklace handing it over. It was made the same style as an arrowhead, except it had a sunburst pendant on it. She examined it for what seemed like several minutes before she handed it back.

"That is the sign of Helios the original sun god. Your horse also bears that sign on his forehead. This necklace works for him as Annabelle's bracelet works for her. They are both descendants of the god's horses. That is why they can see the monsters and the others cannot. You were meant to own them so that they could protect you."

"Is that why they never seem to tire?"

"It doesn't keep them from getting sick though." Annabelle said as she looked over at the horses worried about Oscerr. They were dancing around like they wanted to be anywhere but here.

"Do you know why the items turned when you called their names?" Izabella asked us as we watched the boys dancing around.

"Because that is what they were meant to be. But their true owners had to turn them." Izabella looked at me like I should not have known the answer to that.

"That is partially correct. It is also because you have a form of magik coursing through you." My sister looked at her curiously. Smirking I knew what she was thinking before she said it.

"Do we need wands or something to make them work properly?" Izabella laughed smiling with understanding.

"No. It is not like your books and movies depict. You need an object to make them work at first. After that it is just discipline and knowledge." The moon was high our fire was burning low. "I think it is time to get some sleep. I will keep watch. You two need to rest. You have had a long day. Tomorrow will be just as busy."

The following morning I woke up when the horses snorted whinnying. Automatically my hand went to the hilt of my sword, but Izabella grabbed my wrist before I could draw it out. I had only had it for less than twelve hours. Why had that been so automatic? Probably since I had been having the same dream for over a week now about sparring.

"The horses are spooked from something in the woods. We need to go." Nodding that I understood I walked over to wake up my sister. Rolling up our blankets I strapped them to Delilah. Picked up our backpacks and mounted up. Izabella took out her map to see where we were so far. I had noticed the dots that represented us moving as we did, making it a huge you are here sign. We were on the border of Ohio and Indiana. She wrote a short letter sending it on with a blue light.

"How did you do that?" I asked. Izabella merely looked at me rolling the map up tucking it away continuing on at a trotting pace. We had went about a mile and half when she finally spoke.

"That is how we communicate with each other when we are far away." Nodding at least I had received my answer.

It was near nightfall when we stopped to make camp again. I was really not sure how much more traveling Drake was going to be able to handle. Delilah was holding up fairly well yet. They did not have the unnatural powers of Oscerr and Rocki. I looked them over after we unpacked for camp. Izabella must have read me like the cover of a book.

"You do not think those two will last much longer." It was a statement not a question

"Delilah will be fine for a few more days. She's a pretty tough little horse. Drake on the other hand worries me. He's fifteen years old but he acts like he is thirty. I'm just not sure how much longer his legs will last." Looking him over she checked his legs to make sure they were not sore. He never flinched but just maybe he knew how important it was for us to reach safety.

"He seems to be fine." Physically at the moment sure, but I could tell by the look in his eyes that he was wearing down fast.

After ensuring camp was set for the night I gathered some roots and leaves dumping them in a small bowl Izabella gave me grinding them up. The bowl and little grinder were called a mortar and pestle. Probably something I would end up using quite often I imagine. Adding water to the mix I ground it all up until it made a paste. Walking to Drake I began to slave it on him, his back, shoulders, legs, even his hips seemed to be a little sore. When I was done I sat down on the ground next to the fire taking out a granola bar drinking what was left of the bottle of water I had used to mix up the paste. Annabelle looked between Drake than me looking confused.

"How did you know what to make?" Shrugging I really did not know how I knew.

"I'm not sure how I knew what to use. Whenever I picked something up I would receive a feeling from it. It was strange. That will brush off like fine dirt in the morning. It should buy us a few more days for him." Izabella nodded in agreement.

"You have good instincts. You are in tuned with nature." Shrugging she leaned forward assessing me before she continued. "You understand your surroundings better than you understand people." She was able to gather all that just from looking at me?

"I'll have to agree to that. By the way. Why did we need the stones from my house?"

"I will tell you later. For now sleep. We will worry about it another day." Once again we slept under the stars, and it was cold. At least we had brought blankets with us.

When I woke the next morning I took out Izabella's map we had been using to travel. According to this map we were in lower Kentucky not to the border yet. There was no way I thought. It is not possible for us to have traveled that far yet. If we have than Drake will surely get us to where we are going, than die out of pure exhaustion. I spotted other dots too in other colors. Most of them were ahead of us either in Florida or Georgia.

Another dot caught my attention. This one was a dark blood red traveling north east instead of south east as if it was someone meeting us before we reached our destination. I was starting to assume that it was Florida. I thought about telling Izabella about what I had saw but I was unsure if I should.

Rolling the map up I slid it back where I had found it. After that I pulled out a brush setting to work on Drake with the dried paste on him. Looking at the others I decided to brush them too. So at least you could recognize them again. I gave them each a carrot from a bag I had grabbed while in grandma's house the day we took off.

Returning to the campfire I rolled up my blankets fastening them to Delilah's back. I walked a little away from the camp area to a tree that I could practice my sword work on pretending it was an enemy. The sound of someone stirring reached me so I sheathed my sword working on my yoga sequences instead. A few minutes later Izabella walked to where I was stretching.

"Do you want to actually practice sparring or are you going to wait for the tree to spring to life?" Looking up at her she was smiling even though the comment had been sarcastic.

"I didn't make a sound."

"You do not have to. I could hear the blade swinging." Izabella drew her sword out. Now I had my chance to study it.

"What is the name of your sword?" She lifted it up to her face swinging it out to her side stepping forward making it look like a move used in combat.

"I named it Slash. It was forged for me by my half brother when I was young. We were going to war then too. Now. Prepare yourself." She taught me some of the steps and movements before we started to actually spar each other. I was in good shape, but holy hell. My arm felt like it was going to fall off from the weight of my sword.

Annabelle had woke up wandering over to see what we were up to. I glanced up at her breaking my concentration for a split second and in that split second Izabella was able to disarm me.

"Not bad for your first real sparring lesson." Annabelle laughed at me for being disarmed until I looked up at her.

"Don't laugh. You're next." I was not amused about being disarmed, but I knew that Izabella was good. And that I was new. My sister and I were both surprised at what came next.

"No. Another day. We need to move. We have already been here too long." Saddling the horses we mounted up heading out. I was still pouring sweat from Izabella's lesson.

"Could we stop somewhere? A motel or something? I need a shower. It's been two days and I'm pouring sweat. I would like to change my clothes too." Izabella thought it over for a few minutes as we walked.

"Yes, we can stop somewhere. But we have to be careful. We will need to keep the horses somewhere they will not be seen. Also we will need a different mode of transportation."

"No sweat. My dad taught me how to hotwire cars."

"Maylee!" Annabelle said in astonishment.

"What? This *is* an emergency and I would be bringing it back anyways." I reasoned with her. We traveled until the sun was high which meant that it was around noon.

A small town sign was hanging near the road reading population 500. Well, that was a small town. Don't blink. You might miss it. Hopefully they would at least have a small bed and breakfast. There was an old house not too far from the actual town area with an old fashioned barn outback. The doors creaked horribly as we opened the barn tying the horses inside.

All three of us walked up to the house knocking on the door for several minutes. No one answered. The door to the garage was unlocked as I entered. A car was parked inside, a 1998 Chevy Impala. Red. I hated red. Opening the driver's side door the key was in the ignition. What luck!

"The key is in it! Get in so we can go." Turning the key it started right up sounding a little rough like it could use a good tune up. Annabelle found the door remote opening the garage door. I backed the car out stopping just outside. Closing the door her and Izabella walked out the walk through door to. Driving down the road the car barely moved. The brakes were touchy. We were all worried a cop would see us in a vehicle that they knew, but not the people driving it.

With that in mind I pulled into the first motel we came to in the small town. Oddly enough it was not the only one. Walking into the lobby we paid for a single room for one day even though we would only be there long enough to clean up and leave. The room was small but cozy decorated in tan with red plaid material. I showered first since I was still kind of sweaty and felt really gross.

It felt great to be clean and in clean clothes. I noticed that my sword had turned back into a jackknife before we entered the lobby. Must be a mechanism or something to that effect. It did not take long before we were all clean and ready to go back to the house where we had left the horses.

I just prayed that the boys had behaved and not untied themselves to take off. We pulled the car back into the garage where we had borrowed it from. I pulled ten dollars out of my backpack leaving it on the dashboard for the gas we used. Izabella led the way out to the barn with her eyes open for trouble. Untying the horses we all mounted up walking to the trail on our merry way. Yeah right. I make myself laugh for wishful thinking.

As we re-entered the trail a loud roar came from overhead. Without looking up we knew what it was. That shadow that looked like a dragon, great. I knew it would not be long before it actually caught up with us transforming into the men to capture us. Why they wanted to capture us was almost beyond me. I could understand killing us because of what powers we might have.

We ran the horses until we no longer could hoping that we temporarily lost the creature. Finally stopping we had to let the horses rest while we sat on the leaf strewn ground watching them. Reaching into my backpack I took out a pen and notebook writing a letter to my grandma explaining that we rode off with the horses for a week long trail ride. Folding up the letter I looked at it concentrating on where it needed to go. A glowing blue color appeared around it like Izabella's had done and it disappeared. It did not occur to me that Izabella had been watching me. When I looked up at her, her face registered shock as it had disappeared.

"How did you do that? You have never been taught! It usually takes three to six months for any immortal to learn to do that." Biting the inside of my mouth I did not think I could make it work.

"I don't know. I just did what I thought would work and it did. I didn't think it was actually going to work." It had shocked me that it came so naturally when most took so much time to learn it.

"You just have a gift for figuring things out." Smirking I nodded in agreement.

"Yeah. Let's go with that." Looking over to my sister she was almost asleep. Taking out the box of stones I took each one out examining it. They were just ordinary rocks yet I could feel something from them. Izabella noticed nodding to sit closer so she could explain.

"I can tell you what each one does."

"Okay." Handing her the box she took the first one out holding it for me to see.

"This one is feuer steinsalz or fire stone. From the name you can guess what it does." Indeed. It was red with darker red veins all over. Taking it I thought about the campfire getting low. "Try it." Holding it I thought about the fire in front of us.

"Campfire." The flames grew higher and higher. "Too high." The flames died back down until it was just right. "Stop." The flames stayed at that height.

"Not bad." Izabella commented as she smirked. "You could have done something a little more drastic, but that is a good start. Try this one." She handed me a dark brown one. "This is Erde steinsalz, it controls earth substances." I had to think about what I could possibly do with something like that. Looking at a rock on the ground I concentrated on making it float above the ground. After that I made it break away dissolving into sand. Izabella handed me another one that was pure black. Just holding this one made me uneasy.

"That one will enable you to control the dead or undead depending on what we encounter. You do not have to try that one." Relieved I placed it back in its' box. The next stone was a grayish color with veins of black and white running through it. "This is called a sturm Steinsalz. You can create super cell storms and control everything they do. Again, you do not have to use that one either." Shrugging it would have been interesting to try.

The fourth stone was a pale blue color, almost pastel like. Taking it I could feel something significant with this one, like it could help me no matter what.

"That one has the power to heal. Fittingly it is called Heilen Steinsalz or healing stone. All you have to do is drop it into a glass, bottle or canteen of water and it will make it a healing potion. It could save you from the clasp of death itself, and unlike the flask of potion you have this can be drank more than once a day." This was cool. So if I was injured all I would have to do is take out my water bottle drop it in and drink.

The last one was an interesting mixture of colors. The stone was whitish almost cloudy looking with black veins running through it. Taking it from Izabella I felt more powerful, hyper aware of everything around me.

"This is a very important stone so keep it close. You do not want anyone else to get a hold of it. It is called a steinsalz Unbregrenzte Macht. Or the stone of unlimited power. It only works when you ask it to activate. However. Do not use it for more than twenty minutes or the power will become too much and drain you of life."

"Well, that's comforting. So only when I need a short second wind." She nodded picking up another stone. "There should not be anymore." Taking it out I saw that it was an arrowhead. I had found it on a trail we discovered by accident one time. Making the decision to take the arrowhead back home storing it with the other stones for safekeeping. "Okay, but I'm pretty sure it has no magikal properties." Izabella smiled as she looked up at me.

"That is where you are wrong. Everything has a magikal property. You just have to find out what it is. Find a thick strong branch and bring it back with you." That seemed like an odd request but after everything else I had recently witnessed I was not going to question it.

It did not take long to find one that I liked. A heavy oak branch that was still alive though it had been struck by lightning from the look of it. It took several minutes to finish breaking it off. Walking back with the branch in hand Izabella nodded approvingly handing me the arrowhead.

"Hold them both in your hands, lift and let them down three times and say reveal." I looked at her skeptically but did it anyways. When I looked down it had changed into a bow with a cache of arrows. It had been a long time since I had went bow hunting, but I'm sure it would not take long to tune up.

"Have you ever shot a bow?" Nodding she pointed to a tree fifty feet out. "Shoot the base of that tree." Taking out an arrow I notched it on drawing back taking aim at the base of the tree she had pointed to. After taking careful aim I let it go hitting exactly where it was supposed to.

"Nice shot." She commented as I walked over to retrieve the arrow from the ground. "Since your hunting skills seem to be intact lets practice sparring with your sword." I could not have agreed more. Setting down my new bow and cache of arrows I drew out Star Burst.

The sun began setting when we called it quits for the night. Even my sister had a chance to try it out as she had woke for a few minutes. Annabelle was not quite as good as I was, but I had a few more practices on her. While Izabella worked with my sister's sword lesson I made and applied the paste to Drake again. When we had tied them he had started to limp and his back was sore. Once Izabella and Annabelle were done practicing I walked up to them looking to Drake.

"Could we somehow send Drake back home? He's in pretty bad shape now. Maybe the way you send your letters?

Could we send him back that way?" I figured it was worth a try. Izabella walked over frowning. She must have been thinking the same thing I had been. There was no way Drake would last another day without completely breaking down on us.

"Yes, it is time for him to return. It will take all three of us to do it." I motioned Annabelle over. "Join hands. The open end resting on the horse. Breathe deep, concentrate on where he needs to go. His stall at your grandparents' barn. Okay? Now. Make him go there." We did as she had instructed. Within a couple minutes he was shimmering in the bluish white light disappearing. As we stood feeling drained from what we had just done I realized that the moving dot on the map was bothering me.

"I looked at your map a couple days ago." Izabella looked up curiously as I confessed.

"You sound concerned." Crossing her arms she had the look I had from her so many times now. The look of assessing where I was going with my thoughts.

"There was a dot on the map you had not mentioned to us. Who is it?" Sitting up straight she looked more concerned than before.

"What color was it?"

"It was a dark almost blood red color." Nodding at me she looked distant.

"Where was it when you looked?"

"At least a state away to the west." I was about to ask if we should be worried when she looked up relaxing again.

"Nothing to worry about. Thank you for the information though."

After that we built a woodpile up. Izabella made me use the fire stone to light it to begin learning how my powers worked. Rolling out the blankets we settled down for the night.

"You know. This has been quite an adventure compared to anything I have done with my friends." Annabelle sat next to me on her blankets. For at least half an hour or better we talked about her friends and how school had been going. As we talked I felt as if I was being watched looking around. Izabella looked to me sharply as I did so.

"Maylee. Something wrong?" I shook my head wrapping up the conversation to go to sleep. After another long hard day it did not take long for sleep to take over.

Dante

Days had passed and Izabella still had not answered my messages. Grabbing the only map I had using a location spell I found where Shadow and I were stopped. Frustrated I threw the map to the ground sitting where I stood.

"Why does it feel as if we are going no where?" Snorting Shadow stepped over nudging me carefully.

"You need to rest for more than a few hours Dante. You will need your strength in case they do happen to catch up to us."

"I know." His head jerked up turning to something only he had heard.

"Voices. Over there." Indicating with a toss of his head.

"Are they good or do we need to run?"

"I heard Izabella. If she is with them I do not think we have to worry."

"Right. Unless she wants to kill me as well. Might as well let her." Snorting as he shook his head he nudged me towards the voices.

"Let her know you are here." Shaking my head I stayed where I sat.

"No. I'm too tired." Shaking his head Shadow walked closer to where he heard them before coming back minutes later.

"They are traveling as we are. Three horses, two girls with Izabella." Frowning I stood looking at him thoughtfully.

"Two girls with her?" He nodded. "Did they look similar?"

"Same facial structure. Sisters you are thinking?"

"Yeah. They have to be the ones from the prophecy. Right now they have had no training. I could separate them from Izabella and talk to them. See what they know and how much power they have."

"Why? I thought you were aligning to the council?" Rolling my eyes I nodded.

"I am Shadow. I want to know what kind of fighters the council is recruiting to think they have a chance with no training. Or" Shadow leaned against me as I thought. "How old were they? Young?"

"I would say closer to your age." Nodding I stepped away to walk where he had been to see them for myself. As I stepped carefully through the brush I could hear them talking. Not exactly what was being said though.

Both girls had jet black hair which contrasted Izabella's platinum blonde. As I watched them interact I would notice certain habits or tendencies they had. The girl with long black hair kept glancing to where I was hidden like she knew someone was there. She held herself upright to the point of looking rigid. As she walked around I looked her over. The girl was physically fit yet she had nice curves on her. As she turned I could see she had bright blue eyes. My breath caught slightly when I saw her look directly at me. Izabella caught her attention back as they settled for night. What I wouldn't give to have her. The other girl had shorter hair styled into layers acted younger talking about what had happened at school.

"Okay you two. Enough." Izabella told them as she sat down between them. The girl with shorter hair grabbed a blanket settling down going to sleep while the other held a box looking down at it. What did she have?

"You did well with those today Maylee. It is time to rest now." Why did her name sound so damned familiar? It bothered me as I stood watching her closely. Slowly I backed away walking back to my own camp.

"What did you find out?"

"They are definitely sisters. The one who is my age is called Maylee." Shadow snorted shaking his head.

"You have met her before." Frowning I shook my head.

"I don't remember her."

"Your father wiped your memories a lot. I remember her. Though I never met her. Her sister's name is Annabelle." Shaking my head I could not believe what he was telling me.

"Let me get this straight. I knew her, but my father wiped my memory of her from me. Why?"

"You two were very close in a long distance relationship. I remember one time you visited Michigan to see her." My head began to throb as I tried to remember anything.

"I told you about her?"

"Yes."

"What all did I tell you?" Walking closer he nickered softly nudging my face.

"I will tell you when the time is right. If I told you now you would never believe me nor could you expect her to." Nodding I considered before conceding. "You should settle for night as well. You could use the rest." Agreeing I pulled out my blankets laying by my fire as Shadow shifted into a panther curling up around me.

I woke before the sun rose looking around to make sure my father's army had not caught up. None. Good. Thinking ahead I changed into my fighting gear belting Guardian back on walking closer to Izabella's camp. I knew she would either be surprised I was here or angry. Either way she knew it was because I had changed my mind like she had been begging me to for the past five years. As I walked into their camp area I stepped on a twig I had not saw freezing. One of them had moved when they heard it. Breathing out slowly I walked closer looking at all three of them. It was hard to believe that Izabella had not set up a perimeter for her camp. That was odd. Or maybe she was expecting me to find her. Who knew at this point.

As I stood frozen yet I swept over the rest of the camp before taking another step. Walking to the nearest person sleeping I kneeled down next to her. This was the younger girl. She could not have been more than sixteen. The same age as my brother. Shaking my head I stood walking to the next one. As I kneeled I felt a jolt of recognition. This was her. This was Maylee. Feeling even as she slept that she was powerful I secured her sword before standing. Tapping her foot with my toe I woke her up training my sword at her so she did not get any cute ideas. As soon as her eyes opened with the fire in them I knew I was in over my head. She was hell fire in the flesh. Her eyes flashed when she realized I already had her sword. Just from the way she was reacting. I knew I was in trouble.

Maylee

Something rustling on the ground woke me up. Opening my eyes I noticed there was a person standing over me. Secondly there was something sharp at my throat, a sword. Nice. Now wide awake, fear gripped at me thinking of the hooded figures who wanted to capture us. As my vision focused more I noticed this was a human like us so not the hooded figures. That was one plus to me at this point. Next I realized that this was a guy around my age. Observing him as he stood over me he was dressed in all black tactical type clothing, had shaggy black hair, a light complexion with a slight tan, built as if he was all muscle. Hell. This could end badly as I felt my temper ignite immediately.

If it wasn't for the fact that his sword was at my throat I would have taken a liking to him. He was a good looking guy as I skimmed his facial features. Slowly I reached for my sword. He raised an arm showing that he had already taken it. Dammit! He had taken it before I woke up. With a finger to his lips to signal me to stay quiet. Nodding I stood up. Jerking his head to an area away from the camp he walked in front of me.

"This way." When he spoke I noticed that he had a southern accent. Once out of sound reach of the camp he stopped sheathing his sword looking at me.

"Who the hell are you?" That was the only question on my mind and I might as well be point blank about it. If he was an enemy all I wanted to do was get my sword back and carve him up. Staring at me he smirked throwing my sword back to me.

Well, he couldn't be an enemy if he was giving me my weapons back. Catching my sword I belted it on watching him the entire time. It threw me off that he just watched my every move with his arms crossed. The way Izabella did when she was assessing me. Without warning I drew on him before he could move.

"Now. Who the hell are you?" He did not look very surprised that I had done this but not alarmed either. Calm. How can you be calm when you have a sword pointing in your direction? Smirking in a very annoying way he nodded answering.

"I am Dante. I am like you. A fighter or defender. Whatever the hell they are calling us." I listened to his voice watching his expressions as he spoke. Something was off. He wasn't one of us as I was receiving bad vibes. Though instead of upping my alertness I just watched him closely. Something deep inside was keeping me from just attacking him.

"What are you doing here? Why did you bring me out here?" Looking around he shifted from one foot to another impatiently.

"I have been looking for that shadow creature. It was looming around here so I stopped in. As for bringing you out here? I wanted to talk to you without Izabella butting in constantly."

"How do you know her if you're not immortal?" It was a legit question this time.

"It does not matter. What do you know about the creature?" My gut instinct kicked back in to tell me not to trust this guy. I felt my pocket knowing my stones were all in there. Hopefully I could pull out the right one the first time.

"Why should I share any information with you?" I shot back angrily. Feeling the power each stone emulated I could tell which one was what. Feeling the warmth I knew it was my fire stone. Before he could retort I gripped it tightly.

"Circle!" Sure enough a ring of fire appeared around the two of us. It had distracted him enough I rushed forward to attack him. He automatically fought back looking surprised I had attacked as he countered. This was not like the sparring I had done with Izabella. This felt like a life and death fight. I could tell he was much more skilled than I was. He was able to disarm me knocking Star Burst from my hand. His sword pointed to my throat again as I had attempted to walk forward to retrieve it. Though he did not look angry. Just out of breath.

"Okay. I was not expecting that. Now, put out the fire before you burn down the woods." His voice was forcefully calm as he looked to the circle around us. Smirking I shrugged.

"It's controlled. Don't worry."

"Just put it out." Frowning he lowered his sword slightly raising his eyebrows as if saying five minutes ago.

"Fine." I said stiffly as the stone was still in my hand. "Out." The fire vanished as if it had never been there. He bent down picking up my sword taking a moment to examine it now that it was out of it's scabbard.

"Nice sword. Don't see black iron used hardly anymore." He handed it back to me. Now you would think he would have learned the first time he did that. I accepted it back but kept it at my side. Annabelle and Izabella appeared beside me at that moment. Ha, busted. Izabella looked at Dante with disapproval, or was it hatred? I just was not sure without knowing her better than what I did.

"What are you doing here?" Her voice was barely level. It did not sound forced, but legitimately curious.

"I would ask you the same thing but I can see why now." Pointing to me he asked. "How long has she been training?" As

I listened to his voice it washed over me as though I knew him from somewhere.

"Two, three days. Why?" I told him bluntly answering before Izabella could. He smirked at my tone causing me to smirk back for a moment before I remembered waking to his sword at my throat.

"You're not half bad. A lot of guts I'll give you that. Impressive for the amount of time." The way he carried himself posture wise annoyed me as I found myself disliking him more every time he spoke. Though my head and body were fighting each other with how I felt about him. Dammit. Really? I asked my body as I rose an eyebrow at him like he knew I was fighting an inner struggle.

"I'm still not impressed with you." His smirk faded nodding he turned to Izabella.

"We need to talk."

"Yes. I believe we do." I could hear a twinge of anger in her voice. Dante must have sensed it as he looked weary. They walked down a trail talking very animatedly about something I could not hear from this distance. Probably about him. Maybe he was evil but seen the error of his ways and wants to work for good now. Yeah right. Only in the movies. Annabelle and I walked back to camp retrieving granola bars and bottled water from our backpacks.

We saddled the horses awaiting their return. Delilah was ready for Izabella now. I checked my cell phone for the time; it was one in the afternoon. We kicked back against some big oak trees listening to music closing my eyes for a nap.

Dante

"So. Who are they Izabella?" I asked already knowing full well who they were. I just wanted to confirm it.

"That is none of your concern Dante." Looking at me worriedly she continued. "What the hell were you thinking? Your father's men could have killed you!" Sighing I knew she was going to berate me for what I had done.

"I didn't care Izabella. I just want it to be over. They tried to throw me in charge and I told them no. That he was gone." She was surprised as she stared at me tilting her head.

"Dante." She laid a hand on my arm. I refused to look at her knowing she was worried about me. For the past five years she had helped me out. Now it was time to repay her.

"I will double for the council. If they want me to. I'll do it for any information they want." Shifting her feet she crossed her arms over her chest frowning.

"Really? For how long?" Loosing a breath I did not even realize I was holding I shook my head.

"I don't know. I really don't know how long I could do it. They know I'm done for good after I left off the way I did." Scoffing she glanced back to her camp.

"They want your blood Dante. You are better off just changing now. And I know that it will be difficult for you. But you will be better off in the long run. I just do not know if they will let you back in after what you did." Shaking my head I felt my heart thump harder in my chest thinking about returning to Syracuse.

"Look. If the council wants me to double. I will try to get back into their good graces. But I refuse to lead them." Her nose flared as she sighed shaking her head at me.

"I will let the council know." Nodding I could see the two girls through the trees again. It bothered me that Maylee had fought so well with hardly any training.

"You seriously have not trained her?" Shaking her head Izabella could see how hard I was thinking. "Are they the ones that stupid prophecy foretold?" Raising her eyebrows she smirked slightly.

"Why do you want to know so badly?" Scowling in response I crossed my arms over my chest feeling defensive.

"Curiosity." Raising her chin at me her brows furrowed.

"No. Something else." I raised my eyebrows as she looked at me before back to the girls. Something must have clicked as she went wide eyed muttering under her breath. "It is true. It is foretold of you two being together."

"The prophecy? I doubt that. It's a bunch of bullshit Izabella. None of it is true." Eyes narrowing she stepped closer.

"Really?" She asked as I shook my head at her.

"Really."

"You are changing sides. Which is in the prophecy." Okay. Yeah she had me there. She pointed to Maylee through the trees. "She is the most powerful sorceress I have seen in centuries without any training. Also in the prophecy. You both have siblings. Which is in the prophecy."

"That prophecy is a bunch of bullshit Izabella! I'm not going by that." I had no idea where all my anger was actually coming from but it was from deep. Looking concerned at my sudden anger she was only a foot from me.

"No. But maybe we should. I did not foresee you changing your mind after your father's death. Last I knew you wanted to be done with all of this." Shaking my head I had no interest in talking about that.

"Izabella. I realize that. But Theo attempting to kill me changed that." Nodding she glanced to her camp again. I knew she wanted to return so they could keep moving. Shaking my head I pointed back to her camp. "What is her name?" Scowling Izabella began walking back to camp indicating I follow.

"Her name is Maylee. She has had no training with her powers. And very limited with that sword." Stopping Izabella looked back at me smiling wide. "And she damn near killed you. When you have had years of training. So. You might want to keep your distance. She does not seem to like you much." I smirked as we began walking back thinking how she had handled herself against me. Maylee was attractive to me as I thought about all her features and tendencies.

"I like her. I find her to be" Izabella stopped turning to glare at me her hand closer than comfort allowed to my throat.

"Like her from a distance. She is cold at first. Trust me there. And you are not totally aligned with us since you are willing to spy for the council. That she will be able to sense as well." I rolled my eyes at her.

"Seriously? You think she would be able to sense that?" Looking irritated her cheeks were red as she huffed.

"Yes. It took me days to convince her to leave with me. Her and her sister were already under attack." I felt tired and drained as I stood there pinching the bridge of my nose. Why would they attack them? It made no sense. Lack of sleep was catching up to me. "Just align now Dante. Fully. You are exhausted from running." I felt my nostrils flare as I loosed a deep breath shaking my head. The vein in my temple pulsed with the stress I was placing myself under.

"You know I cannot do that. If I am able to turn one person. Theo might allow me in long enough to gather information for the council." Growling she shook her head.

"You are so damn stubborn. Are you trying to get yourself killed? Because you are certainly on the right path."

"Haven't you figured that out by now? I don't care. They can kill me. I have nothing left to live for." With that I sat down against a boulder just off our path with my head in my hands. Izabella sighed almost growling as she kneeled in front of me.

"What about your sister and mom?" Her voice gentler than it had previously been. I knew she only wanted to help. The way she had helped since I was sixteen.

"The army knows that they are off limits. They do not know anything about what dad did. Or what Matt and I are. They are safe. So if the army wants me dead to save them. They can kill me. I'm done fighting them." I could hear her mutter under her breath as she shifted sitting beside me against the boulder.

"Can I ask you something?" Looking over at her she glanced up the path.

"Anything. I'm an open book." Nodding she looked around the trail to make sure we were not overheard.

"If you did not care whether they killed you or not. Why did you seek me out? Why did you run from them?" I felt my heart thump hard in my chest again. They had made me feel trapped. But that was not the reason I had run. Honestly I did not know.

"I don't know Izabella. I guess it was pure instinct kicking in. I ran into you running away from them. I tried to call you while I was running. Shadow was the one to point out you were close. He heard you last night." Izabella looked me up and down measuringly.

"You really do not know why you ran. Do you? Besides the initial flight instinct of being attacked. I did not hear your calls. That is odd." This was something I did not want to talk about. Shaking my head I stood walking to Shadow. If she did not want me near her precious trainees. I would leave.

"Look" I ran a hand through my hair. "If it makes you feel more at ease. I'll go back. I don't have to go with you. Or them. I wouldn't want to taint them with my presence." As I walked away Izabella huffed grabbing my arm turning me around to face her.

"No. You are not going back to get yourself killed. I think they would do more than that to you. You are better off going with me." Scowling I pried her hand off angrily. I was not about to be told what to do again.

"Like you care? Just let me go and die. I told you. I have nothing" Grabbing me by the front of my shirt she shoved me into a tree my head hitting painfully causing me to see stars momentarily. Just like the first time we had met.

"I know your father really messed with your head. But being suicidal is not the answer. Now listen to me." I had thrown her hand off but now she grabbed my throat pressing her thumb in making it hard to breathe. "Quit. Fighting. Me." Her face was inches from my own. "You know I will tell you the truth. Now pay attention."

"Okay." I choked out. Letting go she let me fall to the ground to gasping for my breath. "What do you want from me?" Touching my neck I knew it would bruise. Izabella was small but physically strong.

"I want you to see your future as it will be if you go with us." Sitting on the ground I shook my head chuckling darkly. What did she think was going to happen?

"Right. Let's see. I change sides. Guard your little leader back there. Die in the final battle protecting her. No thanks." She threatened to choke me again. Holding my hands in surrender before she did. "Fine. What will happen?" Nodding she placed her hand next to my temple touching just with her fingertips.

"Now. Tell me what you see." I sighed watching irritably.

"I'm on the island. On the trail that goes down to the beach." Thankfully I had been on the island years ago when Izabella had saved me. My father had left me for dead when she scooped me up taking me to the island to heal. Unfortunately all I could think about was making sure my mom and sister were safe forcing her to take me home.

"Good. Keep looking." Walking along the trail that led to the beach.

"I'm on the beach now. Just walking along." Next I could see two horses running closer. They were both dark with no tack on. Running up to where I stood one was Shadow the other was a huge black. Similar to the one I had noticed back at Izabella's camp. Looking up at the black horse was the girl from Izabella's camp. It was Maylee. What the hell is this?

"What do you see Dante?" Izabella voice asked. My heart stopped as I watched her. I felt something I had not felt in such a long time I had almost forgotten what it was. Maylee slipped off her horse stepping up to me her arms around my neck smiling. That smile was real. She was talking and we

"Stop. Now Izabella." Stepping back she smiled at me as I sat down on the ground unable to breathe. What the hell was that?

"Now do you see?" Looking up I glared at her for tricking me. After everything I had been through and done. There was no way that girl would ever even look at me like that.

"You are not being fair. That is not my future!" I raised my voice with each word. Izabella smirked momentarily as she looked down at me crossing her arms.

"How do you feel right now? You seem short of breath." Still scowling I stood shakily walking away from her angrily.

"Stop! You are doing this to force me to go with you." Frowning she shook her head following me worriedly.

"Dante. I am not tricking you. Not in any way right now. I showed you what your future would look like if you left here with me." My chest tightened painfully as I rubbed where my heart was thumping hard.

"That is not possible. I'm not. No one could" Raising her eyebrows she walked up in front of me resting her hands on my shoulders to steady me.

"You are angry because I made you feel love Dante. That is something you have not felt in a long time. And it is difficult for you. But yes. That will happen." Now my anger hit the roof making me feel hot.

"No! It is not possible! Stop tricking me!" I shouted at her as she stayed calm. Yanking away from her I walked to Shadow swinging up onto his back. Walking to Shadow she laid a hand on his neck.

"Shadow" He perked up at her. "Do not allow him go back. He does not know what he is doing. I made him feel an emotion he did not like. Now he is angry at everything." Shadow tilted his head back at me nickering.

"I could tell. His energy is different."

"Shut it." He snorted shaking his head.

"Dante. Come with me back to camp. Travel with us to the island. After we are there if you feel the same as you did before I showed you that. I will let you come back without a fight. But

I want you to give that possible future a chance." Growling I followed her to her camp on Shadow.

"Fine. There is zero chances. But I'll go."

"Dante. Breathe and relax." Shadow told me as we walked. He stopped suddenly reaching back he pulled on my pants with his teeth. "Dismount. Now." Exasperated at both of them I dismounted leaning against him still trying to catch my breath. "She really got to you this time. What did she show you?" Shaking my head I stood up walking a few steps.

"She showed me a glimpse into my future. I was walking to the beach on the island. I met up with Maylee there. She was smiling, wrapped her arms around me. We kissed. I pulled out of it knowing I am way too screwed up for someone like her." Shadow snorted as he looked to Izabella who had stopped waiting for us.

"I think you need to give her a chance to get to know you again. You two were together before. You had told me you were in love with her. Than your father wiped your memory. Try to start over with her. You might be surprised." Izabella looked slightly confused as to what we had been discussing.

"Now I am curious. Shadow. Tell me what you know." Nodding he told her everything he knew without letting me hear any of it.

"So. With the both of them having their memories wiped out it will be interesting." Izabella nodded glancing to where I stood impatiently.

"Or she might kill me." He shook his head pulling on my shirt to go to their camp. As I walked back with Izabella slightly ahead of me Maylee looked up at us from her book. Glaring at me she glanced to her sister before standing closing her book. I could tell by her body language I had my work cut out for me on this trip. Sighing I knew what I had to do next if I was spying for the council as I had told Izabella. With paper and pen in hand I wrote a letter to Theo apologizing for what I had done. And what I was prepared to do to help them from the inside.

"Did you send it?" Izabella asked before we rode onto the trail.

"Yeah. We'll see what he says." Nodding at me she walked to the palomino Maylee had just readied. Turning to Shadow he tossed his nose as I stepped back on.

Maylee

I glanced over at Dante as Izabella led him right into our camp with his horse following him. I did not trust him. It had a lot to do with the fact I had woke up with his sword at my throat. Izabella seemed to know him well. Dante's horse reminded me a lot of the shadows as he was a dark grey.

We refrained from running or trotting too much as Delilah was starting to wear down. Tough she may be, but even the toughest have a breaking point. Near sunset I watched as she began stumbling and tripping over nothing. Finally she stumbled so bad her knees hit the ground. I jumped off of Rocki to check her while Izabella stepped off so that Delilah could stand. Izabella unsaddled Delilah while I made sure she had not been seriously injured when she fell. Annabelle and Dante dismounted as well untacking their own horses. After which together they walked off to gather wood for a fire. My back tensed as I watched them walk together to where we could not see them. Izabella noticed stepping in front of me. Shaking my head of the dark thoughts I ripped my attention to Delilah.

"It's time for her to go home." I said quietly as I finished looking her over. She was simply worn out and tired. Annabelle came over once they were back to ask what we were going to do with her. The three of us repeated the process with her as we had done with Drake just the day before. After she shimmered out of sight I looked at Izabella noticing Dante had watched us with curiosity. He was keeping his distance. Looking to Izabella I knew there was no way we could make the boys carry us both.

"What are we going to do now? You don't have a horse to ride. We cannot ride the boys double and carry all the equipment that Delilah had been carrying." Smirking slightly Izabella looked around the camp area.

"Well. There is something I can do. It might take some convincing for you to do it. But I am willing to give it a try." Whistling in the same eerie way she had done at my grandma's when Danny had appeared. Looking up the trail I could hear the sound of a horse running. I nearly dropped! It was Danny! He ran straight to me with his ears pinned straight back rearing and squealing. I walked closer to him so that he stopped. Standing still he nuzzled into my chest pushing me back slightly. He was solid enough to touch this time. This was amazing! I had not been this happy in years smiling wide as I hugged his neck tight.

"What is the condition in which he is here?" Izabella walked up behind me patting his neck.

"That you are the one who rides him." This was too much. I actually had the opportunity to ride him again! Danny is the same height as Rocki at sixteen two hands tall. I led him to a nearby tree stump swinging up onto his back. No saddle, no bridle, complete freedom. The two of us took off running a little ways down the trail before we came back. I slid off letting him wander around since nothing could hurt him. He was already dead.

"You will be able to ride Rocki. He should be okay for you. He's not like this one was." I pointed over to where Danny had stopped to stand guard. Izabella nodded her approval. We rolled out our blankets to rest and sleep. Only I wasn't tired. Taking out my phone I listened to a couple of my rock songs in my play list while reading a book. Dante sat down across from me signaling he was trying to talk to me. Rolling my eyes I ignored him turning my music up louder. Next I know one of my ear buds was taken out of my ear.

"Hey! What the hell did you do that for?" Rolling his eyes in turn he held my ear bud looking irritated.

"You were ignoring me when I was trying to talk to you."

"Yeah? So get the message. I don't want to talk." I turned away from him taking my ear bud back. He walked around to where I could see him again. I was growing aggravated. "What?" I snapped.

"Could we go for a walk? Work out some of that pent up energy you have. Maybe talk?" He was insistent but I could still sense he was irritated about something himself. Teeth grinding in irritation I stood in front of him.

"Fine." I picked up my sword walking past making sure to slam his shoulder as hard as I could. When I was out in front of him he caught up with me still muttering to himself.

"Why are you so angry?" Really? I asked myself looking at him over my shoulder.

"I thought that was kind of obvious." I said letting all sarcasm drip through.

"Why? Because of this morning?" I wondered if he was really that thick or if he was being sincere.

"Part of it. You never did answer my question either." Stopping he looked weary and stressed as if he had been traveling a lot.

"Which one? You asked many." He watched me carefully as my hand stayed on the hilt of my sword in case he tried anything. "I told you who I was and why I was here. What else?" My eyes narrowed on him at his tone.

"I'm not stupid. That shadow creature was not the reason you were here. You say you're one of us. And yet Izabella seems to dislike you. Why?" He looked at me surprised at my conclusion.

"She told me you had good insight." This was a statement. I did not take it as a compliment. "Yes. I know you're not stupid. I cannot tell you why just yet. In good time I will. Just not yet. And for the record. Izabella does not hate me. I have known her for a while. However. I will tell you I am a descendant of the sorcerer Vladimir." I looked at him smirking at his confession. Something gave me the feeling he also had a tough time trusting others.

"That must be one reason why I do not trust you. But only one of many. Vladimir was evil after all." Looking at me exasperated he rolled his eyes explaining his reasoning.

"Yes. But his children were not." He stepped closer looking into my eyes. My heart thundered in my chest reacting to him. Oh stop it I told my body.

"I still don't trust you." I replied taking the step back he had taken closer.

"That's okay. I don't trust you either." His jaw clenched as he told me watching my body language.

"I guess that's what they call a mutual feeling." I stated as his expression changed to quizzical.

"You're not going to ask me why I don't trust you?" Slightly surprised at his response I took the bait.

"No. Should I?" He shook his head glancing to my sword.

"No. But I would feel better if you would quit grabbing for your sword." Without realizing it I had it halfway drawn out. I slid it back down turning to walk back to camp. He walked up behind me grabbing my wrist stopping me to turn to face him. My hand was already in my pocket pulling out Feuer.

"Boundary line." It blew him backwards away from me into a nearby tree. "Out." It quickly vanished not even leaving scorch marks on the ground. I walked toward him as he sat on the ground rubbing the back of his head. "Never! Ever! Grab my arm like that!" He looked up at me slowly standing unsure of how to respond to my reaction.

"Okay." He said slowly. "You can consider me warned. You really didn't have to try to kill me." I almost felt bad, almost. He still held the back of his head. Maybe it knocked some sense into him I mused with myself. "You are much stronger than most after only a few days." I began walking again but he ran stopping in front of me.

"You know. You're getting on my last nerve." Smirking he nodded.

"We need to talk."

"About what?" My temper was surfacing again.

"Your sword."

"What about it?"

"It is made of black iron"

"So? What about it?"

"That's what the forces of Theasis use. Well. A type of it anyway. Yours is not an actual black blade."

"Who? What are you talking about?"

"Theasis. He's the one causing all the problems across the world right now. And he's not even at full power yet. We're going to need all the help we can gather to defeat him."

"Yeah, well it will be used against him this time. I will never join them." My voice had dropped low as my anger had risen. Dante's face showed much relief that I was standing my ground.

"I believe you. Really. So now that we have discussed that. We can go back to camp and get some sleep." He walked beside me all the way back making me uneasy. When we returned I checked on Rocki who was already dozing off.

80

That night I dreamed for the first time since we had been traveling. I did not like what I saw. Dante had informed me that the bad guys used the black iron swords. And in my dream there I was at the front of their army in all black. My sword out. Ready to fight.

The following morning I walked over to where I had set my saddle to pull out the map. I rolled it out, found our dots and of course now Dante's. We were in the middle of Georgia, not too far to go now. I put the map back in the bag as someone was stirring when I stood up. As I turned around I find it had been Dante right behind me. Involuntarily I jumped backwards tripping over my saddle grabbing a branch to stop myself from falling.

"What the hell is your problem? You could have at least let me know you were right behind me." I was breathing hard from trying to catch my balance.

"Sorry." He looked it walking over to his dark grey horse. "That spirit horse of yours. He is just as distrusting as you are. He was standing next to you when I walked up. Pinned his ears at me." Standing up straight Danny was still at my side his ears were still pinned back and his tail was swishing angrily. I smiled at him patting his neck.

"He's a good judge of character. Good boy. You can go. I'm fine." He kept an eye on Dante as he turned to go back to where the other horses were tied.

"He's very protective of you. Not many horses are like that. Even your big black is not that protective of you." Dante walked back to where I stood watching the horses.

"Yeah. Well, it took me a long time to gain his trust. I had him for seven years when I had to put him down. I have really enjoyed being able to ride him again." Glancing over he had taken a drink of water.

"May I ask why you had to put him down?" I watched Danny nibble on some grass wandering around. Looking to Dante I scowled a little as I dredged up that memory.

"His back broke. Top veterinarians could not explain it. They could not figure out why because he was completely healthy. Why are you even asking?" He glanced over at Danny curiously.

"Well. There could have been a dozen things that happened for him to be put down. That is strange. I can tell he really bonded with you." Walking away he rolled up his blankets packing them away placing them by his saddle. Soon after he began pacing around the camp. I kept an eye on him as he did as it looked as if he was assessing everything around us. Sitting against my saddle reading he stopped in front of me suddenly.

"Are you as restless as I am?" I looked up at him feeling irritated but answered all the same.

"Probably. Why?"

"Want to spar? Just swords. No powers." I smirked stowing my book away.

"Sure, let's go." Picking up my sword from the ground beside me I belted it on walking with him a little way from camp. I checked my phone. It was eight in the morning. We started to spar back and forth. More like trying to figure out the other's fighting style intensifying from there.

By the end of it I learned a few new moves, tested my reflexes, and almost disarmed him. Almost. When we stopped to take a break I had a good look at his sword, it was like Annabelle's. Except that the length was the same as mine. On closer inspection it had black worked into the hilt. Barely noticeable. I still did not trust him as we walked back side by side. There was something about him that made me want to put more distance between us than I knew I would be able to. On the flip side I also felt as though I wanted to be near him. My body reacted to him in ways I did not like. Such as wanting to be close to him. Wanting him to accidently brush against me. I was angry at my own body as we walked along stepping away as we walked.

"What is the name of your sword?" He looked over at me unsure to answer. A moment later he looked away.

"I call it Guardian. What about yours?" I touched the hilt as he flinched making me smirk. At least in that aspect I knew he viewed me as an equal.

"Star burst." He laughed.

"Like the candy?" Continuing to laugh I scowled unreasonably angry.

"No. Like how a star looks when it explodes, a star burst. As in it will be the last thing you see when your lights go out." I finished fiercely. He quit laughing looking back at me surprised. By what I'm not sure.

"It should have been something like Destroyer or Wildfire the way you fight." I stopped walking ten feet from camp.

"What is that supposed to mean?" I snapped as he stepped back. Holding his hands up at me he explained.

"I only meant I thought it would be a more aggressive name. Something to fit the way you fight or your personality." Shaking my head I turned continuing to walk to camp.

"Maybe." I finally answered. Annabelle and Izabella were just finishing packing up when we walked into camp. Izabella looked up surprised. Probably at the fact I had willingly walked with him out of camp.

"She did not try to scorch you today?" She asked as she swung up onto Rocki watching Dante cross over to his dark grey.

"No, not today. She's a quick learner. Handles that sword well." Izabella nodded reining Rocki to begin walking down the trail. Dante shrugged at her no comment swinging up onto his horse to follow her.

It felt like the day faded fast and we were moving slow. We stopped to rest around two in the afternoon with Izabella taking out the map to see just where we were on our journey. Annabelle pulled Oscerr up slowing as I noticed she jerked her chin to indicate she wanted to talk away from the other two.

"What is it?" Smirking she nodded to Dante ahead of us.

"When are you two just going to fuck it out?" Angrily I pulled Danny to a stop.

"Annabelle Paige!" The other two glanced back at my voice pausing.

"What? The tension between you two is unbearable. You obviously like each other." The tension on my shoulders intensified as I stared her down.

"Tension yes. But that is not going to happen Anna." Smirking wider yet she glanced to where Izabella and the person in question stood waiting for us. Rolling her eyes she shook her head at me.

"Fine. But you seriously need to with someone. Damn sis." Scowling I could not believe she was having this conversation with me.

"I am not taking advice on sex from my younger sister. Who is not even legal to be having sex might I add." Crossing her arms over her chest she glared at me.

"Tell me you are not serious? I know you were having sex before you were seventeen." Closing my eyes I nodded though mine had not been consensual.

"You know it was because" Pausing her expression changed.

"Shit. I'm sorry Maylee. I did not mean it that way." Shaking my head I walked away from her. "Maylee stop." Shaking my head again I continued until I was behind the other two. My teeth clenched as I kept myself from crying in front of them. Annabelle rode up beside me grabbing my elbow to make me look at her. "I did not mean it that way. You know I didn't." My teeth grinding I nodded walking away from her. I heard Izabella ask her something I could not hear before she appeared at my side.

"Maylee. Are you okay?" Nodding I stayed facing the opposite way as she continued walking past me dismounting Rocki. "We all could use a break. Let the horses rest." Taking out the map she looked it over as Dante and I dismounted. Annabelle was still in her saddle as she watched Izabella. I had a bad feeling about this. "We are just in Florida now. It should not take long for us to arrive at port." She rolled the map back up sliding it into her bag.

"Where are we going?" My sister asked her causing Dante to look at her sharply.

"To a shipyard in the tip of Florida. There is a ship waiting there called the Rockford. It will take us to the island. That is where you will be training." I had to admit that this had been fun. And maybe I was not ready for it to end. The part where my sister began dredging up situations I did not want to think about I was ready to be done with. I was not ready to let Danny go either.

"How long?" Annabelle asked looking fearful. Something told me that the fact she was fearful was not any good. Keeping an eye on her I watched her body language.

"Maybe three hours. Less than that hopefully." Izabella responded as she readjusted Rocki's cinch. Annabelle had been standing next to Izabella when she cued Oscerr running off. I jumped up from the tree I was leaning against screaming at her.

"Annabelle!" She had no intention of slowing down or coming back. "Danny!" He came over as I pointed to my sister running farther away. "Catch them!" He sprinted off at top speed. I strode over to Rocki jumping onto him taking off after them both. Dante was right behind me with his horse to help though I was sure he would be none. I kept kicking Rocki urging him to go faster, but he was not the running type. We started to gain on my sister at last. I watched as Danny ran ahead of them stopping forcing them to stop. Finally catching up to them Danny refused to let them pass. Dismounting Rocki I patted Danny as I walked by him.

"Good boy." Annabelle was positively bawling as I walked up to Oscerr. She looked down at me.

"I want to go home! I don't want anything to do with this anymore!" I looked away from her knowing there was not a thing I could tell her that would make her feel any different. Her sister I might be, but I knew I could not reason with her. Izabella finally caught up to us as Dante dismounted his horse.

"Izabella? Could you talk to her for me? I don't think it would do any good for me to even try." Nodding she stepped forward to where I had been a moment before. "I knew this would happen sooner or later." Dante walked over standing beside me. We both watched as Annabelle dismounted and the two of them walked down the trail a little way. Izabella kept her hand on my sister's back as they walked along talking.

"How old is your sister?" Dante asked surprising me once again that he wanted to speak to me.

"Seventeen a week ago. You have any siblings?" His expression went blank his face suddenly pale.

"Yes. A younger brother and sister."

"Where are they?" Turning he swung onto his horse.

"Home. My sister helps my mom with her gardens." Shaking his head he turned his horse so that he was not facing me staying silent. Short and no real explanation. That was not suspicious at all.

Izabella and my sister finally reemerged. All mounted up heading to our destination. An hour after we had been riding again Dante stopped asking Izabella to lead the rest of the way. An hour and a half later we walked into a shipyard where there was only a single ship at port. It was similar in looks to a cruise ship but scaled down to hold maybe a thousand people.

"There it is." She pointed to it. "That is the Rockford." We walked over to it dismounting the horses. "Wait here." She walked up the ramp coming back ten minutes later motioning for us to board. I stayed rooted to the spot turning to Danny knowing it was time for him to go back. Pulling out the black stone I held it in my hand tightly.

"I release you." He whinnied rearing up disappearing into thin air. I knew he would still watch over me because that was just how he was. Annabelle was waiting for me so I could take Rocki up the ramp behind Oscerr. There were stalls below in the ship's hull. So it was used for traveling to go to battle. It looked like a regular stable down where they had instructed us to go.

Dante

It had only taken a few hours for Theo to write back. In his letter he explained that he had always known there was something going on between my father and myself. Writing that he knew I was not as my father portrayed me to his army. Yet they all seemed to know Matt was a cold blooded killer. Maybe that was how my father had wanted it. For me to lead strategically and for Matt to kill.

"What did they say?" Shadow asked while we were separated from the others for a minute.

"He understands how I feel. That he knew something was wrong he just had not known what." Shadow snorted as we walked along. Glancing up for the first time in a while I watched Maylee on her ghost horse. If it had not been for the fact she needed her saddle to tie her gear on she would have ridden with no tack. Just from watching her I could tell she had the balance to have done it.

"Watching her so closely is only going to irritate her." Shadow commented as I looked back down at him knowing he was right. "Admit it. You're love struck." Making a sound of disgust I shook my head.

"Love struck Shadow? Really?" Tossing his head to say yes. "I admire her for her strength and abilities. Her fire startles me I will admit. She is a force to be reckoned with."

"You two will be great together." I chuckled.

"Yeah. Right. She hates me. That is not happening anytime soon."

"Give her time. She is new at this."

"And untrusting as hell."

"So make her trust you."

"That will be difficult."

"Why? You like her."

"She will know I'm on the other side."

"True. Just try to be friends with her than. Talk to her."

"Fine. I'll try."

"Good."

It was going to be a challenge just convincing her to be friends as every time I approached her was like being thrown back by an invisible barrier. Each time she warmed up by the time we were done talking but she still gave me a distrusting look.

"Have you received anything from them today?" Izabella asked as Maylee had just walked back to camp from a morning sparring session.

"Just a few minutes ago. He wants to meet up in person before I leave." Izabella nodded watching the two girls talk looking to where we stood.

"Keep me informed. Meet with them after everyone is sleeping tonight. We will be in Florida tomorrow." Nodding she walked away looking worried at how tired I was. I could barely sleep anymore with thinking about going back.

"Shadow" He flew down from a nearby tree as I walked away from the camp to meet with Theo.

"Where are you going?"

"I'm meeting up with Theo to discuss what they demand from me to be back in their good graces."

"No." Stopping I looked at him as he shifted into his original form.

"You cannot stand here and tell me what to do Shadow."

89

"I am not going to tell you what to do. I am telling you how dangerous this feels. He's not going to be alone. You know they never fight fair." He had a point.

"I do not have a choice." Snorting irritably he let me mount up running to the meeting place.

Shadow had been right as I walked up to where stood three of them looking none too amused at the sight of me.

"Glad to see you could make it." Keeping my breathing even I tried my best to stay neutral as I stood among them. Theo's eyes glinted like daggers ready to kill me at a moment's notice.

"I never miss a meeting I am summoned to. You should know that." Theo nodded smirking at my response.

"Already back to normal. Time away has done you good. I was afraid you needed an attitude adjustment which is why I brought them." He indicated the men with him.

"Let's just get on with it. What is your demand?" Crossing my arms I already knew there would be a list.

"Well. You did kill some of our men when you left the way you did. Not all of them were your fault as we were attacked by that wild cat as you escaped. None the less it will take more than one demand for you to be back in." Nodding I watched as they assessed my reactions which were none up to now.

"Than tell me so I can get back and started on it."

"If you can turn someone the council is recruiting to our side that would be a good place to start. After that I want you to get friendly with their prodigy we have heard so much about." Frowning I had no clue who he actually meant.

"Their prodigy? Who is it?" Smirking crookedly he stepped closer to me.

"The girl you are traveling with." Confused I shook my head scowling.

"Technically I am traveling with three girls. So which one are you referring to?"

"Izabella is who you met up with correct?"

"Yeah."

"Her two recruits with her. One of them is the prodigy. Do you know which?" Shaking my head I was going to have to lie to them.

"I have only watched them spar with swords. I have not witnessed any powers yet." He nodded.

"Keep an eye on them both." I chuckled at that suggestion.

"The one my age barely speaks to me. Let alone anywhere near her."

"Than she is the one you need to be friendly with."

"What if I can convince her to turn?" Theo smiled wide as a cat who ate the canary.

"If you could convince *her* than you would be leader again."

"No. I want no part in leading Theo. Just made aware of what is going on." That was the single worse mistake I made with Theo. Why had I even offered Maylee to them? To sound as though I have not changed. Looking irritated Theo nodded all the same.

"Fine. As you wish. Turn someone in the next two days. If you succeed I will give you the information you seek."

"Yes sir." Bowing out I turned walking back to Shadow muscles tense waiting for them to change their mind. To attack while my back was turned. When I reached Shadow at the tree line he snorted dipping his head to my chest.

"Your nerves are shot." He commented as I rested a hand on the horn of my saddle taking a deep breath.

"I am aware." After a moment I mounted up taking the reins walking Shadow while my thoughts raced.

91

"Are you actually doing this for the council? Or are you doing it because you don't know anything else?" Yanking the reins to stop he craned his neck to look up at me.

"If I want the council to trust me. I need to give them more information than what I currently have. They will be able to use me to sabotage anything the other side may attempt. And if they try to place a hit on anyone I will know." Squealing in protest he shook his head irritably.

"You should not do this. It is wearing you out. Please just listen. I am here to keep you safe. That is my job Dante." His point was made as I felt more exhausted than I had felt in my life.

"I know. Let's just go. I'm exhausted." Shadow did not speak again as we walked back to our camp. By the time we arrived light was beginning to show in the sky. Not caring I took a nap anyways. An hour later Izabella woke me to find out what happened. I told her what Theo explained and what their demand was. Izabella's eyes narrowed as she glanced to Maylee and Annabelle as they slept.

"Hang out with Annabelle. I think she would turn easily." Scowling I watched as the two girls began to move shaking my head.

"Just give her another reason to hate me why don't you?" Lips in a firm line Izabella stood glancing to Maylee as she sat up from her sleeping bag stretching. Hell. I was officially in hell. When she stretched she had exposed a small amount of skin on her belly before she turned away.

"Maylee does not hate you." Izabella stated drawing my attention back to her as though she knew. "If she did you would be dead already." Raising her eyebrows she turned walking away.

Annabelle was easier to talk to than her sister. Before we packed up to ride the last leg to Florida I approached Annabelle.

As we spoke she asked about my past and what I had done. When I was done she sat silently for a few minutes before looking around. Izabella had pulled Maylee away for a quick sparring lesson while Annabelle and I spoke.

"How do they treat new people?" This was the part I despised. Knowing I had to lie to her just to spy for the council. Maylee was going to hate me forever.

"Very well. I think you would fit in better than with these guys honestly." Nodding she looked up to her sister as she and Izabella walked back. Annabelle looked sad as she watched her sister walking back eyeing us suspiciously.

"My sister wouldn't agree. She sees everything as right and wrong with hardly any grey area." And she was seventeen? Yikes.

"And you see a lot of grey area?" Looking to me she nodded.

"A lot. Izabella has not actually told us why we are leaving except that we were being attacked and she saved us." Leaning closer to her before her sister walked over I added.

"Maybe before we leave to where they are taking us you should run away. Find them. I can tell you where to go if you want."

"I would. Thanks." I knew I should have been happy I had been able to convince Annabelle to leave. But I was not at all as I looked to her sister.

Later in the day as we were crossing into Florida I heard Maylee yell at her sister. Stopping Shadow I turned in my saddle to see what was going on. I was not able to hear what was said. But from the way Maylee had reacted Annabelle said something that cut her to her core. Izabella nodded to dismount to rest the horses while she took Maylee aside to talk. Unfortunately that was when Annabelle attempted to leave. Maylee was able to stop her. I swore under my breath looking to Izabella as she nodded. She knew what I had been doing.

"Close. But not quite." Scowling at me she walked to Maylee who had called for her.

Maylee

All three of us untacked our horses throwing them hay to eat while we sailed to this island. We also made sure they had water to drink. As I walked onto the second deck passing the main office there were loud voices issuing from it. In fact they were almost screaming. One was definitely Izabella's voice that much I could tell. However, I could not hear what exactly it was about. My only guess was that the issue was walking up behind me and my sister.

"Something wrong?" Dante asked as I was still standing next to the door.

"Um, no. Nothing wrong." I continued to walk up the steps emerging onto the main deck. They pulled up the anchor allowing us to begin our journey. I walked to the railing watching the coast of Florida growing farther and farther away. Dante stood beside me watching as well. When I finally noticed he was standing there it had strangely calmed me.

"Do you wonder what will happen to all of this if we fail?" I asked still watching the coast grow smaller.

"It's hard to tell. We will not know until the time comes." His voice was barely above a whisper as we stood there. Good answer I thought. It was growing dark now as we wandered down the stairs to the second deck where all the rooms were. Annabelle met me on the stairs pulling for me to see the room we were going to be staying in. Number thirteen. This I found to be rather amusing. We did not mind, neither of us were superstitious.

The small room reminded me of home. There were oil paintings hanging on white walls, a nightstand with a brass lamp, bunk beds complete with sheets and blankets, all the wood was black cherry. There was even a dresser with six drawers. Like we would even need it. I threw my backpack on the floor next to the nightstand crashing on the bottom bunk.

"I'm saving the fight." I replied upon Annabelle's confusion when I laid out on the bottom bunk. She nodded sitting down at the desk in the room turning on my computer to access the internet checking her e-mail and whatever else accounts.

"Maylee" Annabelle sat across from me on the bottom bunk as I turned to face her.

"Annabelle" She flinched at my tone as I was still angry about the jab she had taken at me on the trail. Closing her eyes for a moment she inhaled deeply before looking at me again.

"I'm sorry. I should never have mentioned your" Shaking my head I turned away from her back to the desk.

"I'm over it Annabelle. It was almost five years ago." Her hand clamped onto my shoulder.

"You say that. But the look on your face when I said it. And your whole demeanor Maylee. It is still on your mind. Talk to me. Please?" Loosing a deep breath I nodded.

"Okay. What do you want to know?" Her nostrils flared as she glanced to the door.

"Have you even had sex since that happened?" Smirking I wanted to laugh but could not manage it with how tired I was.

"Yes Annabelle. In fact I hooked up with a guy from work after I ditched Ethan at the bar. That is not the problem. I promise. With what is happening now. I have to focus on helping to save the world. There will not be time for another person in my life. And that is only if saving the world does not kill me in the end."

"That is not a complete no." She sat up smiling at me. Rolling my eyes I turned back the desk.

***

The motion of the ship did not bother me. Annabelle on the other hand had grade A seasickness. She had been up all night puking her guts out as I slept through it waking me up at ten in the morning. I sat up looking out the window. We were no where near land. In fact it did not even feel like we were moving right now. She informed me about her being up all night sick, which I already knew. At home we said paying homage to the porcelain god since that's what it felt like. She was still a little green looking when I told her it was my turn to use the bathroom but not for the same reason.

Since there was electricity on the ship I plugged in my cell phone so it could charge as it was nearly dead. Looking over I noticed all the clothes that had been in my backpack were gone. When I asked my sister about it she said someone came during the night to collect dirty clothes. They had been delivered this morning clean in the top drawer of the dresser. Well, at least I have clean clothes now. I think a shower is in order too.

Ten minutes after I had finished showering and pulling on my clean clothes someone walked through the hall yelling for everyone to report to the meeting room on the upper deck. We each grabbed our swords belting them on, our items of power, and I pocketed my stones. I left my bow and arrows in the room. There was no sense in taking them.

The meeting room was large like a big corporate building's would be. In the middle was the long rectangular table with chairs lining both sides. There were colored cards every other seat with names on them. We sat down where ours appeared being the first ones in we were able to watch everyone else walk in seating themselves. I noticed that the others had brought their swords and items if they had any. Next observation I made was that we were the only female descendants present. The cards that read our names were the same color as our dots had been on the map. There were six men and Izabella assuming they were the ones who had to find us. Including myself there were nine descendants counting Izabella as Dante's discoverer even though he had actually found us. Izabella sat at the head of the table. The three of us sat to her right. Annabelle, me, and Dante followed by a discoverer from there went by descendant. Izabella stood calling the meeting to order.

"You all know why you are here. Some of you had more difficult journeys than others. But we have all managed to make it in the seven days allowed. We also have one more than we originally planned. The more the better. The more fighters we have the better our chances will be to defeat the enemy. I would like each of you to draw your swords and place them on the table in front of you." She paused as everyone did as she asked them. Walking around the table she began inspecting the swords beginning with the left side working back to us. Skipping over us since we had traveled together. Some time had passed for her to inspect every sword but not too long. Ten minutes tops before she was back to the front of the table.

"Each of you in turn will tell me your first and last name, who you descended, where you are from, and what your powers are." A few of them looked at each other as to say what powers? "Starting with you." She pointed to her left. "Stand and deliver." The guy stood up looking nervous. I would say mid to late twenties, blonde short hair, brown eyes, maybe six foot tall, light complected and built small.

"I am Jake Lang of Hermes, from Bronson Missouri. I have no powers that I am aware of." The next guy that stood up was built like Jake with the exception of gray eyes and darker blonde hair.

"Jarred Woods also of Hermes, from Brooklyn New York. And I also have no powers that I know of." The third stood. Age around mid thirties, short brown hair, green eyes, five foot ten, slightly tan, and looked like he may have worked out a couple times a week to stay in shape.

"I am Ben Plater of Zeus, from DuPont Washington, I create storms." That had to be pretty cool, create a storm. Of course I could do that too with my weather stone. The fourth stood younger than Ben maybe late twenties to early thirties, six foot three, dark brown short hair, brown eyes, thin yet muscular.

"I am Lou Belltin of Zeus, from Billings Montana, I can create lightning out of no where." The next looked fairly young maybe late teens to early twenties like myself. He had a dark complexion, short black hair, a hair over six foot, built like a defensive side football player with dark eyes. Not bad looking at all. I couldn't tell exactly what color his eyes were.

"I am Nathan Kinsly of Hades, from Jeauno Alaska, and I don't know exactly what my powers are but I can make things happen." I smiled as he shrugged sitting down almost wishing I had no idea what my powers were. Nathan wasn't all that sure of himself as the others had been. Though he certainly looked menacing he actually seemed friendly. The final one stood one look and you knew where he was from. I smirked as I observed blue eyes, dark blonde hair slightly overgrown from a short haircut, early to mid twenties, six foot four, and had a surfer's body wow. I bet he had a gorgeous girlfriend back at home.

"I am Todd Crawly of Poseidon, from Miami Florida, and I can control and work with water." Now that I don't think I could do even with my stones making a mental note to ask Todd his age. If he was too young for me I could certainly see my sister with him. That was if he did not have a girlfriend. Dante was next turning pale seemingly glued to his chair. Izabella patiently waited for him to stand to introduce himself. I elbowed him in the ribs hard so he looked over at me.

"Your turn." He nodded standing.

"I am Dante." He stopped looking to Izabella who nodded at him to keep it going. I had not seen him nervous like this. He acted like if they knew who he was they would all converge on him.

"I am Dante of the sorcerer Vladimir, from Syracuse Texas, and I have limited to no powers." He sat down looking like he was about to pass out. I found it odd that he had not shared his last name. Later I would find out exactly why that was. Looking up Izabella nodded that it was okay he did not say.

"You okay?" I asked as he nodded picking up a glass of water taking a drink. Well, my turn. I stood up facing them all, not one bit nervous.

"I am Maylee Elder of Ares and the sorceress Sarita, from Hell Michigan, and I have a few different powers." Sitting down I turned to Izabella who nodded smirking as to say good job. My sister was next looking at me as she stood.

"I am Annabelle Elder also of Ares and the sorceress Sarita from Hell Michigan, but I do not have any powers yet." Sitting down she looked like she wanted to be anywhere but here. Izabella adjourned our meeting saying it had been successful. We all went our separate ways to our compartments to absorb what we had just learned about everyone else which was a lot.

Twenty minutes later there was a knock at our door that Annabelle answered. It was Izabella with Dante who still looked awfully pale. Probably seasick like my sister had been all night.

"Both of you grab your items and come with me." We had not even removed our swords yet. And I still had the stones in my pocket. Grabbing my jar of seashells we followed her into the hall to the upper deck. She led us back to the meeting room except the table was gone as were the windows. "Annabelle, you first. I must test your sword skills to see if you have any underlying powers we have not seen yet." Nervously Annabelle walked toward Izabella drawing Fury to face her. I turned to Dante who was almost green now.

"Are you seasick?" He nodded quickly grabbing a trash can. Yep, that was seasickness all right.

"Sorry." He said once he was done. "I have never liked being on water." Shrugging I knew some people really hated the water.

"Not everyone is comfortable traveling by ship. If it makes you feel better my sister was up all night sick from it." Nodding he walked away from me a ways to get sick again. I watched Annabelle spar with Izabella. She was not half bad. She had a lot of cuts from not moving fast enough. After quite some time something worth while happened. Izabella had disarmed her, but could not step foot near Annabelle because of an invisible self defense barrier. It threw Izabella backwards away from Annabelle. She stood back walking over to Annabelle smiling.

"At least now we know you have some powers."

"Sorry." Annabelle said in a small voice. "I don't know how" Izabella stopped her short.

"This is the only way we can find out if you have them or not. It is perfectly okay." Helping Annabelle to her feet they both walked over to where Dante and I were. I gave my sister a high five for the awesome job she had done. Dante was sitting on the floor with the trash can between his knees green as ever. Izabella looked at him shaking her head.

"I guess you are next Maylee."

In the middle of the room we drew our swords to begin to spar. I was holding my own against her. My session with Dante while we were traveling had done a lot of good.

"You said to use our items right?" I asked her.

"Yes." While I was still sparring I pulled out my stones. Feuer was first.

"Circle!" A ring of flames surrounded the two of us though it did not last long. Izabella extinguished it with water. How did she do that? I asked myself. All right. Let's go. Smirking I pulled out Erde also known as Gios for world. "Tornado!" It engulfed her as she tried and failed to fight nothing but whirling air. "Stop!" Izabella rushed forward continuing our fight. The same stone was in my hand as my thoughts raced. "Lightning" A bolt appeared out of no where electrically charging my sword as I raised it. Izabella's sword met mine mid air the electric charge in mine sent her flying backwards. Her sword flew into the air catching it as I walked forward. Sitting on the floor yet Izabella looked up at me.

"Well done." Smirking I offered my hand to help her up handing her sword back. Walking over to where my sister was standing next to Dante who was sitting and still puking sick. Once again I found myself almost feeling sorry for him. Almost. I was still stinging from the sword to the throat deal the first day we met.

"Is there anything you can give him to make it at least subside?" I asked interested in what she would be able to come up with.

"Do you have your healing stone with you?" Nodding I dug into my pocket showing it to her.

"I try to keep them all on me at all times." Turning to my sister.

"Go down to the kitchen on the third deck. We need a glass of water." Annabelle left walking rather fast. At least I would see if it actually worked.

Only ten minutes had passed when she walked back with a tall glass of water which she handed it to me. Izabella instructed me to drop it into the glass to watch the process of it. At first it looked like a rock in water until it began to glow golden. The water turned metallic pink. Afterward the stone rose out of the glass on its own. Grabbing the stone I studied the glass. Surprisingly the stone was completely dry which weirded me out a little.

"Here, drink this. You will feel better." I handed it to Dante. He looked at it wearily before throwing up again.

"What is it?" He managed to ask afterwards. Not like I'm going to poison you while Izabella is standing right there I thought irritably.

"Do you want to keep getting sick? Just drink it." Slowly he started to drink it down. Setting the glass down beside him he did not move. Slowly his color came back while his breathing was evening out. Finally he stood looking impressed with what had just happened.

"I feel better. What was that stuff?"

"Healing potion. Strictly Izabella's idea." I told him stiffly since I still did not trust him. Nodding he looked around for a minute before asking Izabella.

"Shall we fight than?" She nodded leading the way to the middle of the room. Watching them was interesting to say the least. Whoever had taught him did a good job. They sparred for over an hour until he held out his hand creating an invisible barrier pushing her backwards. Izabella hit the opposite wall hard. Never the less she stood dusting herself off while Dante hit his knees looking as if he was going to pass out. He acted as if it had taken all the energy in him to pull that off. Izabella threw a quizzical glance in his direction walking to me and my sister.

"You are done for the day. Go back to your compartment. There will be another meeting this evening. And could you please help Dante back to his compartment?" Annabelle nodded walking forward immediately. Izabella gave me one of those looks where you just have to give in and do what you really did not want to do.

It took both of us to help him as he was almost lifeless. Depositing him in his compartment he thanked us. Afterwards we walked back to our own compartment to rest. Around one there was a knock on the door as the crew in charge brought lunch to us on a rolling cart. This was because there was no cafeteria and the meeting room was being used for testing. Our lunch consisted of mixed fresh fruit, homemade chicken soup, and fresh bread. We wandered down to check on our horses in the hull.

They were holding out well for being on a ship. Pulling a couple brushes out of the bag I had left by the stalls we brushed them down. It took us almost half an hour to make them look like horses and not tangled up messes. When we were finished we threw them each a leaf of hay. Looking in at Dante's horse I threw him one too. Unlike Dante, I liked his horse. The horse was short built like a foundation quarter horse with dapples all over. He walked right up to the gate like he was expecting his rider but was not disappointed when it was me. I ran a hand over his neck patting him.

"I'm afraid your rider will not be coming down today." The horse threw his head reminding me very much of Danny making me smile before I turned to head back up. As we walked back up the stairs Annabelle stopped turning back to face me.

"We should check on Dante." This surprised me quite a bit.

"Okay. Why?" I asked slowly thinking did I hear that from you? The answer was yes without the why because she led the way right to his compartment door. She knocked on the door looking to me like what?

"Who is it?" He sounded alive. Probably wasn't any better now than he had been when we left him. That did not bother me since I did not like him. Annabelle answered him.

"Annabelle and Maylee. We're here to check on you."

"Come on in. It's not locked." Annabelle opened the door walking in to find him stretched out in a recliner chair in sweats instead of his tactical gear. He was still damn good looking. Biting the inside of my mouth I had to make my brain stop that shit.

"Well at least you're fully conscious now." I said indifferently as he shrugged.

"I've never done that before. It drained me of all of my energy." I stayed by the door not wanting to be near him. "You don't happen to have any more of that healing potion on you do you?" Hesitating I asked myself should I help him or not? If anything went wrong at the meeting we would need him. I saw the way the other discoverers reacted when three of us had sorcerer blood coursing through us. And I was certainly not about to believe the lies Dante was telling me now. He knew he had powers. I found that it bothered me that he was lying about it.

"Somehow. I find that hard to believe. But yes. I have my healing stone." I could tell he was still trying to figure me out. And I was not going to make it easy. Annabelle handed me a glass of water dropping the stone into it I repeated what I had done that morning. When it floated out I handed the glass to him. This time he gulped it right down not thinking twice.

"Much better. Thanks." I took the glass saying nothing. Annabelle told him we went down to see the horses. He looked disappointed that he could not have gone, but looked like he felt better when she told him we gave his horse hay too.

"What is his name?" I wanted to know. Dante stared at me for a moment since I had barely spoken since entering the room.

"His name is Shadow." His eyes narrowed on me as if I was asking him to jump off the ship. He was just trying to figure out why I wanted to know is all.

"I'm not surprised. We better get going. See you at the meeting." I opened the door walking down the hallway before Annabelle came out catching up quickly. Frowning I knew she wanted to be friends with him. Once in our compartment we could hear the testing going on in the meeting room. It was interesting. There were a couple yelling matches though we could not hear exactly what they were saying. After that I decided to get out my phone so I could listen to my music. As I put the ear buds in Annabelle looked over at me.

"Why do you hate him so much?" I arched an eyebrow at her.

"Why don't you?" I retorted back. She let out an exasperated breath rolling her eyes.

"He's not bad Maylee. He's actually really nice."

"And he also works for the wrong side." She stared at me measuringly. Her eyes were storm clouded as she attempted to make her point.

"He's not with them anymore. He told me that." She looked sincere wanting to believe him. I just smirked. Yeah. Right.

"I don't believe that. He's just doing his job Annabelle. He certainly has you convinced. But I am not so easily swayed. Sorry." With that I put my ear buds in turning up the volume so

I could not hear her argue back. The first song on was one about war. How ironic since that's how this all felt about now.

***

Evidently I was tired as Annabelle woke me up by shaking my shoulder. I took an ear bud out.

"The meeting is in five minutes." I nodded turning off my music standing up stretching. Together we walked up the stairs into the meeting room to where we had been earlier. Automatically I drew star burst setting it down on the table. Annabelle followed suit with fury and Dante with guardian. Izabella walked in taking her spot at the head of the table but stayed standing resting her hands on it.

"What have you found out about your descendant that you did not know before?" She began with the left side again working around to us. They each took a turn explaining the fighting skills they had and the traces of powers or none at all depending on who it was. Neither of the descendants of Hermes had any kind of powers.

Finally it was Izabella's turn to tell them about the three of us. She told them about Annabelle's self defensive barrier that stopped her. The long fight with Dante that ended with the barrier that threw her backwards. Than there was me. My circle of flames, the tornado that had engulfed her, my electrically charged sword that jolted and threw her backwards.

Apparently I also had a barrier of some kind around me I had not known about. As I watched the faces of the others they seemed to be afraid of me. The only exception was the three with me. Izabella had noticed this leaning close to me.

"Maylee. Would you, Annabelle and Dante wait outside the door for a minute. I need to speak to everyone. Someone will let you back in when we are done." Rolling my eyes I nodded. The three of us left standing on the deck by the door. I kept my ear against the door trying to hear what they were talking about. Unable to hear what they were saying I finally gave up sitting by the door. Annabelle sat beside me but Dante stayed standing up across from us. The door finally opened again.

"You can come back in now." It was one of the immortals. I did not remember his name but he seemed friendly enough. I could feel the tension in the air as we walked back in. It could have been cut with a knife as we sat down at our places. Our swords were being held by another of Izabella's peers. He looked tough, weather worn, mean around mid forties age wise with short brown and gray hair. He was just a big guy.

"I would like to see them fight for myself. I want to see if they have the powers you say they have." Izabella looked at him calmly almost to the point of smiling.

"Okay. You can fight each of them yourself. Just like I did. Can you handle that?" Ouch. I think that was a challenge.

"I would love to." He threw the swords down on the table picking Annabelle's back up.

"Annabelle right?" She nodded as he walked up to her handing her sword to her. "You are first."

Everyone stood moving against the wall. The table was moved aside. Annabelle looked to me nervously.

"What do I do?" I did not realize it but I was tensed up. They chose to pick on my little sister first which made me furious.

"Give him hell." She nodded in agreement standing at the ready. As I watched she had learned a lot from Izabella in the short amount of time we'd had to train with her. She was fighting like she had done this her whole life and it was amazing. I could tell she was growing tired. Her eyes looked like storm clouds. Almost like she was gathering energy from somewhere else attacking harder. As she fought her defense shield went up deflecting the man's sword. Afterwards the shield collapsed and he was able to go after her. Fury landed on the floor with a clatter. Annabelle bent down picking it up breathing fast and deep. Her opponent tired out more. Izabella walked up to her handing her a glass of water.

"You learned fast. Well done." Annabelle sheathed her sword walking over to me. I gave her a half hug.

"Good job." I looked to Izabella who gave a small smile as in yep I taught them. She turned to the man.

"Now. I think you should challenge Maylee or Dante. They are much more advanced than young Annabelle." He looked at her shaking his head. "No? Than who else would like to challenge them?" She stared at each settling on the one who had brought Nathan the descendant of Hades.

"Randall. You're the best swordsman here. You can take on Dante." Randall nodded walking to the middle of the floor as Izabella handed Dante guardian. It was hard to determine what was on his mind as he stood ready. He glanced over to me before he concentrated on his opponent. Frowning I glanced to Izabella. Something deep down was trying to tell me something.

"Izabella." She glanced up at me as Dante and Randall began their duel.

"Not right now Maylee." Rolling my eyes I watched the two fight. It did not take long. If Randall was the best than I hated to see anyone else. Annabelle stood at my side as we watched the fight.

"He's really good." Smirking I glanced over to her.

"Yeah. I'm sure where ever he was from taught him well." My sister made a sound of impatience at that.

"Could you just try"

"No." My voice forced out angrily turning to her. Izabella glanced up at us from the fight as we talked. "I will not try to be nice or his friend. And you know exactly why I feel that way."

"He is not him. Get over yourself." Before I could even say a word she walked away through the crowd. Growling I turned to walk after her only for Izabella to grab my elbow hard on the way through. Dante had disarmed his opponent not even breaking a sweat. Randall looked embarrassed. Apparently he did not lose often.

"Let go." I growled at her as Dante walked back over to us smirking, like he needed to inflate that ego anymore. Izabella did not react to him as she had with Annabelle looking to me instead.

"You are next Maylee." She said simply ignoring my growl handing Star burst to me looking up at our group. Dante looked concerned at the fact I was flaming angry but did not say anything instead looking for my sister. "I think I better do the honors against you." They all nodded in agreement. Now I could turn all my pent up anger onto her instead? I had really wanted the chance to take on the guy who had bullied my sister. "And Maylee" I looked up at Izabella. "Do not hold back." Smiling wide at that knowing it was not a problem.

"If that is what you want." She nodded when I glanced up from my sword. Taking out my stones I placed the healing stone back as it would not help me in this fight. I could hear Dante talking to Izabella as she walked by him.

"Do all these guys a favor. Show them what you can really do." Izabella shouted from the other side. Smiling wider yet I looked at some of the faces showing much doubt. My sister arched an eyebrow as if asking us she held back? I nodded at her as she raised her eyebrows looking around crossing her arms in front of her to watch. Dante was intensely watching as we stood ready waiting for our signal.

"Sword work first or use my powers from the beginning?"

"Sword work first. At least for the first few minutes."

Right from the beginning it was intense. It was like I was fighting for my life instead of showing these idiots what I could do. We exchanged blows, attacked, dodged, dived and twisted. When I thought it had been plenty long enough I looked down at Feuer and Erde.

"Circle!" A ring of flames and wind combined surrounded us. I kept the stones in my hand as we fought. Looking to feuer. "Circle out." The flames died but the wind kept up. "Sword" Star burst erupted in golden flames which caught Izabella off guard momentarily as she kept attacking. Looking down at Sturm I thought about what I could do with it. "Waves" The water outside began churning, rising, and falling jerking the ship around. The ship was really heaving now. "Stop" It was instantaneous as it just stopped. We kept right on fighting. Although it was strange that she had eliminated my circle of wind already.

"Sword out." What did I have left? The one that controlled the dead. That should be interesting. "Guard me" Ghosts came from below the deck surrounding me. Izabella could not get through them. Catching my breath I instructed them back to where they had came. The ghosts left right away with Izabella rushing at me. Tiring out I had one more stone I could use yet as I looked down.

"Activate" It felt like I had completely refueled. With renewed energy I attacked aggressively. Using Erde once again "Lightning." The bolt came from the ceiling traveling down my sword making it glow. Apparently Izabella forgot that was what happened the last time we sparred. Swinging hard our blades met.

Izabella flew backwards instantly hitting the opposite wall hard not letting go of her sword. Two of her peers rushed forward to help her up. I walked forward to stay on the attack. The two men walked in front of Izabella to stop me. Stopping I noticed Izabella held a hand up signaling me to stop.

"That is enough." I dropped my hand to my side relaxing. My sister and Dante came to my side as Izabella stood.

"Deactivate" Pocketing the stones I instantly felt drained, exhausted, and almost collapsed. She must have known I was using that one. Standing before me she was also breathing hard with her hands on her knees.

"Your lightning traveled through me when our blades met. By all means I should have dropped my sword but the electricity made me grip it harder instead. That was a very good move." Smiling a little she fully stood.

"I was not trying to do that. I was just trying to do what I did this morning."

"You did. But with the power stone activated it intensified it by ten." That thought had not occurred to me. That had made every move more powerful too.

"Sorry." I apologized causing her to frown.

"Why are you sorry? That could keep you alive in battle. Never be sorry for being more powerful than you think you are." The table moved back to its spot on the floor. We all sat down again except for Izabella who stayed standing. "Would anyone else like to test their skills or question me about them?" They all looked up at her together.

"No." I was whipped, ready for bed, and wanted to leave. Pulling my healing stone out I pulled a glass of water to myself. Dropping it into the water like I had done twice already. The water turned, my stone floated out and I drank it. I pocketed the stone feeling much better after the potion. At least I felt okay and not completely drained. When I looked up everyone had been watching me. Everyone. Their expressions were mixed. Some looked afraid while others were interested. The only ones in the room who looked proud of what I had done was Izabella and to my shock Dante.

"What?" I asked. They all looked away from me to Izabella. Annabelle tapped my arm so that I turned to her.

"They are all afraid of you." She whispered to me. "And after seeing what you just did. So am I." Great I thought. Now I've scared my own sister. I looked to my left at Dante who was smirking and looking rather smug.

"Impressive. Better than you were this morning." Raising my eyebrows I was not amused by his tone.

"I wasn't showing off." I told him stiffly. Taken aback he raised his eyebrows looking serious.

"I know. Take it easy. I just have never seen anyone do that before. At least not with your amount of training. Or lack there of." I relaxed slightly keeping an eye on him. My feelings of him being on the other side had eased some. Just not enough to justify attempting to be friends like my sister and now Izabella were pressuring me to be.

***

After our demonstration of skills or more about my demonstration of powers there was much whispering and muttering. If there was a crowd they would part before me as though afraid I would attack them. Did they actually think I would attack with no good reason? I had never been one to pick fights. I just finished them.

Through the morons on board I had heard that my sister had those powers, but did not know how to use them. They did not realize it was the stones I possessed that gave me those abilities. I never heard anything of it, but that did not mean anything.

There were only three people besides myself that knew about them. And two of them did not know what each one did. Dante only knew of my stones because I had used them against him. Thinking back to the meeting room the night before. I must have looked pretty fierce as he was trying to make friends with me. Of course he had actually been trying to be friends since the day we met.

We had been traveling at sea for nearly five days. Each day we had a meeting in the morning and at night. There were no more challenges to any of us after what happened on the second day. The meetings were completely boring compared to that first one. I almost wished someone would challenge me just so I could fight. Before the meeting on the fifth night I decided to go see the horses without my sister tagging along. Her nagging about giving Dante a chance at being friends was tiresome.

I needed time away from people in general. I brushed Rocki down while he munched on some hay I had given him. When he was clean of straw and bedding I packed the brush away walking up the stairs for the meeting. Something caught my eye causing me to stop turning to see what it was. Drawing star burst I thought the worst walking back to the stalls. There was nothing there as I looked around. Sheathing my sword I began walking to the stairs again.

Something still felt wrong. Walking back again I checked each of the horses thinking it was coming from one of them. Checking each one over by hand Rocki was fine as he was still eating as was Oscerr but I checked him thoroughly just in case. Next I walked to Shadow's stall. He was lying down occasionally trying to stand up than would lie back down. I checked his water, he had not touched it since that morning. His hay had not been touched either. Entering his stall carefully he looked at me wide eyed as he didn't know me or what my intentions were. Talking to him softly I reached down grabbing his halter attaching a lead rope to pull him up to his feet. He no more stood than was on his way back down. Nice, a sick horse on a ship.

Pulling out my cell phone I texted Annabelle to bring me what I would need to help Shadow. And to tell Dante to get his ass down here since this was his horse. Within five minutes he was running down the steps. At that point I was struggling to keep Shadow on his feet.

"What's wrong?" I could hear a trace of panic in his voice. I could not answer because I was afraid if I even broke my concentration Shadow would be down again. Finally he quit struggling so hard.

"Are you going to just stand there or help me keep him on his feet?" Dante jumped forward to help talking to his horse holding his halter as we kept him walking. Annabelle came hurrying down the steps arms full with everything I had requested.

"Help Dante keep him up and walking. I need my first aid kit." She set everything on a tack trunk next to the stalls hurrying over to help. I was always prepared for something to happen. Taking out a small box I had brought vet wrap, gloves, a needle, syringe, and a bottle of tranquilizer.

Uncapping the needle I stuck it in the bottle, attached the syringe and drew out two milliliters withdrawing the needle testing it to make sure there was not air in it. I signaled for them to stop walking up to his neck finding where I would need to administer. As I was about to insert the needle Dante grabbed my wrist hard stopping me.

"What are you doing?" He asked looking panicked. I understood that he was afraid of what I was doing. He did not know me. And I had a needle about to go into his horse's neck. Staying calm I knew I would have done the same thing in his position.

"It is only tranquilizer. It will make him relax and easier to handle. Horses that are tranquilized normally stay on their feet and will take less effort from us to keep him up." Letting go he stepped back still looking unsure. For that reason I did not proceed yet staying where I was.

"I was a veterinarian's assistant for two years. I know what I'm doing. Okay?" He nodded but I knew he was still unsure. Finally I proceeded finding the vein I needed again administering Shadow with the shot. "This will allow me to get the tube to his stomach to pump the mineral oil into him. I've had horses my entire life. If nothing else right now. Just trust me on this. I'm not saying you have to trust me once we leave here. But right now this horse's life depends on what you allow me to do." Still unsure he nodded breathing out a sigh as he watched my expressions.

After several minutes Shadow's head was hanging down. Grabbing the tube I started to send the mineral oil to his stomach. My sister retrieved the funnel filling the bucket while I held the tube in place. Once the oil was gone we followed it with warm water. Unhooking the funnel we had to make sure it all went down and was not going to come back up. Nothing happened so I pulled the tube out throwing it aside over a stall door.

Next I checked his sides for bloating or hard areas. There was no bloating that I could find nor any hard areas. It must have been an impaction that had formed within the last few hours. Grabbing the gloves I knew what I had to do next which was to check where the impaction was located in his intestines. Believe me it was only my two years as an assistant that I knew exactly what I was doing. I was taught very well by the vet we used. In all that time all I refused to do was to hold a horse while he had to euthanize it. As I did that part of the examination Annabelle was fidgety.

"What is it?" She finally asked.

"An impaction. A bad one. But it hasn't been there very long so he should come out of it in a few hours." I did a check of his vitals, his gums were barely pink, pulse was high, he was breathing hard partially from the tranquilizer, but his temperature was within normal range. We stayed with him until the tranquilizer began wearing off so we could begin walking him. Within another hour he stopped moving altogether. We tried to make him move but he just refused but he finally urinated.

"That's a good sign." I commented as we continued to walk him. Eventually he also defecated or pooped. They kept him walking while I checked it with a stick, it was dry. That had to have been what was left of the impaction.

"Okay. Stop him for a minute. Annabelle. Grab a bucket and see if he'll drink." She walked into his stall retrieving his water bucket placing it in front of him. He lowered his head drinking the whole bucket so she refilled it automatically giving it back to him. He drank another half a bucket.

"He's improving. Stay with him in his stall for a couple more hours. I'm going to bed. Come get me if he gets bad again." Dante nodded staring at Shadow in deep thought. I began walking up the stairs when I heard him say something.

"Wait" I stopped turning around as he walked up to me. "Thank you. I don't know what I would have done without you." Raising my eyebrows at the fact he was being genuine I replied.

"You're welcome. Take care of him." Turning I continued up the stairs stopping short of the top. I walked back down part way to where he had not moved staring at his horse's stall. "I just have one question for you." He looked up at me than back over to Shadow. "How could you own a horse and not know what to do?" When he looked back to me again his face was red. Almost like he did not know why he didn't know.

"It's not that I didn't know. I just never had to deal with it."

"Right. I'm guessing you're one of those who just call the vet when your horse begins to act the least bit funny than leave." I turned to leave again.

"Wait." Sighing I turned back again as he shook his head looking conflicted. "Look. Someday I will tell you. I will explain why I don't know. I will explain everything. I am grateful for what you did for him. I owe you for that. I just can't tell you anything about myself right now." I nodded walking back upstairs too tired to even retort. Annabelle had already went up an hour before. As I reached the top stair I was met by an irate looking Izabella. Oh shit. The meeting.

"Why were you not at the meeting?" I looked straight back at her coolly feeling tired and fairly cranky.

"Well. I was tending to a very sick horse actually."

"And that took all three of you?" Was she seriously going to give me this attitude right now?

"Actually. Yes it did. Shadow coliced and it took all of us to keep him up and moving. Dante held him, I treated him and my sister brought me what I needed to help him."

Izabella let out a deep breath as if she had been holding it. Looking exhausted she shook her head.

"I cannot stay angry with you. You did save the horse."

"That sounds about right. He would have been dead by morning if I had not checked on him while I was down there."

"How is he now?"

"Pulling out of it. He drank a bucket and a half of water a little while ago."

"Annabelle is already in your compartment sleeping. You look like you could use it too. Where is Dante? Or should I ask?" She knew I still did not like him.

"He's staying with Shadow like I told him to." Smirking she knew I found it amusing he had to stay with the horses.

"Okay, I will go down there and talk to him too. I will have the two of you excused from the morning meeting. Go get some sleep."

"Thanks."

"And Maylee." Stopping I turned back tiredly. "I know Dante makes you uneasy. But he is one of us. And he would like to be your friend and ally. Not your enemy as you keep treating him." Shaking my head I rolled my eyes irritably.

"Not you too."

"Maylee. I know your instincts are great. But this is going to be the one and only time I tell you to go against them."

"No." I told her strongly. "Until he proves to me he means well and not still working for the other side." Izabella hung her head.

"You really are stubborn." Nodding in acknowledgement I started to head up to the compartment only to have her pull me around to face her. "Maylee. I have to ask you and I am going to be dead serious." Frowning I nodded.

"Okay. What?"

"Do you remember having any kind of fencing or sword play lessons?" Now I was completely confused.

"No. Why are you asking? I told you when you first met us I had never had any formal training." Sighing she glanced to the hull where I knew Dante still remained to keep an eye on his horse.

"What if I told you. That I think you had training but cannot remember because your memory was wiped out." Irritated I shook my head at her.

"What the hell are you trying to get at? Is this a way to make me be friends with him?"

"No. It is not Maylee. But I do think at one point or another you should allow me to test you for memory recall."

"No. I don't want to remember something that was wiped out. If it was than it was probably for a damned good reason. And I want it to stay that way." Crossing her arms she frowned.

"Your attitude is not directed at that exactly but something in your past has happened to make you as sharp as you are." I chuckled smirking darkly.

"You could say that." Without another word I turned walking again.

"Maylee" Izabella's voice sounded dangerous as I stopped. Every muscle in my body tensed as I turned back to her.

"Izabella. I'm tired. And getting very pissy. Could we please have this conversation. Another time." Raising her eyebrows at me she stepped closer.

"No Maylee. We have this conversation now. Come with me." Walking to the main office I had saw her in she shut the door behind us. "I need to know your past. As much as possible before we port." Chuckling sarcastically I rested my hands on my hips.

"You seriously think I am going to tell you everything right now?" Sighing she sat behind the desk.

"For your own sake. And your sister's. Yes." Damn her. Huffing irritably I sat down looking at the floor.

"What exactly are you looking for in my past?" Leaning onto her desk towards me she searched my face.

"Why do you not trust anyone?" Ouch. Just cut to the chase. Angrily I sat back crossing my arms.

"Long story Izabella. Truly it is." Smirking she sat back looking at me.

"I have time." My body began to tremble at my lack of rest making it difficult.

"Izabella"

"NO." She cut across as she noticed my reaction to the gesture. "You are going to tell me whether you want to or not. We can stay in this office all night if I have to. But you will tell me what happened."

"Okay. Fine." Taking a deep breath I told her everything I could remember.

It was almost four in the morning when Izabella finally allowed me to go back to my room. My sister was dead asleep when I walked in. I barely hit the pillow and I was out.

The following morning I was woke up by the compartment door slamming shut. Opening my eyes slowly I sat up Annabelle standing next to me.

"It's about time you woke up. It's nearly eleven. You never sleep that long." Instantly I jumped out of bed quickly dressing without showering. I was almost out the door when she spoke again. "I already checked him. He's fine." Freezing in place I turned back to her.

"You're sure?" She gave me a knowing look.

"I'm perfectly capable. Yes. You don't have to go."

"I'll feel better if I do." Without another word I was out the door on my way down to where the horses were. As I walked down the stairs I could see Shadow was eating some hay. Just to make sure I went into his stall checking everything. It was just something I felt I needed to do. Feeling he was fine as my sister had said I looked around seeing that everything I had used the night before spread out everywhere.

Gathering it all up I put it all away hoping I would not need it again for a very long time. I walked back to the compartment laying in bed again. As much sleep I had the night before I should not have been tired. I slept for another few hours.

This time when I woke it was four in the afternoon. Groaning I dragged myself out of bed, dragged a brush through my tangled mop of hair walking out the door. I stepped onto the main deck to my right my sister and Dante were talking about something. They had not noticed my presence as I walked to the railing on my left leaning against it watching the clouds in the sky. Annabelle appeared at my right arm.

"I thought you were going to sleep the day away." I smiled.

"Nah, I never could sleep like that. I might have been tired, but I'm not that tired." Suddenly Dante appeared at my left side cautiously as if I might do something.

"I hope you did not mind that Annabelle checked on Shadow. You were still sleeping when I came up for you. I figured you needed the rest." He flinched slightly like I would hit or attack him because of this information.

"That's fine. Did she also tell you he cannot have grain for at least three days?"

"Yeah, she did. Are you all rested up now?" I nodded with raised eyebrows thinking like you would care. Though what Izabella told me the night before ran through my mind.

"We are supposed to be at the island first thing in the morning." Annabelle informed me as I turned back to watch the ocean. There was an occasional dolphin jumping out of the water. My sister laid her head against my shoulder. "I'm homesick." I wrapped my arm around her shoulders.

"I know. Maybe I should have let you go home." Pulling away slightly she looked at me.

"You could not have left me alone." I bit my lip knowing she was right.

"Yeah, you're right. But maybe when this is over you can go back to having a normal life." She scowled at me.

"My life? What about you? With those powers and abilities?" As I looked at her eyes they had that storm clouded look. It made me uneasy as I shifted my feet as they only looked that way when she was angry.

"I could never go back to a normal life after all this. Although you might get a kick out of me using my powers against people at work or threaten them with a scary sword. No. When this is over I will stay on the island. Or wherever I'm needed." She nodded not amused by my answer but did not try to push the issue. They called for the evening meeting the three of us walking in together.

Dante

O nce on the ship in our compartments I wrote to Theo immediately informing him that Annabelle had turned to their side. Asking what they wanted next. Within minutes there was a flash as he had written back already. The letter congratulated me for turning Annabelle followed by instructions.

***

The next time Annabelle is with you without her sister show her the next letter behind this one. It should convince her to go to base in Texas. Once there we will give her an assignment. If she passes we will pardon all wrongs you have committed. If she fails. You will be executed sight seen.

Curious as to what they would inform her to convince her to go to base. And which base? Surely not the main base in Dallas? Closing my eyes I flipped to the page behind my letter. Unlike the handwritten letter Theo had sent this one was typed. Signed by. No. Fucking. Way. No. Not him. Crumpling the letters I threw them both in the trash leaning onto the desk bracing myself. Dammit. Shaking my head I called for Izabella as my body shook in protest of what I knew still must be done.

"Where is the letter?" When she walked in. Realizing how I felt she gripped my shoulder pushing me into the desk chair. "What is it Dante?"

"The letters are in the trash there. I should never have agreed to this. I should have known" Stopping I shook my head rubbing my face roughly before looking up at Izabella.

"I tried to tell you this would be difficult. Obviously the letters held information that bothered you." Nodding I took them from the trash can straightening them out showing her the letter meant for Annabelle. Taking them cautiously she looked it over before scowling when she was done reading. "I see the problem. The Master. You remember him. Yes?" Nodding I glanced to the letter.

"Yeah. He was the one who sent me home to die Izabella. Only to change his mind a year later. He sent me home the day after I ascended at sixteen. Once I was seventeen he wanted me back to help train recruits in Dallas. Where he wants Annabelle to report for further orders." Shaking my head I could not allow this to go any further. "I'm done. I am not sending a young girl to her death at that damn place." Izabella nodded handing the letters back.

"I understand your feelings on the man. I do. But I have my orders as well. You know that. The council will not take you quitting so quickly lightly."

"What would they do? Kill me like he was before you helped?" Her face set grimly as she stepped to the door signaling me to stay quiet. I heard Maylee and Annabelle talking just outside my door since they were right across the hall. Izabella saw my face as I heard their voices going wide eyed.

"Her entire presence is affecting you." Nodding in agreement she thought for a moment. "You have to give Annabelle that letter Dante. If you want to protect Maylee. Give her that letter." Shaking my head I looked up at her.

"She will hate me for this. You know that." Frowning she placed a hand on the doorknob to leave.

"Annabelle will forgive you for sending her. Trust me. You both want the same result here."

"What do you mean?"

"Give her the letter. I have a meeting to attend. And for the gods sake get some rest. Or I will give you something to make you sleep."

"Okay." The meetings on board were far from dull as the others who recruited our group were doubting Izabella about Maylee. She took it all into stride allowing them to challenge us one by one. I was totally awestruck when I watched Maylee and Izabella demonstrate for the whole ship. My chest ached where my heart thumped harder than usual.

"Do you like my sister?" Annabelle asked as we watched. Sighing I stepped back trying to focus on anything else.

"No. Why?" Frowning her eyes turned dark as she assessed what I said.

"You're lying." Impatiently I turned to her as she crossed her arms over her chest.

"Why are you asking?"

"She won't turn like I did. I guarantee that." Her voice was low as everyone watched Izabella and her sister battle. Agreeing I nodded.

"I know that. They only want me to watch her and report what kind of powers she possesses. Nothing more. Alright?" Without another word she nodded watching the fight again.

Days passed with the sea and my stomach fighting for which would win. I had not been down to the hull to see Shadow for at least a day. When I tried to communicate with him I received nothing. My compartment door flew open as Annabelle looked panicked.

"Shadow is sick. You need to get down there. My sister is helping him right now. Go!" Scrambling I did not have to be told twice.

It had been a long night as for the first time I could remember I had to rely on someone I barely knew to help me.

126

Maylee had been great. My admiration for her just kept going up as a result. When she had walked to the stairs I stopped her to thank her. I had to stop myself as I just wanted to hug her but knew she would kill me. She had began to relax around me more at last. It was already starting to become difficult to keep my distance from her.

The morning after Shadow had been sick I went back to my compartment after Annabelle checked him over meticulously telling me her sister would approve for him to have hay. Nodding I made sure he had water, threw him just one flake of hay before retiring. Izabella woke me around two telling me we needed to talk already.

"What now? Haven't I done enough?" Frowning she gestured for me to take a seat.

"I interrogated Maylee last night about her past. It is not good. And I can see why she guards herself as she does." At the mention of her name I was wide awake.

"You interrogated her? After everything she did last night? Izabella. Why would you do that?" Smirking she folded her arms across her chest.

"I had my reasons. There were chunks of her memory missing. Just as I had suspected. But the worthwhile part occurred toward the end of our conversation." Rolling my eyes irritably I could not believe she had done this.

"And that would be what?" Sighing she sat down before looking at me evenly.

"She was very badly abused by a past boyfriend." I felt my chest ache at that admission.

"In what way?"

"Physical, mental, emotional. You name it. He did it to her."

"And that is why she guards herself like she does. Why did you even ask her about that?" Looking to the door there were a lot of people walking through before she responded.

"I was following up something her sister shot at her while you were sparring Randall." Frowning again I nodded implying my question. "What Annabelle responded back was definitely a dig at Maylee's actions. And not at all fair to her. The sad part was Annabelle knew exactly what happened and still used it to hurt Maylee."

"That was why she was fuming when I was done. And why you knew you had to be the one to face her or she might have hurt someone." Izabella nodded at what I said. "The conversation was about me. Wasn't it?"

"Yes. It was. Annabelle was trying to talk her into being friends with you. She is very stubborn and adamant about not getting too close. But after our conversation last night I can truly understand why."

"What did Annabelle tell her that pissed her off so badly?" Shaking her head she stood rubbing her face.

"Look. I will help when I can. But I refuse to get in between the two of you and act as a mediator. Just talk to her."

"What did Annabelle tell her?" Frustrated Izabella shook her head again.

"That you were not him and to get over herself." Words that could cut like a knife to any wound still healing.

"Yeah. I would have been pissed off too. Damn. She is nasty already. I hate to see her once she turns fully." Nodding Izabella walked out. Sitting in the chair my mind was going a million miles a minute. Staying away from Maylee until she decided to give me a chance was going to be difficult. Sitting back in the chair I dozed off again.

Maylee

The meeting had went well but I felt that certain information had been withheld from us. When we arrived back at our compartment I powered on my computer jumping on the internet. I checked my e-mail first, mostly junk, how typical. Logging out the computer took me to the news page. Oh my god!

"Annabelle! Come here. Like now!" She rushed right over.

"What?" I pointed to the screen.

"Apparently we are missing fugitives because of my truck." Reading the article all the way through I laughed.

"What is so funny?"

"They think we may have headed to Arizona."

"Why Arizona?"

"How do I know? Wait, it says here. Our mother suspects that is where we went due to the scrutiny we were under with the local show grounds and were running away. She suspects we may be in a hospital under false names out of state. Wow, she went far this time." Annabelle shook her head rolling her eyes irritably.

"That would be mom. You know she has to be dramatic. Anything else?"

"There was some flash flooding in our area. Florida had some fifty foot waves hitting the beach for ten minutes four days ago. That's it, nothing too major." She looked at the screen over my shoulder just to make sure I had not missed anything smirking for the first time in days.

"What?"

"The waves were from you. When you and Izabella were sparring on the second day."

"Maybe." The ship had rocked from that.

"What are you thinking?" I was too easy to read. Maybe I could take some lessons on that from Dante. He was difficult to read and mostly emotionless. At least seemingly. I closed out of the internet looking at my computer handing it to Annabelle.

"Here, I'm thinking I want you to have this. I do not need them or want them anymore." She took them as I looked at my phone. Better keep it just in case I need it one day. Shutting it off I pushed it to the bottom of my backpack packing our supplies from the tables and drawers.

"Maylee" Setting the laptop on her bunk she crossed her arms over her chest looking concerned. "Why are you giving me your laptop? You're not going to" Smirking I shook my head standing in front of her.

"I will have no use for them once we are on the island. I have a feeling I will be too busy training to peruse the mundane internet." Sighing she nodded.

"Okay. But if you ever want it back. Just let me know." I wandered down to the hull where the horses were stabled. Grabbing the brushes and first aid kit I packed them into my bag with everything else.

We arrived at port to the island as we had been told before we woke. Annabelle and I dressed at top speed stuffing our pajamas into our already full backpacks. Running out the door swinging our bags over our shoulders rushing down to the hull where horses were stabled. Dante was not far behind us. All three of us saddled up waiting for the signal to take them up to the main deck. The horses were more than ready for solid ground. When the ship finally dropped the ramps we made our way up.

"Whoa." I said as we stopped on the main deck looking all around. The island was beautiful! It looked like Hawaii. Except the buildings looked like they were straight out of the 1500s. Walking down the ramp that led to solid land the horses all lunged forward wanting to run the instant they felt dirt. We managed to keep them in check, although Rocki had dragged me a few feet before he stopped. When I looked over Dante had grabbed a hold of Rocki's bit close to his mouth nodding once I noticed letting go.

"Thanks" Turning he walked to where Izabella walked onto the land in front of us.

"Before you have any ideas of exploring the place. Everyone has to meet with the chief. He is the one in charge of the island and keeps it running. Now. The descendants you traveled here with are not the only ones on this island training. Just the last group to arrive." We all nodded following her along a well beaten trail. It brought us right up to an old stone house on a hill overlooking the entire island. And I do mean the entire island.

There was a hundred foot round pen by the house. The three of us led the horses over untacking them letting all three loose. It was fun to watch them as they ran, bucked, crow hopped, and jumped sideways. They were happy to be out of their stalls. Izabella led us into the cabin. It was bigger inside than it appeared on the outside.

All the descendants and their discoverers were gathered around a desk when we walked up. A few of them looked at us wearily but moved aside to let us through none the less. A man standing by the desk looking to be in his late fifties, wispy gray hair covered by a military hat, five foot eight, light complected, heavier set, though he looked pleasant to be around. He walked forward upon the sight of us.

"Izabella! Welcome back!" Shaking her hand he gestured for her to stand at his right side. She motioned for us to walk up too. We were pretty much in the same formation as we had been while on the ship. The chief nodded to Izabella who clapped her hands three times. The desk turned into an oval table chairs appearing behind us.

We all were seated placing our swords on the table making it feel like king Arthur's court of knights. There was an empty seat to the left of the chief. It seemed odd since everyone I knew was here. The chief cleared his throat.

"You all know why you are here by now. We are being threatened by a force that has not existed in nearly a thousand years. Some of you may know his name. In his human form he is known as Theasis. He is evil, powerful, and most certainly manipulative. He has the power to bend one's mind to thinking like him before you know it. His thoughts become your thoughts. As some of you know he has been sending shadows to do his work. This is to make his job later on easier. He has even sent spies to us. They are among our descendants as he had wanted them on his side worse than others."

He paused looking to Izabella who nodded before he continued on. I figured he must have been talking about Dante.

"Immortals, descendants of the gods, and others are the only ones who can stop him. Mortals can only see freak accidents and nature at its worst. During the hurricane in Florida our ship was not damaged because it was protected against him. Our sources tell us he will not be in full power until the alignment of the planets on December 21, but we must act now to weaken their forces. The ship being enchanted though. I do have to ask. What were the waves pounding against it my scouts told me about?" He smiled as Izabella nodded over to me.

"That was courtesy of Maylee. Everyone aboard wanted to see if she really had the powers I told them she harbored. I think she succeeded in showing them." He laughed light heartedly.

"Good! We can use another like Izabella here. Listen to her. You will go far and learn a lot." I nodded in agreement. The door opened with another man walking in sitting in the empty chair on the chief's left side. The chief leaned over talking to him. It was pretty back and forth. Not mean or aggressive at all. The chief gave one final nod and the conversation was over.

He was around six foot ten maybe eleven, dark complected with short sandy colored hair. He had really muscular arms from hard work and was maybe around thirty. Wow. Maybe Annabelle had a point. Maybe I did need to sleep with a guy for stress relief. And the way Kamran kept eyeing me. it was a thought. He was definitely not bad looking as he glanced over to me, up to Izabella, than around to everyone there.

"Attention everyone. This is Kamran. He will be your defensive coordinator. In other words teaching you to fight with swords, knives, bows and anything else you may end up using. You will have a schedule to follow depending on your skill and power level. You will also be trained to use the powers you have inherited from the god you descended. Your training will begin in two days. This way you will have a chance to rest and settle in. I will be watching you all. Good luck."

That was our dismissal. Good. We stood to leave but Izabella signaled us to stay. She walked up to Kamran smiling they hugged each other. They must know each other really well, maybe work together. They talked for a minute before walking over to the three of us. He looked between me and my sister

133

first crossing his arms giving the same look Izabella had when she was assessing me.

"So. You are the two from Michigan? I heard you had some real kick ass powers." Holding his hand out to shake my hand. I accepted noticing that he had a strong grip and I was lost for what to say.

"Did you?" I asked finally making my voice work.

"Yeah, I cannot wait to work with you. From what I heard you three will be the most advanced I teach." He pointed to Dante who in turn lost all color.

"You on the other hand. I'm not sure what I can teach you. Apparently you have already been well trained somewhere."

"Not for anything like this. I still have much to learn." Yeah. You're a good liar. Even I could tell that. Either way Kamran ignored his answer.

"Well, I will see you in two days to begin training. I'm sure I will see you around here before that." With one last look over me he began walking out. My arms broke out in goose bumps at the look I had received from him. Pretty sure he had been seriously checking me out. Izabella must have remembered something because she jumped stopping him to talk.

Glancing up at Dante I remembered how he had drained of color when the chief spoke. When Kamran had just confronted him a moment ago he was the same way. The two moments definitely made me think that he was not on our side as Izabella had tried to convince me. He was only spying on us for the evil scum that was trying to kill everyone. Kamran walked back over with Izabella after a few minutes standing in front of me. This time I felt uneasy as he stood too close for comfort with his arms crossed over his chest.

"I want you to take a look at Maylee's sword. Maylee. Show him please." Oh hell. Now I would hear it from him too. Maybe

Dante was not the one they needed to worry about. Maybe it was me. Nodding I slowly drew it out handing it over to him. He gripped it by the blade examining it closely.

"What about it?" I actually sighed in relief. If he was not tripping out than it cannot be too bad. "It's not a dark blade if that is what you are afraid of. It is just designed to look this way. It is quite strange. I have never seen one made like this. It is made of black iron, but not completely because there is steel in it. Very unusual. Unheard of. But there is nothing dark or cursed about it." Shrugging he handed it back to me brushing my hand as he did. I could have swore he noticed that I involuntarily flinched smirking at the fact. At the same time I was physically relieved that my sword was not evil.

Izabella and Kamran walked outside together talking in the mean time. While they did that the three of us walked out to the corral saddling up to go for a ride to explore the island. Annabelle and I did not take long. We were ready mounted up to go. My sister insisted we wait for her new friend before we rode off. Dante was taking his sweet time. In mid throw of saddling Shadow he stopped swinging his saddle back over the fence.

"What is your deal?" I asked irritably. He looked up at me deep in thought.

"I need to talk them. Alone." With that he walked back to the house. Shadow's reaction was nearly comical. He looked up watching him intently.

"What about me?" Okay. That was weird. I think I just heard what he was thinking. I turned to my sister.

"Did you hear that?"

"Yeah. I heard what Dante said." Frowning I shook my head at her glancing to Shadow.

135

"No. Something else." Looking concerned she frowned shaking her head.

"No. Why?" I shook my head waiting for Dante for nearly twenty minutes. Looking to my watch it had stopped the moment we stepped foot on the island. Weird.

"Let's just go Annabelle. He can catch up to us." I took one last glance at Shadow. "Sorry boy." Before we started out. Shadow had other ideas as he untied himself running after us. He ran right up beside me causing Rocki to pin his ears flat angrily reaching to bite him. Shadow pinned his own back shaking his head. Rocki stopped looking at him ears forward. They were communicating

"Shadow. No. Dammit. Come here." Reaching for the lead he yanked it out of my reach. He threw his head around rearing up with his ears pinned back.

"No!" I heard it distinctly this time. This was too strange. Could I hear his thoughts?

"Okay. You do not want me to touch you. Got it. Sorry about what I had to do on the ship." He stopped throwing his fit looking at me walking up beside us.

"Maylee no. You saved my life. I trust you. Just. Watch yourself here. Not everyone has your best intentions at heart." Why he had actually felt compelled to warn me?

"Thanks for the warning. But I had already been doing that. Or are you talking about your owner?" He flicked his head.

"No. But I cannot tell you what he does not want told. Only warn you of what could happen here."

"Okay. I understand. Have you been here before?"

"No. Dante was. A long time ago. Izabella was protecting him. But he insisted she allowed him to leave. To return home." Frowning I glanced to my sister.

"Okay. So. He's not the bad guy. What is he to you?"

"Dante has owned me for a long time. Helped to raise me when I was only a foal." Now I understood his reaction to when Shadow coliced.

"That's why he panicked when you were sick. He did not want to lose you."

"Yes. Now please. No more questions. He will have to tell you himself when the time is right." Nodding at him I replied.

"Fair enough." Shadow turned running back down to the corral to wait for his rider to return for him. I loosed a deep breath before I turned continuing down the trail.

Annabelle and I chose the trail leading the way to the beach where we dismounted. I removed Rocki's saddle and bridle. Annabelle followed suit with Oscerr. Leading them to a large boulder mounting up without any tack. We rode out into the water staying along the edge. Not wanting to go out far with everything that going on. Annabelle had not heard Shadow's thoughts as I had so we talked about what he had told me.

She wanted to trust Dante. I on the other hand just kept drawing myself farther away from him. I guess this is where the old saying applies keep your friends close and your enemies closer. We rode further into the water until the boys had to swim. Momentarily forgetting about the creatures that could be lurking there. It was a lot of fun. Something we had never had a chance to do before.

We swam back to the beach onto the sand drying off in the bright warm sun. It did not take long for all of us to dry off. Saddling back up we decided to ride down another trail. This one traveled through the forest. I had saw it on the way to the Chief's house. It was amazing! There were exotic fruit trees like pineapple, kiwi, bananas, and some stuff I had never saw before. I was examining what looked to be a cocoa tree when we could hear something coming through the trees. Not too sure of what it could be we moved the horses around drawing our swords to be ready. Breaking through the branches it was Shadow with Dante on board.

"Whoa! Guys. Really? All I did was stay behind and now you're ready to attack me?" I looked to Shadow as I sheathed my sword.

"Sorry. We didn't know what was coming."

"You're apologizing to him? But not me?" Dante asked me looking confused. Shrugging I smirked as Shadow tossed his head.

"Yes. I still don't like you. Or trust you. I did find out that I can hear your horse's thoughts. We had pretty good conversation." He looked shocked glancing to Shadow before up to me his expression leery of what may have been said.

"What did he tell you?" His face became set as in he was probably furious with him.

"Don't worry. Nothing that makes me too uneasy. Or I didn't know already." Shadow looked to me giving a small nod.

"Thank you." I heard from him before I looked back to Dante.

"So what took so long?" He looked around dismounting to join us on the ground.

"I had a long talk with the chief about some things." The look on my face must have told the story. "I will tell you everything in time. I'm just not ready for you to know yet. Okay?" I had to think that one over for a minute before I nodded. I looked over to Rocki whose voice came into my mind as Shadow's had earlier.

"Would you like me to kick him for you?" I snickered glancing up to Dante.

"No. That's okay." I thought back to him. "Just understand this. I will not trust you until you tell us." Dante nodded looking none too amused. Annabelle sheathed her sword just before we mounted our horses continuing our little exploration.

We made our way into the town to find it was in the very middle of the island. As I said the buildings looked like they were straight out of the 1500s and they were stunning. The streets were all made of cobblestones which was something we rarely seen now a days.

As far as how people dressed? It was modern. Regular jeans, t-shirt or whatever they wanted. I did see a few who dressed as if from the late 1800s. Other than that it was all pretty modern. Electricity included. We met with Izabella by a rather large building nearly out of town. She motioned for us to go there pointing out behind the building.

"There is a stable for the horses out there if that is where you want to keep them. You will each have your own apartment in this building we are in front of. Everything you need will be in the rooms, furniture, beds. Your belongings have already been taken up. Food is also supplied. If you want to make your own you can, if not we can deliver it to you pre made." Annabelle was excited before worried.

"Can my sister come to my apartment when I cook? She can just not very well. She prefers to see how it is cooked and where it is from." Izabella nodded.

"That is fine. Now take care of your horses and unpack your belongings. Meet me back here in two hours for the grand tour. One more thing. Just in case you were thinking about letting your horses wander instead of staying in the stable. There are dragons that stay on this island. Anything that moves when they are hungry is fair game." As she walked away I looked over at my sister in disbelief.

"Is she serious? Dragons? Really?" After that without any hesitation we walked to the stable.

139

"A wise choice I think." I could not tell which one had thought it but I agreed. After the horses were all settled into their new stalls I turned to Rocki pointing at him.

"Be good for the people who will be feeding you. No biting or escaping." I pointed to Oscerr. "And no kicking." He lowered his head flicking his ears back and forth.

"Why not?" I rolled my eyes at him taking care of our tack where we were told. My emergency kit among tack since you just never know when you're going to need it.

We walked back to the building our apartments were located through the doors. It really reminded me of a castle from medieval times yet it was modern. There was a clerk's desk at the front walking up to it the clerk had noticed us. He reached behind him bringing out three keys.

"You are all on the third floor. The number is on your key." He went back to organizing some files as we all looked at each other like how did he know who we were? Shrugging we went down the hall to the elevator. There were stairs but we took the elevator instead as we were tired.

We stepped out onto the third floor looking both ways. There were only four rooms on this floor. Two rooms on each side. These rooms should be big than. On the left were rooms nine and eleven, to the right was ten and twelve. Annabelle had ten and I had twelve so we were next to each other. Dante had eleven. Great right across from me. We went to our respective door unlocking them walking in at the same time.

"Wow" I said looking around my apartment shutting the door behind me. It could have passed as my parent's place back in Michigan, except it was all done the way I had always wanted. It was more like a small house. There was no television but I doubted I would have time to watch it anyways. I explored the kitchen finding everything I would need for cooking and herbs I was assuming to make some potions with.

The bedroom was next on my list. The bed was king size. Much bigger than I had before with hand made quilts and lots of pillows. A desk for when I decided to write in my notebook, a huge dresser made of cedar wood with a mirror on top of it. Like I would ever use it, I did not care how I looked. There was a small bookshelf with a few leather bound books. I did not take the time to pick them up and look at them. I went back out to the living area. The couch seated three made of smooth dark brown leather. I sat on it for a minute, it was really comfortable. In the corner of the living room there was a small home gym. Hell yeah. There was a small rack of dumbbells, a bench, a squat rack with plates laying beside it. The barbell was an Olympic model. This was an amazing set up. After looking over the gym area I grabbed my backpack from the floor taking it into the bedroom to unpack.

Unzipping all the compartments I dumped it all out on the bed to sort through it. My Ziploc bags of money fell out. I had forgotten about them. Picking up one of the bags I counted out five hundred dollars since I needed a few things and I was sure my sister would too. First thing would be more clothes, and other essentials. It did not take long before I had everything packed away with my now empty backpack over the chair to my desk. I would use it for missions from now on.

There was a knock at the door walking over to open it. Annabelle stood there waiting for me looking overly anxious.

"Come in." I stood aside. She looked around nodding,

"Nice" Before asking me to see her apartment. It was similar to mine, different colors, patterns, and she had a T.V. She did watch movies a lot so it made sense to me. We walked out to the elevator to meet Izabella by the corner. She was already waiting for us when we arrived.

Dante walked out behind us moments later. I could not tell what he was thinking. He was so expressionless most times. How boring but probably useful. Izabella gave us the tour of where we would study, train, the buildings and field. Finally we came across a store to buy supplies at.

"You will not wear clothes like you wore on the way here for training. For all training you will wear the issued mission gear given to you tomorrow morning." Annabelle and I looked at each other. This really was beginning to be like one of our books.

"What about when we are not in training?" Shaking her head she turned to the training field.

"You can wear what you want when not in training. We will have the shoemaker in town take everyone's measurements for custom boots." Frowning I crossed my arms.

"So we can't even wear our own boots?" Smirking she crossed her arms over her chest looking to my boots.

"The sole of your riding boots are too thick for the amount of moving around you have to do in combat. The ones we will have made for you are made to move with you."

"Right. And how much are those going to cost us each?" Smirking she glanced to the chief's place.

"Nothing. The shoemaker said he would make them free of charge." Nodding Annabelle shrugged as we walked along coming across a general store.

"What do we buy with?" Since I was not sure what they used here.

"Did you bring money?" I checked my pocket to make sure it had not fallen out.

"Yeah, but I wasn't sure what exactly was used here." Izabella nodded.

"We take all forms of money, American, the Euro, pesos, pounds, anything with value. You can even barter if you do not have money." I was relieved to hear this.

"Good, I brought all my money from home with me." Annabelle looked at me with raised eyebrows.

"All of it?" She asked surprised.

"Well, most of it. I withdrew it the day before we left." She looked uneasy shifting her feet.

"Could I borrow some? I need clothes and shampoo and well the list just keeps going."

"Why do you think I brought it? Can we go in now or do we need to wait?" Izabella looked at the store.

"I still have much to show you. Could it wait until we are done with the tour?" We looked at each other nodding at the same time. "Good." She said continuing on.

The town was absolutely huge, and we found out if we needed anything they did not have there they could order it. When the tour was over my sister and I went back to the merchandise store buying what we needed. It came to nearly three hundred dollars which did not shock me at all. Without hesitation I dug into my pocket pulling out the money from earlier. Loaded down with everything we bought we headed back to the apartments. After we had unpacked all I wanted was to go to bed. It had been a long day. Now they were about to be tough too.

Dante

Once we arrived on the island my nerves were worse than before. Gathering in the cottage for the meeting as everyone was introduced. Having been here once before I knew who the chief and Kamran were immediately but had to act as if I did not.

Izabella stopped her half brother to examine Maylee's sword as she had thought it was dark. I could tell it was not, but it put Izabella at ease to have Kamran look at it. As we stood looking at her sword I could tell he was paying too close attention to Maylee making sure to touch her hand when giving back her sword. Izabella noticed as well frowning as she let us leave. All of us walked out but I stopped going back.

"Dante. I see you have made it back to us at last." The chief commented as he looked at another map.

"Yes. I know it has taken a lot of time. But I am here now. And I'm trying to help." He nodded slowly walking around his desk as Izabella and Kamran stood behind him. If I was easily intimidated that would have done it.

"Are you? Or are you just here to spy on us for them?" He stopped inches from me as he asked. Taking a deep breath I had to steady myself.

"I'm here to help the council. They can use me to obtain information from them." He mumbled stepping back smoking his pipe.

"What kind of information do you think we might need from them that we could not gain anywhere else?"

144

"My father led that army until he died. They trust me. They tell me ideas and training they don't tell others." The chief nodded walking away from me.

"Okay. Prove it."

"How would you like me to prove it?"

"Izabella informed me that they asked you to turn one of our recruits. You were successful. Correct?"

"Yes."

"What is her first assignment?"

"They did not tell me."

"So they do not trust you. Do they?"

"They do."

"Than what are they asking of her?" He slammed his hand onto his desk. I never flinched but Izabella jumped looking to me wide eyed.

"They want her to bring her sister to headquarters in Texas."

"When?"

"They never said when. Just as soon as possible." Silently he looked to the map again before glancing back to Kamran who nodded to him.

"You are dismissed." Walking out I felt my heartbeat quicken shutting the door. As I saddled Shadow Izabella walked out to the corral looking livid.

"Why did you do that?" Scowling I looked up at her.

"Do what?" Sighing she shook her head.

"Withhold information. Important information." Dropping my hands I turned to her feeling more tired than ever.

"It wasn't on purpose. I didn't think that was important right now. Annabelle is not strong enough to take her sister on like that." Looking angry she stood up straight.

"She is not strong enough. However. If Annabelle begins to catch wind that you are informing the council of everything. You will become more of an enemy to her. You will lose any chance you have at all at being friends with her." My body began to tremble as lack of sleep and breaking nerves were finally catching up.

"Dammit Izabella." Leaning on the fence I took a few deep breaths.

"You should never have agreed to this." She told me quietly as I tried to regain my composure.

"I didn't know I was going to be interrogated once I arrived here. Sorry." Glaring at me she shook her head.

"Your father really did a good job of brainwashing you."

"What the hell is that supposed to mean?" I asked angrily.

"He taught you to manipulate everything. Even if you do not realize that was what you did when the chief was asking you questions. That was why he questioned you to begin with. You gave him the hole he needed to think you are here to spy on us."

"I'm not!" I growled back only becoming more agitated.

"I know that. Look at me." Izabella was already calm again as I looked at her as asked. "From now on. You tell them everything. Even if you yourself do not think it matters. Am I clear?"

"Yes." Nodding she crossed her arms.

"I have put myself on the line for you. Do not make me regret it."

"You won't." She nodded walking away as I finished tacking up Shadow to catch up to Annabelle and Maylee.

"What did you do to piss her off?" Shadow asked as we walked the trails.

"I failed to mention what Annabelle's first assignment was."

146

"Why?"

"Something just did not feel right."

"You realize that makes them not trust you. Right?" Rolling my eyes I knew he was right.

"I know. I messed up. Izabella already reprimanded me." Tossing his head slightly he stopped.

"I know. And you. You are not okay right now."

"No."

"Than we should stay away from the girls for a while longer. At least until you can pull yourself together."

"Agreed." We met up with them after half an hour or so. Together we rode all over the island for a while. I stayed to the back behind the other two as we rode the trails. Shadow tilted his head up at me just before we arrived at the apartment building we were staying.

"Would you just talk to her? You are too obvious up there watching her."

"I should stay away. With the council forcing me to spy." Stopping as Shadow stopped huffing.

"You volunteered. Which you should have never done to begin with. Especially after escaping Theo the way we did. You knew there would be repercussions."

When I arrived in my assigned apartment there was already a letter waiting on the kitchen counter from Theo. Sighing I picked it up reading it.

***

The sooner you send the girl the better. If she is not here within a month we will send someone for you.

I knew what that meant. They would send someone here to kill me. Throwing myself into a chair I kept looking at the letter thinking about Maylee.

Maylee

I woke up when someone knocked on my door. Rolling out of bed I walked sleepily out to see who it was. It was my sister opening the door to let her in.

"I was sleeping. What do you want?" She raised her eyebrows at me surprised.

"It's ten in the morning. And you were not up yet? I came over for breakfast." I looked up at the clock on the kitchen wall. Damn. It was five after ten now. I must have been beyond tired.

"Remind me to buy an alarm clock at the store today." She nodded sitting at the counter on one of the bar stools. I walked to the cupboard taking out a frying pan holding it up.

"How do eggs and toast sound?"

"After nothing but toaster pastries and granola bars? Any real food is good." I laughed agreeing with her. Opening the refrigerator I took out the carton of eggs, a bowl of butter, and a loaf of bread that I had to slice. Within minutes we were enjoying our eggs and toast. When we were done I put the dishes in the sink. I would wash them up later. Annabelle returned to her own apartment while I showered and dressed.

We met in the hall an hour later walking down to the stable together. We walked right past Shadow's stall. He called me back to talk to him. He asked about Dante and if I had seen him today. Shadow seemed disappointed but he did not think it. We brushed the boys giving them their favorite treat, carrots. After that we went to the store so I could buy an alarm clock. While we were there I also decided to buy some workout shorts and tank tops. I had not had time to pack mine when we left the house. Annabelle smirked as I chose all black shorts, leggings, tank tops and sports bras.

"You do see that there are other colors and patterns here right?" Looking up at the shelves I nodded.

"I am aware." I heard her make a sound as she turned walking another way in the clothing area. She held up a push up bra. It was a nice one. I could not argue that.

"Before you say anything. It's for me. Not you. Although I'm sure you could use"

"Enough" I told her firmly. Wide eyed she nodded looking through the rack. Closing my eyes I walked around looking at pajama sets. There were a few I liked. I settled for two sets that were string tank tops with shorts. One set of dark purple and another in black. Annabelle smiled when she saw the sets saying nothing. We returned to the apartment complex with our purchases. Afterward we went for a walk down some trails that led to the mountains.

Annabelle wanted to trust Dante. To be friends with him. Not me. There were just too many bad vibes. Even though he had seemed genuinely grateful I had helped his horse telling me he would talk to me eventually. My gut told me not to trust him. As my sister and I walked along I had become aware of the same ill feeling from her. It was not something I was going to like at all.

Suddenly something large flew over us startling me as I jumped sideways. I watched it fly toward the smallest mountain, away from us. It was a dragon. Izabella had told us that they were here. I thought she was joking. I should have known better. We followed the path it had flown to the small mountain where it landed walking around. There was someone on its back jumping off when we walked up toward them. He walked right up to us.

"You two must be the sisters from Michigan. Maylee and Annabelle right?" I was growing used to the fact everyone here seemed to know us without introducing ourselves.

"Yeah. That's us." He held a hand out introducing himself.

"My name is William. Nice to finally meet you in person." We took our turns shaking his hand.

"Likewise. You ride these dragons?" He glanced over at the one he had been with.

"Well. We train them. Not necessarily ride them. I am not his owner or master." I felt my forehead crease.

"What do you mean not its owner?" He was patient while explaining this because we were so new.

"Us immortals. Spend our years training them until the right person comes along. If they match up to someone we train them together. Right now we have eight unclaimed dragons. With nine new descendants arriving yesterday more will choose to bond. "

I looked over at the nearest dragon. It was pitch black, silver ridges going down its neck along its back with spikes of the same color on its tail. I felt stupid for asking, but I wanted to know.

"Are there different breeds or colors?" Annabelle before I did making me look over to her questioningly. William smirked as I was sure it was not the first time he had been asked that.

"No. There is only one breed. They all look like that one there except their ridges and spikes are a different color." Too cool. You could fly at night without ever being seen.

"How do you know it's the right person?"

"A very good question. When close enough to their match that particular person's sword glows." He looked to us smiling as he pointed to Annabelle. "Like that." I looked over. Sure enough her sword was glowing faintly silver. This was awesome. William walked up beside her.

"Come meet the dragon you will be training with." He glanced over as I felt something behind me. I wanted to jump or run, but I slowly turned around facing another dragon. My heart was thumping so hard it felt like it was breaking out of my chest.

My sword glowed a faint gold color. This dragon was like my sister's but had gold ridges and spikes. Our first full day here and we already have dragons to train with too. Talk about a full schedule. I looked to William taking a cautious step back releasing my muscles.

"What are their names?" He pointed to the one Annabelle would be training with.

"That is Albay, and that is Marlo." Their names began with the same letter as ours did. He seemed to have noticed this pattern too.

"Anyways. If you also notice. The color of ridges on the dragon is the color your sword glows when you were near." I had somewhat noticed. Marlo's trainer walked out of the side of the mountain introducing himself as Winston. He was not as friendly as William but he was willing to teach me.

The trainers had us board our dragons riding along to teach us how to navigate. We flew everywhere over the island. You could cover a huge area with them. They even flew us over the ocean for a little ways. This had to be how they had kept track of the Rockford when we were sailing here. They would just ride a dragon flying across the ocean. Literally.

We flew back to the island landing on the mountain we had started on. I don't think it's called dismounting when you have to jump off and not just step down. Izabella, Kamran, and the chief were waiting for us to return at the mountain top. Oh no, I thought. I don't remember anything about a meeting today. Apparently my sister was thinking the same thing.

"Did we do something wrong?" Izabella walked up to us.

"No. You did nothing wrong. We just did not expect you to find your dragons so soon. But since you have. They will be added into your training schedules. We looked up to see the dragons being flown as in they were being taught basics and were curious to see who it was. We should have known it was the two of you."

Izabella was impassive. Why was everyone around us so good at that? Seemingly emotionless? I was always extremely readable and it always got me into trouble. Kamran stepped in front of me so close we were almost touching.

"Now I can teach you to fight from dragon back too." He sounded like he was going to have fun. It sounded like a lot of work to me. Annabelle and I looked at each other smiling. It would be interesting. The chief spoke up next.

"I have a favor to ask of the two of you." That sounded slightly foreboding.

"Okay. What is it?" I asked as he started walking down the trail. We all followed. He glanced back as he walked to make sure we were there.

"Keep an eye on Dante." I stopped dead in my tracks. They must suspect him.

"Why? Do you think he is a spy for the other side?" The Chief looked to Izabella who shrugged.

"I told you she just knows things. She has amazing instincts." He turned back to me shaking it off.

"We suspect. Yes. But that is all for now. We cannot seem to be able to prove it. Just find out what you can from him. He seems to be drawn to you Maylee." Wide eyed I'm sure I had not just heard that correctly.

"Me?" Just to make sure I did hear that right. "Why would he even want to be around me? I almost roasted him the first day we met. And I have let him know I do not like him. I definitely do not trust him." The chief chuckled confusing me.

"He did mention that when he talked to me yesterday. He actually does not want to be here. Feels that he does not belong. That maybe because he feels guilty about being a spy or maybe he is just honest about himself."

"No." I said a little louder than intended. "He has some deep dark secrets. I was informed to not trust him. Now you are telling me to get close to him? Seriously? Can't you just make him leave?" Izabella scowled when I mentioned him leaving. She was on the same give him a chance bullshit Annabelle was on.

"Yes. I want you to get close to him." The chief stated calmly. "Just give it time. He might open up to you. Just try Maylee. Get the information we need from him. You do not have to be best friends or anything like that."

"What if I refuse?" Izabella was wide eyed looking at me as the chief stared in disbelief.

"I have others that could watch him. After talking to Izabella we thought you were best to make him open up more. As I said. He seems to be drawn to you."

"So you wouldn't kill me or kick me off the island for telling you absolutely not?" The chief looked unsettled but nodded all the same.

"Very well. If you do not wish to do this I will find another. Maybe your sister?" I nodded glancing over to her.

"She seems to think they are friends. Certainly more friendly with him than I have been. He should be okay with her."

"Than it is settled. Annabelle will obtain the information we need. Good luck training Maylee." I watched him walk away talking to my sister.

"I thought you would want an assignment like that." Izabella said standing beside me with her half brother crossing her arms.

"If it had been anyone else? Yes. But I cannot stand him and the bad vibes that roll off of him. I just want to concentrate on learning what I need to know."

"You know Maylee. He is not bad." Stopping I turned to her.

"Than you go watch him." Her face tightened at my tone.

"Maylee. I know your instincts are good. But listen. Certain things will feel that way when you first arrive here. Instead watch and learn."

"You knew him before he found us." She nodded glancing to her brother who was on my other side now. "Why didn't he use his powers against me when I attacked him?" Izabella was quick to answer that.

"He chooses not to use them. He resents his powers. Look. He has been trying to convince us that he does not work for them anymore. His story checks out, but I want to be completely sure first." With that she gave Kamran a look turning to walk back where we had been.

"Izabella" Stopping she turned back. "When we have time could you show us where to pick up our mission gear?" Smirking she nodded.

"Go to the shoemaker today for your measurements for your boots. Next door is a supply store for your issued mission gear. You will have two sets. You will also wear armor after a few weeks. I will see you later." With that she walked away.

"They want to believe the best in people. They can be wrong. You just have to be careful." Kamran laid a hand on my shoulder looking down at me. His thumb pressed my pressure point momentarily. I had not realized he was still beside me. "Maybe we could meet up later? I like you." Keeping my breathing even I laid my hand over his pushing it off my shoulder.

"Kamran. While I think you are attractive. I am going to say no. I want to concentrate on my training." Smirking he yanked me up against him holding me there. I had not realized just how large Kamran was to me.

"What if I do not accept your answer?" Glancing to my side I knew Izabella was not far.

"Than I would say you are someone I would not waste my time on to begin with. I escaped one abusive asshole in my life. I refuse to be involved with another." His chest rumbled with a growl as he released me.

"I would never hurt you like that." Straightening myself out I shook my head at him.

"I do not know you well enough to know. From now on. Leave me alone unless I am in training." He nodded giving a look that felt like an indication of what he would like to have done. Nodding we went our separate ways. As I walked someone grabbed my arm. Not thinking about it I swung out to find it was my sister.

"Sorry!" Annabelle jumped back looking wide eyed.

"What has you so jumpy?" I did not think anyone would believe me.

"Everything. Why don't we go relax?" Agreeing we walked further up the trail. My adrenaline was still coming down as we sat on a couple of large boulders facing one another.

"So why are they setting you up to watch him?" She shook her head.

"He seems to trust us more than he does them."

"Great. Well let's go back up to the cavern. We have a lot to learn." As I stood up Annabelle looked at me worriedly.

"Are you going to tell me why you have been shaking for the last half hour?" I shook my head trying to smile at her.

"It is nothing for you to worry about. Nothing that I can't handle. Okay?" Nodding she still looked apprehensive.

We learned that the dragons could go a day or two without food or water. They hunted for themselves so we never had to worry about feeding them. They could fly up to three hundred miles without resting, depending on the weather. With Erde I could help out with weather conditions. Only one thing they would not do and that was fly through thunderstorms because the lightning could strike them down. The thunder threw off their sense of direction which made sense to me. They would be really useful when we went to battle.

I wish we could take pictures and send them to everyone at home. Mess with me now please. My dragon will either char you or eat you alive. That would be fantastic! There were a couple more dragons in the air as we went back into the air to learn more about flying.

The trainers were teaching us barrel rolls when I could have swore the name of one of the other dragons was Dillon. That would make him Dante's. Riding dragons was a lot different from riding a horse. Mostly because of their bodies were so big. There was a notch on their neck that was like a saddle you sat on. The scales even curved to keep your legs in position while flying. The trainers let us take a break for lunch.

We hit the street market in town since I still had money in my pocket left over from this morning. We found a side stand that sold sandwiches and drinks. I bought three sandwiches with drinks taking them to the apartment complex. Once on our floor Annabelle knocked on Dante's door. No answer. Maybe he went to see Shadow? I reached out to Shadow with my mind finding that it actually worked.

"Yes Maylee?" He answered.

"Is Dante down there?"

"No. He has not been down here at all yet." Hmm. Odd. I thought it over. "I could break out to find him."

"No, I'll find him. Thanks anyways." I turned to my sister. "Let's go check the training field."

We walked down to where Izabella had showed us was the training field. There were people practicing sword progressions. They were either sparring against someone or against a stuffed opponent. That must be one of the groups Izabella had spoke about. I looked closely at their swords until my eyes finally recognized guardian.

"Over there." I pointed walking in that general direction. From how he looked he had been out here most of the day already. He saw us walking down stopping what he was doing breathing hard wiping sweat out of his face with his shirt. Like it would do much good. His shirt was soaked with sweat. But holy hell when he wiped his face. The man had muscle. I actually had to bite the inside f my mouth to keep my cool.

"How long have you been out here?" I asked as he looked fairly worn out.

"Since this morning." I handed him a bottle of water. "Thanks. I do feel slightly dehydrated." Nodding acknowledgement I also handed him the sandwich walking toward the edge of the woods to sit in the shade. He followed us slowly not knowing what to think of the fact I was nice to him. After a few minutes eating in silence he spoke up. "Where

157

have you two been all day?" We exchanged glances smirking knowing how he would react to what we were about to say.

"Learning to fly dragons." His reaction was nearly comical. Almost choking on some water he had just taken a swig of.

"What? You are not serious." I glared at him.

"Have I ever not been serious? Yes. We have been flying all over the island today. You have not seen them in the air?" He shrugged considering for moment.

"I guess. There were four flying when I saw them." Frowning he glanced to his sword. "Something weird happened when they flew over."

"Let me guess. Your sword lit up red?" His eyes widened in surprise actually showing emotion. There's a change.

"How did you know?"

"Ours glowed when we met our dragons. Mine was a pale golden color and Annabelle's was a faint silver. Makes sense to me since one of them flying with us had red ridges and spikes." Nodding he drank some more water before asking.

"Where are they?" Annabelle was devouring her sandwich leaving me to answer him. Raising my eyebrows at her she shrugged.

"On the smallest mountain. We are just taking a break. Annabelle wanted to know what you were up to." He looked at me as though measuring me up looking back to the training field. Annabelle choked on her water she had just taken a drink from glaring at me. "What?" I mouthed back without sound. She rolled her eyes annoyed. Observing without staring at Dante I could tell that he was much more relaxed around me than he was my sister. Another oddity as I was always blunt or snarky to him. A total bitch in short. Still annoyed with me she spoke.

"You should come back up with us. That way all three of us can train on them together." Annabelle suggested as he nodded looking around.

"I could use a break from this." Taking that as a yes we led the way back up to the mountain. We were greeted by our two dragon trainers.

"Hey guys. This is Dante." They greeted him at which his sword lit up. Of course they had noticed.

"Looks like we have another one. The one your looking for is over there. His name is Dillon. The trainer's name is Hector. Go on over and meet them. Meet us in the air." After all their introductions we all were flying around the island a few times learning about the dragons.

It was nearly sunset when we landed back on the mountain saying our good nights to the instructors walking back to our apartments for the night. I was certainly sore from all that flying around and the maneuvering. I thought riding the horses was hard work. The three of us talked about the dragons all the way to the doors of our apartments. Oddly enough Dante walked at my side while Annabelle dropped back behind us.

Dante had loved flying saying it suited him much better than sailing. When we walked to our apartments there were papers taped to our doors. They were our training schedules. At least for the first day of training we all had to start out together for assessment. Adjusting our training accordingly once completed. It seemed as if they wanted to keep the three of us together as our assessments were scheduled at the same time and place. I knew my sister's sword skills were no where near Dante's. Or mine for that matter. They would be sure Annabelle was close to Dante to keep an eye on him.

Before I went to bed I wondered if my telepathy would work with Izabella calling her. Moments later there was a soft knock on my door. Looking out the peephole it was her. Opening the door I felt my face burn at what I was about to tell her. Her face showed concern as she laid a hand on my shoulder.

"Is something wrong Maylee?" I nodded feeling my face warm more.

"I need to talk to you about something." Walking past me she stood by my kitchen counter crossing her arms over her chest.

"Okay. Can you be more specific?" Shaking my head I sat beside her at the counter on a barstool. Sighing Izabella set to work in my kitchen handing me a cup of something hot. "Drink it. You will feel better." She waited until I had drank half of the cup before saying a word. "Did someone try to hurt you?" I fixed my eyes on my cup feeling like a coward for calling her to my apartment.

"No."

"There must be something. What happened that you felt you needed to call me here this time of night?" It was demanding yet gentle at the same time.

"I cannot train with my sister and Dante." I heard her make an amused sound shaking her head.

"Because she is gaining his trust for information?"

"No. Because after today I will never look at Kamran the same. I can't train with him. I want to train with you. Please?" Confused she sat beside me.

"Why can you not train with Kamran?"

"He made me uneasy after you all left earlier." She laid her hand on my shoulder.

"Maylee, look at me." When I looked up she was not angry with me as I thought she would be. "Tomorrow. You have to report to the training field. I will not be far. If he attempts anything. Call me. Okay?" I nodded acknowledgement as she stood walking out of my apartment. Sleep was uneasy that night.

I had set my alarm for eight in the morning. Unfortunately I was wide awake at five. Shaking my head at the way I had reacted the day before I knew I had to toughen up. In more ways than one. Physically I would have to workout. I needed to be in better shape along with mentally stronger. Throwing my blanket off I stood pulling out my workout clothes dressing. Looking at the clock it was only five thirty. Quietly I walked out of my apartment down the stairs to go to the street. Daylight was breaking illuminating the streets. Walking fast the first block I turned running the trail to the beach. By the time I had reached the beach I was out of breath stopping by the water. Hands on my knees it took a few minutes to catch my breath before I began running back. According to my watch that had been two miles. Fuck. I have work to do.

When I arrived back at the apartment complex Izabella was waiting by the main entrance on the street.

"Is this part of your new routine? Or is this because you could not sleep?" Hands on my hips I tried to slow my breathing.

"Both. I had planned on starting to run. Just not this early in the morning." Turning she signaled for us to go upstairs.

"I am not going to your apartment Maylee. I just wanted you off main street at the very moment."

"Why" Before I could finish my sentence Kamran walked by reading a paper. As he did I felt my breathing almost stop.

"Maylee" Izabella called my attention back.

"Yeah." She frowned turning to look up to where my apartment was.

"Stop holding your breath." Shaking her head she looked back to me. "Also. I have a feeling you will have to take over befriending Dante soon." Scowling I rolled my eyes as I started up to my apartment.

"Why? Pretty sure my sister has it under control."

"No. She does not." Grabbing my wrist she stopped me just before the door to the third floor.

"What are you"

"Listen!" She whispered loudly to me jerking her head to the door. There were two voices very heatedly talking. Arguing actually.

"If you had done as your boss had told you than I wouldn't have to do it! You don't know how good you had it before." It sounded like Annabelle. Tilting my head I listened closer.

"And I am telling you. They are not worth it. You don't know what they did to me. The amount of time they tortured me." Dante. Damn. He was quiet as he spoke. It did not sound angry quiet. It sounded hurt quiet. What did they do to him?

"I don't give a damn what you think they did to you! Come near my sister and I will kill you myself!" I heard him laugh.

"With what skills? I have years of training. You can barely hold that sword. And its not even a full size sword. At least your sister can do that much." I smirked as the last part sounded like a taunt.

"Go to hell Dante. Where you belong. And stay the hell away from my sister. Got it?"

"Why would I stay away from her? She barely speaks to me now. Let alone hang around me unless she is with you. Besides. Someone needs to warn her that her brat sister has turned sides. You are going to get her killed!"

"Don't even think about it! And I'm not going to get her killed. They only want her powers."

"How the hell do you think they get them?" When I turned to say something to Izabella she was already gone. Rolling my eyes I took the last ten steps to the door loudly throwing the door open. They were no where to be seen. I kept my eyes on my own door acting as if I had never heard them. So that had been why those vibes were rolling off my sister the day before. She had turned against us. Irritated I showered before making breakfast for myself and my sister. I could not let her know I knew she had changed. I had literally just buttered the toast for her omelet when there was a knock on my door.

Answering the door she was not the only one standing there. Dante was too. They were both red in the face. Annabelle's eyes were storm clouded the way they turn when she was mad. I assumed they had been arguing again. I did not need this right now.

"Good morning. I made omelets for breakfast." Walking past me into my apartment. "And what do you want?" I asked Dante. When he looked at me an air of darkness crossed his face shaking his head.

"Nothing. I'm going to see Shadow. Later." He walked away with one last glance back at my sister who was sitting at the counter. I scowled watching him walk down the hall to the staircase.

"Well good morning to you too." I slammed the door shut. As I shut it Dante looked like he was about to walk back to my doorway. I let it go walking to the counter where Annabelle was working on her omelet.

"What was going on between you two? You both looked red hot about something. I thought you were supposed to be friends with him?" She looked at me darkly shrugging indifferently.

"He was asking about you. I didn't want to tell him anything."

"Like what?" I was genuinely curious.

163

"I don't know. I ignored him after the first stupid question."

"And that was?"

"What were you doing today. And when." Shifting my feet I placed my hands on my hips staring at her.

"You blew up at him for that? Why?" It was obvious that she did not understand the complications of having to baby sit him. She looked down ashamed of having done it.

"Sorry." I just looked at her pointing.

"I'm not the one you should be apologizing to. The chief asked you to keep an eye on him. Blowing up and sending him away defeats that purpose in many ways Annabelle. That is the opposite of what they want you doing." I looked around the apartment grabbing a hooded sweatshirt pulling it on over my tank top.

"I'm going to the stables to talk to him. You stay here and cool it." Standing quickly she grabbed my elbow on my way by.

"Maylee no. Let him blow off. You don't like him anyways. Why waste your time? Unless you actually do want to" Raising my eyebrows at her I pulled her hand off my arm gently.

"Annabelle. The chief asked you to keep him close. To get information from him. If you can't stop arguing with him about everything including me for some stupid reason. Than I guess I will have to do damage control for you. Just don't mess up again. Because you are right. I don't like him. And the less time I have to be around him the better."

"Or Maybe your attitude towards him right now is just foreplay. I still think you two should just"

"Enough!" I yelled scowling angrily. Her face fell realizing I was legitimately angry. "I have had it with your shit about him and I. Where is that coming from?" Her jaw worked in anger before she looked at me.

"I'm sorry Maylee. I'm just. Stressed. And you're here so I take it out on you. He really likes you. A lot." Frowning I shook my head sitting beside her.

"I understand. All of this is stressful. I get that. But as far as Dante and I. He is your assignment. How he feels about me has nothing to do with your job. And you know damn well the feeling is not mutual." She smirked momentarily nodding.

"Okay. I'm just worried about you. You were so jumpy yesterday. Did something happen?" Sighing I nodded.

"Yes. Once all of you went your separate ways Kamran tried to"

"What! I swear if he hurt you"

"Annabelle" She stopped sitting back down. "I'm fine. He did not do anything. Just the look he gave when I walked away indicated what he wanted to do." Her face set in a way I knew she was angry.

"But you're okay?" Smirking at her I nodded.

"Yes. Now. I am going to walk down to the stable. Talk to your assignment to do damage control. Than I have to change before assessment at nine. You good now?" Rolling her eyes looking more annoyed than before she nodded.

"Yeah. I'm good. Just be careful with him. He is not who you think he is." Nodding I walked out the door to the staircase. It did not take long to find him as he was brushing and talking to Shadow. Stopping where I knew he could not see me I listened in on their conversation. Dante sounded torn about something like it was a life or death decision. I listened in on Shadow's thoughts as they talked knowing I should not have. Walking closer I let them know I was in the building. At least it was a fair warning. Dante looked up to see who it was before back to Shadow.

"Look, I'm sorry about my sister. She has been very easily upset lately. If there is something wrong. Maybe I could help?" He kept brushing. I watched as eventually he glanced up again. I could tell he was angry. For someone who normally was so controlling of their emotions he was letting go now. I knew he wanted to tell me about my sister, but he also knew I would not believe him. And until she revealed to me what she wanted I had to keep acting that way.

"Maylee. Stop it. Just go away. I don't want you near me. Please just go." By the time he spoke the last part he sounded tired.

"No. Just give me a chance to explain something. Before you do anything." Irritably he waved for me to continue. "I don't know what is going on between you and my sister, but if there is anything I can do to help with the problem" He laughed forcibly.

"I can't even begin to tell you the problem. I would love to. But I am a hundred percent sure you would not believe me in a million years." Raising my eyebrows I crossed my arms.

"Try me." He shook his head looking angrier.

"No. Just leave me alone." His jaw was working as I stayed rooted to where I stood.

"He's not angry at you Maylee." Shadow told me. Dante heard him looking down slapping his shoulder. Shadow pinned his ears, shifted his feet pushing Dante into the stall wall.

"Really Shadow!" More furious yet he threw down the brush that he had been using. Grabbing a hand full of mane he swung up onto Shadow's back. He kicked him to move, but he would not budge. "Shadow! Come on!" I could tell this was just making things worse. Shadow tossed his head angrily backing up into the wall of his stall before rearing up. I cringed slightly as he rolled off his back landing in a heap as a result. It would have been comical except the fact he was so pissed off. He stood up dusting himself off looking at me evilly. "Get the hell away from me!" Turning he started walking away but not before Shadow stood in his way not allowing him to pass. This made it easy for me to walk right up to him.

"What exactly is your problem? What have I done to you?" He clenched his fists arms drawn back like he was going to fight.

"Nothing. Just leave me alone." Over his shoulder Shadow nodded at me nosing Dante closer to me well within hitting range. Dante turned to him. "Stop it Shadow!" Shadow squealed pinning his ears back from being yelled at causing Dante to take a step back. He turned to leave again. This time I grabbed his wrist pulling him to a stop. What I found odd was the electricity that traveled through me when I grabbed his wrist. I wasn't sure if it was his anger, my annoyance or something else.

"Will you stop acting so damn dramatic?! Everyone has their own issues! Would you at least give me a chance to listen to what you have to say?" He ripped his wrist away from me angrily drawing Guardian pointing it at me. I was only somewhat surprised. Not completely because it was him after all.

"You want a fight?" I pulled my jackknife from my pocket allowing it to erupt into Star burst. "Than you will get one." I took a swing at him with my sword. He ducked out of the way of the oncoming blade looking at me as if he had not expected me to actually do it.

"What are you doing?" He asked only a hint of anger left in his voice. I swung again nearly hitting him because he did not move fast enough.

"You wanted a fight! So you will have one!" He backed up a few steps as his shoulders dropped sheathing his sword.

"It's not you I want to fight." Sighing heavily he turned sitting on a wooden box in front of Shadow's stall. I kept my stance in case he changed his mind though as I watched him he was not going to. Shrugging I sheathed my sword walking over sitting beside him.

"Than tell me what the hell is your problem? What did you two fight about in the hall before I opened the door?" He looked down at the ground but I could still see his face as anger set in once again.

"I just asked her what you were going to do today after assessment. And that I wanted to talk to you. She just blew up." I nodded as it matched what Annabelle had told me before I left.

"Yeah. She blew up on me too. I think she's just really stressed out. She's never been away from home like this."

"Or maybe it was something else." He said glancing over at me.

"Like what?" Frowning his jaw was working angrily.

"There is something about me you already don't like. Maybe I could tell you a small part of it. Both Izabella and the chief know everything about me. I know they set you to keep an eye on me, right?" Smirking for once I shook my head.

"No. They asked me to and I refused. Do they have a good reason? Yes, I think they do. I mean you seem well trained and yet you will not tell anyone where or how." He ran a hand over his hair looking straight ahead taking a deep breath before looking up at me.

"They have every reason to watch me." Smirking I stood looking to where he still sat surprised I had moved so quickly.

"I know they do. And I am almost totally sure why." His face drained of color as he stood in front of me.

"Alright. What do you think?" He sounded genuinely curious causing me to smirk in response.

"I think you were brought up to fight. Anyone who has combat training can see that. You use your sword like it's already an extension of your arm. From what I have been told is a huge hint. You worked for the dark side. Whether it was your choice or not I don't know but I can feel their energy on you. And lastly. You were sent here by them to watch me." His body tensed more as he stood facing me.

"Maylee"

"I'm not done." My voice had growled as he stopped in his tracks voice barely audible. "They sent you to watch me because I am the one person they are threatened by. And honestly I do not see why. At this point I barely know anything. But tell them what you want. I could care less what they do to me." Shaking his head his face was unreadable once again. Taking a deep breath his shoulders dropped in defeat.

"I am not here to spy on you. I am here because I turned on them. This was the only safe place I had left. Izabella knew I would be useful to their cause. So please understand? I mean you no harm." Damn! I thought. At least my first instincts had been right on. I had started to feel more comfortable around him which I found odd. Maybe it was actually because he was telling the truth?

"Strangely. I do understand. Are you going to be okay? Or should I draw my sword for another round?" I smirked at my own use of irony so that he even smiled a little.

When we left the stable he was in a much better mood. Almost like a weight had been lifted off his shoulders. I had the feeling there were many more weights there just yet. I met up with my sister who was still acting surly on our walk to the training field as our schedules had instructed us. As we walked down Izabella was out there already sparring someone I had not met before. Watching her I realized how good she was. How I beat her I still had no idea. Off to the west of the field looked to be a military type obstacle course. Anyone who had already been evaluated for weapons were over there. Now it was our turn for weapon evaluations by Kamran. Which was just great. He wanted to test each of us individually. As soon as he was within ten feet of me I tensed. My adrenaline began to pump remembering the day before. Glancing over I could see Dante looking between Kamran and myself as if trying to figure out why I was so tense.

"I think I will take the pro first." Kamran commented gesturing to Dante who just looked at him none too amused.

"I'm not a pro." Dante told him flatly.

"Maybe you do not think so. But you managed to disarm one of my best swordsman in twenty minutes when you were on the ship. Correct?"

"Well, yeah but" Kamran cut him off.

"Alright than. Let's go." He led us down the field a little ways into a stone circle. Looking behind us Izabella was not far just as she had told me. "Besides myself. Izabella is the best. There is only one who I cannot beat and that is the chief." He drew his sword signaling for them to begin.

They started out sparring slow gradually increasing their speed until they were almost a blur to watch. I was not sure how much time had passed. It seemed like an hour. I figured they would end it in a draw. Instead they kept fighting. Izabella had been watching walking over standing with Annabelle and myself.

"How long have they been going?" I looked over at my sister's watch to check the time. It was four o'clock.

"Around two hours." Her jaw tightened. Unsure I assumed anger as she began walking over to where they were still full on fighting.

"That is enough." She stepped in between them. I would not have dared do that, too dangerous. Holding her arms out on each side of her. "Enough!" They both stopped as she turned to

Kamran. "You should have called a draw after an hour. Not kept going. You could have killed him." She was pointing to Dante who at that moment collapsed to his knees from exhaustion gasping for air. Izabella threw me a water bottle to give him. Since him and my sister were not jiving at the moment I figured I had better suck it up and do it instead. Opening the water I handed it to him. He drained the whole thing. Hesitating I handed him the flask of healing potion I had telling him to take one drink from it. His breathing eased up quite a bit. Annabelle walked over looking dark as she gave me another bottle of water for him. Frowning I noticed her eyes were storm clouds.

"Why didn't you stop?" I asked turning from her as he took a drink of the water before looking up at me.

"I was taught that you did not stop until your opponent is disarmed or dead. When I was against an instructor I was taught that I did not stop until they told me. Needless to say I had some pretty intense sword lessons." Izabella shook her head turning back to Kamran pointing.

"I was only testing him. Chill out Izabella. I was ready to ease up when you stepped in." I looked to Dante angered by Kamran's lie.

"Was he or is he just saying that?" He looked over to Kamran thoughtfully.

"No. He was starting to ease up. We probably would have been done in another few minutes. Don't worry about me. I was trained hard. I'll be fine." He did seem to be recovering fairly fast.

"Okay." I said every now and again glancing over at him. Kamran walked up to Annabelle.

"You're next. Come on." She walked away from my side glancing back. I walked up to Kamran not caring who he was or what he had tried the day before.

171

"Pull that stunt again and I will come after you with all my being." I said low and dangerously to the point he stepped back away from me. "Especially if you do it to her." I pointed to my sister walking back to where Dante and Izabella were standing. Dante was smirking.

"What?" I snapped as I stood by him to watch my sister spar as he shook his head.

"I think you scare him." Frowning slightly I looked over to him.

"Right. I don't think so."

"I do. He stepped back from you." Arching an eyebrow I kept watching. Dante also added. "There was also the fact you had flames around you. That may have had something to do with it." My jaw was hanging loose.

"What? I had flames around me?"

"Yes. You really didn't know?" I rolled my eyes.

"Obviously." Smirking yet he crossed his arms over his chest.

"It must be something you do when you're really upset. You didn't even need your fire stone to do it."

"I wasn't trying to do it." He actually laughed. It was a nice laugh since I had never heard it from him before. Ah hell I was in trouble now looking him over checking him out. Damn. I felt my face warm knowing I had to force myself to ignore him.

"Sorry. I just think it was funny. Mostly because it was not me on the receiving end of it this time. You were pretty scary." Izabella looked over at us raising her eyebrows at me.

"That was a new power." She said it casually as if this kind of thing happened everyday.

"Yeah. Dante told me. I had no clue." She looked slightly concerned.

"You could not feel it?"

172

"No. I think it was because I was angry. I felt hot anyways. I just thought it was my temper." I was being honest as I really had not felt it.

"Usually extreme situations do bring out powers we do not know we have." She walked away to watch my sister and Kamran closer.

"Are you sure you are okay?" I asked Dante again. Smirking he replied.

"Yes. I'm fine really. I will say this though."

"What's that?"

"I can't wait for him to take you on."

"And why is that?"

"Because I think you can kick his ass. Even without your powers." Now it was my turn to laugh.

"I doubt it."

"I don't." He responded seriously. He was earning points. I will say that. Again. I had to stop. I have training to concentrate on. Closing my eyes I felt my nostrils flare with my breath out.

I turned just in time to see my sister's sword go flying through the air. It had only been ten minutes. Kamran looked over to Izabella.

"You are right. She is a natural but she needs time and training."

Annabelle walked over to where her sword was picking it up. She looked at me proceeding to stomp off toward town. I let her go as I badly wanted to face Kamran myself. Walking forward I drew Star burst approaching him quickly. A panicked look crossed Izabella's face as she ran out in front of me.

"Maylee no! Stop, please." Kamran looked at her quizzically laughing.

"Let her attack as she is. She will not beat me." My jaw clenched angrily as I thought back to the day before. What an arrogant jackass. We'll see who's left standing as I walked forward again. Unlike when he went against Dante we began fast as my anger burned hot.

I was aiming to kill if I had the chance barely on the defensive. I put a lot of force into my blows aiming at his arm hitting it as I had planned. Without missing a beat he switched hands. He was not as good left handed but I did not care. I kept attacking. Stopping he stepped back away from me holding a hand up signaling me to stop as well.

"Enough."

"What?! You battled Dante until you were both ready to drop! But not me? Am I not good enough?"

"Easy Maylee." Turning I had to know who had told me. Only to find it was Dante. "You almost hit him several times. You actually hit his arm. And you have been going for just over two hours." I looked to Izabella who nodded in agreement.

"Maylee" Kamran said to get my attention. "No one has ever been able to attack me like that. And you did. You actually injured my sword arm. So either you are naturally that good. Or I have grown slow. Who taught you?"

"Izabella did on our way to Florida. And believe me I'm not that good."

"I beg to differ. My arm says otherwise."

"I thought you just said"

"I was joking. It was a bad one. Must be I made you bring out your inner warrior or something." I looked at the ground since it felt like his gaze was about burning me.

"Yeah. Must be." I was not about to apologize. The sun was starting to set watching as the colors turned.

"How about we go rest for the night?" I glanced over to Dante. He had been trying extra hard all day to keep me talking to him. It made me feel as though he might deserve the chance

Izabella was pushing me to give him. Asking myself I found that I was actually okay about being comfortable around him. My problem now was my adrenaline pumping so that I was too wound up to hang around him.

"I would. But I'm still too wound up."

"You could try." Good point I thought shaking my head again.

"Nah. I need to walk off my excess energy. I'll catch you later okay?" He gave a single nod looking to Izabella before he walked to town alone. Izabella walked up beside me tilting her head slightly.

"Are you going to give him a chance? Or are you just trying to keep him distant?" Smirking I began walking onto the trail.

"I need more time before I give him a chance Izabella. He's not as bad as I thought." Nodding she glanced back for a moment.

"It is plain to see he likes you."

"Right."

"You do not think so?" Stopping I sat on a boulder just off the trail.

"I don't know what to think anymore. Honestly? As of now I think it is best I just learn what I need to learn and worry about him later."

"Fair enough. Staying out here or going back soon?"

"I'll start back in a bit. I'm still catching my breath."

"Alright. Be careful." Nodding I watched her exit the trail walking back to town. Taking a deep breath I stood walking the opposite way further into the trail. It began to grow dark as I arrived at the building slightly chilled. As I walked up to my door to enter Dante opened his door frowning at me.

"You're back pretty late. Are you okay?" I could hear his concern smirking at him.

"I'm fine. Really. But thanks for asking." He nodded but did not move. I looked to my sister's door. "Do you know if she came back yet?" Shaking his head he frowned.

"I haven't seen her yet." I nodded walking into my apartment. Izabella had told me Dante liked me. She had been talking me into giving him a chance. Well we were beginning to be friends now.

"Why?" I asked myself out loud falling onto my bed and asleep. Izabella had told me day two onward would be with her training. The very first day she met me to the entrance path to her cottage.

"We will focus on controlling your fire this first week. Once you have control of those powers we will work on the others." Sighing I nodded.

"Okay. But. Can I ask questions first?" Smirking she nodded as we began walking around to the back of the cottage. "The few of us that came here on the Rockford can't possibly be all you have to help fight this war. You have to have an actual army for this." Izabella led me to an open area past her herb garden.

"Yes. We do. The council has been recruiting for over a year." She stopped turning to face me.

"Where are they?" Smirking she shrugged.

"The council did not inform me of that. You are my focus right now Maylee. What other questions do you have so that we can train." I felt my jaw tighten nodding the same.

"Everyone that came here were descendants of greek gods. What about the other ancient gods?"

"They are training elsewhere. Do not worry Maylee. We have everyone we need now." Sighing I nodded.

"Okay. Why do we use swords and medieval weapons? Why not guns and bombs?"

"They can be manipulated by our magik. Our weapons are made so that they cannot be manipulated in that manner." Shaking my head it made sense.

"Okay. What do you want me to do for control?"

"I want you to focus. Make your fire appear. After that you must be able to keep it contained. To feed or snuff it out. We will spend some time on your focus. We will also begin identifying plants for teas, potions and tinctures."

Nodding I knew we would be working on more than my powers.

"What about sword work?" Smirking she shook her head once.

"You insist that you have never had lessons. Yet. You are as good as Dante with your sword." Sighing I knew she wanted to touch on my missing memories again.

"Izabella"

"I know. You do not want to know about your missing memories."

"No. I don't. If someone erased them there must have been damn good reason." Nodding she pointed to some rocks nearby.

"Follow me. We need to stay isolated in case your fire rolls out of control." Agreeing we walked to the plateau not far from her cottage. "We will practice with swords after you are done with powers. We may be an hour or we might be all day. Either way you will be exhausted when we are done. And we will do this every day until you can use your powers as easily as breathing while you fight." Breathing out hard I nodded.

"Okay. Fire first than." My fire was easy to draw up to use. Controlling it was proving more difficult the longer I had to hold it.

A whole week flew by training with Izabella and watching as my sister's friendship with Dante fell apart. After my morning runs I would catch Dante watching me as he was already on the training field before anyone else. Arriving at Izabella's she led me to the back part where we began with some minor spells for repairs.

We sparred for an hour before we changed over to plants learning to identify them. After identifying each one Izabella would ask what they were used for. I aced every single one earning myself an early out to go back to my apartment. I began walking back the same trail I used earlier. As I was walking I felt weak. Breathing heavily I felt everything around me. Even the air felt heavy as I sat on the ground trembling from the weakness. What had caused this?

"Maylee" I heard a voice call. Shaking still I looked around to see who it could be or where it had issued from. A few feet away Shadow walked up to where I sat.

"Shadow. Please tell me" Snorting he shook his head just a little.

"He is not with me." I nodded wiping the tears from my eyes. "Come on. I will take you back." Blowing my nose I stood grabbing a handful of his mane just standing there. "Come now. You need to get back. It is growing far too cold with the dark for you to stay out much longer."

"Okay." Finally I managed to swing up onto his back. Steadily he made his way to the apartment building stopping in front of the main entrance. As I slid off Izabella walked up crossing her arms over her chest.

"What happened for this to occur? I have never witnessed you help anyone besides your charge." It hit me she was talking to Shadow not me as she stepped forward gripping my upper arm to steady me.

"I owe her my life. The least I could do was assist her when no one else could." With that he walked into the dark.

"What is he talking about Maylee?" Shaking my head I glanced around us.

"Could we go to my apartment before I explain? Please?" Lip thinning in barely contained anger she nodded assisting me the entire way. Once in my apartment I could hear music on the street looking out the window. Izabella set down a cup on the table signaling I sit to drink.

"Now. Explain what happened to you tonight." I opened up explaining what had happened out in the woods after training that day. When I was done she stood looking out the window. "Are you going to be okay?" Turning she watched my face as I nodded.

"Yes. I am fine." Walking to my door she looked me over again.

"You should go to the stable to see your horse. You have not been there in a day or two. It would do you some good." Nodding I agreed. "Not tonight. Shadow is right. Rest." She added closing the door behind her. Exhaling hard I nodded knowing she was absolutely right. I found myself doing exactly that even after Shadow had told me to stay inside for the night. With Izabella agreeing. I found it difficult to stay inside with the sounds outside growing louder. I walked to the stable to see Rocki instead of being social and hanging with everyone else in the town square. All the descendants were hanging out to get to know each other.

"Maylee" Rocki rested his head on my back as I hugged his neck. "What is wrong?"

"Something doesn't feel right. I want to be around everyone. I just feel off."

179

"Why don't you hop on and we will go for a ride on the beach. The moon is nice and bright tonight." Nodding I slid on from the tack trunk. He stopped at the beach allowing me to watch the tide ebb in and flow back out. Taking some deep breaths I slowly calmed before making our way back.

I woke not feeling great. And of course today was obstacle course, cardio, spells and power control. My whole body was aching like I had fallen ten stories. Walking through the gate Izabella watched me closely as I stopped in front of her.

"Are you okay?"

"Yeah. I think I slept wrong." Nodding she let me go right after cardio training to rest.

Dante

Keeping myself together around Annabelle and Izabella was becoming increasingly difficult. Theo had sent Annabelle a letter directly so that I did not know what was going on. Before we had a chance to begin training she jumped my case about turning to side with the council. Since that morning she had became hostile towards me.

Only half an hour later Maylee came into the barn to what I figured was to recover something her sister had done. I wanted to tell her everything but unable to I became angry at myself. In the end I spilled more than I should have to her. Annabelle had threatened punishment if I spent too much time with her sister. As a result I tried to push her away. It worked.

Angrily I stormed off to my apartment only to run into Izabella.

"Hey. Why are you so pissed off?" Genuinely concerned she grabbed my shoulder to look at me. "Dante. What is going on with you?"

"What do you mean?"

"Is Maylee the reason you can not seem to concentrate? Are you getting too close to her?" Rolling my eyes I shook my head.

"No. And no. Annabelle threatened to rat me out to our superiors if I am around Maylee too much." Crossing her arms she shifted her feet assessing me.

"You love her." Scowling I looked to her sharply.

"What?" Smirking Izabella stepped closer.

"You love Maylee."

"Izabella seriously." Raising her eyebrows daring me to protest.

"Dante. When I showed you that vision of the future it was with her. Get closer to her. Stop being afraid." Shaking my head I felt ready to explode in frustration. Reaching out Izabella stopped me in my tracks.

"Let go!" I roared at her angrily. Her face set irritably as she stood in place after I threw her hand off. "I am not afraid of her."

"I never said you were afraid of her Dante. You are afraid of your own emotions." Sighing she grabbed my arm forcing me to follow her to her house.

"Why do you say that?" I asked her tiredly. Smirking she indicated me to sit.

"Because every time we have any kind of conversation concerning her you get angry or quiet. Now out with it. What are you afraid of with her? Of actually having someone" She stopped in her tracks knowing she had found the problem. "That is the problem. Dammit."

"I appreciate your help Izabella. But this is something you can not help with. Really. Maybe when this all calms down she will look at me. But not now. I am not even a thought in her mind." Sitting back in her own chair she raised her eyebrows at me shaking her head before leaning closer.

"She actually does like you Dante. Her instincts tell her to not trust you. That is all. She wants to trust you. She just cannot bring herself to. I think if you stopped doubling for the council she would warm up to you faster." Making a sound of annoyance I nodded in agreement.

"That might happen sooner than we planned anyways."

"I heard you and Annabelle fighting the other day."

"Yeah. Theo wants her to tell him if I'm turning." Izabella looked away in thought.

"Try to hang in there a little longer. Alright?"

"Yeah. I'll try." With one more nod I knew I was dismissed. Walking back to my apartment I saw what looked like Shadow carrying Maylee on his back. Stopping in my tracks confused I thought to him. "Do you have Maylee with you?"

"Yes. She needed assistance. I saw what happened. I offered her my help to ensure she was safe."

"Safe? What happened?"

"She does not want you to know. The first question she asked was if you were with me."

"Is she okay?"

"Yes. I am taking her to the apartment building now. You should go to the town square and socialize. It looks like the chief is organizing a party for all of you."

"Maybe if Maylee was there and her brat sister stayed away I would."

"Maylee will not be there tonight. She needs to rest. Just go. You need to talk to at least a few of the others." Rolling my eyes even though I knew he could not see me I nodded acknowledgement.

Two days later I was on my way to the training field when Izabella stopped me.

"Before you report this morning practice is post-poned for a few hours." Frowning I shook my head. I was always an hour early to workout before the others arrived.

"I know I more than likely do not want to know the reason. But. I'll take the bait. Why is practice post-poned?" Her nostrils flared causing me to frown. She was angry.

"Kamran has been summoned to see the council this morning." Nodding that actually made sense.

"Good. Have you seen the way he looks at Maylee?" Her eyes flashed as she dropped her hands.

"That is why he was summoned. He has been told she is off limits. The other night he cast a spell on her." Immediately my anger was radiating.

"He did what?!" Frustrated she exhaled loudly shaking her head as she rubbed her neck.

"Just do me a favor. Go retrieve her from my place. Bring her here and explain why on the way." Closing my eyes I nodded glancing to where her cottage was.

"Alright."

"And Dante." Turning I stopped for a second. "You need to start acting interested in her now."

"I am."

"Than actually act like it." Walking to Izabella's I knew Maylee would be there waiting for her one on one studies. She was far too advanced to train with the actual army. Kamran had tried several times to talk me into lessons with the chief as they knew I was good with a sword as well. The chief himself had approached me about giving the beginners lessons. I turned that down as well. Just like Maylee I could not afford to have any distractions.

Although having her as a distraction would be nice. Dammit. Those thoughts needed to stay buried as I saw her waiting at Izabella's as I ran up to meet her. For the first time since we had arrived I noticed she was changing. She seemed happy at the moment. Content. And she had lost weight which she had not needed to. But it made her shape even more pronounced. I skimmed her over as I approached. Damn she looked great in her mission gear. That ass. Dammit. Again. Those thoughts.

Maylee

I walked to Izabella's cottage for practice. When I arrived she was not there as I walked all over to find her.

"Maylee!" Dante's voice reached me as I watched him walk in my direction meeting me part way from the training field. Without realizing it I felt a jolt run through my body as he walked closer.

"Have you seen Izabella?" He frowned looking to the field for a moment.

"She's leading practice. Kamran never showed up." Frowning at the news that I found to be strange.

"That's odd." He nodded in agreement.

"Come on. Izabella was sending me to retrieve you." We walked to the field side by side. I flinched when I felt our hands brush against each other.

"I haven't practiced with anyone besides Izabella since I have been here." Dante smirked as we walked closer to the field where I could see Izabella.

"I think it will do everyone good to see you down here. Maybe they will pull their heads out of their asses and work harder." Smirking slightly I cocked an eyebrow at him.

"They are not improving I take it?" Sighing in answer he shook his head.

"Not like they should be for as many practices we have had." Nodding we walked to where Izabella stood.

"I want you two to work together on the basics while I attempt to get the others to do something besides stand like statues." I wanted to protest that I did not want to practice with him. Especially once my sister was down there watching closely.

"Maybe I should leave." I commented as Dante and I began to spar noticing the death looks from my sister. He shook his head turning his back to her.

"No. Those looks are directed to me. Not you." Frowning as we practiced I glanced up again.

"Why?" Rolling his eyes he shook his head.

"It's fine." Growling at him I shoved him back hard causing him to lose his balance. Catching himself he scowled marching back up to me angrily.

"Make it interesting." I told him smirking. Shaking his head he smirked back.

"Damn you. I can't even be mad." Izabella walked over crossing her arms.

"You are supposed to be sparring. Not talking." We both nodded at her.

"My sister keeps glaring at us. Maybe you could partner us with different people?" I asked trying to make it not sound like I was being a jerk since it was for both of our sakes.

"No. Annabelle will have to get over it. You two are the most advanced here. Just keep practicing." Exasperated we both nodded continuing our practice. As the session wore on I could tell Dante was growing agitated.

"Are you okay?" I finally asked stopping to lean on my sword. He nodded glancing back to my sister.

"I'm fine. For now." Frowning I glanced to my sister as well as she glared at him. Shaking his head he walked away towards Izabella. Watching them interact I could tell he was angry about something. Izabella was not relenting. Finally she pointed to town and he strode away as she walked to me.

"What did I do?" Frowning she shook her head.

"Not you Maylee. Your sister. She keeps glaring at him and it has him on edge. You can go if you want too. Talk to him without your sister around." Nodding I sheathed my sword walking into town as well. As I walked the trail I noticed he had not gone too far. Just enough to stay out of view of the field sitting on a large tree stump.

"I'm sorry Maylee." Dante told me rubbing his face tiredly.

"It's okay. Izabella let me go too. There's not anyone else I can practice with." Sighing he shook his head.

"Your sister seems to hate me more than you do." I choked out a laugh.

"Okay. I am going to straighten that out right now. I do not hate you. I never have. I don't trust you. There is a huge difference. Nor do I know you all that well." Nodding he glanced to town standing up.

"Do you have a hard time trusting people in general or just certain ones?" Frowning I crossed my arms.

"In general. Why?" Sighing he shook his head.

"No reason. I'll see you later." Exasperated I walked up beside him as he walked with long strides.

"Why are you asking me those questions?" Stopping he looked frustrated for the first time since I had known him.

"I'm just trying to get to know you. Asking people questions is not something I am very good at." Smirking I nodded knowing I could be the same way.

"That's all you had to say." Crossing my arms again I turned walking back towards the field to watch everyone else. When I glanced back Dante had gone. Sighing I walked back to the field watching practice. Annabelle immediately seen where I stood. Her eyes darkened. She wanted Dante dead. I could see it in her face.

After my lessons for the day I walked to the stable taking Rocki down to the beach as dusk was approaching. I watched the waves thinking about what I had learned. And how far I still had to go.

"What has you upset?" Sighing in frustration I leaned against his side.

"There is just a lot going through my mind." Snorting he tossed his head turning to nuzzle my arm.

"You like Dante. Don't you?" Shaking my head I pushed his nose away.

"I don't know yet. Why don't you go back to the stable. I'm staying out here longer to think."

"Maylee. No. It is not safe for you alone. Izabella warned you." Sighing I knew he was right.

"Alright. Take me into town." Sliding onto him from a nearby stump he walked down the trail.

"Why don't you go to the party they are having tonight?" Frowning I looked down the trail to where I could hear music.

"Another party? Why?"

"So all of you descendants can get to know one another and relax with what lies ahead." Rolling my eyes I agreed to go.

Once there I slid down from his back looking around the town square. Staying back from the dancing I watched everyone. Finally I was able to spot my sister. She was dancing with Kyle from wherever he was from. I knew he was foreign. It made me smirk as I watched them for a moment before turning to make sure Rocki was gone. I began walking down the nearest trail.

"Maylee" Stopping at my name recognizing the voice I turned back as Dante walked up to me. "I'm surprised to see you here. I didn't think this was your kind of scene." Sighing as I looked down the trail I answered.

"It's not. I was leaving." Frowning he looked down the trail as well.

"You just got here. I saw you with your horse." Rolling my eyes I nodded.

"He refused to leave me on the trail alone. That is why I am even here."

"He's smart. There are a lot of dangers on this island when it is dark." I gave a single nod before turning to walk away. He grabbed my wrist stopping me. "Just stay for a bit. So we can talk?" Raising my eyebrows I shrugged.

"A couple minutes is about all I can handle of this music." He chuckled.

"I can agree with that." With that he gestured for us to sit by the fountain.

"Let me take a guess at classical music." His lips tugged at a single corner looking around nervously. "Not good with crowds." Sighing he shook his head.

"Yes and yes. My mom used classical when she gardened. I never expanded my listening beyond that." Nodding I noticed the vein in his neck pulsing hard. He was stressed out.

"You're under a lot of stress. Why?" Frowning he turned to me brow furrowed.

"How do you know?"

"The vein in your neck pulses out and your breathing is light." He let a surprise of breath out.

"You observe a lot for never being taught how."

"So Izabella has told me." Smirking he nodded.

"My turn. Music wise. I'm guessing the harder stuff like rock or death metal." It was my turn to smirk.

"Yeah."

"You're not good with crowds either. Which was why you were trying to leave the moment your horse left."

Ruby M. Knight

"Correct again. On that note. I do want to leave." Frowning he looked up taking a deep breath causing me to look up as well. My sister was watching us looking none too amused. That was not what bothered me. What bothered me was that her eyes looked black.

"I think we better part ways for both our sakes." Nodding in agreement he walked to the apartment building as I walked to the trail again. Annabelle caught up to me within steps.

"Why were you talking to him?" Stopping I turned to her.

"Maybe you haven't noticed Annabelle. But I am older than you. And I do not have to tell you anything about what I am doing." Glaring at me she glanced to where we barely saw Dante.

"I thought you hated him."

"I told you. I do not hate him. I don't trust him."

"You looked pretty trusting to me when you were talking." Scowling she was on my last nerve.

"How so?" I asked crossing my arms. Raising her eyebrows she pointed her chin to where we had been sitting.

"Pretty secluded spot for someone who doesn't trust people." Rolling my eyes I turned walking away.

"Good night Annabelle."

"I wasn't done." Turning back slightly I waved at her.

"I am." She never tried to stop me but I could hear her mumbling and stomping as I walked. Once on the beach I watched the waves ebbing in and out calming me. When the moon was high I began walking back to town where the music had finally stopped.

As I walked the trail back out of no where someone wrapped their arms around me from behind pinning my arms down. I kicked as hard as I could flinging my head backwards. None of my blows hit. I was slammed into a tree hard feeling the back of my head bounce off painfully. My vision blurred as a result as I landed on the ground. I tried to stand only to be met with a knee to my rib cage multiple times. Shaking my head as I landed on my hands and knees they gripped my hair pulling me to my feet. Breathing hard I spit blood where I could see movement.

"Bitch!" The man threw me into another tree hard following with a punch to my face. Falling to the ground I coughed attempting to catch my breath. Their foot caught my shoulder kicking me to my back staying on my throat. "You will pay for that." With my vision still affected I could not see who was pinning me to the ground.

"Get away!" I screamed finding my voice at last. My head ached sharply. I heard a chuckle before my wrists were bound together over my head.

"I think not. I need you out of my way." The unfamiliar voice told me sitting over top of me.

"Let go!" I felt a hard back hand across the face almost knocking me unconscious.

"You have a choice Maylee. Give up fighting now. Or I will make sure you do not fight again." Breathing hard I struggled against him. My vision began to come back to see the man sitting over top of me. He was about the build of Kamran just not as tall. He wore a mask so that I could not see his face but I could see his eyes. They were deep gold full of hate staring back.

"Why would I give up? If they send someone to kill me than I guess you should get on with it. I refuse to stop fighting." A growl issued as he back handed me a second time. My head ached worse as I saw stars.

"Dumb bitch. Fine. I hope you like resting in bed for the rest of your life." Lifting me off the ground by my wrists he hooked them onto something hanging me up. My toes scraped the ground as my vision was blurred again. Gripping my leg he broke my left knee with a crack that echoed in the woods. Screaming my body hurt in ways I never had before. "Give up"

"No!" I screamed. I felt him hit my rib cage multiple times until I coughed up blood. Cutting my wrists free I fell hard on my broken knee. He kicked me to my back sitting over top of me yet again.

"You are not really in any position to negotiate at this point. Now are you Maylee?"

"Get off of me." I choked out when my voice would actually work.

"Since you are indisposed at this point. I might as well have more fun." Instead of hitting or breaking more bones he pulled my pants down to my knees. No. This was not happening. His hands closed on my throat not allowing my voice to work.

"Stop!" I choked struggling against him. There was no strength left in my body from the beating he gave prior to raping me.

"Do not cry Maylee." I hated this man. I would find out who he was. And I will kill him continuing to attempt to fight. Instead he closed my throat off more thrusting his hips into mine harder. "Just enjoy it. You're fighting it. Come on Maylee." My vision began to blur from lack of oxygen until he let up keeping his hand resting on my throat. As I was able to see again I attempted to fight earning myself yet another hit to the face. "Not a word to anyone about this. Am I clear?" In more pain than ever I cried. He laughed kicking me in the ribcage walking away. I had started to stand when he walked back grabbing my throat pinning me to a tree. Struggling for breath I tried to elbow his face.

"Oh and I will be back. I promise. I can't wait to fuck you again." He kissed me before letting me fall to the ground choking for breath. He laughed before disappearing into thin air. I was totally numb as I laid there shaking attempting to sit up on my knees before a boot appeared kicking my head knocking me unconscious. I felt warmth around me with the whine of a dog.

"Izabella is coming Maylee." Shadows voice told me before I was out once again.

Opening my eyes slowly I looked at my surroundings. Izabella's house from what I saw. My breathing was much better as I sat up slowly. My ribs were still sore. Pulling the blankets back there were huge purple bruises.

"I brought you here since everything I needed to heal you would be here." Izabella walked up next to me inspecting my neck.

"Thank you." Sighing she pulled up a stool looking at me levelly.

"Who did this?" Tears formed in my eyes as I thought about how much it seemed the man wanted to kill me.

"I could not see his face. He knew my name."

"Okay. If you feel up to it you can go to your own apartment." Nodding she helped me to my feet. "I healed most of your injuries. Others take a few days rather than immediately."

"Like my ribs?" Wide eyed she nodded once worriedly.

"Yes. Maylee. All of your ribs were broken. Whoever this was"

"Does not want me to fight."

"Is that what he told you? How do you know it was a man?"

"Yes. That is what he told me. Can we go to my apartment before we talk about it. Please? I need a shower."

"Of course." She shimmered us right to the door of my apartment. Slowly I walked to my room gathering my clothes to take my shower.

When I came out she had a cup sitting on the counter for me.

"Move your hair." Shaking her head she sat beside me. "Why did you not call for me to help you?" Scowling I hit the counter with my fist angrily.

"My powers would not work! I screamed. I fought and I struggled as hard as I could. I just wasn't strong enough. I hate this Izabella. I hate the man who did this. For doing this to me." She wrapped her arms around me holding me against her as I sobbed. There was a knock on my door. Standing Izabella answered it.

"Who was it?" I asked once she sat back down.

"Your sister. I told her you were not feeling well and were possibly contagious so she needed to stay away." I nodded. Likely she wanted to talk more in depth about what we had discussed at the party earlier. "I will stay with you for the night. Okay?" I nodded again as she helped me to my bed.

"It's not that late is it?" Izabella glanced to my window.

"No. You need to rest after an attack such as the one you withstood. Maylee. You are lucky to be alive. Now sleep. Heal your body." Nodding I turned in the bed drifting to sleep.

When I woke in the morning I could hear voices in my kitchen. Heated and calm voices both. Slowly I managed to slide out of bed pulling on a robe walking to my bedroom door. Looking through a crack in my door I could see Izabella and no way. Dante. Seriously? What is he doing in my apartment?

"What happened to her Izabella? I could hear her screaming last night. And do not lie to me." He was concerned about me? Seriously?

"I stayed with her through the whole night. She never screamed Dante. Unless"

"What?"

194

"You are connecting to her."

"Maybe. But you know she is pushing me away. She has no memory from that time."

"I know."

"I want to see her." I heard footsteps as I opened my door stepping out. In front of me was a very shocked Dante as he saw my face.

"Oh. My. God. Who did this to you? I will kill them." I shook my head walking past him to Izabella. When I turned back to face him he was inches away still looking at me.

"I don't know. I was walking down the trail and was attacked from behind. I hit the back of my head on something. Please. Just leave. I'll be back in training tomorrow. Okay?" He was frozen to the spot.

"If you know who did it. You need to tell me Maylee." The look on his face was murderous as I realized I had taken my robe away from my neck.

"I'll be okay." He grabbed my wrist so that I could not move away from him as he was taking in my injuries.

"They choked you. Dammit tell me!" I actually cringed when he yelled so forcefully. He was angry. I could not believe it.

"Dante" I looked at him levelly but tears were close as I thought about my attack. "Please just leave. I will be okay." Shaking his head he pulled me into an embrace. I stiffened to pull away but embraced him instead.

"Dammit." Pulling back he took my hand into his as we stood there.

"What are you doing?" Slowly my trembling subsided as he released my hand looking pale.

"Helping you." Reluctantly he left looking at Izabella worriedly as his jaw worked in buried anger.

"He is very worried about you." Nodding I walked to the counter.

"Yeah. I could tell."

"Are you going to tell me this time? Or am I going to find out the hard way?" I began to cry even though I was mostly angry about the whole situation.

"I was attacked from behind. This man grabbed me around my midsection and threw me into something. My head bounced off of it. I was dazed. He beat my ribs in. And my face." Shaking my head I paused taking a breath. "He kept choking me to stop me from screaming. Than he" Frowning I could not stop myself from sobbing. I stopped remembering every detail taking a deep breath to steady myself.

"Who Maylee."

"I don't know who attacked me. He had golden eyes. I was not strong enough to make him stop. I have never heard his voice before." Izabella nodded looking distant.

"I am sorry for what that man did to you. I truly am. You did not deserve it." She leaned forward laying a hand on my arm. "I know this is not something you will want to consider, but I can wipe this attack from your memory. And heal all of your injuries. It would be like it never happened." Looking to the floor I shook my head feeling determined.

"No. I don't want that. I just hate what happened. He made my body want him to. I hate myself for that." She held me as I sobbed again. Pulling me back she looked me in the eyes.

"No. Stop that. Your body was reacting the way it thought it was supposed to. It happens. You did not want him to do that. Okay? This was not your fault. I will talk to Kamran about your attack. He can help us find out who it was." It had been nagging at me that she knew I had been on the beach that night.

"How did you know where I was last night?"

"A friend of ours told me you were attacked. He followed you to the beach."

"Who?" Confused I had not noticed anyone.

"You will find out soon enough." A little later Izabella helped me to bed giving me a cup of healing potion. As I fell asleep I heard her say something but was out before I could ask.

It was morning when I woke my alarm blaring out. Sitting up my injuries from my attack were mostly healed. Walking to the kitchen Izabella was already there with a cup waiting for me.

"Is this a pity thing? Or because we are friends?" Smiling she slid the cup to me.

"We are friends Maylee. Drink that. It will heal those bruises faster." I nodded to her walking back to my room to change for my run. "Where do you think you are going?" Confused I pointed to the door.

"I've been running in the morning. Remember?" Nodding she looked at the clock.

"After what you went through two days ago you should not be running. You were in rough shape Maylee."

"I feel fine now. My ribs ache a little but that is all." Nodding she waved me off letting me go for my run. As I ran the trail to the beach I felt as though I was being watched. Once on the beach I stopped to catch my breath glancing without moving my head to see who was there. I could barely make out what looked like a horse.

"Shadow?" I thought to him. The horse's head raised slightly.

"Yes."

"Are you following me?"

"Yes. I am. To make sure you are not attacked again."

"Dante ask you to watch me?"

"Yes. But I also wanted to watch for myself. I was the one who saw your attack. I stayed with you until Izabella arrived to heal you." I felt my face drain of blood. Not because it had been Shadow that had witnessed my attack. More that Dante could have known everything.

"Please tell me you did not tell Dante you know exactly what happened?"

"No. I did not. If you do not want him to know I was not giving him that information."

"Thank you."

"He cares about you Maylee. I have not seen him so beside himself as he is now about your attack."

"Shadow. Please. I can't deal with that right now."

"I know. Watch yourself. And start back. I will not be far behind."

"Okay. Thanks." I ran back walking as I approached the front door only to have someone slam their arm out in front of me. Stopping I looked over to Kamran as he shoved me back away from the door pinning me against the building by my shoulder.

"Leave me alone." I told him stiffly as he frowned looking at my face.

"No. Izabella told me what happened." Turning I walked under his arm to the door only for him to grab my elbow pulling me back to face him. "Maylee. Do you know who it was?" Looking straight back at him I answered.

"No. I don't know Kamran. If I did I would kill the man myself. He was built similar to you. He had golden colored eyes. But it was definitely not a voice I have heard before." He nodded looking me over.

"Izabella did a good job healing you. Although there is still a bruise" He stopped touching the base of my neck stepping away. "You were choked. Dammit." His anger began coming off in waves as mine did.

"I fought the best I could for how I was attacked Kamran. I promise you that." Shaking his head he made me stand in front of him.

"Why the hell didn't you use your powers against this man?"

"They didn't work against him Kamran! I couldn't reach my stones. He pinned my wrists over my head. He tried to cave my ribcage in." He nodded looking up as Izabella appeared at my side.

"Maylee. Go to your apartment. My brother and I are going to talk about what happened to you." He nodded allowing me to leave as well. Around the corner I almost collided with Dante.

"I'm sorry!" I stopped wiping away a few tears that had leaked out. "I'm sorry. I wasn't paying attention." He shrugged. As Kamran did he saw the base of my neck frowning though I saw anger in his eyes.

"How do you feel today?"

"Not too bad." Gripping my elbow he helped me up to my apartment. The whole time he helped me to our floor I could feel how worried he was.

"You ran too hard today. Especially after what happened." He took my key opening the door to my apartment helping me sit down. "Are you sure you're okay?" I was not even paying any attention as he handed me a glass of water.

"I'm fine. Just a little shook up yet." Kneeling in front of me Dante looked beyond worried once again as he looked over my injuries from two nights before. I had become incredibly at ease around him.

"You are totally sure it wasn't Kamran?" I smirked as I tried to stand but he stood pushing me back down to sit.

"I'm fine. Honestly. And I am totally positive it wasn't Kamran. He was just as pissed about the fact I had been choked as you were yesterday when you saw it." Frowning he reached up pushing my hair out of my face. Suddenly I felt dizzy before blacking out.

"Dammit." I heard him say as I felt him pick me up carrying me to my bed laying me down again covering me up.

I woke around sunset slowly sitting up to see if there was anyone in my room. Throwing the covers off I noticed I was still in my workout clothes. Walking to the kitchen I was shaky sitting at the counter trying to clear my head. My door opened slowly looking up to see Izabella walking in.

"How do you feel?"

"Well. Confused as hell. Why did I just sleep the day away? Or why did you let me?" Sighing she walked up.

"I asked Dante to give you a sleeping potion when he brought you up to your room. He was against it. But he also knew I was doing it for your own good."

"Why? I managed myself just fine."

"I know that. I needed time to talk to the chief to tell him what had happened. Kamran is investigating your attack." I nodded.

"What about my sister?" Her brow furrowed as she looked to my door.

"I honestly do not think we will have to worry about your sister."

"Why do you think that?"

"She is not in her apartment."

"This day could just get worse couldn't it? I'm going to the stable. She might be down there." Grabbing my shoulder she stopped me short of the door.

"Ask her horse. It will work from here."

"Oscerr. Is Annabelle with you?"

"Yes. We are on our way down to the beach. I'll bring her back safe."

"Thanks." Looking up Izabella stood at the door to leave.

"She is with her horse?"

"Yeah, riding down the beach. He said he would be sure to bring her back safely."

"Good. I will be back in the morning to go with you on your morning run."

"Why? I don't need to have an escort everywhere I go Izabella. Someone is going to notice." Standing in the doorway she glanced to her right before back to me.

"No one will notice. I know how to make it look as though I am not there to those who do not need to know." I laughed sarcastically.

"Who would even believe me?"

"You actually care what they think? I did not think you cared what anyone thought?"

"I don't want them to think I am weak."

"That they know you are not. Those who witnessed our fight on the ship know you are not weak. Most want to be your ally. Last I counted there were at least three."

"Three? Three of them want to be my ally?"

"They wanted to train with you. You were far too advanced for two of them and the third you keep at a distance." Rolling my eyes I turned to go to my bedroom hearing my front door shut.

Screaming in fear I woke in a cold sweat breathing as if I had ran in a marathon. Looking to the clock it was only 4 in the morning.

"Dammit." I swore at myself laying back down trying to go back to sleep. When that did not work I swung out of bed pulling on my workout clothes. Quietly I walked down the stairs into the lobby of the apartment building.

"Where do you think you are going this time of morning?" The voice was male but familiar as I froze turning to the chief.

"I can't sleep. I was going for a run." Taking a puff off his pipe he looked to the clock.

"I believe Izabella said she was to accompany you for that." This was growing irritating.

"She did. And I told her that I do not want the others to think I am weak. I already do not train with them."

"They all know you are too advanced to train with them. As is Dante. But he insists on staying with the group. For the reason Izabella is with you they would not think that."

"Dante is better than I am with my sword. That makes no sense." I told him utterly confused at why he would do that.

"Well. He wanted Izabella to train him, but he knew if she was training you that she would not have time for both of you." And he knew I did not trust him I wanted to say, but was able to refrain from doing so. The chief looked over my shoulder waving as Izabella walked through the door.

"She wanted to go half an hour ago but I kept her here until you arrived." Again I rolled my eyes at the fact they were insisting I needed to be watched like a child.

"Good. Ready?"

"I've been ready." She frowned as she glanced over at me.

"I think it is time to start pushing you harder." Agreeing with her we began our run. Instead of the trail to the beach I had been taking she made me run the entire east side of the island.

When I returned to my apartment I was tired and sore. Izabella reminded me to be at her place in two hours for sword practice. As I passed my sister's apartment I stopped knocking on her door. Nothing. Maybe she was not awake yet. Shrugging I entered my own apartment taking a shower before making breakfast for both of us.

In the kitchen I was making pancakes and sausage for our breakfast when a knock came from my door. About time. I thought thinking about my sister the night before. When I opened the door it was not my sister, but Dante. I felt my face drain of color as I remembered what Izabella had told me.

"Hey. What do you"

"Maylee stop." He grabbed the door as I was about to shut it on him. My adrenaline began to hum thinking of my attack. Dante was not as big as that guy was, but he could be just as strong. That I was sure of.

"Izabella isn't here right now." Tilting his head at me he looked worried again stepping closer to me.

"I'm not looking for Izabella. I wanted to check on you. Especially as out of it as you were yesterday." I bit my lip nervously as I noticed he had began to reach for my hand but stopped.

"I'll be fine. Really. And thanks for helping me yesterday." He gave a curt nod turning to walk down the stairs. Slowly I shut the door resting my head against it softly thumping my forehead against it.

"No. No. No." I told myself. Do not get mixed up with him right now. As I was about to walk away from the door there was another knock. Opening the door standing before me was Nathan. The descendant from Alaska.

"Can I help you?" His gaze went from straight at me to the floor as if afraid of me.

"I was told by Izabella to have you report to the stable immediately." Frowning I turned to grab my weapons belting on my sword.

"What happened?" I asked him as he walked beside me down the stairs.

"She said your sister's horse is missing from the stable. That he never came back last night as he was supposed to."

"Okay. Thanks!" At that I sprinted down to the barn. "Rocki! Where is Oscerr?"

"I don't know. Annabelle took him out yesterday and they never returned."

"Great. I'll be there in a second. We have to find them." As I rounded the corner I almost ran into Dante. He side stepped just before we would have collided.

"Sorry. That's twice I've done that to you."

"It's fine." I heard him say as I ripped my horse's gate open swinging up onto his back. "Aren't you going to tack him up first?" He asked as I walked by.

"I don't have time. I have to find my sister."

"I'll help. Hold up." Beside us was Shadow with Dante on board giving a nod he was ready we both ran from the barn down to the beach. We found hoof prints, but they were old maybe from last night. "We will never find her this way. We might as well ride the dragons and search by air. We'll cover more area that way too." Dante suggested to me.

"No. Hold on just a second." Stopping for a moment I thought to Oscerr. "Where are you?"

"On the beach. We are both injured. Hurry." Panic gripped me as I looked down the beach.

"Where on the beach?"

"South side. By the palms and driftwood."

"The south end and they are both hurt. Let's go!" Rocki did not have to be told twice as he stretched out running as hard as he could. Shadow was barely keeping up with his huge strides.

I could hear Oscerr before we arrived as he screeched in pain. He had one leg held in the air causing me to panic thinking it may be broke. Rocki had not even stopped when I jumped off running to Oscerr to check his leg. I checked it thoroughly. Not broke. His tendon had bowed and he had popped a splint. My sister could not be too far away. I knew she would not just leave her horse injured.

Through the trees and brush we found her unconscious only ten feet away. I checked her pulse. It was weak at best. She must have been here for a while. Izabella made her way through the brush shaking her head.

"I can heal her if you want me to." I stepped aside quickly.

"Yes." I finally managed to spit out. Kneeling down beside her Izabella placed one hand over her head. The other over her chest. I could hear her saying words, but not what they were. Nothing I could recognize. Izabella sat back on her heels as Annabelle's breathing became steady before she suddenly sat up fast looking around.

"How did I? Ouch! My head hurts. Where's Oscerr?" She looked over to me as I pointed over to him.

"Over there. What did you do to him?" Instantly she started crying hysterically.

"I wanted to get away. I was running him when he tripped. That's all I can remember. Well. I remember coming off. I hit the ground hard. Other than that I just woke up." That was concerning. She had to have a concussion. A bad one at that.

"When did you takeoff?"

"Right after training yesterday. I was waiting for you but Izabella said you weren't feeling good." Nice, Izabella must have healed her from a head injury. Nodding I kneeled beside her.

"Other than your head where do you hurt?"

"My whole body. My back and head mostly." Dante started to walk toward closer but I stopped him by shaking my head. I did not need another fight between the two of them. Izabella helped Annabelle to her feet slowly supporting her to walk to her house.

"I will take her back to my house to keep an eye on her. I can further heal her injuries. And see how long it will take for them to heal."

"Take Rocki. You will get there faster." Smirking Izabella shook her head.

"I would. But I travel without horse or walking Maylee. Take that horse back to the stable. Tend to his injuries and report to training. You will come to my house as planned." I nodded. Izabella disappeared with Annabelle into thin air. Shaking my head I turned to Dante looking to Oscerr.

"This might take a while."

"I'll help. If you want me to." I nodded appreciatively. Though I was sure Izabella had already implied as much.

"Thanks. I'm going to need it." Taking turns we led Oscerr back to the stable. One of us would lead him while the other rested. Shadow and Rocki followed along. It felt like it took hours, but it had been one. Once in the stable I gathered my first aid supplies wrapping his leg to help it heal. When I was done I stepped back to take a better look.

"I think that will do for now." Turning I was surprised to see that Dante had stayed while I fixed Oscerr's leg. "I thought you left already." He shrugged. "Well. We better get to where we are supposed to be or else they will hunt us down." He rolled his eyes nodding in agreement. As we were about to part ways he stopped.

"Maylee wait." Turning to me he glanced down to the training field.

"You should go so you don't get in trouble." I told him quietly. Frowning he shook his head.

"You should come down to the training field with me. Just for today. I think it would do you some good. Change in scenery." Glancing to the road I felt unsure.

"I don't know if that is a good idea. I'm supposed to"

"Have a babysitter. Yeah I know. And I know why. No one will try anything if you're with me down there. Or Kamran either. Come on." Taking my elbow he gently pulled me to follow him. Surprisingly I followed the pressure as he pulled me along beside him. He had no idea that Kamran was the last person on the planet I wanted to see.

"You don't know who it was." Glancing over as he pulled me along he cocked an eyebrow at me.

"And according to you. You don't either." His strides slowed to a stop pulling me to face him. "But you do. You know who it was. Don't you?" I met his gaze evenly as he asked.

"No. I honestly do not. Izabella and Kamran are investigating." Frowning he nodded searching my face almost as if searching for a lie. He was only inches away to where I could feel his breath before he slowly pulled back pulling me along behind him to continue on. I felt my face warm up as it truly felt as if he had intended on kissing me and stopped himself. That had to take a shit ton of self control.

When we walked onto the training field everyone was already full blown practicing as they attacked stuffed dummies. There was only one who was battling another person, and I did not recognize who it was. Kamran was on top of a small knoll watching everyone before looking straight at us. I felt my adrenaline kick in hard when he pinned me with his eyes. The pressure on my elbow increased as Dante pulled me to keep moving until we were at the back of all the rows.

"Take a deep breath Maylee. Just focus on your steps. The basics. Just like before." Nodding I shifted to draw my sword taking my stance.

"Well about time my two best fighters made it down to practice." I rolled my eyes feeling like my heart was jumping out of my chest. Dante shook his head at me as if telling me to relax. He didn't know about the issues I had been having with Kamran. "You will not learn anything with these boys. Dante I have told you"

"Go to the chief or Izabella. Yeah. I know. I don't care." Kamran glared at him as he turned to walk away. Instead he turned back gripping my wrist hard.

"I need to talk to you. Alone." Automatically I yanked away backing up. What was his deal? Dante stepped between us glaring at Kamran.

"Leave. Her. Alone." He growled deeply so that I had to make sure it was him that had said it. Kamran smirked arrogantly.

"I do as I want boy. Now move so I can teach her a lesson." Dante stayed planted where he was. I laid a hand on his arm causing him to glance back.

"It's okay. Let him show his true colors in front of everyone on the island. I can hold my own. I showed him that before." Kamran's arrogance faltered as anger crossed his face. Waves of nervousness were coming off of Dante as Kamran and I circled in the middle of the training field. Everyone stopped what they were doing watching the two of us.

"You actually think you can beat me little girl?" He taunted as we took our stances to face each other. Smirking I adjusted my grip on my sword with a swing.

"No. I know I can." In a flash he attacked. Everything was a blur as we exchanged blows, I deflected and attacked. It was repetitive as time wore on. I began counting the order in which he was attacking finding his rhythm. Smirking I knew how to counter him as I stepped forward attacking as he was about to attack me. Throwing him off his order I slashed his side twisting around holding my sword to his throat.

"In a fair fight. I hold my own very well." Kamran was irate as I held my sword in place not allowing him to move as the crowd around us clapped and cheered.

"Sheath your sword Maylee." Izabella said behind me sounding angry. Stepping back I sheathed my sword not taking my eyes off of Kamran. If looks could kill. I would have been dead.

"You and Dante to my house. Now." Walking backwards I refused to take my eyes off of Kamran until I knew he was not coming after me. I felt a hand on my wrist pulling me to follow knowing it had to be Dante.

"He was pissed I beat him." Dante was smirking as he glanced back behind us.

"More than pissed. He was irate. You made him look bad and have only had how many formal lessons? Like five?"

"Well. More than that."

"But still. And I'm in trouble as well." I frowned looking over at him as we slowed approaching Izabella's house.

"For what?"

"Taking you down there." He looked ashamed of himself. As he was about to say something a voice came from behind us that made me cringe.

"What. The. Hell. Were you thinking?" Closing my eyes I turned to face Izabella who was furious.

"He attempted to make an example out of me and I showed him up."

"Was Kamran the one who hurt you?" Dante cut in suddenly.

"No!" I responded quickly. As I was about to turn to him Izabella grabbed my arm shoving me into the house in front of her.

"Izabella please. I had to do something." Sitting in a chair she pinched the bridge of her nose.

"You two will be the death of me." Letting go she looked up at us. "Sit. Both of you. Now."

"It was my fault Izabella." Dante told her as he stood in front of us both. "I told her she should go there with me. I didn't think anyone would mess with her if they knew she was with me. I didn't know Kamran would be such an ass." Leaning forward with her elbows on her knees she looked at us thoughtfully.

"I think I know why." Izabella looked at me levelly. "As do you Maylee. Why he acted as he did." Rolling my eyes I nodded. Dante looked confused.

"I think so. But besides the other day he has hardly spoke to me."

"What the hell are you two talking about? Is this about your attack?" Shaking my head Izabella nodded for me to tell him.

"No. It has nothing to do with my attack Dante." Looking up at him he tilted his head gauging my expressions.

"If it has to do with your sister" I began to chuckle.

"No. Not Annabelle." Izabella cleared her throat.

"Anyways. There is also the fact he is investigating who possibly attacked you. And he was more slightly pissed you were with Dante. On top of that you showed him up. So" Sitting back in her chair she sighed. "You successfully pissed off my brother. Congratulations. Usually that spot is reserved for me or Aliyah." Shaking her head she smirked. "For future advice you two. Stay away from him. You damaged his pride and ego fairly well today. Dante, you can train with the chief one on one."

"But what about you? Can't I train"

"No. I am training Maylee. She has more to learn than you."

"I can help. I don't care how." Izabella looked to me questioningly.

"What? What are you looking at me for?" Izabella glanced to Dante momentarily.

"I am leaving it up to you. He actually does know quite a bit and could help us." I felt my face drain of color causing me to shiver involuntarily. It probably would be good for me to learn from someone else. On the other hand. It was probably another attempt to throw us together.

"I don't know." I was expecting him to be irritated or make a sound of protest. Neither came to pass.

"It's okay. I can train with the chief. I do know a lot. But honestly I don't know if I could teach you. I kind of do things my own way." He told us. His tone made me cringe. He was upset with me but not telling us.

"No kidding." Izabella commented looking up at him pointedly. "But for today. You two will train together with me. The chief is fitting Kamran with a leash after what he saw today." Shocked I stood from my chair.

"He saw what happened?" Izabella frowned at my reaction looking between the two of us.

"Yes. I called for him when I looked down to the field and saw Kamran grabbing your arm to pull you away from Dante."

"Oh god. I feel sick." She frowned glancing to the wall.

"Maylee. You are fine. They needed to see what he was doing. Besides as you said you showed him up and he was beside himself because he lost to you." I was still shaking as I sat with my elbows on my knees. "He will get over it eventually." I nodded as she stood walking to her kitchen cabinet. "Over here you two." Standing we both walked to the counter though I kept my distance from Dante. He noticed tensing even though we had started talking more. Today I was just tense all around. "I am going to teach you one useful potion everyday this week. For two hours you will learn about ingredients and properties. Sword work, and finally working with your powers."

Two hours later my head felt like it might explode. Izabella had released us for lunch and to report back to her by one. On the way to my apartment I stopped at one of the small cafes ordering a large salad with chicken and iced tea opting to eat outside while it was so nice out.

"Do you care if I sit with you?" Dante asked holding his plate. I felt my face warm but nodded to the seat across from me.

"Sit. I don't mind." Something was on his mind as he had not touched his food.

"Can I ask you something?" Looking up from my food I swallowed the bite I had just taken.

"Depends on what you want to ask." Glancing up he checked the crowd before looking at me.

"I know Kamran is investigating who attacked you. And that it did happen. I saw myself how you looked when I was in your apartment the morning after. How was anyone able to do that after how you fought today?" I sighed pushing what was left of my food away. "No. Maylee. Don't. I wasn't trying"

"He grabbed me from behind." I told him quietly as he stumbled on his words. "I was walking down the trail after we were done talking. I walked down to the beach for some time alone. When I was walking back someone wrapped their arms around me throwing me into a tree or something. They bounced the back of my head off of it so my vision was blurred. He beat the hell out of me. Izabella said every single rib was cracked or broken. He choked me out a couple times. I lost consciousness once. When I came to the man was sitting over top of me pinning my wrists over my head." He shook his head as he looked over at me concerned.

"I'm sorry you were attacked." Shaking my head at him I smirked.

"Not your fault. I'll be fine."

"I'm sorry. I should never have asked. I didn't think" I looked up at him as he turned to stand to leave.

"Stop apologizing. And sit back down." He stopped talking at last frowning but sat back down. We talked for another few minutes before realizing the clock was chiming one telling us we had to go back to Izabella's.

As we walked we could see down onto the training field I had started thinking about what Annabelle had pulled taking off on her horse. I had been walking along not paying attention to Dante, but I knew he was close to my right arm.

"I don't know what my sister was thinking taking off like she did last night. And injuring her horse in the process." I shook my head worried sick about her recent behavior. She had changed. Her personality and the way she acted. Dante must have been reading the look on my face.

"She will be fine. Izabella's taking care of her."

"Yeah, I know. I just have this feeling something is going to happen."

"What do you mean?" He stopped me turning me to face him. I knew I would have to lie to him to make him think I still did not suspect she had turned.

"My sister. She's just so home sick. I hope she doesn't do anything too stupid." He opened his mouth to say something but I closed my eyes turning to continue our walk. He stayed silent the rest of the way there.

Izabella pushed us both using our powers even though Dante had told her he refused to use his she made him anyways. The controlling exercise for today had been a protective barrier against all attacks. The only one I could hold for long and only against certain ones was only ten feet around. Not great for when you are battling for your life. Dante actually did better. His was the same size as mine but held against all attacks. He waited for me to walk back to the apartments until I checked my sister. She was still sleeping soundly when I walked out the front door.

After we were pushed so hard today I was ready to go to bed and rest up for tomorrow.

"Has she been pushing you like that with your powers already? Or was that just starting today?" Dante asked curiously as we walked.

"Just today. She made me learn to control my fire the first couple weeks. Once I could maintain it she made me learn to snuff it out or feed it." Without another word we arrived at our building going our separate ways. I was out the moment I hit my pillow. But the nightmares began with the man who attacked haunting me. It seemed as though there was never escaping what he had said to me when he was done. That he would be back to do more to me.

There was heavy pounding sound that at first I thought it was part of a dream I was having. It became louder and more insistent waking me up realizing someone was at my door. At first I panicked thinking I overslept looking at the clock it was only four in the morning.

"Who the hell could that be?" I threw my blankets off pulling my robe on over my pajamas opening the door to

Izabella. "It's only four in the morning. What's going on?" As I focused more I could see she was panic stricken.

"Annabelle is gone!" Okay. Now I'm fully awake. She had my full undivided attention.

"What! How? When?"

"She must have woke up and left while I was sleeping. I am so sorry. I even scryed for her but she is not on the island. She was heading northwest over the Atlantic." That threw me into more of a panic. What if she was attacked by the other side while traveling?

"She could be attacked or captured. Or killed! And how could she be flying? Never mind I already know the answer to that. She's flying her dragon. Dammit." Izabella laid a hand on my shoulder to gain my attention.

"We cannot go after her if that is what you are thinking."

"Why not?" I asked testily. It did not faze her that I was.

"Someone cannot be brought here against their will. Just give her a few days. She will be back. Albay will keep her safe. Do not worry." But I did worry, it was in my job description as big sister. My cell phone.

"Hold that thought." I ran into my room digging through the desk drawer. Grasping my phone I turned it on. Izabella met me at the couch closing the door when she walked in. I dialed my sister's number hitting send. She did not answer so I left her a nice little voicemail.

"Annabelle Paige! How dare you! How dare you leave like this. You had better bring your sorry ass back here right now or when you do come back you will not like me!"

I ended the call tossing my phone aside frustrated that she had done something so stupid. Leaning against the wall I sank to the floor crying. I had too many emotions running through me. This was too much. First I'm attacked where I had never felt safer. Now my sister flees the island home sick. Izabella crouched down beside me.

"She will be fine. Her dragon will see that no harm comes to her. That is what they are trained for." She wrapped an arm around my shoulders as I wiped the tears away standing. "Maylee, I am sorry. Have a seat at the counter. I will make you some tea." Shaking my head I could feel rage from deep within rising. Without warning I turned punching the wall in front of me several times. Occasionally screaming with rage whenever I felt like it. Izabella stood there with her arms crossed watching me punching holes in the wall. At one point she walked away opening the door to my apartment. Shocked at Dante's presence I stopped resting my forehead against the wall. I heard him ask closing the door behind him.

"What is going on?" He saw the holes I had punched in the wall looking to Izabella. My hands began to ache from hitting the walls. Tears were running down my face which only refueled my anger. Screaming with rage I began hitting the walls again. Dante walked to Izabella confused at my behavior.

"What happened?" She pointed at the holes I had made.

"To the wall? Or why Maylee is taking them out with her bare hands?"

"Just tell me what is going on." I heard him tell her irritably.

"Annabelle took off on her dragon without informing us she was leaving. I woke up to check on her and she was gone. I scryed for her but she was already off the island somewhere over the Atlantic going northwest."

I had stopped punching the walls tiring out resting again. Dante wandered over to where I was now standing whistling low with his arms crossed.

"You sure are making a mess of the place." He looked over the entire wall admiring it. "Personally, I would have used a sledge hammer. It would have been easier on the hands." Was he actually talking me down? This was a first. I should record it somewhere to keep track as that tactic had never worked on me. He never told me to calm down, or not be so upset. Either phrase would have only made it worse. I looked down at my hands. They were all black and blue with blood running down my wrists. That also had calmed me down knowing they were likely broken.

"Yeah. It would have been." I turned my back to the wall sinking to the floor looking up at him. "Sorry I woke you up." Tiredly he smiled a little.

"I would be surprised if anyone could sleep through that. You were loud." Izabella walked over kneeling down to examine my hands.

"We need to heal your hands." Nodding I stood up on my own following her to my kitchen counter. Walking around she found the pot she wanted. Measuring out different herbs before mixing in some water. Dante walked up leaning against the counter at my side. Izabella was boiling some water separate from what was already mixed.

"She left in the dead of night?" He asked quietly turning to face me.

"Yeah. Why?" Frowning he seemed to be thinking about it.

"I thought I heard a door open and close around two this morning. I thought I was just hearing things in my sleep. I guess I should have got up and checked. Sorry." Shaking my head I winced at how sore my hands were. Sighing he reached over taking my wrist gently looking at my knuckles.

"You did not know. If I would have heard it I would have just turned over and went back to sleep. It is not anyone's fault but my sister's. And I should have known. I knew how she was starting to feel about all of this. Maybe this is all my fault. I

217

should have seen it coming." My brain finally registered he had my wrist feeling my face warm that he was touching me before pulling away. Izabella had mixed everything together in a large bowl setting it in front of me.

"You cannot see everything. No one can. Now set your hands in that bowl." Izabella told me as my hands healed in the potion she had made. It only took a total of five minutes for them to fully heal. "You can remove your hands from the bowl. They should be healed." Taking them out of the bowl I stretched my hands cracking my knuckles to make sure everything would still work.

"Well. We might as well start on what you were teaching me this morning since we are here. When we're done I will go for my run." She nodded agreeing with me.

"Dante you may join us for this if Maylee is okay with you in her apartment." Startled she was pinning me to the spot I turned to him. He had talked me down when Izabella could not.

"Yes. I am okay with that."

"Good. We can start with the simple healing potion I just made for your hands. It is for bones, muscles, cartilage, and tendons. There are different healing potions and spells based on the type of injury." Izabella ended up using my apartment as our learning center for the morning. I had everything she needed to mix some of the potions she was showing us. Dante and I took turns mixing each one as she had done.

We finished for the day around noon dismissing Dante. Once he left I realized that I had been in my pajamas the entire time we worked. Pausing once the door closed behind him I shook my head.

"Are you going to change for your run now or run as you are? You might cause some of the men to run into stationary objects if you run that way." Smiling she knew why my face heated now.

"He was in my apartment for hours while I looked like this." Crossing her arms over her chest she frowned nodding.

"Yes. Why are you upset?" It took a moment for me to gather my thoughts enough to explain.

"Izabella. This is my safe space. Where no one can hurt me. And someone I cannot bring myself to trust. Was in my apartment. All morning. Right beside me." Shaking her head she gripped my shoulder forcing me to sit in a chair.

"Enough"

"Izabella" Looking irritated she shook her head.

"No. I left it up to you for him to be in your apartment. You were more than comfortable while I was brewing your healing potion. I saw him look at your hand. Now what is the actual problem?" Raising my eyebrows at her I looked down to my pajamas.

"Oh I don't fucking know Izabella. Maybe I should have realized sooner I was half naked the whole time he was here." Izabella laughed.

"Maylee. Trust me. He realized it." Closing my eyes I shook my head.

"This is not funny"

"The way you are reacting to the situation is. He handled your presence as you are dressed better than you are handling the fact he was here. Now. If I had to guess. I would say the feeling is mutual. You like him. Besides. It is not like you were naked." As I was about to protest she shook her head. "Go change. I will wait outside." I must have made Izabella mad. She made me run half the island before she allowed me to slow or stop. "Your stamina is finally starting to build up." Nodding I was still breathing hard as she had not let me take any walking breaks the whole time.

"Well. When you start pushing me that hard my body doesn't have much choice does it?" I heard her laugh a little.

"Well. You could choose to walk when I tell you to keep going if you really wanted to." Rolling my eyes I walked up the stairs to my apartment.

"What time do I need to report to your house for sword practice?"

"In about four hours. You already had your potions lesson. Go for a ride and clear your mind. You are thinking about far too much." Nodding in agreement I showered changing into my jeans and t-shirt to go ride Rocki. Never knowing what I may run into I pocketed my stones and Star burst in jackknife form to keep it concealed.

When I walked into the stable Dante had both of our horses saddled and ready to go. Oh shit. Rocki allowed him to saddle him.

"If you don't mind. I would like to ride along with you." I shrugged. Why not? If my horse allowed him to touch him I should allow it.

"Sure, you saddled them up. Only I have just one request." Cocking an eyebrow at me he shifted his feet looking slightly uneasy.

"What's that?"

"We don't run unless the horses want to." He looked at Shadow who nodded in agreement.

"I'll agree to that."

The two of us walked the familiar trail down to the beach just taking in how nice it was. He walked right beside me the whole time looking everything over.

"What are you thinking?" Dante asked as I looked around. There was something or someone watching us.

"Let's just get to the beach. I will explain why when we are there." We rode onto the beach sand stopping as I pulled out the black stone that controlled the undead. Dante looked at the stone wearily.

"What are you doing?" I gripped the stone hard.

"Someone is watching us and I want to know who." No reaction from him as I looked in the general direction that I felt the presence coming from. It was not Kamran as I had come to know his energy. This was something else.

"Reveal." I was about shocked when Danny walked out of the woods. "Danny? Why are you watching me?" He tossed his head like he always did when he was irritated.

"Protecting you."

"From what?" He turned his head toward Dante.

"People from both sides."

"He still doesn't like me does he?" Dante asked as I looked to him.

"You could say that. What else?"

"I have also been watching your sister. And I warn you. When she comes back you are to not trust her."

"Why? She's my sister." He disappeared without answering my question. I had to think this one over for a minute. "Dante?"

"What?"

"You could hear him. Couldn't you?" He turned away from me scowling.

"Yes. I could hear him." I figured I might as well ask.

"You have more power than you let onto. I can feel the energy of it. Why don't you use them more?" Shaking his head I could almost feel him close off.

"I don't want to talk about it." He started walking along the beach as I followed not bringing the subject up again.

It was four days total that Annabelle was gone before she returned. Four days that Dante and I had been hanging around each other more. I knew that was not good for me. Annabelle was walking up to our apartment building as Izabella and I were on our way back to my apartment after my sword lesson. She smiled when she saw me. I however did not seeing as I was still fairly angry with her for what she had done. She ran up giving me a big hug apologizing over and over. I pulled away from her angrily.

"Why did you leave?" Her shoulders dropped frowning.

"I wanted to go home. I missed our family, and my friends. I'm sorry I left the way I did."

"Did you actually go home and stay? Or did you just watch them through the windows?"

"No. I stayed for a couple days. I had to sneak out to come back."

"How exactly did you hide Albay? Dad would have noticed a dragon in his garage."

"He stayed in the woods outback. No one noticed him." I shook my head still completely disgusted walking around her to continue to the apartment building. She started to follow me only to stop standing frozen in place. I glanced back after a good amount of space only to see her face turning red as Dante walked onto the road from the chief's.

"Great." I said to myself stopping to turn around walking back to where they stood. Before I could take one step Izabella grabbed my shoulder to stop me.

"No. Just watch. What happens between the two of them is their problem. You have your own to deal with."

222

"Izabella. She is my sister. No matter what she does. Let me go." When I looked back to what was going on Annabelle drew fury pointing it at Dante as he spoke to her. Dante turned pale reaching for Guardian. Izabella had let go of me without realizing it so I hurried forward stepping in between them.

"Stop. Both of you! Now what is going on?" Annabelle narrowed her eyes at Dante as he had stopped drawing his sword when I stepped between them. I knew the only reason he did was because it was me standing between them. "Annabelle?" Her jaw worked as I looked to her with her eyes that were black. When I saw that my stomach dropped out telling me what had happened.

"Maylee. This does not concern you. Move. Now." Was all she would say to me.

"What do you mean it does not concern me? You are about to attack someone with no reason." Taking her eyes off of Dante she looked at me as though I had no idea what was going on.

"No reason? That's rich. You totally hate him and you're telling me he is on our side?" Taking a step closer to her I nodded.

"Annabelle. Enough. I did not hate him. I just did not trust him. You know it is hard for me to trust people. And you know why as well. We have had this discussion. Now. Do us all a favor. And sheath your sword. I want you to come back to my place and we will talk over lunch." Angrily she rolled her eyes but did as I asked. Sighing relief I turned to Dante. He had already relaxed exchanging looks with Izabella.

"For my sanity and so you two do not do this again. Please. Just stay away from each other." I glared at my sister who begrudgingly nodded before looking to Dante. He was beyond tense to the point Izabella looked about ready to step in to help.

"Annabelle. Please go with Izabella back to my apartment. I need to speak with Dante. I'll catch up." Izabella nodded taking my sister's elbow to make sure she did as she was told.

"Maylee don't" Holding my hand up I stopped him.

"I stopped you both. To prevent you both from doing anything stupid that you would regret. I don't know what is going on between the two of you. And you do not owe me an explanation. My sister's battles are her own and I will not interfere as long as she stays level headed. But when she attempts to attack someone that is where I stop her." He looked angry but it was not directed to me as he took a deep breath.

"I would tell you Maylee. But I know you would never believe me. Especially since she is your sister and you barely know me. I get that. Really I do. Thanks." Turning he walked away not glancing back even once. Dammit. Damn them both for making this so difficult. Beginning the walk to my apartment my chest ached terribly making it difficult to breathe. Approaching town Kamran walked up to me glancing to the buildings behind him. My nerves shot throughout my body remembering what Izabella had told me after our angry sparring session. I did not need his crap on top of what I had going on with my sister and friend. Ugh. Yeah. Friend. In the last four days with my sister gone I had grown comfortable around him.

"Kamran. Look, I'm sorry about" He shook his head looking to the ground.

"Do not be sorry for what happened a few days ago." I felt myself begin to tremble as we stood only feet apart. Taking my hand I looked up at him. "I was not angry that you beat me. I was angry you were with Dante. And I should not have been. I know there was nothing between us. I have never been jealous before and I was. I am sorry for that."

"Kamran. Dante is a friend. Just starting to be my friend. You have no right to be jealous. And you're not really a friend either." He smirked glancing over his shoulder.

"I know." He reached his hand out to rest on the side of my face. Before he could I stepped back away from him.

"Kamran. No. Do not touch me."

"I know you do not like me." I nodded understandingly. He allowed me to walk away. I walked quickly as we left almost running into my apartment letting Izabella know what had just happened with Kamran. My chest ached sharply when I walked through the door. Izabella noticed immediately.

"What is wrong?" Shaking my head I sat on the couch as my sister looked on from the kitchen.

"Nothing. Maybe I ran too hard today." Frowning she sat beside me examining me top to bottom. Annabelle walked over watching with curiosity. When she was done there was a smirk on her face as she stood crossing her arms in front of her.

"I know what it is and it is not from working out too hard. Or from Kamran being such an ass to you either." Rolling my eyes I really did not want to know the answer.

"Than keep it to yourself. I have enough problems to worry about." She nodded in agreement as we talked to my sister for a while before she decided to go to her own apartment to rest.

"Izabella." She looked up from the counter after Annabelle had left.

"Yes."

"I need to go for another run. I need to clear my head."

"Change your clothes and we will go now if that is what you want." I was already in my bedroom to change before she could finish her sentence. Before we were done we ran the entire perimeter of the island.

"Now that is pushing it Maylee. Ease up. Walk down this next trail."

"I'm not going to ease up until this war is over. It is tearing everyone apart." As we walked I began to feel shaky.

"When was the last time you ate?" Izabella asked as she held my elbow to steady me.

"I can't remember. Why?" Stopping I looked at her as she looked me up and down.

"You have lost a lot of weight. Your clothes are hanging off of you." Waving her off I continued to walk.

"Pretty sure I can't lose too much in only a couple weeks Izabella." She stayed silent as we walked. Sighing I was trying to catch my breath from running so hard. "I think it was Kamran who was trying to work spells on me." She nodded turning to continue our walk. As we approached the apartments the chief walked into our path.

"Izabella, Maylee. Do you have a moment?"

"Sure. What's going on?"

"I think it is time to send you on your first mission." My brain froze. I did not feel I was ready for that yet.

"Me? On a mission? Are you sure?" I wanted to make sure he had the right person here.

"Yes, but you are not going alone." Well that was a relief to say the least.

"Who is going with me?" I had started to wonder who he would want to send me with? He looked as if he was still trying to figure it out for himself yet than looked up at me thoughtfully.

"I think you should take your sister." I frowned at that thinking great the fight is on. That would have to go on the backburner until we came back.

"What is the mission?"

"You will fly over South America to see how bad things are going there. Than over the U.S. Word has reached us that California has had a massive quake and has began to split at the fault line already." That is awesome and we're only in freaking April.

"When do we leave?"

"Tomorrow. You will have seven days to come back. After that we will send someone to find you in case you are in trouble." I sniggered glancing to Izabella.

"Yeah, I doubt that will happen." He looked at me as if he was ready to reprimand me from acting stupid.

"You will meet myself and Izabella at my cabin before dawn." Nodding I turned to leave. "And Maylee" I stopped. "Do not tell anyone besides Annabelle about your mission." He looked stern.

"Got it. Thank you." Turning he walked back down the street disappearing into the crowd.

"You know what is going to happen. I will make sure that you are well prepared for what is to come." My stomach sank as this was part of a bigger plan. And from what I could see, it could be a disaster.

"I'm going to visit the stable before I go to my apartment." Izabella made a sound of impatience but nodded allowing me to go.

Rocki and Oscerr were more than happy to see me. I told them that Annabelle and I might be gone for a bit. As I told them they understood not even asking why we were leaving them there. My chest ached again as I walked into Rocki's stall leaning against him stroking his mane.

"This is harder than I expected." Turning his head he nuzzled me.

"You are doing fine."

227

"It does not feel that way. I'm between a rock and a hard place with no way out but to take the hit and find out what happens when it's over."

"It will be okay. Just be careful." With one last hug around his neck I turned walking back to my apartment out of the stable. As I walked by Shadow's stall I noticed it was empty. Where was he now?

"Shadow?" I thought out to him. "Where are you?"

"Not far. Almost back." He responded.

"By yourself or with your owner?"

"Dante is with me."

I stood by the big door entrance waiting for them to walk through. It did not take long as Shadow walked in but without his rider. I took a step out to look around. Shadow stopped short of his stall tossing his head.

"Where is he?"

"Behind you." He replied pawing the ground nervously.

I turned around in time to find Dante with Guardian drawn out in front of him. I backed up drawing Star burst as I did so but upon seeing my blade he dropped Guardian to his side.

"Why were you hiding in the dark?" He asked suspiciously as I sheathed my sword.

"Why did you have your sword trained at me?" Taking a step back we both looked around.

"Well. It's dark out. I could sense something in the doorway but not who or even what."

"So, let me get this straight. You were going to run me through even if you could not see who or what I was?" He narrowed his eyes at me a vein in his neck was pulsing out. Not from anger though that was what underneath it was. No, something had him strung out.

"No, I waited until I could see you in the light. If I had not we would not be having our conversation right now." I nodded so what was he expecting?

"Why? Were you expecting someone?" I could tell he was getting exasperated about being questioned so in depth.

"Just never mind. Why were you here?" He snapped slightly causing me to raise my eyebrows as I began walking toward the door. It was the first time he had ever done that to me and meant it. Usually he was trying to make me talk to him.

"Last time I checked I had a horse here." Shifting his feet he began walking behind me.

"Sorry. I forgot." He said in a level voice as if he really meant it. I stopped turning to him scowling.

"You seem to be forgetting a lot of things." I commented as I continued walking. Opening his mouth to retort he stopped walking off to a trail.

After I was on our floor I stopped by Annabelle's apartment knocking on the door. No answer, oh well. I'll try again in a few hours to tell her about our mission. I went into my own apartment instead. Izabella was waiting when I arrived to discuss everything. Afterwards I set my alarm and went to check Annabelle's apartment again. This time she answered surprised yet eager to go on the mission. After that I went to bed. Something was still bothering me, Annabelle's eyes earlier today. I had only seen them stormy when she was angry, but earlier they were like that when she was fine. They were black when I stepped between her and Dante.

I went to sleep recounting the exchanges between the two of them, how he had turned pale when she told him something I had not heard. It was difficult to act as though I did not know she had turned. At the stable Dante acted strung out. Something was definitely going on between the two of them.

I woke up startled as my alarm blared out turning over to shut it off. Sitting up I was drenched in a cold sweat. I really hope that was just a dream. Lying back down for a minute I was thinking about my dream. It had been snowy, so it must be about the future. It looked like the Appalachian or Colorado mountain ranges. One thing was for certain, I had better keep a close eye on both my sister and friend. I rubbed my forehead with my hands trying to forget it all.

Finally I threw the covers off getting up and around. I would talk to Izabella later on about that. Dressing quickly I grabbed an apple out of the bowl on the counter, that would do for today. I was growing sick of cooking all the time now. A knock sounded at the door as I stood rolling my eyes knowing I would have to tolerate my sister's games for the next few days.

"It's your sister. Remember me?" She said irritated annoying me from the start.

"Well, I cannot be so sure. My sister would not have taken off like you did without telling me or anyone else for that matter." I said lightly but knew that would further annoy her as well. She was silent for a minute. Probably to change her tactic or choosing her words carefully.

"I told you I was sorry." She said through clenched teeth as if it pained her to do so. I looked through the hole again. I still couldn't see her. I finally opened the door letting her in, but kept the door open. Walking in she turned facing me looking thoroughly annoyed.

"And you can keep saying it until you are blue in the face. I did not appreciate the way you left." She looked down sheepishly before back to me with a slight smile on her face.

"I could see that. Did anyone besides the wall get taken out?" Gesturing to the wall.

"No, just the wall. And when you came back I wanted to repeat the process to you, but I knew I couldn't." She was angry instantly. Why I do not really know. Her eyes turned black as she glared. So I was not just seeing things.

"You would turn on me?" She asked angrily while I just looked at her like what is your problem?

"Turn on you? I have not turned on you. *You* left. Remember? Not me." My temper was kicking in. Of course I could tell we were sisters and her temper could match mine if she needed it to.

"Is that why you started spending all your time with that traitor?" She spat. What the hell? Frowning I tilted my head slightly listening to her tone.

"Traitor? You mean Dante?" I asked slightly misconstrued.

"Yes! He is against us. Everything we are doing here." She was leading me into something here. I could feel it. I thought over what she said knowing I had to just play along. At least for now to see where she was going with this.

"I have only been around him two or three times. And those were while you were gone. He has been helpful actually."

"So that is your response? Why you are around him at all?"

"Yes. Something happened a couple days before you took off on Oscerr. I was attacked. Shadow alerted Dante about it and he sent Izabella to help me. He has been checking up on me since. That is it. Now, tell me about your trip." As she stared measuring me up her eyes turned back to their original hazel color.

"You were attacked? By who?"

"I will tell you the same thing I told everyone else. I don't know. Okay? I don't want to talk about it." Nodding she frowned but went into details about her trip home.

231

"I have something to tell you about time here." She reached for her phone sliding it open to look at the date and time. "What is today?" I had to think about that knowing Izabella had told me time was different here compared to home. I had not seen a calendar since we had been here. I started going over the amount of time we had spent traveling, than at sea, and finally on the island itself. It was April 24th when we left, it had been around three weeks maybe a little over.

"Should be May twentieth or something like that." She raised her eyebrows.

"When was the last time you looked at your phone?" I shrugged striding to the table picking it up to look at the date. June 15, 2015 8:00 am

"It must be malfunctioning." Annabelle gave me a yeah right kind of look handing me a newspaper from when she had been gone.

"Read the headline and date on that." I took it reading the date June 15th 2015. I grew wide eyed reading it. "Time slows down here. Not us, but time itself. How long was I gone from here?" I looked up from the paper.

"Four days total." She made a face.

"Yeah, I was actually gone for two weeks." I was in shock. That was slightly more than what Izabella had told me it was.

"Wow. Okay, so how were mom and dad holding up?" Mom I did not care too much about. It was more about our dad.

"Dad was nuts, glad I was back. Glad to see me and that I was okay. He took me to the mall to go shopping and everything. And of course mom could have cared less. Unfortunately, I met some people while I was gone too. They told me things were about to get worse." Now she had my undivided attention.

"Worse? You mean worse than the weather and other catastrophes they are causing?"

"Yeah. They actually said our house was going to be engulfed in a mudslide and it would kill our parents." She sounded serious as I searched her eyes deciding whether to believe her or not.

"That is not possible. That ground is completely solid. It would take over a month of torrential rainfall for it to be engulfed in a mudslide." I crossed my arms as it just wasn't possible.

"I know. But I still panicked at first." She turned away from me before I could get a good look at her face when she said it.

"Well. I have something to tell you now that we have gotten through that." I was somewhat reluctant to tell her.

"What?"

"We need to get moving for our mission." Her face lit up at once knowing she wanted to get away from here again anyways. She walked out the door to grab her bag so we could leave within the next half hour. Looking to the clock I knew Izabella would be in the lobby to send us off. With my own backpack I walked out of my apartment almost running right into Dante.

"Holy hell! You scared me." I said breathing hard from the surprise of it. He looked almost as surprised as I felt but distracted too.

"Sorry about that." He apologized looking up to my face. "I'm sorry about last night too. I've just been really jumpy lately. I reacted before I thought about it." He looked sorry as out of no where a bouquet of orange carnations, light purple lilac and white calla lily's appeared handing them to me. "For you." Taking them I was stunned. The flowers were beautiful.

"I accept your apology." I said slowly looking at the flowers. "But you didn't have to give me these." I smelled them. I loved carnations and orange was my favorite color. Had he known somehow? "You hate using your powers." I stated as I studied his expression. "So why use them to give me flowers?" Nothing as he shrugged though I could have sworn I saw a twitch of a smile.

"There are still many things you do not know about me." Glancing over his shoulder he must have been listening for my sister. "One day I will tell you everything. If you would allow me." Smirking I nodded as he kept glancing to my sister's apartment.

"Hopefully soon. Trust me when I say we all have secrets most people do not know." Frowning he looked me over for a moment stepping closer. My heart was pounding in my throat as I could almost feel his breath on me.

"You think you have secrets?" His right hand rested on my arm as we stood close shock after shock traveling through my body at the touch.

"Maybe not as many as you. But yes."

"Interesting." Smirking he leaned closer yet stopping as we both heard Annabelle's door begin to open. "Sorry." Turning he walked down the stairs rather quickly. Why had he actually given these to me? Rolling my eyes I already knew the answer to that as Izabella had told me time and again to give him a chance. To at the least be friends with him and I had done that. A moment before Annabelle started opening the door he was leaning closer. Probably to kiss me but had to run because of my sister.

Annabelle walked out of her apartment looking to me expectantly.

"Where did the flowers come from?" She had sounded genuinely curious though the look on her face showed she already suspected.

"Dante gave them to me. He apologized for almost slicing me open at the stable last night." Scowling she looked to the stairway door than back to me.

"With flowers? Seriously." Rolling her eyes she walked down the stairs throwing the door open before her angrily. Damn. She was pissed. Sighing I stepped into my apartment long enough to put the bouquet in a vase before running after my sister.

"You have everything?" Izabella asked us both once we were in the lobby of the apartment building. Both of us nodded though Annabelle still looked moody as hell. Frowning slightly Izabella noticed.

"Annabelle, could you go ahead and pack up both your dragons? I need to speak with your sister for a few minutes."

"Sure." Taking my backpack she walked down the street turning to the mountain trail.

"She is pissed at you. What happened between you before you came down here?"

"I know what the problem is and it is not my fault." I replied crossing my arms in front of me.

"Which problem? Her issue with Dante or the fact she's turned against us?"

"I'm almost completely sure those two problems are one in the same. She was pissed he gave me some flowers before we came down here." Izabella smirked crossing her arms over her chest looking up at me.

"He gave you flowers?"

"Yeah. I was slightly shocked."

"What kind?" Frowning I was not quite following what she was asking.

"Carnations, lilac and calla lily's."

"Smart."

"Why does it matter?"

"Do you know the meaning of each one?"

"No. I just like orange carnations. Why?"

"Back in the ancient times when men really liked a woman they would give them a bouquet of flowers. They were made up of two kinds. The flower that particular woman preferred and calla lily's. The calla lily's represent their interest in asking you to be with them." After Izabella told me this my chest began to ache dully thinking about him.

"So. That was his way of asking me out without actually asking?" Shaking her head Izabella smirked again.

"No. He will ask you in due time." Nodding I glanced to the mountain where my sister was waiting for us.

"I think if Annabelle had not walked out when she did he was going to kiss me." Izabella smirked.

"Yeah maybe. Anyways. Back to your sister. Do you have real proof that she has turned?"

"Her eyes turned black yesterday Izabella. For me that is more than enough proof. I'm sure that she has a plan to have me captured."

"I have heard that they do. So this is what we are going to do about it." It only took a few minutes for us to formulate a plan to keep me from being captured in the event it was tried. After that we walked to the mountain where my sister was impatiently waiting for me so we could leave.

"Wait up you two." The chief's voice came as he walked over the hill so that we could see him. My stomach dropped when I saw Kamran only steps behind him looking angry.

"Izabella. You can go. I need to speak with Maylee before they leave." Izabella nodded curtly glaring at Kamran as she walked out. He watched her go looking back to me smiling wide.

"Maylee, Kamran has made you a dagger to match your sword. I will let him explain." As Kamran stepped closer I grew more tense like a tightly wound rubber band ready to break.

"It has many magickal properties. It can heal any wound from the inside out when traced, draw out poisons and only truly works for either the maker or the person it was given to." He held it to me in a wide open hand as I looked at it. The dagger was literally my sword in much smaller form.

"May I look at it?" He gave a small nod as I carefully picked it up from his hand admiring his work. He had done a fantastic job on it.

"It is yours to keep." Taking a step back he kept his arms in front of him.

"Thank you. It is beautiful, you did a great job on it." He smiled taking the compliment. "We better get going." They both gave a nod as I walked to Marlo to fly out.

"Maylee wait." Kamran's voice came from directly behind me causing me to freeze as I turned. Annabelle was watching as she saw how tense I had become.

"You know I asked you to stay away from me." I whispered to him trying to keep my anger in check.

"I know." Glancing to my sister he looked back to me. Stepping closer again my nerves were shooting.

"Kamran. I need to go. Please. Do not say any more. I do not want to hear it." Turning again he grabbed my elbow turning me back to face him.

"That does not mean that I cannot care about what happens to you. Be careful out there."

"Kamran. Don't ever touch me again." He smirked crookedly.

"Do not worry. I will not."

"Thanks." I gave him one last look before I climbed onto Marlo's back. Annabelle looked at me worriedly.

"Are you okay?" Turning she made a face.

"I'm fine. I want lots of distance between us and this island for a few days." Kamran really had to get over me. The strange feeling in my chest was back as we flew away that had nothing to do with Kamran. When it did this I had unconsciously been thinking about Dante.

Dante

Tension between Annabelle and I continued to worsen as the days went by. One night just after dark Shadow contacted me.

"Dante. Send Izabella to the trails. Now." He sounded almost panicked as he told me.

"Why? What is going on?"

"Someone is being attacked. Send her!"

"Alright." Closing my mind to him I reached out to Izabella. "Shadow told me someone is being attacked on the trails and to hurry."

"On my way."

Just before I went to bed for the night I could hear someone struggling to help someone outside my door. Looking out I could see Maylee leaning on Izabella injured. It was Maylee who Shadow had saw being attacked. I wanted to walk out and ask what had happened but I stopped myself. Even though she had relaxed around me now was not the time.

"Shadow. Why didn't you tell me it was Maylee who was being attacked?"

"Because I knew you wouldn't be able to handle seeing her in the condition she was in when Izabella found her." I could barely sleep that night thinking about her. We had been talking earlier in the night. Only the fact Annabelle had noticed we were together talking made us separate. It would not have bothered me if I wasn't still trying to get information from them yet. I knocked on Maylee's door first thing in the morning only to be greeted by Izabella.

"She is sleeping. Leave her alone for now." My muscles tightened more at the tone of her voice.

"What happened to her?" Sliding by her I entered Maylee's apartment looking to her bedroom.

"Nothing. She will be okay."

"Bullshit Izabella. I saw you bring her up here last night. She was injured badly. What happened?" Sighing she leaned against the couch looking at me evenly.

"That is for her to tell you if she feels up to it."

"What happened to her Izabella? I could hear her screaming last night. And do not lie to me." Izabella frowned crossing her arms over her chest staring at me.

"I stayed with her through the whole night. She never screamed Dante. Unless"

"What?"

"You are connecting to her."

"Maybe. But you know she is pushing me away. She has no memory from that time."

"I know."

"I want to see her." The bedroom door opened slowly as Maylee walked out looking between us. I was in shock as I saw her face in the light. Someone had used her as a punching bag. Before I knew it I was standing directly in front of her.

"Who. Did. This? I will kill them." Looking as if she wanted nothing more than to just cry she shook her head walking to Izabella. I followed her as she turned to face me.

"I don't know. I was walking down the trail and was attacked from behind. I hit the back of my head on something. Please. Just leave. I'll be back in training tomorrow. Okay?"

"You know who did it. Tell me Maylee." I had never known the level of angry I could reach until she dropped her robe from her neck revealing a dark purple mark from being choked.

"I'll be okay." Without thinking I grabbed her wrist so that she could not move away as I looked her over. She was in a black tank top and shorts under her robe as I mentally noted all her injuries.

"They choked you. Dammit tell me!" I felt my voice change with my anger causing Maylee to cringe.

"Dante" She looked back levelly but tears forming as she tried to find the words. "Please just leave. I will be okay." Shaking my head I tried to pull her into an embrace. At first she stiffened but relented holding me back burying her head into the crook of my neck crying. She only stayed there for a moment before pulling away.

"Dammit." I took her hand into mine as we stood there.

"What are you doing?" Slowly her trembling subsided as I attempted to take away her shock. Releasing her hand I felt slightly shaky myself as I had not ate yet.

"Helping you." Was all I could manage as I felt my jaw work at how angry I was. Everything just kept declining from there.

Later in the morning Izabella came in to check on me.

"You looked pretty shook up yourself Dante. Are you feeling okay?" Shaking my head as I sat on the love seat.

"No. My nerves are shot. Annabelle is giving me a run for my money right now. I am fighting as hard as I can to stay in. But if she keeps this up they are going to send someone to kill me."

"If they did come here to kill you we would not allow them to. You should know that." Scowling I stood in front of her angrily.

"No one should have been able to access the island who would brutally attack Maylee either. And yet here we are." I could tell I hit a nerve with that one as she balled her fists at her side biting back her own anger.

"We have no idea how that happened. Kamran and I are both investigating it as deeply as possible."

"Any ideas who it was?" Shaking her head she sat across from me.

"You want to help her?" I tried not to choke as I barked a laugh.

"Yes. What do you want me to do?"

"I know that she will insist on going for her morning run tomorrow. By than she will be healed enough. When she comes back she will need assistance to her apartment. I know her body will be running on fumes. Meet her at the entrance to this building and help her to her apartment. Once you have done that make her some tea and slip this sleeping tonic into it." Frowning I almost agreed before knowing why.

"Okay. Why does she need a sleeping tonic?"

"She is barely sleeping. Nightmares from her attack. And when she does it is fitful to say the least."

"What happened to her Izabella? You need to tell me. I agreed to what you asked. Now you at least owe me an explanation." Crossing her arms she raised her chin at me standing from where she was.

"I owe you nothing kid. I told you what would happen if you came here. If you would have moved quicker she would never have been attacked." Scowling I stood in front of her.

"That is totally unfair Izabella. You knew when I told you I would spy for the council she would know and stay away from me. And she has. Her damn sister has about blown my whole

plan because they have been in direct correspondence to her."
Smirking Izabella pushed me back a step.

"Yes and no Dante. Did she know? Yes. Is that why she distanced herself from you? Yes. And did Annabelle pretty much blow your plans? Maybe. That is yet to be seen. You have almost blown it yourself." Scowling more I threw my hands in the air.

"Than please explain how the hell I was ever going to manage both without one side or the other messing it up." Sighing she looked at me evenly.

"The council set you up to fail. They knew you would never be able to maintain it for long."

"Why?"

"They wanted to know the lengths you would go to keep your ties to your father's army."

"In other words they wanted to know if I was truly with them or not?"

"Yes." I chuckled darkly.

"And what is their conclusion?"

"That you put yourself on the line for the council. And you refused to jeopardize Maylee in the process." My throat went dry as she told me.

"So what do they want me to do? Salvage my connection so they can use it? Or break away?" Gripping my shoulders she made me look at her.

"Hang in there just a little longer. Alright?" Nodding I agreed leaving the apartment.

The next day I realized Annabelle had not came back from her trip she had taken around the island. She had been angry with me when she left. Maylee had come running down to the stable jumping right onto her black taking off to find her. She was barely healed and running after her brat sister. Shaking my head I helped her look as she rode her horse looking like black lightning.

Annabelle was injured when we found her. Izabella healed her taking her to her house for further healing. Maylee asked me to help take the horse back as he was injured as well from a fall he had taken. I watched her as she took great care of this horse. Standing she was startled I had stayed to wait for her. I accompanied her to Izabella's only to stop at the training field where I was supposed to be going. Whenever I looked at Maylee I felt at ease for the first time in months. It was a feeling I did not want to leave as she stared down at the field before telling me I should go. Dammit. I wanted so badly to kiss her still. Instead I had her go with me onto the field knowing Izabella would kill me for it.

At first we began to spar but I could tell that Maylee's attention was not on our sparring as she looked past me to where Kamran was striding up to us. Remembering what Izabella had told me and what I had saw for myself I was angry just for him walking up. Before we were done him and Maylee fought. It was nerve racking for me as I watched them. Damn she was good for the amount of training she had been through so far. Involuntarily I cringed when Izabella screamed at the two of them. Maylee had just finished the fight defeating Kamran anyways. The looks Izabella gave me after we were all at her house should have killed me on the spot.

That night Annabelle left the island to go to headquarters in Texas. I knew she had been readying to leave. It had shocked Maylee she had just up and left waking up most of the apartment complex as she bare handedly deconstructed the walls. I had been able to talk to her enough to calm down. Izabella thanked me as she assisted Maylee to heal her broken hands. Sighing I shook my head keeping my distance as I realized Maylee was still in her pajamas. Looking away from the two of them I swore under my breath. She was wearing a black spaghetti strap tank top that hugged her body with shorts that barely covered her ass. Izabella glanced to me as she finished healing Maylee smirking at how difficult a time I was having. After her hands were healed she cracked her knuckles one by one. When she did I had found myself looking at her chest instead turning away again. Maylee frowned probably thinking I just did not want to be here. That was not the case. I was at my wit's end behaving myself. To further torture me Izabella decided to keep us there to teach us the potion she had just used. After that was done I returned to my own apartment finding a letter on my counter. It was from Theo.

***

Your new recruit has arrived at headquarters one week ahead of your time frame. Congratulations for that. However. She has been talking to us about some concerns she has about you siding against us. Meet with us in another week. I will send exact time and location the day of the meeting.

Theo

Crumpling the letter up I felt exhausted flopping onto my couch looking to the clock. There was no way that the meeting they wanted was going to go well. Rubbing my temples I stood going to the stable to see Shadow.

"Why don't we go for a ride around the island? You look exhausted by the way." Shaking my head I knew how bad I must look.

"Sure." As I finished tightening his cinch he tossed his head looking back at me.

"Saddle up Maylee's horse too." Frowning I glanced to the big black gelding as he pinned his ears at me.

"Yeah. Not happening. He hates me." Snorting as he shook his head Shadow walked up to the stall.

"Let him saddle you for Maylee to ride with us."

"Why should I? If she does not like him." Flicking his tail Shadow looked to me for a second.

"It will be good for us all."

"Just this once than." Shadow backed away allowing me to walk the black out to saddle him. I had just finished up when Maylee walked through the door surprised I already had her horse ready.

Using the time Annabelle was gone I tried to stay close to Maylee. She had become more relaxed around me joking around. We would walk the trail to our lessons together before splitting off. She would split off to Izabella's and I walked to the chief's as decided by them since the incident with Kamran. It was nice that we could just idly chat without having to worry about someone interrupting or glaring at us.

As I was walking back to meet up with Maylee I saw Annabelle walking beside her. Feeling my presence she stopped turning to face me instead. The look on her face told me everything. Not only that, but her eyes were black in color as she watched me approach.

"You met with my superiors while you were away?"

"I did. Funny they seemed to dislike you more than I do."

"Annabelle. Listen to me. You have to tell me what your first task is going to be. And what they plan on doing with your sister." Smirking oddly she stood up straight glaring.

"My first task is easy. As far as my sister goes. You do not need to know." Frowning I did not like where this was going.

"I'm supposed to meet with them in a few days. If you don't want to tell me they will."

"My task. Yeah. About that. They want me to report everything you do to them. And if I find you reporting to the council I am to kill you." I could feel my color drain as Maylee stepped in between us when Annabelle drew her sword on me.

"Stop. Both of you! Now what is going on?" Annabelle narrowed her eyes at me more yet as her sister stood there. "Annabelle?" Her jaw working as Maylee turned her back to me.

"Maylee. This does not concern you. Move. Now." Annabelle told her coolly. The tone she used made me go cold again.

"What do you mean it does not concern me? You are about to attack someone with no reason." Annabelle laughed at her sister.

"No reason? That's rich. You totally hate him and you're telling me he is on our side?" Maylee stepped closer to her nodding.

"I know. And I did not hate him. I just did not trust him. You know it is hard for me to trust people. And you know why as well. So do us all a favor. And sheath your sword than you can come back to my place and talk over lunch." Angrily she rolled her eyes but did as her sister asked. I was looking to Izabella as Maylee swung to me crossing her arms. "For my sanity and so you two do not do this again. Please. Just stay away from each other." I was tense to the point Izabella looked about ready to step up but nodded for Maylee to handle it instead.

"Annabelle. Please go with Izabella back to my apartment. I need to speak with Dante. I'll catch up." Izabella nodded taking Annabelle's elbow to make sure she did as she was told.

"Maylee don't" Holding her hand up she stopped me from saying anymore.

"I stopped you both to prevent you both from doing anything stupid that you would regret. I don't know what is going on between the two of you. And you do not owe me an explanation. My sister's battles are her own and I will not interfere as long as she stays level headed. But when she attempts to attack someone that is where I stop her." I wanted to tell her everything but I knew that was not going to happen. Taking a deep breath I tried to steady myself.

"I would tell you Maylee. But I know you would never believe me. Especially since she is your sister and you barely even know me. I get that. Really I do. Thanks." Turning I walked away from her not giving her a chance to say anymore. I felt bad enough for being short with her as my chest ached once again. Dammit. This was crazy. Once I was in my apartment a letter appeared from Theo as promised.

***

Our meeting will take place tonight at the old cemetery where
your father is buried. Be there at 9

248

Theo

G reat. Nine at night their time was only a few hours away here. Knowing that I walked down to the stable to take Shadow with me.

"Where are we going this time?"

"I have to leave the island for a few hours to meet with Theo." Shadow snorted his dislike for the situation.

"When were you informing us of this meeting?" Izabella asked walking in looking angry. Finishing the knot I was working on I turned to her shoving the letter into her hand.

"Now. Before I leave."

"Dante. Stop." Turning she walked up looking around. "You know what may happen today. Be careful."

"They will try to kill me. I will be ready this time." Nodding she allowed me to leave.

Arriving at the cemetery felt foreboding as hell knowing I may end up in this very ground before the end of the night.

"You actually showed up." Rolling my eyes I held my hands out to my sides.

"You expected me to stand you up? Why?" Walking closer Theo looked me over assesingly.

"Well. If you had not shown I would have suspected you had changed sides on us." Scowling I stayed where I was. His tone implied he already knew I had changed.

"Why would I switch now?"

"You have been growing closer to Maylee."

"You told me to so that we would know the extent of her powers."

"Correct of course. But. You are getting attached."

"What are you talking about?" Smirking he walked closer yet.

"Your aura has changed colors Dante. Seems to me you are quite how should I word this. Close but not close enough."

"Theo. What are you saying right now?" Every muscle in my body tightened. My blood began to run cold at his words.

"You have a few options. One is you turn her over to us and you are back in free and clear." Shaking my head I knew that was not going to happen.

"She would never blindly follow me somewhere. Try again." Smirking he walked around some more.

"Option two. Her sister can bring her to us and you are out totally. Should you appear anywhere near any of us we will kill you on sight." Swallowing hard I kept looking for others. "It is only us tonight. Stop acting so nervous Dante. It is very unlike you."

"Things change." He nodded as he stopped in front of me.

"As do minds. You want nothing to do with us. You can stop pretending. I will not kill you tonight. Though if you step foot back here the command is open."

"I'm not turning against you." Theo smirked walking up in front of me stopping as he assessed my words.

"Yes. You are. Stop pretending Dante. Your father never let you lie to us. Nor did he tolerate when you did." I could hardly breathe as we stood toe to toe. My nerves were shot from all of this.

"I'm not trying" Without warning Theo punched me in the jaw hard enough I staggered sideways.

"Stop talking." Shaking his hand he frowned. "I will say one thing. Your dad taught you to take a hit. Your jaw is glass." Standing upright I bit down my growl of anger.

"Theo. I just need more time to gather the information you want. Maylee is just beginning to warm up to me. I can gain a better grasp if you allow me more time." Sighing heavily he gave a single nod.

"You have one week. One week to report back or you are done. Am I clear?"

"Yes sir. Understood. What are your plans for Maylee?"

"You are no longer really one of us Dante. That is not something you need to know. They consider you a traitor already for what you did when you left. So be ready to fight. We are done. We will meet back in another week." Theo walked out not looking back though he looked Shadow over on his way. My heart was pounding in my throat as I quickly mounted up to leave.

"You got lucky Dante."

"I know."

"No. You did not. You thought he was going to kill you."

Once back on the island I felt as though I was dragging my feet. How would I explain this to Izabella? The council had been counting on me for inside information. As we approached the stable I felt someone there. Sliding down from Shadow I sent him in first drawing Guardian before entering. Still unable to see who I was facing I recognized Star burst. Maylee. She looked shocked I had almost ran her through. I had been expecting Annabelle since she wanted me dead. Taking the closest trail to Izabella's I knocked on her door. There was no answer so I sat on the steps on her porch until I heard her walk up an hour or so later. Frowning she stopped in front of me.

"You look like hell. What happened?" Standing up I looked up at her.

"Theo wanted to dismiss me. He allowed me to leave without any attempt to kill me. But he said the others may try even though I'm technically with them yet." Gesturing we go in the house I followed her. I sat in one of the arm chairs. Izabella sat across from me making me look at her.

"You are done than? No more information." Shaking my head I couldn't even look at her.

"No. He wouldn't tell me anything. He just wants more information about how Maylee's powers work." I managed though not very audible. Standing quickly she grabbed my shoulders shaking me slightly.

"Would you snap the hell out of it?" Standing up I pushed her back away from me.

"This gives the damned council every right and reason to have me executed. What do you think is on my mind?" Taking a deep breath she gestured for me to sit back down.

"They are not going to execute you."

"How do you know?" Smirking she looked to her desk as a letter appeared.

"They told me so. The council knew you would not be able to hold that cover long once they found out it was Annabelle who had turned. She had been informing your colleagues there about you talking to me. And hanging around her sister. You are very lucky they did not execute you tonight. The council says you are relieved of your duty and free to train with the others." Swallowing hard I nodded.

"They are going to take Maylee. Theo told me as much while I was there. He wouldn't tell me what for. He wants to meet one more time before I'm officially done." Izabella muttered before walking a little ways.

252

"The council is sending her and Annabelle on a mission tomorrow morning. I will talk to Maylee about a plan to escape in case they try anything."

"Good." Frowning Izabella walked back again.

"What else is on your mind?"

"I don't know. I think I have actually fallen for her." Izabella smiled kneeling in front of me.

"Maylee?" I nodded as she stood again. "Go to your apartment and rest."

"What about"

"She will be fine. Maylee is smart and cunning."

"Alright." As I was walking out the door Izabella stopped me.

"You might want to give her some flowers before she leaves. And apologize for almost killing her for crying out loud." Rolling my eyes I had already planned as much.

"I will." She nodded smirking as I walked down the path to the apartment building. As I walked along I decided to stop by the stable to talk to Shadow. He had told me when I met Maylee on the trail we had been together before. Now I wanted answers. His head shot up as I walked through the door ears flicking back and forth listening.

"You told Izabella about your meeting with Theo?" Nodding I sat on the tack trunk in front of his stall.

"I have questions Shadow. And I was hoping you could answer at least a few of them." He snorted softly resting his head on my shoulder.

"They must be about Maylee." Smirking over my shoulder I nodded.

"Yes. I have been slowly spending more time with her. And maybe I'm crazy but I feel like we have a connection already. Any time I would touch her bare skin like her wrist or hand I

253

felt shocks go through my body. And tonight when I thought Theo was going to execute me. She was all I could think about." I heard him sigh heavily.

"You two were very close before. But it was over two years ago. Your father thought if he kept you two separated after your memories were wiped he was in the clear. But it was not that easy. As close as the two of you were. There were still bits and pieces you remembered. Now. You came to me to ask other questions as well. I cannot answer them all. Is there anything specific you want to know my friend?"

"Actually. Yes. Did I ever tell you what type of flowers she liked?" I heard him make a sound that if human would have been a short laugh.

"You did." With that he informed me exactly what I gave her and the reason why.

Maylee

Once we were over the ocean it did not take long to hit South America. Flying low we had a glimpse of the damage that had been done most recently. There was so much damage that it made me homesick. I feared what home could look like now.

We finished sweeping through before dawn landing in Texas to rest. We spent most of the day wandering the streets of Dallas while the dragons rested up. While we were walking down a more desolate street I had the feeling we were being watched. We looked normal. We had our swords in cover form. It made me feel odd. I had grown used to it at my side when and if needed.

I nudged Annabelle jerking my head toward another street. She was acting nervous. I thought she could feel it too. From behind someone took my arm by the elbow firmly.

"Just keep walking. And don't try anything." My instincts told me to turn and fight. Something else told me to just do as he said. I really wished I had that dagger up my sleeve not down in my boot.

I glanced over at Annabelle. She was just walking with us acting even more nervous. They had not even taken a hold of her. She was walking freely. She *had* flipped sides. This would be a good time to know more than I do about magik. I was escorted into the side door of an abandoned building. Just inside the man relinquished his grip on my arm. There were several dark hooded figures standing in the room as though they had been waiting for us.

"What do you want?" I asked coldly as one of them walked up to me.

"Just to talk." His voice sounded familiar.

"Well, to just talk. You sure forced me into this place." I held my arms out like here. The figure turned to my sister.

"Annabelle. Why is your sister here?" She looked at the floor.

"I was going to ditch her but they caught up with me before I could." He turned away shaking his head.

"No matter. Maybe we can talk her into joining us too?" I was furious at my sister right now as I covered it by laughing.

"Don't count on it." I told him thinking about what Izabella and I had planned. "Well. On second thought. What do you have to say?" He recounted how he and one other had discovered the existence of Theasis. That they worked to bring him back fully restored. How it had failed killing the man who had first attempted it. This man never did tell me his name or the name of the other follower. Just about what had happened and how angry they all were when the son of the man who died ran off leaving them without their rightful leader. That had definitely peaked my interest but he did not say any more about it. I kept thinking back to how Dante had said he had ran from them. It almost had to be him. How Izabella had said he resented his powers because of what he had been forced to do with them.

This man told me how they were building up followers. That was why we had not found very many. I listened intently as I was picking up a lot of information. With an agreement to prove my loyalty they allowed me to leave to go back to the clearing where the dragons were. I did not like this part of the plan but it would be very useful later on.

My task was to find stones of power, like the ones I had. They told me to find the stones and return to the building with them. That they would be in the hills of Tennessee. I left my sister in the clearing as I flew in that direction not taking over forty five minutes to arrive. I sent a message to Izabella about the task. That my sister had indeed flipped sides with proof now. And to be ready when I returned because it was about to turn ugly.

The power of the stones was strong as I landed with a thump on one of the hills. Taking out my own stones beginning with Erde knowing what I had to do.

"Reveal your stones." The ground trembled with the stones rising to the surface. I gathered them placing them in a small bag. There was more than one set here. Out of curiosity I gathered them as well coming up with a clever plan. I also gathered six regular stones, wrote a fake letter and sent it on. I also called on Danny, since he was undead he could get the second set to Izabella without being intercepted. I threw the other set into my backpack climbing back onto Marlo flying back to the clearing in Texas.

As I walked into the building something did not feel right. Annabelle had been gone when I landed. Not a good sign as I continued walking into the building. I entered the door immediately grabbed by the throat and shoved against the wall with a dark blade against my rib cage.

"Don't move too fast. I might make a mess out of you." This man said almost laughing as I scowled. He must have been one of the followers from earlier.

"What the hell are you doing?" I asked angrily while the figure from earlier walked closer to me.

"You betrayed us." I just looked at him shaking my head.

"No. I didn't. The council tracks everything I do. They had asked me what I was doing. I told them. And sent fake stones to make them think I was doing it for them." The sword against my ribs began to cut into my skin. I wanted to yell in pain but refrained from doing so. "Just check the stones you intercepted. The ones that I sent to them. Than check my backpack for the real ones." He turned picking up my backpack taking the stones out comparing them to the ones they had from the fake letter I had sent.

"They are ordinary stones." I nodded at him. The one who had me against the wall released me removing his sword from my ribs. I could see blood on his blade, it had cut me. I just couldn't feel it right now. He jiggled the real stones in the palm of his hand looking up at me.

"I think we have a new ally on our hands. I like the way you think. You are much better than your sister. She failed at her task." I had wondered what her task had been. Obviously I had not been a part of it.

"I'm glad to hear I could be of service. Just out of curiosity though. What was her task?" He turned around walking toward a table to put the stones down.

"That is between her and our superior." Well that didn't work.

"What would you like me to do now?" He was silent turning back to me.

"Go back to your island. Tell them you found the stones but were attacked before sending them and you lost them." I smirked at his plan because I wasn't playing for much longer. I had a plan of my own.

"That sounds good. Only one problem."

"What's that?" He asked curiously.

"It would not look good if I was caught and walked away without a scratch on me." He considered that for a moment.

"You are right of course." Giving a nod to his men they began advancing onto me. My pleasure I thought as I pulled out Star burst erupting into full form. It startled the first guy who had started after me for a moment before our blades met in the air. It did not take long before I defeated him sprinting to the table to grab the stones headed for the exit. The rest of them chased after me. The hooded figure yelled at them to not kill me but capture alive. I had nearly paused when I heard him yell that to his men. Why did they need me alive? I figured they were going to kill me outright. He had to have known I had no intention of siding with them. I finally made it out the door running back to the clearing. Pretty sure that was the fastest I had ever ran. Sure glad Izabella had pushed me so hard in training. Hopping onto Marlo we flew back to the island. Once over the ocean I sent another message to Izabella telling her I was on my way back.

Once over the island I flew to the mountain where unfortunately my sister had beat me standing at the top. With her dragon Albay, the chief, Kamran, and Izabella. Well, I'm crazy not stupid. I flew over them landing by the stable instead knowing it would take them at least a few minutes to run there. Running into the stable I flung Rocki's stall door open walking him out. I hopped on running him down the trails with no saddle and no bridle. Instead of sticking to the trail we cut into the thick forest stopping in a small clearing after a while. Who ever came in after me would have to walk in on foot so that I had plenty of warning.

It did not take long before I could hear the rustling of trees. Someone was coming. My hand jumped to the hilt of my sword ready for when whoever it was walked out if I needed it. Within moments Izabella appeared through a small grove of trees looking worried. I still did not let my guard down. After all, Annabelle could have followed her in here. She looked me over in a hard measuring way.

"What happened to you?" I looked up at her from where I had just sat down to catch my breath holding my ribs.

"I barely escaped."

"I knew you were coming back. You sent me the message. Did you manage to retrieve the stones or did you have to run for it?" Reaching into my backpack I pulled out the second set I had found.

"Right here. You can imagine how irate they were when I stole them and ran." She took the stones examining them for a moment.

"So how much information did you obtain?" I grew wide eyed.

"A lot. At least I think it's a lot. More than I knew anyways. I'm sure you probably knew. Don't go far with those. I want to keep them safe. They're my sister's stones and frankly I don't want her to have them." Izabella nodded shoving them back into my bag for me.

"Okay. So what kind of forces do they have?" She asked.

"Anyone and everyone. They have descendants that we could not find. That's a lot of power against us. Not all of them have powers. None of them did anything against me except for a hand around my throat and a sword to my ribs." And at that exact moment my ribs felt like they had been laced open. Where I had been holding them blood was coming out from under my fingers. It was a black oozy blood. Not thick and red.

I knew that sword had been a cursed blade. Looking up to Izabella everything was beginning to go black. My body felt limp as I slumped over on a fallen tree I had been sitting on. There was nothing but blackness as I could not feel anything. So was I dead? Or cursed? Either way. I was in bad shape.

***

I found myself drifting around in a limbo between life and death. Must be a coma of some kind. Yet, I was still able to think clearly. Still aware of my surroundings so I knew that I couldn't be dead. Izabella and I knew we would have to trick my sister into thinking I was dead and out of the way. For the time being I am out of the way. I had warned Izabella that I thought they were trying to take Dante out as well. That way they could move him away from my sister. I was worried they had given her more power than she could handle instructing her to kill him. That had to have been her first task that she had failed. She couldn't do it. Annabelle was not the killing type.

I could sense Rocki and Danny near grazing quietly. Izabella placed them there to protect me. Mostly to keep my sister away. In fact they had almost attacked her. I was rather amused. Especially when I heard what Danny had been thinking when he charged after her.

I could feel the presence of two people walking closer. Not sure exactly who it was I sent the boys to find out for me. I could hear Izabella talking rapidly. She sounded like she was panicking. That was not good. Next I heard a yell. It must have been Dante from Danny running after him.

"Danny no. He may be the only one who can help me now." Danny snorted angrily but relented since I could hear them walking closer.

"Is she dead?" I heard Dante ask. His voice was strained as I had known for some time that he cared about me. Izabella had been pushing me to give him a chance. After my last relationship before I came here I was too afraid to invest in someone when I had a job to do.

"No, but as close as you want to be. She is actually in between life and death. Like a coma. I have tried to heal her. Nothing has worked. I have tried everything that I know on her." I could hear the sadness in her voice pleading for me to wake up. I felt someone standing close. My chest tightened again. Dante. He was the reason that had been happening.

"Maylee please. Fight this. Come back to us. We need you." His voice was so strained as he spoke it almost made me hurt. "I need you." He whispered taking my hand into his. As I read his emotions he had fallen in love with me. That. I had not expected. That seemed different from interested in dating to actually being in love. The question I had to ask myself was could I love him? Oddly enough I felt calm about the thought of us in a relationship and frankly that scared me even more. I knew nothing about him except of what I had come to know on the island. I guess I should at least try after this was all over. Because I had consciously used my powers Dante could sense I was aware of him there. That actually gave me an idea which I conveyed out to Rocki.

"Tell him to use his powers. I think they will work where Izabella's would not." I heard him relay the message. Dante stepped away from my side tensing.

"No. I can't." He said darkly sounding angry at me for even thinking it.

"If she believes you can do it than at least try!" Izabella yelled.

"Dammit I can't!" He yelled back his voice deeper than usual.

"Why not? I know you can do it. You choose not to." I heard him take a long deep breath before answering.

"Bad things happen when I use them. People are hurt or killed. That you know as well." He must have been a mercenary

262

for them. He really did not want to use his powers. That was a strong feeling from him. I heard one of them walk a few steps. I assumed it was Izabella since it did not feel like he had moved at all.

"This time is different. You would be helping. Saving her life. Now. Use them!" She had used a convincing voice yelling at him angrily. I could tell he did not want to do it.

"Dammit." I heard him say under his breath.

"If you care about her as much as you have confided to me these last two weeks you will do it."

"You know I did not lie about that. I do feel that way about her. But I know she has no feelings for me." I heard Izabella snicker.

"She has you fooled. Keeping her distance so that she is not hurt is more like it." Yeah. Look where we are now I thought as I overheard them. "Now, heal her." Growling in anger I felt his hands take mine. Dante took a deep breath before he spoke.

"Feuer y Feuer, Erde y Erde, Heilen Unbregrenzte macht, macht y Heilen." He let go after a moment. I started to feel warm. It came in slow waves. Like my body was warming back to normal temperature. I was finally able to open my eyes looking around wildly breathing like I had fallen from ten feet in the air. I was choking while trying to breathe turning to my side. My breathing evened out after a few moments. I sat up straight looking over to the two of them. Izabella looked astounded.

"It worked." She said wondrously. Dante was still standing beside me when I lifted my right hand looked over at him curling my hand up I hit him with a closed fist full in the face. He stepped back fast rubbing his jaw looking pissed off.

"What the hell was that for?!" He asked angrily still holding his jaw.

"For not doing that sooner. Thanks anyways." I swung my legs over the edge of the tree I had been laying on. Izabella was trying to not laugh at what I had done barely suppressing a smile.

"Well. You're welcome. I guess. Did you have to hit me so damn hard? Dammit that hurt!" I raised my eyebrows at him.

"You're not knocked out are you?" He considered for a moment.

"So what now?" I reached down to my boot where my dagger was sheathed pulling it out. He saw the glint of silver backing away hands held up in surrender.

"Whoa! I just saved your ass! Now you're going to kill me?" I just looked at him with narrowed eyes like you're stupid. Izabella laid a hand on his shoulder.

"She has to use that blade to heal the cut. Kamran worked many magikal properties into it when he created it." He looked angrier than he had after I sucker punched him.

"Kamran gave that to you?" His voice with barely concealed rage.

"Yes." I said so quietly Izabella sat beside me.

"Why would he give you something like that?" Dante's anger was barely under control as I looked up at him.

"He wanted me to have more than one weapon in case I was captured. Which I was. And I almost didn't make it back." I whispered the last part knowing how angry Dante was that Kamran had given me something so valuable.

Tears running down my face I lifted my shirt to trace the wound. Dante grabbed my wrist stopping me so that I looked up at him.

"I'm not angry at you Maylee." His eyes searched mine as he stood close enough he was almost touching me.

"You should be." Confused he frowned.

"Because you punched me? Honestly I probably deserved it."

"No." I wanted to keep talking but was beginning to feel woozy. Dante leaned closer than away looking to Izabella.

"We will have to talk when you feel more up to it."

"Thanks." I told him stiffly slightly irritated though I was not sure why. Izabella nodded to me as he removed his hand from my dagger to allow me to trace the cut. It was black and oozy as I placed the dagger tip in the cut tracing it. It hurt like I cannot even describe. There was no pain like it. When I was finished there was only a thin white scar where the cut had been. I looked at the dagger after the last trace as it lit up white. After that I blacked out completely unconscious.

I woke with a start trying to sit up. Izabella was over me in an instant pushing my shoulders back down.

"Stay in bed. You are going to be weak. Even with your healing potion it will take several days to recover from an injury like the one you suffered." I finally relaxed back onto the pillows around me. Looking around I was in a bed. The place looked familiar enough.

"Where am I?" I asked her when it was bothering me. Izabella walked back into the room mixing something in a medium sized bowl looking up at me.

"Dante's apartment." She said flatly. I sat up straight in a hurry.

"What!" I yelled. "My sister is down the hall!" She walked closer to me.

"Calm down Maylee. She's not there anymore." That had my attention.

"Wait. What?" I asked confused.

"She moved down to a cabin by the training field yesterday. We faked your funeral while you were indisposed." Well. I guess that explained a lot. Dante walked in frowning when he saw that I was talking to Izabella. He had to have heard me yelling. If not than he was hard of hearing.

"About time sleeping beauty." He walked up to the end of the bed smirking at me. I just stared at him. Yeah. I bet he was happy all right. I was in his apartment. And in his bed.

"How long have I been out exactly?" I asked out of curiosity.

"Around four days I believe it has been." He was holding a cup of something steaming hot in his hands. Coffee maybe?

"Could I get some of that?" I asked as nicely as I could as he looked down at me apprehensively.

"Are you going to sucker punch me again?" I leaned against the pillows behind me crossing my arms.

"You deserved it." I said shortly. He thought it over for a minute.

"Maybe. What do you take in your coffee than?" I sat up straight again as I told him. Minutes later he was back with it.

It was another three days to heal further. When ever I had tried to stand up I would nearly fall upon standing. One morning I had woke from a nightmare screaming in a cold sweat. Dante ran in to see what was going on as I tried to calm down.

"Sorry." I apologized gathering my knees to my chest. "It was just a nightmare. I'm fine." Frowning he sat beside me on the bed laying his hand on my back.

"From what?" His voice had been so gentle I broke open.

"My attack. From when I was attacked. It happened so fast. I feel like I should have been able to defend myself better. That I didn't do everything possible." It was what my nightmares were always about anymore.

"I'm sorry about your nightmares. That you were attacked." He pushed my hair back as it was in my face. My heart was thumping so damn hard at his touch I hated it for betraying me. "I need to go." As I tried to stand I collapsed. Dante caught me picking me up laying me back in his bed.

"You are fine right where you are. Give yourself time to heal. Okay?" Shaking I nodded turning to my side to try and sleep. When I woke later that morning he was sleeping in a chair beside the bed. It made me smile that he had done it to put me more at ease.

On the fourth morning I was finally able to walk around on my own. Neither Izabella or Dante were awake just yet. I found my backpack taking out some clean clothes heading to the bathroom to take my first shower in nearly a week.

It felt great. I didn't realize just how much dirt I'd had on me from all the traveling. On top of that I had stayed in the forest for a day or two. I pulled on my clean clothes, brushing my hair before walking out of the bathroom almost into Dante.

"Wow! You look human again." He remarked smartly with a grin. I put one hand on my hip.

"Shut up and hand over my coffee." Smiling he handed one of the cups he was holding to me.

"Someone's feeling better." I walked past him into the living room area sitting on the couch. "At least you're not trying to knock me out again." I looked up from taking a drink smirking.

"Not yet. Give me another day or two."

"Figures." I kept my smile grabbing a paper skimming through it. He had watched me for the last few minutes. It was beginning to get on my nerves. I looked up over the paper.

"What?" I asked snippily he shook his head sitting back in his chair.

"Nothing. Nothing at all." I just glared at him irritated. Yeah right.

"Whatever." I said looking back to my paper. It did not take long to finish reading placing it back on the table. Grabbing my backpack once again I began checking the pockets for my stones. They weren't there. I went through every single pocket.

"What are you looking for?" Dante finally asked.

"My stones." I told him still looking through my bag not caring about what he seen.

"Yeah. About them." He said cautiously as I turned around fast.

"What happened to them?!" I was furious. Rubbing the back of his neck he walked to the counter.

"When I brought you back a few days ago they dissolved absorbing into you. Except this one." He held up the stone. It was the one that was black with white veins running through it. That was the stone that controlled the dead. "What does this one do?" I took it holding it up to examine it as if I had not seen it in forever.

"It allows me to control the dead. Or ghosts." Nodding comprehendingly.

"That's how you surrounded Izabella on the ship." He said more to himself than to me.

"I have only used it twice." He looked up at me like I wasn't supposed to have heard him.

"Really?"

"Yeah. You were with me both times. The ship like you said. And when we were on the trails I called for Danny."

"Your ghost horse." I still wasn't keen on the idea of being around him. On the other hand he had saved my life and truly had feelings for me. I made a face at him sitting back down on the couch.

"I remember too." Came Izabella's voice startling me as I reached for my sword. My hand on the hilt when I realized who it was. She held up her hands in surrender.

"Easy Maylee."

"God you scared me. I didn't even hear the door open." Izabella shook her head.

"No. You did not. I have other ways of traveling around besides walking." I sat back down as she sat beside me looking me over in a quick glance. "Speaking of traveling. I wanted to talk to both of you." She looked from me to Dante as if we did not understand.

"You both need to leave the island for a while." I nodded as it made sense to me with what was happening.

"Where do we go?"

"Place to place. Stay moving. Stay in contact wit me." She said indifferently.

"Will we sail or fly?" I wanted it all narrowed down.

"Fly. It is much more efficient and faster than your horses. Though I am going to suggest you go to Texas first." Bad idea to mention that for both of us evidently.

"What?!" Both myself and Dante yelled at the same time looking at each other.

"We can't go there. They will be looking for me as soon as they know I'm in the area!" He was close to panicking. I now realized he truly had switched sides.

"And I'm supposed to be dead." Izabella looked withdrawn and tired at our outbursts.

"Yes, I know." She stood up walking around for a minute. "Dante when you left you left your stones. Correct?" She asked Dante. He looked down to the floor.

"No, I didn't. I've had full powers since I ascended at sixteen. As for my items. I only had one besides my sword and

269

I still have him." He looked up at me. "At least thanks to you Maylee." I looked at him confused.

"What?"

"Shadow" He said simply. "He is a shape shifting kelpie. On command he will protect me at all cost. He can turn into almost anything. Sometimes he does it automatically and I don't have to say anything." Hmm, well that was most definitely interesting.

"He told me he was the one who saw my attack. I had not seen him anywhere. But when I regained consciousness once I heard a dog whine. That was when I heard Shadow tell me Izabella was on her way." Smirking Dante nodded.

"Wolf. He told he saw the moment your attacker kicked you. You could of told me about your attack the morning I came to check on you." My body jolted when I realized he was angry I had not told him myself.

"And you should have told me you knew my sister had changed sides but you didn't." He scoffed shaking his head.

"You would never have believed me." Raising his eyebrows he looked to Izabella hesitantly.

"Exactly. Neither would you." Crossing his arms over his chest he tilted his head for a moment.

"Actually. I would have. I've been here before. I didn't know there was anyone here who would attack someone." I laughed harshly.

"Seriously?" Wearily he sat on the arm of his couch.

"In my defense I figured you would be fine. With your powers and reflexes I never would have thought" Stopping he looked away from me angry with himself.

"Stop. Both of you." Izabella intervened looking from one to the other. As I was about to say something she shot me a look. Rubbing her temples she stood looking between us.

"I swear. If the two of you do not just give in I will have to take action." I felt my blood drain from my face.

"What do you mean?" She growled making me stand up next to her doing the same to Dante.

"What I mean is that you two have a very strong connection. You have feelings for each other and refuse to acknowledge it. Maylee." She said pointedly. Pinching the bridge of my nose this was growing old from her.

"I have enough going on right now. I don't want to have to worry about" She put her hand up for me to stop talking. Dante was walking out of the apartment with big strides. My chest began to ache sharply. Izabella held my shoulders looking into my eyes.

"This is not something he expected Maylee. He did not even want to be here. I made him leave with us the day he ran into us." Shaking my head I could barely grasp what she was telling me.

"Why?" She glanced over her shoulder to the door.

"Because if I had not made him he was going back to the other side. And they would have killed him the moment he stepped foot on their property. He wanted to go back for that reason. He told me he had no reason to live. What I showed him that day gave him a sliver of light to hold on."

"And what was that?" She smiled wide.

"A future with many possibilities." I nodded turning from her yanking workout clothes from my backpack. "You are not running if that is what you were thinking." Rolling my eyes I turned to her.

"I have to do something. I have too much pent up energy. Not to mention I pissed him off without even meaning to." Sighing she grabbed the clothes away from me steering me to the kitchen.

"He is not angry with you Maylee. He wants to be close to you. And you are pushing him away. Even if you do not mean to."

"What else am I supposed to do!" I snapped feeling on edge. "I'm working my ass off to fight. I am learning all these damn potions and ingredients with their damn properties so I know what they will do for me. On top of that I have to learn to use these damned powers I have and how to control them to help win a war that is only months away!" Breathing hard I sat down feeling lightheaded. Standing in front of me Izabella gripped my shoulders as sobs wracked my body.

"It is a lot. Especially for you when you have not had any kind of experience with these things. I apologize for how unfair it is. That we have such high expectations. But I also know if we can fly over these last few bumps in the road you will be fine." I laughed sarcastically feeling ready to lose it.

"Bumps in the road? That's what my attack was? Or my sister turning against me? Or"

"Enough." She snapped at me. "Just go rest in bed. I will tell you where you are both going tomorrow morning." With that she stomped out leaving me alone in someone else's place. Shaking yet I laid in the bed attempting sleep.

The bed was warm as it had taken some time for me to fall asleep. Waking more I realized it was that warm because Dante was sleeping beside me. My heart threatened to leap from my chest as I realized I had been curled up around him and him to me. I did not know what to do as I attempted to sit up only to realize I was still very tired. Yet my adrenaline was thrumming enough I was wide awake. Without another thought I reached for my sword in its jackknife form flipping it out grabbing him by the front of his shirt holding it to his throat.

"What the hell are you doing?" He jolted realizing my knife was at his throat though he did not panic.

"Easy. Take your knife away and I will move. Okay?" Breathing hard I sat back watching him carefully until he was standing.

"What gave you the idea that you could just climb into bed with me? I am not" Without warning he grabbed the knife from my hand throwing it into the door casing without even looking. It sank halfway down the blade.

"Calm your ass down. I was trying to do you a favor. It did work after all." Scowling I stood from the bed crossing my arms.

"What are you talking about?" Exasperated he shook his head indicating the bed.

"You were having nightmares again." He told me quietly. Quickly he walked in front of me as I had began to relax. Shaking my head I turned to walk out of the room but not before he gripped my wrist gently. "Maylee, just stop. Please. I promise I will not do anything to you. I would never hurt you. And I will not take advantage of you." That I knew to be true. Shaking slightly I knew our connection was growing stronger the more time we were close like this. "Look I'm sorry if I upset you. I just want to help you." Shaking my head I turned to face him crossing my arms over my chest holding my elbows.

"No. You do not have to apologize. I should be apologizing for pulling my knife on you. It was a reflex. And I should never have done it. I'm sorry." He smirked taking my hand looking at the lines.

"And no matter what Izabella tells you. You owe me nothing. I owe you. Got it?" Frowning I did not understand that.

"What do you mean?"

"Well. You saved Shadow for me on the ship. And you saved me the day your sister returned. Her mission was to kill

273

me and take you back with her. She failed at both because of you." I was lost for words and had no idea how to act if we dated. This just seemed awkward. Sighing I turned to walk out only to be stopped again as he gripped my elbow.

"Dante. I am not an easy person to get along with. You deserve someone better." Sliding his hand down my arm he gripped my hand tight pulling me back to face him looking fierce.

"No. Look at me." Taking my face in his hands he made me look as I shifted to try and move startled by the fact he so easily could make me stay in place. "Stop. Why do you think that?" Tears of anger welled in my eyes thinking of when I was attacked.

"I have not had any luck with this kind of shit. Alright? Until I get to know you better that is all I am telling you." He sighed bowing his head nodding.

"Okay. You need to go back to bed. I'll go back to the couch."

"No. I'm awake now. It's fine." I walked to the kitchen picking up my back pack closing it up walking to the front door. "I'm leaving. I need to go somewhere I can't hurt anyone. Or mess everything up." He followed quickly grabbing my elbow before I could take another step.

"Maylee no." Before I could turn the handle he had my backpack in his hand tossing it aside. Taking my hand he pulled me away from the door. His hands cupped my face holding it looking at me as I shook my head. "Stop this. You are not hurting anyone. Look at me." Without a second thought I pushed him away hard as my adrenaline had kicked in. As soon as he had touched my face my flight instinct kicked in. Barely keeping his balance he stood walking up to me again. This time my hand drew back slapping him hard enough to cause his head

274

to whip sideways. Breathing hard it took a moment to realize what I had done. Slowly he looked up at me with burning eyes. I knew that look. He was pissed off as hell I had struck him. "I'm sorry." Turning back to the door I leaned against it ready to open it to leave. "I'm sorry Dante. This is why I can't be with anyone." A tear made its way down my face as I finally stood to open the door. Before I had the chance his hand wrapped around my wrist gently.

"Maylee. Please just stop." Pulling me around to face him I looked to the floor unable to meet his eyes. Slowly his other hand came up under my chin to make me look at him. "I know you didn't mean it." Any anger from what I had done was completely gone.

"You have no idea how bad I feel right now." Smirking in his annoying as hell way he nodded.

"I honestly had not expected it either. Look at me." Before I knew it I could feel his warm soft lips on mine. We connected. I wanted to kiss him as he tilted my head back for a deeper kiss. My hands rested on his sides as we kissed in front of the door. Pulling away slightly he kissed down my neck and collar bone moving one hand from my face to my shoulder pulling me closer. Once back to my lips we kissed deeply again. The ache in my chest melted. Breathing hard he stopped touching foreheads one hand on my face the other on my hip rubbing my bare skin under my tank top.

"I shouldn't have done that." His breath was ragged as he shook his head not letting go of me. I could feel myself ready to sob as we stood together like that. Our connection was so strong. Slowly I reached for his hand on my hip entwining our fingers together.

"Why not?" Looking up into his eyes I could see a lot of hidden anger, hurt and anguish.

275

"Maylee. Look." Pausing he was trying to find the words he was looking for. "I have admired you since the day we met. But I knew you hated me. So I stayed away." Frowning I gripped his hand tighter pulling him a step closer.

"We had this discussion Dante. I never hated you." He scoffed shrugging still not looking at me.

"I know we have. But when we were traveling to Florida you glared at me whenever I would look at you. I just figured it was because you hated me." Smirking I knew he was keeping me talking so I would not leave. And it was working.

"There are very few people I would waste hate on Dante. You are not on that list. It was never hate. I have a very difficult time trusting people. And I have legit reasons for that." Nodding he brought me up against him by my hips our hands still together.

"I figured that out once we were here and I talked to you more. The more we talked the better you were." I kept looking at his face to catch him lying. It never came to pass. He was being totally truthful right now.

"Why me? Don't you have a girlfriend back home?" He laughed sounding humored.

"No. No girlfriends back home. Why are you asking?" Confused I shook my head looking away. After what we had just been doing. Kissing so intensely. Now I questioned him. Taking my face in his hands he made me look at him.

"Maylee. I know we don't know each other that well. But in the time we have been around each other I have" He stopped as he thought of what to say.

"You shouldn't." Scowling he looked at me evenly.

"Shouldn't what?"

"Care about me. Not at all. I know that I am just a means to an end. The one they need to win the war right? So that means

I will die before it is all done with. You shouldn't waste your time on me." Chuckling he smirked in that way that annoyed me again before pulling me tightly against him.

"I can waste my time on whoever I wish to waste it on. And as far as I'm concerned. You are not anyone I would pass up in a hundred lifetimes. I do care about you. I want to be with you like this. I won't do anything more unless you want to." My whole body trembled at what he was laying before me. If nothing else this could be a small copse of happiness before I die in the war. Nodding at his words I replied.

"I'm willing to give it a shot." Without another word we were kissing deeply again. Suddenly he lifted me up carrying me to the bedroom. Once on the bed we felt each other kissing with so much intensity. It felt as though our bodies were meant to fit together this way which felt odd but familiar. Laying over me he was smiling wider than I had seen since I had known him.

"What is it?" He seemed out of breath as we lay there.

"I want you more than anything. Especially since we are both ready."

"I am sensing a but in there." Smirking he shook his head.

"No. I just know everything you have been through already. I want to make sure you are okay." Laughing I bit his lip before pulling back.

"If I wasn't we wouldn't be at this point." Frowning I slid back slightly. "That's not it. You're afraid I might lose control of my powers." Sighing he pulled me back to him.

"It's legit reasoning." I nodded in agreement.

"It is. But I know how to handle it. Unless you have changed your mind?" Shock flashed in his eyes as he pulled me against him before kissing me deeply pushing me back down onto the bed.

"Oh no. I want you." He managed pulling back. My hips came off the bed again wanting him. I knew we were worked up. He had my hands over my head as I arched up to him. Out of no where I was having flashbacks. I couldn't separate them from what I was doing no matter how hard I tried. And finally I couldn't do it anymore.

"Stop!" I had not said it out loud but I had screamed it in my head. He stopped sitting back away from me looking concerned. Taking my face in his hands he searched my eyes.

"I promise I will not hurt you. I love you Maylee." I couldn't breathe as what he said sunk in. Love. God no. I had feelings for him but I had not faced what they actually were just yet. I had been keeping it all pushed down to focus on the war.

"I know you would never hurt me Dante." Looking away from him I had felt so alive with him only moments before. But suddenly what had been done to me had come back out of no where. "I just. I just can't. I'm so sorry." Before I could move he stopped me gripping my wrist gently.

"You have nothing to be sorry for Maylee. We were just carried away and went further than either of us had planned. It's okay. Just stay with me. Please?" Looking to him I nodded lying back in bed.

"That's not what my problem was Dante." Holding my forehead I rubbed with my hands feeling the tears in my eyes as I looked up at him. Realizing I was down to my bra and panties I wrapped the bed sheet around me. "I had flashbacks to my attack." Sliding closer he wrapped his arms around me holding me tightly.

"Your attack?" He asked trying to figure it out. It finally occurred to me Izabella had probably not told him everything.

"Yes." Frowning he sat up looking at me.

"What do you mean?"

"I don't want to talk about it. Please. I wish I could change what happened."

"That's okay. Just relax and try to sleep. I will protect you from now on." Holding each other we slowly drifted to sleep.

When I woke up Dante was sitting up talking to Izabella as quietly as possible.

"It just happened. I had not meant for us to go that far. She freaked out. I feel like shit for making her feel that way."

"I am sure she will be fine. Just try to take it slower next time. You have to remember she was only attacked two weeks ago."

"I know. I keep forgetting. As guarded as she keeps herself I was surprised she even let me kiss her. And I said something I should not have as well."

"And that would be what?"

"I told her I loved her."

"Why is that bad?"

"Izabella. You didn't see the look on her face. I should never have said anything." Slowly I rolled to my back stretching out looking over to them.

"What time is it?" Izabella jerked her head at Dante. Barely glancing back he nodded leaving the room. "What did I do?" My friend looked at me as I imagined a mother would look at her child when they had been injured and wanted to know if they were in trouble. Sitting beside me she looked straight at me knowingly.

"You did not do anything Maylee. Do not look and sound so worried. You never cared before." Sighing I stood to walk to the bathroom barely able to stand she helped me there and back before we continued the conversation.

"He's angry with me. Isn't he?" Izabella laughed.

"No. I do not think he ever could be angry with you. He feels terrible about last night." Crossing my arms I shivered involuntarily.

"It wasn't his fault. Not at all. I shouldn't have reacted the way I did. I told him that."

"Okay. What happened? He told me *it* happened too fast. And neither of you have told me what *it* actually was." Feeling ashamed of the way I acted I could not even look at her as I told her.

"I tried to leave yesterday after I woke up. He had came back after you left. When I woke up he was in bed with me. I was curled up around him. He told me I had been screaming in my sleep. That I was having nightmares again. So he stayed with me to make sure I was okay." Turning I picked up the blanket wrapping it around my shoulders feeling cold.

"Maylee. What happened?" Nodding I looked at the floor.

"I pulled my knife on him. He kept his cool. I sure as hell didn't. So I tried to leave. He stopped me. I pushed him away to leave anyway. When he stepped in front of me I slapped him. I felt horrible. He didn't deserve it. I certainly do not deserve him as patient as he was. I told him he deserved better." Pausing I finally looked up at Izabella. She was thinking as I spoke looking to me when I stopped.

"Why would you tell him that? That boy loves you. I do not know how you cannot see that. He would do damn near anything for you." I felt tears build in my eyes as I nodded.

"I know he does. And I do not deserve to be loved by him. Or any man. I know I'm damaged goods because of what has happened to me. The nightmares I have are of my attack happening again and again. I grabbed my bag and tried to leave." Pausing again I knew the look on her face as she wanted to interrupt but decided against it as I continued. "He stopped me taking my bag away and we kissed. We had an instant connection. I had never felt anything that intense. And we were so close to having sex. And I wanted to be with him. He even paused to make sure that was what I had wanted. But out of no where. Absolutely no where. Images from my attack played in my head and I freaked out." I held my head in my hands. "He was really great about it. Stopped instantly. Still wanted me to stay with him. But I can't Izabella. I can't be with him. Not when those images come back to me like that." I heard her sigh sitting back in her chair stretching out.

"When I said the two of you were going to be the death of me. I meant it." Standing from the chair she kneeled in front of me smiling genuinely. "It is difficult for me to see you both in so much pain over the same thing. To give you both advice when all you need to do is talk to each other and work it out." Shaking my head I felt angry at her for suggesting we talk it out. I had told him I would die. That he should not bother with me. When he still wanted to be with me I felt hope. Now I was just angry again.

"I can't deal with this right now. Send me away for training. I don't care where." Making an impatient sound she stood up.

"You have to deal with it no matter what eventually. When I send you away for training, he will be with you. Get over it and stop feeling sorry for yourself." With that she walked out. I heard her snap at Dante before she left as well. Knowing I was the center of both their anger I stood pulling on my clothes walking out of the bedroom. Dante was in the bathroom when I grabbed my bag walking out the door without saying a word to him.

"Where the hell do you think you are going?" I heard Dante's voice behind me as I was about to walk out into the street from the apartment building.

281

"Away from here. Anywhere to be alone because evidently that is what is best for me." My voice had more anger behind it than I had intended towards him.

"Because of me. Because of what happened last night." Angrily I turned to face him.

"No. Because of my attack. That had nothing to do with you. What I am going through right now has nothing to do with you Dante. Honestly. Maybe eventually we will be able to be together. Just. Not now. I'm sorry." Turning I walked to the stable each stride growing longer. I could not stay here. Everywhere I looked I was reminded of my sister's betrayal. I was a mess. Working through that was not fair to Dante.

Once there I sat on my tack trunk in front of Rocki's stall with my head in my hands.

"What is it Maylee?" Rocki asked draping his head over his stall door. Looking at him over my shoulder I shook my head.

"I have to leave. I can't. I can't stay." Rocki snorted looking up sharply. Sighing I knew it had to be Dante here to stop me. Only for Shadow to walk up in front of me softly nosing my shoulder.

"No Maylee. I know you feel overwhelmed. The last thing you should do is isolate yourself. You have friends who will help." Shaking my head I stroked his soft nose with tears in my eyes.

"Friends. Everyone thinks I am dead Shadow. Except Izabella and your owner. Just sitting in the stable right now I am jeopardizing my own life." I saw a flash of light looking up. Shadow was gone. In his place was a large black german shepherd. Frowning I sat back before reaching out to pet his head. Jumping up beside me he laid down resting his head on my lap.

"It is still me Maylee." Smirking I nodded.

"It was you that kept me warm until Izabella found me the night of my attack." Sitting up he kissed my face before jumping down.

"Yes." Closing my eyes I stroked his ears. "He knows how badly hurt you were. Dante is my charge to protect. I can choose to protect someone besides him if I feel they need it."

"Did you follow me the night of my attack?"

"No. I was on my way to the stable when I heard you scream. I flew down the trail. At first I could not find you. When I finally did find you were barely alive. I contacted Dante to send Izabella. He did not know who I was protecting." Nodding he whined.

"Thank you Shadow. I owe you." Sneezing he was a horse again in a flash.

"No. I was protecting you from harm. You saved my life on the ship on our way here. You are my charge just as much as Dante is now." My stomach clenched thinking about him. "He loves you Maylee. Nothing you say to him will drive him away." Breathing out hard I shook my head.

"I can't be near him Shadow. There is a lot about me you do not know. I have a past. This attack. Was not the first time I have been hurt like that." In another flash he was a dog again jumping up beside me lying down his head on my lap.

"I am sorry Maylee. I did not know."

"I know you didn't. I am not using that as an excuse to stay away from Dante. I wanted you to know so you know why I do not feel I can stay with him." Sighing he hopped down sitting in front of me with his ears down.

"I know you feel that way. So I will tell you an uncomfortable truth. You two need each other." Closing my eyes I nodded.

"I understand. Just not right now." Standing I picked up my backpack.

"Maylee. You have to stay. You are not fully recovered. Please. Return to the apartment. Just talk to him." Pressing my lip into a line I nodded before walking to leave the stable. At the entrance Dante stood leaning against the doorway with his arms crossed over his chest. How long had he been there? What all did he hear? Glancing back to Shadow he nodded.

"What did you tell him?"

"Nothing about our conversation just now." Frowning he looked between the two of us. In a flash of light Shadow was a horse again walking up to the two of us. Dante sighed standing up straight blocking me from leaving.

"I can't let you leave. Not like this." Rolling my eyes I stepped around him only for him to step in my way again.

"Dante. What do you want?" Smirking he stood inches from me causing a shiver to travel down my spine.

"There are many things I want." I swallowed hard looking away.

"Not with" He placed a finger over my lips to hush me. Closing my eyes I attempted to walk around him again. His hand gripped my wrist hard stopping me from walking away.

"Maylee stop. For both our sanity. Please. We need to stay together." Taking his hand away he looked to the trail for a moment.

"Dante. You know nothing about me. Just what you have seen since we have been here. The few moments we have spoke. Please. Let me leave." Sighing he stepped closer grabbing my backpack pulling me back into the stable around the corner of the door against the wall. His hands rested on either side of me his body not allowing me to move. My body began to shake. I was pushing it from my recovery from the mission. Frowning Dante realized it laying a hand on my side to support me.

"I would go crazy if I didn't know where you were. You can't tell me you would not be the same way." Our connection was too strong to stay away from each other for long. I could feel it more all the time.

"I can't. What are we supposed to do?" He smirked stepping closer taking my hand entwining it with his.

"We are going to stay together. Fight as we need to. We will have each other's backs. We can be whatever you want." I chuckled as his hand came up to cup my cheek.

"Dante. Stop." Smiling he tipped my chin up to him.

"Maylee. Look at me." Breathing out through my nostrils slowly I looked at him levelly. Leaning closer he kissed me gently. "You need to come back to the apartment to rest. Please Maylee. Come back with me." Slowly he leaned down his lips onto mine a second time. I could melt into him. Dropping my bag I wrapped my arms around the back of his neck as he lifted me up against the wall to deepen our kiss. After a few minutes we stopped foreheads touching. We were both smiling wide.

"Damn. Okay. Umm. Sorry." His eyes were bright as he looked back at me. He whispered into my ear.

"No. Do not be sorry. We will catch fire one day." Stepping back he took my hand into his walking back to his apartment. His smile was contagious as neither of us could stop. Izabella met us halfway smiling herself that we were walking together.

"You are both set to leave for Ireland tomorrow. That is where the council is located. My half sister Aliyah will be training you both there. She is tough but will do you both justice." We both nodded as she led us back to town.

285

"And where are you three going?" My blood froze in my veins at that voice. Stopping he walked around in front of us looking from me to Izabella. Dante frowned at how tense I was.

"They will be leaving tomorrow to train with Aliyah." He smiled at that information pinning me with his eyes.

"Really? Does she know she is teaching them both?" Izabella sighed as Dante pulled me behind him slightly. My muscles tensed more knowing that move was protectively.

"Have you found out who attacked Maylee yet?" Glancing to Dante he shook his head. I could almost tell what he was thinking as he watched Dante and I holding hands. He seemed aggravated though he was barely containing it.

"No. Whoever it was had a very different energy from anyone who is here currently. Why is Aliyah training them? As much as they need they could stay here longer." Izabella glanced back as I stepped up beside Dante watching Kamran carefully.

"The both of them have the potential to be as good as we are." Now he looked angry as he stepped closer to us.

"You are sending them because you think I have a bad influence on her?" Izabella chuckled frowning at his temper.

"No. I am sending them away so that we can concentrate on those who need much more help than they do." He nodded still looking angry as I shook Dante loose walking up in front of Kamran surprising us all including him.

"Just help those kids Kamran. They don't have the instincts I do. And they may never reach their full potential for any battle if you don't concentrate on improving them now." He smirked crookedly stepping closer to me looking down as he was almost two feet taller.

"There is much more to it than that. Trust me." He looked me up and down hungrily. I wanted to step back but I held my ground. Leaning down he whispered to me making my skin crawl. "I wish this war was never brought about. I would never have had to deal with training kids who will never be ready. You two will be fine. He's done this his whole life. And your instincts make it seem as if you have. But the others? We might as well kill them now. They will all die anyways." Pausing he glanced up to Dante and Izabella. "And for the record Maylee. You will come to me eventually. You will be mine." With that he turned walking away. I felt all breath driven out of me.

"Maylee?" Dante took my hand but I couldn't feel it. "Maylee. What did he tell you?" Turning to them both I felt lightheaded just before the world went black.

"What did he tell her to make her turn ghost white?" I heard Dante ask as I regained consciousness in a warm bed. Dante's bed. He must have carried me back to his apartment.

"I have a few ideas. We will wait for her to wake up to ask her." Shaking my head as I stood walking out to where they were sitting. Dante met me within steps.

"Are you okay?" Nodding I walked straight to Izabella.

"I need to talk to you about what Kamran told me on the way back here." I replied quietly.

"Maylee. Look at me." Dante said taking my hand. Shaking my head I walked away with my hands on my hips.

"Let me talk to Izabella. Than I will be able to calm down. Please Dante." He nodded backing off as I turned to Izabella.

"What did he tell you?"

"He basically told me he doesn't want to bother training the other descendants. That they will die anyway so he shouldn't bother at all." She nodded looking solemn as I was still quiet.

"What else?" Shaking my head I looked to the floor.

"That's all I'm concerned about." Looking up at her she gave a single nod before standing.

"He said something else to you. You tensed. When he said it. What was it?"

"I don't want to talk about it. Just make sure he trains them properly." Nodding she walked out of the apartment. Dante walked up from the bedroom glancing to the door.

"Everything okay?" I nodded sitting at the kitchen island.

"Yeah. Fine. For now anyways."

"Something is on your mind. You can tell me."

"I know." Sighing he pulled the stool out next to me sitting down.

"What all is really bothering you?" Resting my chin on my hand I looked over at him.

"Can you handle it if I tell you?"

"Of course."

"There are a few things that are bothering me fairly badly. First of all I'm sorry about how Kamran acts around you. It's my fault." Frowning he rolled his eyes.

"How do you figure?"

"He seems to think I should be with him even after I told him to stay away. Izabella had to tell him to leave me alone. He actually cast a spell on me. Shadow had to help me back here because of it." I heard him chuckle softly.

"That does actually explain a lot. He is super jealous when he sees you with me." Smirking I nodded.

"Yeah. The day I went to the field with you"

"Was why he yanked you away from me." Again I nodded.

"Yeah. He's an ass." Feeling overwhelmed I stood walking to the door.

"Hey. Where are you going?" Standing he had grabbed my wrist to stop me.

"Back to my own apartment." Frowning he stood face to face with me.

"Why?"

"Because you" Shaking his head he looked away for a moment.

"I was just processing. It took a moment is all. Okay?" Nodding he pulled me into an embrace. "Now" He pulled back looking at me smiling. "I would like for you to move into my apartment. Permanently." Smirking I sighed.

"Are you sure?" Resting his hands on my hips he pulled me close.

"Very sure."

"Okay." Leaning down he kissed me lightly.

"Anything else you want to talk about?" Resting my head against his chest I looked up at him.

"Since you want me to move in. You should know about my nightmares. At least what they are always about."

"You said before they were about your attack." Sitting back down I gestured he do the same.

"It is not what Izabella told you. There was more to it than that. In fact you may not want to be with me when I tell you everything." Scowling he took my hands into his.

"Whatever happened to you is horrible. I know that. But it will not keep me from wanting to be with you." I shook my head looking at the floor.

"Dante. When I was attacked. I was not just beat up." Taking a moment to gather my thoughts I continued. "I was down at the beach watching the water from Rocki's back. I sent him back to the stable without me because I wanted to walk the trails. Rocki would not allow me insisting he drop me off in town. After he was gone to the stable I walked back to the beach alone. That was when you stopped me and we talked. After that I made my way back to the beach." I heard him sigh shaking his head.

"Even after I told you I agreed with him and you shouldn't be out alone." He stated quietly as I looked up at him. His face was neutral but his eyes were angry.

"Yes. I know. What happened is partially my own fault." Shaking his head he gripped my hands tighter momentarily.

"No. There should never have been anyone here who would have hurt you like that. Anyways." Knowing what he meant I continued on.

"I was on my way back to town when someone wrapped their arms around me pulling me to the ground. The back of my head bounced off of the ground making me black out. When I was able to see again a man was standing in front of me. He threw me into trees, kneed my ribs, punched me in the face. My magik would not work against him. I was able to elbow his face as he hung me up on a tree by my wrists. He just beat me from there telling me to not fight in this war. I told him no. He let me down from the tree and hit me in the face again choking me." Stopping I could feel the sob coming as I remembered every detail. Exactly what that man had done to me.

"Maylee" Dante pulled me to him in a tight embrace. "It's okay. You don't have to tell me any more. It is obviously too painful for you." Pulling back hard I looked up at him as tears flowed from my eyes.

"No. You don't understand. I never wanted this to happen. I did not want him to touch me. I didn't want any of this." Shaking his head he pulled me back to him holding me tighter.

"No. No, Maylee. No one ever deserves to have that happen to them. You did not deserve what happened."

"I hate whoever that man was. I hate him for what he did to me." I sobbed against Dante as he held me.

"I know you do. Maylee. You survived it. You're still here." I was literally trembling as I remembered. Taking a breath to steady myself I finally managed to make my voice work. "He raped me. When he was done he grabbed me by the throat again. He told me not to tell anyone or he would hurt me worse. And that he would be back again. I tried to stand after he was gone. He reappeared and kicked me in the temple knocking me out." I felt Izabella's hand on my shoulder making me jump as she had left half an hour before.

"You need to rest Maylee." I nodded as Dante led me to the bed his hand on my lower back. My body was trembling from a combination of what I told him and not fully recovered from my injuries.

"You see now? I am damaged. Too damaged to be with someone that would care about me the way you do."

"No. Maylee. This is not going to keep me from you. We will deal with it together. Okay?" Shaking my head I rolled to my side away from him going to sleep.

It was daylight when I woke up. This time as I became more aware I could feel Dante's arms holding me against him tightly. Almost as if I would get up during the night and run away. I would have. But I was still much too weak to try that just yet. As the day before had proved.

"Awake?" He asked as I stretched out turning to look at him.

"Yeah." Smiling he pushed my hair from my face leaning over to kiss me but I turned my head.

"Hey. Maylee. Don't do that." Looking back to him I glared once out of bed to go to the bathroom. When I opened the door to walk out he stopped me in the doorway.

"Dante please. Just stay away from me." Shaking his head he leaned down to touch our foreheads together his hands on my hips to keep me still.

"I can't stay away from you. I tried that. It didn't work. You know the same would happen to you over time." Tears spilled down my cheeks as I knew I wanted to be with him. He kept telling me he wanted to be with me. It was myself that felt I should not be with him.

"I know you keep saying that. And I know that you mean it. But we need to be realistic here. With what happened to me. I will never be any good to you." When I looked at him he had his arms crossed as his jaw worked. He was angry. Maybe that was what it would take to drive him away.

"And why is that? Give me a good reason. And it had better be a damned good one."

"There will be times we won't be able to have sex because I might freak out. The first time we tried. I really wanted to. But images from my attack started coming back to me. We had to stop doing everything. And trust me. I didn't want to stop." He sighed as he laid his hands on my shoulders.

"It has not been long since your attack. Those things take time to heal from. I have not ever been attacked like that, but I was beaten everyday by my father when he was alive. Almost to death once though I do not remember it." I was surprised something like that had happened to him as he seemed so strong.

"Your father abused you?" He nodded looking distant meaning he was telling me the truth not just to make me feel better.

"If it had not been for Izabella I would have died the first time I met her."

"You two knew each other before this. I figured that out. For how long?" Taking my elbow he walked a few steps.

"Around five years. I was only sixteen when she stumbled onto me." The way he said it sounded very ominous.

"You don't have to tell me about it." I told him quietly as he looked back to me.

"You really would not want to know. I was in a bad way. Maybe another time we will talk about it. But not now." He tipped my head up by my chin looking into my eyes as I stared back at his. His eyes were such a bright green they could have been fake. Leaning down to me I felt his lips on mine. They were warm and soft as I leaned into him allowing him to deepen the kiss. His arms tightened around me picking me up setting me down on the couch. He sat down having me straddle his lap to continue. We were on fire as he moved my hips against him. He kissed down my neck and across my collar bone nipping at my ear as he went. My body arched into him more. I wanted him as much as he wanted me. Now he was trying to prove it. Breathless I pulled back looking at his face taking in his features.

"We should stop before we go further. I know you are not ready just yet." Nodding in agreement I stood sitting beside him instead.

Around night time I retrieved my backpack pulling out sweatpants and a long sleeve shirt for bed changing in the bathroom. I was nervous as we actually went to bed at the same time. Usually I went to bed and he snuggled up to me later. I felt my face turn red as I stood at the side of the bed unsure of our situation. Smiling he laid in bed patting the space beside him.

"You're actually nervous." Suddenly it must have dawned on him why I was that nervous. "Have you ever been in a long term relationship?" My face felt hot as I thought about my past.

293

"Well. Yes." I said quietly. "I did have one boyfriend but it turned out to be a disaster. He wasn't" Stopping before I could remember more Dante sat up resting his arms on his knees watching me.

"You need to rest. Lie down Maylee." Glancing up he turned to his side away from me.

"I'm sorry." Turning to look at me I knew he had heard me even though I had whispered it. Turning I walked out of the bedroom almost running to the front door.

"Maylee stop!" My hand was on the knob my forehead against the door as I heard his strained voice calling me. His arms wrapped around my waist pulling me away from the door turning me to face him. Without a word with one arm around my waist we walked back to the bedroom.

"Get in bed. You need to rest. Please. Lay down." Nodding I did as he asked. Turning the light out he laid on the other side turning to face me when he was settled going to sleep without a word.

When I woke we were tangled together but it was ridiculously comfortable. As I lay awake I studied his face and how he breathed.

"You can move if you want you know." He said before opening his eyes smirking at me amused.

"I'm comfortable where I'm at." Smiling crookedly he tightened his grip around me.

"Good. Because I didn't want to move." He kissed the top of my head which for some reason instantly made me relax into him more. After a bit I looked up at him not knowing what to think.

"What is it?" Shrugging I had no idea. Pulling my chin up he kissed me lightly looking at me as if asking permission to do it again. He kissed again. I kissed him back wanting him as much as I felt he wanted me. If we kept it up we would be further than the first time.

Breathing hard we both stopped looking at each other knowing we were about to the point I was possibly not ready for. Smiling wide he leaned down over me pulling me against him tightly. Instead of tensing as I thought I would I wanted him to continue. Breathing harder he noticed why I was reacting that way smiling as he kissed me.

"Dante" Unable to contain the urge he sat back pulling my sweats off along with his. Feeling as though I could not catch my breath he leaned over me stroking his hand up and down my leg before kissing my inner thigh. Whatever I had done before was nothing compared to now.

"I told you we would catch fire." My hands on his sides I felt something rough along his back. Flinching he grabbed my hand kissing it instead.

"What was that?" Shaking his head ever so slightly he took both my wrists pinning them over my head.

"Nothing to worry about." Smiling my hips came up off the bed.

His teeth grazed my collar bone. As he had earlier I clenched my teeth hissing as I wanted him tipping my head back. The wicked things we did as this went on was by far amazing. Once we were done I slid to his side as he wrapped his arms around my midsection pulling me tightly against him.

"That was amazing." Breathless he turned to his side facing me kissing my cheek as he looked at me. His thumb gently rubbing my collarbone.

"Yes it was." I told him smiling so much it hurt.

"I love you Maylee. Believe me when I tell you that." Immediately my whole body tensed when he said those words. That killed the amazing mood we had set.

295

"I do believe you. I just. I am not sure how I feel." He nodded tensing himself but began to relax after a while as we laid there holding each other.

"Why did you pull my hand away earlier?" He let loose a hard breath before sitting up on his elbows to look at me evenly.

"Because I didn't want you to know about my scars. But now as we have connected on another level." Taking my hand he helped me sit up before him turning his back to me. There were several scars on his back from what could have been from whipping. Reaching out I touched the one that looked the worse. The one I must have grazed earlier as he flinched when I touched it.

"Did. Did your father do this to you?" Without a word he nodded. "I'm sorry. That he did that to you." Turning to me he smirked taking my hand into his.

"Don't be. If you don't find my scars to be repulsive than I can live with it."

"I never saw them when we were practicing. When you pulled your shirt off."

"I used a glamour to cover them. That was something I learned from a young age." Taking his hand into mine I nodded before softly kissing his cheek. "What did Kamran say to you on our way back here?" Sitting back from him I sighed. Not this again.

"I'm not afraid of him. And he didn't say anything about my attack." Frowning at how defensive I had become he slid back slightly.

"I know you're not afraid of him. He is just physically much stronger." He lifted my chin to look at him. "What did he tell you?"

"He just said we were better off leaving for training because the others will never be at our level. That they will likely all die in battle anyways. He basically said we should kill them now because they will all die anyway." I stopped as his words haunted me.

"Maylee. What all did he tell you?" His voice sounded harsher as he must have been angry about it.

"Dante please." Closing my eyes I tried to push what he told me out of my head. "It was an empty threat. I'm not worried about it." Sighing in frustration he pulled me up closer rubbing his nose along my neck.

"You have to trust me enough to tell me everything. That includes what you think only you can deal with." Pulling back he looked into my eyes as I shook my head.

"Okay. But promise you won't fly off the handle." Raising his eyebrows at me he glanced to the door.

"No promises."

"Dante." Shrugging I knew he was not about to leave me alone about it. "He told me that I will come to him eventually. That I will be his." Dante pulled away from me standing from the bed in a hurry. Looking up he was dressed belting on his weapons.

"NO! Dante!" I jumped out of bed grabbing his arm. "Please. Do not go looking for him. I don't want you to get hurt." He pulled away storming to the door wrenching it open. Izabella stood looking at us as he was about to walk out. Concerned she crossed her arms looking between us.

"I would ask what this is about. But I think I have an idea."

"Did she tell you what Kamran told her last night?" There was so much hate and anger in his voice that I barely recognized it.

"Dante. Stop. Please." Izabella raised her eyebrows as she must have realized I was begging him to stop acting this way.

"Yes. Maylee told me what he said."

"I shouldn't have told you what he said."

"No. I asked you. I do not want you to hide things like that from me." Gripping my shoulders I was angry as tears welled in my eyes.

"I'm sorry Dante. It's not like I" Shaking his head his hands cupped my face holding me in place looking at him.

"I know. Look at me. I am not mad at you. I'm worried about you. There's a difference." My tears never fell but I felt as bad as if they had.

"The council would like you both to go on a small mission before you report to them for further training. I think you should leave today. As soon as you are packed would be best. I do not feel like breaking up a fight." She looked to Dante meaningfully. "Dante go start packing. I want to talk to Maylee for a moment." Taking my elbow she led me to the living room. It had just occurred to me I was wrapped in his bed sheet feeling my face heat up.

"Did you two" Rubbing the back of my neck I nodded.

"Yeah. We did." Her face tightened but she said nothing about it.

"Do you feel okay?" I nodded. Suddenly she gripped my shoulders looking into my face. "I know that look. Do not even think about it."

"About what?"

"Running away. Kamran would be the first sent to find you. And we would never reach you in time if you ran. And once we did find you. And if you were attacked. There would be one hell of a fight between him and Dante. And even with the two being even on strength. Kamran has more combat training and uses his powers as if he knew what you were going to do before you did. So. Go on this mission. Stay with Dante. Do not run off. I will be in touch with both of you. Okay?" I nodded walking to the bedroom to pack my clothes as Dante was just finishing up with his.

"What did she want?"

"Just to ask if everything was okay." Grabbing clothes I went to the bathroom to dress. Dante was right at the door when I opened it.

"There was something else. I think she saw what I'm seeing right now. You have a look on your face that I have only seen once before. So what is bothering you?" Smirking I was irritated that I was so readable.

"So you've noticed. What do you think is bothering me?" I asked him crossing my arms shifting my feet. He sighed standing inches from me his hands resting on my hips.

"I noticed because I have watched you. Since the day I met you. I have watched you. How you act to certain people or situations. The look you have is one I seen when we were on our way to the island. When everyone was giving us shit about you having so much power." I sighed nodding to him laying my arms over his shoulders.

"You really were watching me. Even though I was a bitch to you." He nodded acknowledging that fact.

"I knew why though. You guard yourself so heavily. And it is not for show like some girls. You do it as easily as most people breathe which tells me certain people have always treated you badly. And when someone is good to you. You honestly don't know how to handle it." I was blown away at how accurate he was. What all he had figured out in just a four week period.

"Damn. You really were watching me." Nodding he moved my hair to kiss my neck.

"Yes. I was. For many, many reasons." I could feel his breath on my neck as he spoke. "You were going to run away." He whispered nipping my collarbone.

"Yes." I almost cried unable to look at him. "I thought it would be best for us both. But Izabella told me to stay with you. She told me to be extra careful when we arrive anywhere new." He sighed heavily. Kissing me deeply he tangled his hand into my hair before touching our foreheads together.

"I'm glad she told you that. You should finish packing so we can leave." Pulling back he let go smiling as he let me pack my clothes alone to think about everything. He had been right as had Izabella. I had thought about running away while we were traveling. But not for the reason Izabella had thought. I was still coming to terms with what I felt for Dante. He had told me several times that he loved me. I also knew I had strong feelings for him. It was that I did not want to admit to myself or to him what exactly it was. Closing my bag I knew I would have to admit it to myself soon as we had just made love in his bed. Taking a deep breath I was ready to leave.

Walking out of the bedroom Dante met me at the door taking my hand as we opened the door to leave. Suddenly he ducked back inside pushing me back behind him.

"What are you" He turned placing his hand over my mouth.

"Listen." Listening I could hear Kamran angrily yelling at what sounded like Izabella. Who was equally angry as they argued. I could only hear words now and again but it was enough I knew what it was about. Pulling against Dante I tried to leave but he only gripped me tighter.

"Let me go." I whispered angrily but he shook his head scowling.

"No. You are safer with me." I yanked free running down the hall past the two of them down the stairs as fast as I could. Once in the lobby I shoved the door open into the street. I kept running all the way to the stable until I was between Shadow and Rocki's stalls. Opening Rocki's gate before shutting it behind me

I sat in the corner of his stall knowing he would never let anyone who meant harm to me inside. I heard the door open slowly with careful footsteps before there was a light hand on my shoulder. Jumping I looked over to see Dante. His face set in a way I knew he was angry with me for what I had done.

"I'm sorry. I couldn't breathe. I had to leave. I'm so sorry." I felt him sit down next to me wrapping his arm around my shoulders bringing me against him.

"I know. It's okay."

"You thought I was running away. I just couldn't be near Kamran. I'm so sorry."

"Maylee" He whispered to me as he held me. "Stop apologizing. I understand." I felt him pull away standing up beside me pulling me to my feet. "Come on." Nodding I followed the pressure of his hand as he pulled me along to the mountain. As we walked inside he kept looking around.

"Get your dragons packed. Now." Izabella's voice sounded angry as she walked out of the dark.

"Why? What is going on?" Looking to the opening of the cave she grabbed my arm pulling me into the shadows.

"Your sister seems to know what we are doing. We have to disguise you until you are gone. Put this on and keep your hood up." She told me handing me a heavy black cloak. My senses began to go crazy.

"Fly to the coast of Ireland. That is where the council is located." Nodding I looked to the cave entrance.

"She's coming." Izabella squeezed my arm hard silently telling me to stay quiet as I mounted Marlo. Dante hopped onto Dillon as quickly as he could turning to the exit.

"Let's just get out of here." He said out loud. My thoughts were racing telling me we needed to leave quickly. I could visibly see Dante tensing up looking around for something he could not see.

"You feel it too?" Glancing to me he nodded before he resumed looking around.

"And just what do you think you are doing?" A figure stepped out of the shadows at the entrance of the cave. Annabelle. Dante reached for Guardian drawing it pointing it at her.

"You! You have caused this! You killed your own sister!" She chuckled. Yeah chuckled! Remind me to strangle her later. Wait. I can do one better. I can torture her with my powers. When I learn to use them for battle.

I had already been warned that it was better to keep my mouth shut if this happened by Izabella. I sent a couple telepathic messages to Dante since Izabella was still in the cavern out of view. We had wanted them to think I was her, laughable since she had almost silver hair. If mine fell out of its band at all I was dead. Again.

"That might be." My sister finally spoke again. "But you are still on my list. Who is this with you? Izabella? That's too funny. At least you tried to escape." I reached for Star burst, but froze when I heard a resounding No from Dante. It was odd how we were using telepathy so much. We had barely used it with each other with the exception of the day I freaked out on him almost walking out.

Looking at my sister I read evil plans, fighting, a great force we knew called Theasis, and that she had to kill Dante to fulfill her first task. But why had they set that task to her? I still couldn't figure that one out. I pulled out of her mind looking around. We were surrounded. Damn. She was good. Now she was walking towards Dante. My stomach knotted up knowing what she could do to him.

"I asked you a question!" She yelled at him. Dante just looked at her pure hatred on his face. It did not even look like him anymore.

"Yeah, you did. That does not mean I'm going to answer you!" He yelled back at her. She just threw back her head laughing. It was really annoying.

Kind of like those shows you watch where the evil person laughs so much you just want to shut them up.

"I'll just go see for myself than." She said simply walking up to me looking at Marlo with great skepticism. "This was Maylee's dragon. How come he's letting you ride him?" She asked looking up towards me.

I stayed silent. Even as she drew fury on me I stayed still. Even when she swung it up at me I did not move. Looking me up and down before turning walking away.

"Seize them both. Keep her alive." She walked back to the edge of the cave, her warriors closed in on us. A hooded figure appeared at my side, Izabella. She took my sword for a moment before giving it back. She must have swapped our swords around. This way my sword would not blow up our plan. I looked around but she was gone already. Dante was ready to fight as I could feel his energy rise significantly as he swung Guardian preparing to fight.

I drew out the silver sword raising it up as they charged at us. There were ten of them and only the two of us. Some match. I had tried to not use my powers. The injury I had recovered from was weakening me already. There was no way I had fully healed yet.

Somehow we were defeating them. One by one they fell until Dante had the last one in a headlock with a knife to his throat. Annabelle was furious.

"That was not supposed to happen!" She screamed drawing Fury again stepping forward. Dante lunged forward first but I stopped him throwing my arm out in front of him. I signaled to him that I wanted this fight through our telepathic link stopping he did not back away or sheath his sword.

I knew what to do. Lunging forward I twisted around grazing her arm. She was shocked that I had been so quick. I took advantage walking up behind her. My arm wrapped around her neck choking her out. Not killing her though I wanted to. I pulled my dagger sliding it across her face cutting her cheekbone. I relinquished my grip backing away elbowing her in the ribs hard. After that we turned quickly mounting the dragons once again flying away. We were well over the ocean before I remembered my sword.

"Oh shit!" I yelled using my voice for the first time since we had entered the cave. "My sword!" I looked to Dante who frowned.

"What about it?"

"Izabella switched ours before we fought. That way they wouldn't know it was me." I could not see his face too well. We were flying after all.

"Check it now." He told me evenly.

"What?" I asked confused.

"Just do it." He said though I was still confused. I pulled out my sword as it still looked like Izabella's. It lit up white leaving Star burst. I was astounded by this. I had so much to learn feeling I did not have enough time to learn it all.

"How did she do that?" I asked still looking at it. Even as we flew I could see him smiling.

"We were ready for something like that. She cast a spell on your sword to make it look like hers until we left the island. Even after your up close confrontation with Annabelle I don't think they thought it was you." Well that was a relief.

"Good" With a deep sigh of relief to really let it sink in.

"So did Izabella tell you where we are supposed to be going?" He asked looking to me I nodded.

"Yeah. We are to fly to the coast of Ireland. She said that was where the council was located." I couldn't see his reaction.

"Sounds about right. Ireland will be quite interesting. There is a lot of history in that place."

"I know. I have heard some stories about that place. Personally I like all their symbols and language."

"You know. It all originates from sorcery and witch craft." I looked over at him.

"Really?" Witch craft? Is he really serious? Well I have powers so I guess I cannot doubt it much.

"Any symbols used to the day were used for that. And they are still used today by religions across the world." I laughed to myself.

"Like runes, hieroglyphics, and Japanese?" He laughed at me.

"Not Japanese, but the runes and hieroglyphics yes." Since we were on a long flight I might as well ask as much as I could to see what he knew.

"Is sorcery and witch craft the same?" He looked over at me sharply any sign of humor gone.

"No, but they are similar. They both use runes, spells, and potions but to answer a few general questions from those who don't know much about it. There are no sacrifices in witchcraft. They do however have gatherings to celebrate their holidays. Than there is also the three fold law, do you know what that is?" I nodded.

"Yeah. There is none of that in what we do. In sorcery there are no sacrifices except for your own life to learn the craft. No one knows everything." That had sounded like a warning. He must know I wanted to learn more. "There are certain things that we cannot do." I figured there would be limits like with anything else. "We cannot stop or alter time, bring back the dead, cure a medically incurable disease, or slow time down." Made sense to me as I thought it over more.

"Okay. Are sorcerers and witches related somehow?" He hesitated with that one.

"That I'm not sure about. You would have to ask someone else. Either someone from the council or maybe even Izabella could answer that." I nodded again figuring I should probably stop interrogating him about everything.

"If you have other questions just ask." He stated looking over to me. "I forget you are new to all this. It never occurred to me you would have this many questions. You never asked Izabella?"

"It had never occurred to me to ask her. So, the sorcerer and sorceress that we descended. The ones Izabella talked about. What were they to each other? Brother and sister or husband and wife?"

"From what I understood they were husband and wife. They had two kids together. The kids were born immortal and helped destroy their father when he tried to take over the world." That was interesting. They had two kids?

"Are they still around? The kids I mean." Perplexed he looked at me through the air.

"I have no idea. I have never heard their names." Really?

"I think we know one of them. I just did not realize it until now." Now he was confused.

"What? Who?" I knew he was going to be angry and upset with what I was about to say. But it was the truth.

"Kamran." I could not even bring myself to look at him as I said the name that caused me to tense up.

"Yeah. That explains a lot of things about him. And why he took such a liking to you as well." Confused I looked over to him.

"What do you mean?" He smirked slightly as we flew.

"Did Izabella ever show you pictures of what your ancestor looked like?" Thinking back I had never asked.

"No."

"You look a hell of a lot like her. Appearance wise."

"I'll take your word for it until I see for myself."

"That actually does explain a lot. That dagger he made you that matches your sword. It would take a great deal of magikal skill to do that. More than any regular magikal being would have." I took a chance looking down as we were still over the ocean with a long way to fly. It was freezing up here pulling my cloak tighter around me to keep warm.

"Okay. One more and I promise I'm done interrogating you." He shrugged.

"I would not say you have been interrogating me. But ask anyway." Looking to me expectantly.

"Where did you learn all this? It's still a long flight." Even from where I was I could see and feel him tense. He had confided to me that his father had beaten him on a daily basis. That he and Izabella had known each other for five years when he met my sister and I on the trail.

"It is a long flight. To keep the answer short. My dad and others."

"Sorry. I shouldn't pry." The way he had said it made me sorry I had asked.

"It's fine. You just want to know more about me." Yeah especially since we just had sex in his bed in his apartment. And I hardly know him. That was a stupid move on my part.

"Maylee, stop thinking like that."

"Will you quit doing that!" I yelled forgetting that he could read my mind at will.

"Sorry. If you closed your mind to your thoughts I would not be able to do it. Just try this. Clear your mind like you do to meditate. Concentrate on something you can see to block me out." If he keeps it up I might as well try it.

Clearing my mind I looked down at the sea. It was like a big black wall. Thinking I could feel him in my thoughts I pushed it back.

"Hey!" He yelled at me causing me to jump. I looked over as he was climbing back onto Dillon. "I said block. Not push." I felt my face hot from embarrassment.

"Sorry, I didn't realize I could do that." He was actually mad at me for it. Just one more to add to the list of things he could be mad at me for.

"Stop thinking like that. I know you didn't mean it."

"No. I didn't." Suddenly I felt my anger coming off of me in heated waves for almost no reason. Unfortunately I was actually engulfed in flames. I turned them off realizing I needed to learn to keep that in check.

"Damn" I heard him say turning back.

What?" He looked at me skeptically again.

"I guess being a descendant of Ares gives you the temper, but the magik makes you down right scary when you are pissed off." I felt guilty for my bad temper for the first time in a long time.

"Sorry. I just can't seem to keep it all in check."

"Well. You need to learn that. I need to learn other stuff. So I guess that makes us even."

"Like to use your powers instead of not using them when you need to. Right?" Rolling his eyes irritably he nodded.

We flew silently for what felt like forever when land was finally coming into view. Dillon and Marlo landed us in Ireland along the coast. It was nice. When I slid off my knees gave way forcing me to sit on my butt in wet beach sand. Instead of standing up to walk it off I sat there. Dante wandered over kneeling beside me.

"Are you okay?" Sounding concerned I looked up at him.

"Well, that is a loaded question." I told him as he looked around.

"Yeah, well you have been sitting there like that for almost ten minutes." I shrugged looking around in the sand finding some seashells collecting them to add to what I had already. I sat for another minute before I tried to stand. Dante offered his hand which I refused.

"No." I thought to him openly. I was finally up walking toward the wood line when my ribs throbbed sharply. I stopped bending over slowly dropping down to one knee. Dante rushed to my side immediately.

"They hurt again? It should not affect you like this." I looked up at him as he was genuinely concerned border line panicked about my condition. My breathing was shallow and labored from the pain.

"Not telling me anything I don't know." I managed through grit teeth. Minutes passed before the pain finally began to subside. Slowly standing up straight I kept my hand pressed to my ribs.

"I need to know how to make the pain stop." He looked me over quickly before turning toward the woods walking right at my side.

"First let's make camp so we can both rest." He reached to take my elbow to assist me while walking. Unfortunately it caused a flashback to when I was attacked. I was not sure why. Of all the shit that it could have been causing my adrenaline to kick in. He must have realized what happened as he quickly let go apologizing. I shrugged swallowing hard as I felt nauseas.

"It's okay. From time to time that is bound to happen without reminders. Like if I had not successfully fought my way out of that building in Dallas. I'm sure my sister could have wreaked some serious havoc on this war. I mean she is already. But I was able to stay ahead of her." I sat on the cool ground covered in deep green grass. Smiling I could not believe I was actually in Ireland. Dante kept close watch of me as if I might drop dead.

"I'll have to agree to that." I scowled looking to him confused. Agree to what? About my sister? Or that I might drop dead? I quickly remembered the mental block I was supposed to be working on.

Dante finished piecing the tent together stepping back to take a look at his work.

"I think a good order of sleep is on its way." I nodded in agreement. There was a zippered divider in the middle of the tent.

"Let's just hope it does not rain." I said looking at top of the tent. Dante turned to me looking confused.

"Why?"

"Because it is not water proof." I said thinking it was pretty obvious.

"No. They are not. A simple spell fixed that." He stated glancing the tent over.

"What kind?" I asked interested.

"From elements and enemies. You will learn all of this soon enough. Just rest for now."

"Okay." I replied as I yawned crawling onto the air mattress under the blankets. Sleep was almost immediate. Strange enough I had no dreams at all.

When I woke the next morning I felt as though someone was watching me. Too comfortable to move I realized Dante was not in the tent.

"How long have you been awake?" I asked as he stood just outside the tent entrance.

"Not long. Come on. We need to keep moving." I turned in my blankets.

"Uh Uh."

"Fine. You have five minutes and the tent comes down around you." Looking up I glared at him as he walked away. I threw the blankets off rolling them up. My ribs were aching already. Stepping out of the tent I was buckling my sword on when I looked up.

"Whoa" This place looked exactly like the pictures they show you. Except that you always think they are photo shopped. The beautiful beach, green grass, the cliffs. It was just amazing. Out of the corner of my eye I saw the tent crumple to the ground and roll up on its own. I turned looking to where it had just been set up.

"One day you have to teach me how to do that." He looked up confused.

"What?" I just looked at him. He had just used his powers and did not realize it or what? I pointed to where the tent had just been set up.

"The tent. You just used magik to put it away." A crease appeared on his forehead.

"Yeah. So?" I arched an eyebrow as he was so frustrating!

"Never mind." I said turning to my bags to make sure everything was there. We spent a few minutes in silence while we both did this with everything we had there. Since I no longer had my stones I was not sure on how to call for Danny. Well, I'll have to give this a shot. I sat down on the ground as if I were meditating.

"Reveal yourself." Opening my eyes I looked around. There he was galloping down the beach toward us. The sight of him here like this was awesome. Having done that made me wonder what else I could do without actually holding the stones.

Taking up the reins I swung up into the saddle waiting for Dante to be ready. He looked around whistling. A big gray owl flew out of the trees landing in front of him. The owl hooted surrounded by light growing larger until the light died revealing Shadow. I looked at Dante who was attaching his bags onto his saddle before he swung up walking over to where I was standing.

We rode along the beach. It was like a dream come true. At riding Danny along the beach with Dante beside us. I still had not come to terms with my feelings but I knew it had to be soon. When we were apart or when I made him angry my chest would ache. With that happening I knew it was serious.

I decided to ride into the ocean itself until Danny had to swim. Dante stayed on the beach keeping Shadow on a tight rein since he wanted to join in.

"Just ignore him and come out." I thought out to him across the water.

"I heard that!" Dante yelled to me.

"Than quit being paranoid and let him come out to swim." I could see he was irritated even from out here. None the less

312

he let the reins go slack. Shadow ran into the water quickly catching up with me and Danny.

"Lighten up." I told Dante as he looked cross about being out here. Hmm. What could I do out here with my powers? Thinking almost to the point I spoke it. "Circle" We were surrounded by flames. With a wave of Dante's hand they were gone. "Hey! I was just testing myself." He looked at me but instead of being angry like I figured he probably would be he was more worn out.

"That kind of stunt will get us noticed." He stated matter of factly.

"Sorry" I said. And I meant it. I had not thought of someone noticing coming to see who did it.

"Come on. Let's get out of the water." Him and Shadow led the way as Danny and myself followed. Wait a minute. I don't follow anyone! I kicked Danny forward through the water passing Shadow hitting the beach at a gallop. It was pure freedom as we ran along the water line. Looking behind me to see where the other two were.

When I did I realized that Shadow was not quite as fast as Danny so I stopped waiting for them to catch up. When they were within ten feet of us I kicked Danny into a run again.

"Come on!" I thought back to Dante. *"Either catch up or stop me."*

"Would you just stop!" Came his voice so angrily that I stopped immediately. They almost ran into us. "I didn't mean while I was right behind you!" He yelled. My hands rested on my hips while I scowled at him.

"You told me to stop!" I yelled back. We had a five minute starring contest. He finally looked away walking closer with Shadow.

"You need to be more careful about where you use your powers and who you are around." I just kept glaring at him readying my sarcastic voice.

"Yes, because it must be so tough being stuck here with a complete novice in magik. Who should be dead by the way." I paused to see his reaction. At first he was angry which was what I wanted but upon the should be dead part it quickly dissipated. Concerned he stepped closer to us shaking his head.

"But since I AM ALIVE I would like to enjoy what freedom I have while I can. So quit ragging on me! I don't just know things the way you do." I finished almost screaming at him. I felt so angry but I could not figure out where it had came from. Also I was enveloped in flames. Again. Dammit. I thought I had gained control of that training with Izabella. Looking to Dante his expression went from somewhat calm to alert.

"Put your flames out! Now! I think someone saw us." He said pointing to where he had seen people. I looked as well as they were on horseback coming at us at top speed.

"Come on! Let's run for it." I watched them as they ran closer.

"No." I said simply.

"Maylee! We cannot be caught!" He yelled almost panicking. I turned in my saddle to look at him

"I know they are not evil. I just want to hear what they have to say. If they try anything we can leave. All right?" Shadow stood still as if he understood what I was saying. Dante would not face me so I could not see what his expression was. The feeling of exasperation and anger however could have drown me. The two riders slowed down as they approached.

"You two have come far. Follow us." They were definitely Irish. The one who spoke had used English with a very thick Irish accent.

"They are probably from the council." I thought to him. Looking over he gave a curt nod.

"Maybe." Scowling I raised an eyebrow at him as we followed the riders.

"Could you be more uptight? Relax." I saw his nose wrinkle hearing a small growl of anger issue from him. Whoa. Someone is pissy today.

"You think?" Pulling Danny to a stop I scowled staring at him. It took a moment for him to realize I had stopped before spinning Shadow around walking back. "Maylee. We do not know who they are. This could be a trap. I know you have no experience with any of this. But this does not feel right." Looking up the riders had stopped to wait for us.

"Do you trust me?" I knew asking him was a long shot. He scoffed shaking his head at me irritably.

"Maylee. That is not a fair question and you know it."

"I know. Just. I believe they are with the council Izabella told us about. Nothing about them is sending red flags." Closing his eyes for a moment he sighed glancing to the riders.

"Okay" I barely heard him as he turned walking in the direction the riders were waiting. Shaking my head Danny turned his looking up at me before snorting following Shadow.

The riders looked almost identical. Leading us to a cove inset into the cliffs dismounting their horses they waited for us to follow suit. The woman had bright green eyes, long red hair, a pale complexion, she reminded me of Izabella with her eyes and complexion. I wondered if they were related but I was not about to ask. The man with her also had green eyes, his red hair of course was short, also pale complected. They were both around five foot seven and gangly. The girl spoke first again.

"Izabella told us you would be coming. She wanted us to keep an eye on you." She looked to me. "You are Maylee?" I nodded slowly. "She said you were recovering from a serious injury. A dark blade cut your ribcage open six inches. Has it been bothering you?" I rubbed my rib cage subconsciously.

"Yeah. Slightly." I admitted.

"Slightly Maylee?" Came Dante's voice as he walked up beside me. "You could barely stand on your own yesterday when they were hurting. And this morning I saw you holding them. That is why I wanted you to take it easy." I crossed my arms over my chest irritably. I guess we were both in moods today.

"I don't know how to take it easy." I told him stubbornly.

"I noticed." He replied sarcastically causing me to turn toward him.

"You know what?" My temper flared quickly. The woman walked in between us pointing at me.

"Enough!" She looked from one to the other. I did not realize she had dismounted her horse. "You two bicker like an old married couple." What she had said caught my attention.

"Excuse you?" She smiled wide at my tone. Nodding the man dismounted his horse. Looking to Dante he indicated we do the same. Dante shot a look as he dismounted. I would hear about this later non stop. The woman held her hand out to introduce herself.

"I am Keira. Izabella's half sister if you have not already guessed. I am a member of the council. This is Chris. He is also a member of the council." Nodding I glanced to Dante who crossed his arms over his chest. Assessing their words. Always assessing.

"Well, one of us has to."

"Could you not pick a god damn fight right now?" I snapped. I saw his jaw clenching and unclenching as he stared at me. His anger emanated in drowning waves.

"I'm not picking a fight. It is reasonable to keep your senses open. We do not know these people. This could be a trap."

"So you mentioned already." Keira watched as we stared each other down arguing telepathically.

"Are you two done arguing?" Shaking my head at him I scoffed looking to her.

"Izabella told you we would arrive today?" Keira nodded as both her and Chris stared at me. Remembering what Dante had taught me the night before I blocked them out of my mind. I could tell they plainly did not like Dante. They did not have to say anything to figure that out. I was unsure why.

"Who taught you to block your thoughts?" Chris asked as I looked to him my arms crossed from my arguing with Dante.

"Does it matter?" I responded coldly causing him to take a step back from me.

"No. Whoever taught you did a good job." He said before turning to walk toward the rocks. Out of the corner of my eye I swore I saw Dante smirking so I turned to face him.

"What's so funny?" I asked him my mood was just plain shit at this point.

"You." He said shortly. My temper was spiking more.

"What?" Looking at me perplexed he smirked at me.

"I just think it is funny that you mouthed off at a member of the council and didn't even think twice about it." My anger began to subside replaced by shame feeling my face heat.

"I didn't think. That's the problem." I sat on a nearby rock running my hand over Danny's shoulder. Dante walked over sitting next to me wrapping an arm around my waist. "I'm not meant for this." I told him simply shaking my head. "I mean. Why the hell do I even try? I can't do anything right. I'm not that powerful. I'm not what they need." I was now mad at

317

myself. How could I have been so stupid? Dante stood up in front of me taking my shoulders looking into my eyes.

"You are meant to do this. Or you would not have the powers you possess. Or fight the way you can. You are more powerful than you give yourself credit for. I know for a fact. I've been on the receiving end of it a few times. And you are far from stupid." I sat up straight looking up at him. He had read my mind as well.

"When I created the ring of fire in the water. All you did was wave your hand and they disappeared. If that was all you had to do to banish them than I am not that powerful." He looked concerned as I admitted.

"That is because you are not fully healed. And contrary to what you think it took great effort to banish your fire." I shook my head feeling overwhelmed. Back on the island I had been fine. That was just initial training. The council taking over was crunch time.

"Yeah. Okay." I stood to walk away he released my shoulders allowing me to walk. I quickly sat back down as my ribs were aching again. I held them tight as if that would really help. Cursing a lot in my head my breathing was too constricted to say anything out loud. Before long I had tears streaming down my face from the pain. It bothered me that I could not breathe. Dante wrapped his arm around my waist until I was sitting stably on the same rock. I had to give him credit as he was showing he cared about me. I finally looked up at him.

"Just kill me would you?" My voice cracked. He half smirked for a quick second.

"That would be too easy for you." He replied as Keira walked over examining my ribs. She said something to herself turning to Dante.

"I will be right back." My breathing finally eased up a little as the pain slowly receded. Keira reappeared with a brown glass bottle and a wash cloth in front of me opening the bottle pouring some liquid onto the cloth. "This may be painful. It is the last of the poison leaving your body." Lifting my shirt she looked at my ribs placing the cloth on them. I screamed in pain. Dante wrapped his arms around my shoulders to stop me from moving. Minutes passed when Keira finally removed the cloth. Even the ache that had been there since I had healed was gone. The scar was there. But the pain was gone.

"Thank you. I did not even realize how much it had been draining me." Dante just looked at me.

"*I told you so.*" Rolling my eyes at him I nodded.

"So what now?" I asked turning to Keira. The cloth she had used on my injury disappeared before she spoke.

"You meet the one who will be furthering you in your magik."

We followed her to the rock wall of the cliffs where a door opened. Looking around as we walked inside down a stone passageway. Now I was feeling bad vibes.

"*What do you think?*" I asked Dante.

"*I told you from the beginning what I thought.*" He replied back.

Regardless we followed Keira and Chris deeper into the cliff until we came to a room on one side of the stone hall. Keira opened the door. It was an office room with a desk, bookshelves, oil paintings of landscapes, and a crystal chandelier lighting it all.

Sitting behind the desk was an older woman reading an American newspaper, right on the cover was a picture of the destruction left behind from a line of tornados that ripped through the Midwest. She looked up over the paper at us folded it up setting it on her desk.

"Maylee, Dante. Welcome. Have a seat." She was around forty years old, five foot three, slender, pale skin, dark gray hair, her face looked young. I glanced to Dante quizzically.

"How did she know our names?" He remained silent not acknowledging anything. This woman looked so familiar but I could not place her. She looked directly at me as if she was assessing me. Probably because she was.

"Maylee. You have great power. You have only tapped into it." She looked to Dante. "The same cannot be said for you Dante. You have power but do not wish to use it. That is fine. For now." She looked to me again. "Do you know who I am?" Dante and I looked at each other shaking our heads. She stood from her chair walking around her desk standing in front of it.

"I am Sarita." I had to pick my jaw up off the floor. No way! I looked to Dante. He had turned chalk white.

"How do you know who we are?" I asked her. She smiled walking around her desk sitting back down.

"I know of you. I do not know you. I have heard of your powers through various sources. Both of you." She stopped looking to Dante again. "I know you mean well by not using your powers Dante, but you need to use them. There will be a time that both of you will have to perform the same level of magik at the same time. If you do not than we may not be here much longer." Some color had returned to Dante's face as he processed what he was told.

"So. You're. You're not going to kill me?" She looked at him genuinely surprised as he stuttered.

"Why would I kill you? I do not want them ruling the world. Or destroying it for that matter. I happen to like it here." He finally relaxed. "You were able to save Maylee with your powers. So the outcome is not always bad." He shifted his feet around looking at the ground.

"Only because she told me to."

I wanted to laugh because that had sounded awfully childish. She looked to me as I had raised my eyebrows at his reaction barely suppressing a smirk.

"You both have telepathic powers too. My husband and I shared that power as well." Once again I was shocked by this revelation though I should not have been.

"Is that power only active around certain people?" I wanted to know just in case anything happened to us.

"Yes. My abilities ceased when my husband was killed. He was an asshole that last century he was alive. I have no idea what he was thinking." That's scary. So were Dante and I meant to be together? A good question I thought. I had so many others in her presence.

"You have other questions?" Startled I jerked to attention. How had she known? I thought she said she did not possess that ability now? Yet I swore I could have felt someone in my mind. I shrugged it off.

"A lot of them." I said almost exasperated just thinking about it. I was not entirely sure which to ask first.

"Do witches and sorcerers share the same blood? I know that sorcery and witch craft are different and everything." She sat back in her chair looking amused.

"They are similar craft wise. The same magikal blood type. Yes. They are related by magikal means only. To be blood related yourself? No. The defining line between a witch or sorcerer or sorceress is that a witch can have powers and use them right from when they are born. A sorcerer or sorceress has to hold their stones of power before they become fully active unless born from two sorcerer parents. Once they are active and you use them often they dissolve binding into your blood. Hence giving you full powers." She nodded to me. "Your

321

powers are fully active." She looked over to Dante. "As are yours." He looked up surprised she knew nodding.

"I have had full powers since I was sixteen."

"Well. Since I have two fully powered sorcerers here. I might as well teach you a few things. I know Izabella did not have lot of time to teach you. And Maylee" She paused for my full attention. "You need to gain control of your fire element. When you are angry you are enveloped in flames. You can thank Ares for the temper. I will be able to teach you to wield it for battle as needed." She paused again. This time to gain Dante's attention.

"You control yours too well." He set his jaw.

"I don't want to use them." He told her quietly. She nodded to acknowledge he admitted to it.

"Too bad. I am not giving you a choice. You will use them." He stared at her in disbelief.

"If you knew" She cut him off mid sentence.

"I do know. Do you want a chance to fight them? To save the place you call home?" He looked frustrated searching for words.

"Yes, but"

"You will use them. And unlock your full potential." He opened his mouth to argue back. "End of discussion." He closed his mouth grinding his teeth. I could feel his anger.

She watched him intently for a moment like she was expecting him to do something. He stood walking out of the office. I thought that gesture alone would make her angry. "Is he always like that?" She asked as I sighed.

"About his powers? Yes." She jerked her head towards the door.

"Go talk to him." I stood glancing to the door crossing my arms over my chest.

"I'm not chasing him down." I told her defiantly.

"Maylee" She raised her voice. I guess I did not want her angry. Uncrossing my arms I rolled my eyes walking out the door to go after him. He had not made it too far. Only twenty feet down the hall looking tired.

"Dante wait up!" I called. He stopped turning back for me to catch up. Once I caught up we walked together. "Where are you going?" We walked farther and farther from the door.

"Just for a walk. That's what I do when I need to clear my head." Yeah or run away from it. Right? Act tough around everyone but what you really want to do is run for your life. He looked over slowing.

"I heard that." He said quietly stopping.

"Heard what?" Looking a little frustrated he shook his head.

"What you were thinking." Ah dammit. I kept forgetting about the telepathic communication shit. Breathing out a hard exasperated breath I knew I had to explain this.

"Sorry. I keep forgetting about the whole telepathic reading of the minds. What is your deal than? I know you do not run from a fight. I have witnessed that a time or two." He was silent looking agitated.

"Maybe you're right as far as my powers go. And I will fight them. But in my own way. Not how they want me to." Sighing in frustration I turned to face him.

"Dante" I raised my voice sharply at him. Looking down I had grabbed his arm to prevent him from walking away.

"What?" He asked angrily. I let out a low growl. He was acting like a petulant child.

"Stop this." Anger flashed into his eyes at my tone of voice.

"Why? I'm admitting to it aren't I? That I resent my powers. Because I do Maylee. I despise my powers." I felt my temper flaring up knowing both of us angry could spell disaster.

"Dante. I am still here thanks to you. Now quit being so damn pissy so we can go learn what we can while we are here." Right after I had said he was being pissy he grew angrier breaking loose of my grip glaring at me. "That does it!" I screamed in anger waves of flames erupted around me. They burned hotter than usual as golden lightning crackled around me. A black cloud loomed over Dante's head. Wind gusted through the hall. One look from him with eyes flashing stopped it all. The cloud disappeared wind dying instantly. Now I was irate. My vision tunneled down to focus solely on him. My flames turning blue and white. The lightning now black. Raising my hand I grabbed one of the bolts to throw. Suddenly Dante walked up grabbing my wrist hard.

"What are you doing!?!" I screamed feeling my voice strain. "Fight me! That's what you want!" Cooling off slightly at his lack of fight my flames resorted back to their usual red and orange. The lightning disappeared.

"No. It's not." I could barely hear him. "Maylee. It is not you I want to fight. I'm only fighting myself. What I have to do. You do not realize it, but you were about to kill yourself with your own power." My flames disappeared from my shock of being told this.

"What?" He released my arm standing in front of me worried.

"Right now. If you would have kept on like that. You would have destroyed yourself. Not just been hurt or battling." I hung my head. My temper was too fly off the handle when it activated my powers. Taking a deep breath I nodded looking at him evenly.

"I really need to gain control of my powers when I'm angry. I'm only somewhat sorry though. You were acting so ridiculous! It made me mad." He lightened up smirking as my anger subsided further yet.

"I know. I'm sorry." He looked up behind me a dark look crossing his face. Grabbing my wrist he pulled me behind him protectively. Sarita had walked out of her office. And she looked positively furious.

"Are you two done now?" Sounding calm she sure did not look it. Within the next minute she was all calm and serene again. She looked at me pointedly. "That was quite the fireworks display." Looking to Dante she pointed her finger at him. "And you. You are lucky to have stopped her." He looked to the ground shamefully.

"I know." Sarita stood straight slipping a small laugh.

"No. You did not know. I was watching you both. She scares you when she is in flames. Had it been me in your place though. I probably would have been too." Looking back to me she smirked. "You are formidable when you are in that state."

"Really?" I asked in shock. "I can't be that bad." Dante looked at me taking a step back with raised eyebrows.

"I don't want to be near you when that happens again." I felt so confused. Was this good or bad?

"You were beyond control Maylee. That is good for when you are in battle against our enemies, but not with those on your own side. You could have destroyed the both of you if he had not stopped you." I felt so ashamed of myself. I had really allowed my anger to run me.

"Sorry. I guess controlling my anger with my powers will be the first thing I learn." She nodded in agreement.

325

"Yes, I do believe so. You were drawn to this place because of its magikal energy. Come now, I will show you where you will both be staying while you are in training."

We walked back down the stone hall. I could not believe that Sarita was actually alive, here, and teaching us. This could not be real. In fact I was sure Izabella had told me she died shortly after Vladimir was killed. This had to be a dirty trick someone was playing on us. But who would do this besides the evil side?

Our rooms reminded me of jail cells except that they were more comfortable. At this point I am certain that we are in jail. I rattled my brain remembering that I had indeed asked Izabella about my ancestor not long after she had found us. I opened the door to my room peeking out to see if anyone was there. No one in sight. Well I am not staying in there if I don't have to. I walked a little ways down the hall knocking on Dante's door. It opened instantly.

"We need to talk." I told him. He nodded in agreement stepping aside to let me in. "I think this was a set up." I said as soon as the door was shut. He crossed his arms as he stared at me.

"I tried to tell you it was." I threw my hands in the air angry at myself.

"Yes. You did. Now how do we escape?" He smirked in that annoying way he did when he was ahead on something.

"I have a plan." I figured that.

"Okay. What?"

"If you completely let your powers loose. Like earlier. I am almost certain that they will let us go." He sounded sure enough about it.

"You're sure?" I asked hesitantly.

"Well, not one hundred percent. But it's worth a shot."

"Okay. Before we do that don't you think we should try to contact Izabella?"

"We can try. But if she doesn't reply or show up by morning we will go with my plan instead."

"Okay. How should we go about making me lose control?" We both took a minute to think it over. "My sister." I told him as he looked up wearily knowing that I could truly fly off the handle about that.

"Okay" He said slowly. "Is that really the best idea? I mean you already about blow up just thinking about it. Do you think I'll be able to stop you in a full rage?" Nodding as I stared at him.

"You will be able to. I'm not worried about that." I told him confidently. Shaking his head I knew he did not like the idea.

"Yeah, like earlier when you almost exploded. I barely stopped you." He looked worried as I crossed my arms narrowing my eyes at him.

"Can we forget about that?" He sat in one of the chairs looking relaxed as he looked at me thoughtfully.

"No. I won't let you." May as well leave it at that. The fact that he was still worried about what had nearly happened was making my brain go a million miles an hour. I sat down in an arm chair across from him resting my elbows on my knees. From those thoughts I switched to our current situation. If they kept us separated we wouldn't know where the other was. Dante must have been reading my thoughts. This time I could feel it. I threw my wall up sitting straight as he was still watching me.

"What are you thinking?" I bit my lip still trying to figure out something different. This was the best I had.

"If we are separated. We should meet somewhere. Reunite. Than we can leave from there. I was thinking South Carolina along the coast. Wait a week before leaving if the other doesn't show up." He thought it over for a minute before nodding in agreement.

"Sounds like a plan. We'll go with that." That was settled.

"Could I stay here for the night? Just on the floor or something. This place is really creeping me out." He smirked as he looked at me.

"All the time we were together in my apartment and now you actually ask? You will absolutely not sleep on the floor. You will sleep in the bed. With me if you want." I felt my face warm remembering two nights ago. We had sex in his bed.

"If you want me to." My voice had been so quiet I was not sure if he heard me. Taking my hand he gave it a squeeze.

"I do want you to stay with me. Especially in bed." Smirking I could not help but smile back at him as he pulled me to my feet to change for night. Climbing into bed I was cold shivering as he climbed in wrapping his arms around me kissing my temple.

"Good night." I smiled snuggling into him more.

"Good night."

I was the first of the two of us to wake in the morning. Dante was asleep looking peaceful as we were again curled right around each other. I swung out of bed noiselessly walking to the small bathroom to wash my face and brush my teeth. When I walked out Dante was awake sitting up in bed.

"Mornin" He said groggily standing up taking his turn in the bathroom. I went to the tiny kitchen area. Luckily there was coffee. Dante had just walked out of the bathroom when there was a knock at the door. Looking to me he strode over to answer it.

"Okay. We'll be there." He shut the door walking over taking his cup. "That was Keira. They want us on the beach ASAP." I took a deep breath.

"Okay. Ready?" He nodded.

"Yeah. I think so." We walked out the door down the stone path that led out to the beach where we had been the night before. As we walked I twined my fingers with his. He gave my hand a squeeze. The door opened into the cove. Only Sarita was standing there waiting. I could sense that we were surrounded rreleasing Dante's hand drawing my sword. Dante had done the same.

"Invisible wall." I thought sending it up. Dante glanced over knowing I had done it. We could communicate very well telepathically at this point.

"What are we learning today?" He asked her as she looked at him like she was straight out of a psychiatric ward.

"To defend yourselves." Raising her arms she signaled something. My senses were telling me everything but stay still. I looked up at the top of the cliff. We were surrounded by archers.

To each side warriors with swords and more archers. Fuck my life. We might actually die. One of the archers shot an arrow. It merely glanced off my barrier. Dante turned grabbing my wrist.

"Come on! We have to run. The plan is not going to work!" He pulled me to start running. Finally I followed him down the beach. As we ran away everything crumbled falling into a heap of rubble. I stopped as it collapsed like a chain reaction. Dante kept pulling my arm.

"No" I told him walking back to the heaping mess. As I walked everything went back into place as if it had never happened. I stopped by some boulders in the cove. He finally caught up with me looking at the cliff with astonishment. It all looked completely untouched. We had been surrounded. Dante walked up investigating the cliff wall.

"No door. But it was here." I climbed onto one of the rocks sitting down for meditation. The wind picked up water spraying a little. When I opened my eyes Dante was standing in front of me. Looking at me in astonishment.

"Were you just standing there watching me the whole time?"

"No. Not the whole time. That was interesting though."

"How's that?" He shifted his feet as he looked around before sitting down beside me.

"You were levitating." I looked at him in pure disbelief.

"Yeah. Right. Good one." I said almost laughing before I realized he was not joking. "You're not joking." He shook his head. So now I could levitate? That was strange. "Okay. What the hell was that all about? A test? A dirty trick from the enemy?"

"It's hard to tell. We should leave. Go somewhere else. Than try to get in touch with Izabella again." At this point I completely agreed.

"Okay. Since this seemed to be a total bust. Where are we going to go?"

"You want me to choose?"

"I'm asking aren't I?" He took a moment to think.

"Russia. It's a big country. There are lots of places to hide."

"Okay. Let's go." I jumped down from the rock. We were walking along when the door in the cliff opened once again. Looking at each other confused we were unsure of what could be next.

"What the hell." I said turning around to see what was happening.

"This cannot be good." Looking at him we could have went along without that comment. The sound of marching men was issuing from the passageway. In the light we could see they were heavily armed with swords, spears, and bows covered in full battle armor. The fake Sarita was leading them. Great. They stopped as she ordered them to surround us again. We were in trouble. We were in a bad way as back to back we stood ready to fight.

"You have a plan now?" I asked over my shoulder.

"Yeah. Use everything you've learned with your temper and I will use my powers. This time anyways." Rolling my eyes I smirked.

"Just remember. I don't know a whole helluva lot yet."

"That might be, but your instincts are damn accurate. Lead with what your gut tells you. I'll do my best to keep up."

I had to open up my mind so we could communicate as easily as talking. The men began to advance at us with their swords drawn closing in. We already had ours out as they had surrounded us. Together we commanded a blast of wind to knock them down followed by a blast of fire. So not only did it blow them away, it burned them as well.

The number had declined from twenty of them to twelve more to our favor. I thought about the fact that I had actually levitated earlier looking to a boulder. Holding my hand out the boulder rose from the ground tilting and twisting in place. If it had not been for the fact that we were currently battling literally for our lives this would be beyond epic.

Drawing my arm back throwing it as if I had been holding a stone. The boulder crushed a couple of the men. I repeated this method until we were down to five of them. Time to fight by sword. Star burst lit up in flames advancing onto two of the soldiers fighting like I had done it all my life.

I was finally able to hit one of them in the midsection. The feel of resistance and scrapping bone was odd making me shiver in response. The soldier disappeared in a shimmer. Swinging out again I hit another who also shimmered out of existence. I turned around to see how Dante was holding up. He was fighting two soldiers. Stepping in I made it an even one on one. With a well placed swing I hit my soldier in the side disappearing as the others had. Just one left. I turned to go after the fake Sarita but when I turned to make my move Dante had been disarmed by his opponent. Dammit. Turning back he was on his knees holding his arm to him. The soldier was holding his sword to his throat about to run him through.

"No!" I screamed knowing I could never make it in time to save him. When I screamed the ground shook splitting just underneath the soldier causing him to fall into the chasm disappearing. Dante threw himself backwards to prevent himself from following. In shock I had been able to cause the rift I closed it up. Turning once again to confront the woman as my anger was growing. She still looked calm which only further infuriated me.

"Your turn!" I yelled lengthening my stride walking to her as quick as possible. Before I could even take a swing at her she shimmered out smiling wide. Screaming in rage my flames were coming off in huge waves. Lighting struck around me leaving holes and burn marks. The ground began trembling. I could not remember being so pissed off in my life as I screamed feeling my voice ready to break.

"Come back here and face me!" I screamed as loud as possible feeling my voice was ready to crack from the strain. Exploding in complete rage all the rocks floated into the air orbiting around me. The sky turned pitch black. Pointing my sword where the woman had been moments ago lightning struck the spot several times leaving the ground blacker than the sky.

Dante

Holy. Fucking. Gods. Maylee had opened a chasm swallowing a soldier as he closed in on killing me. I could feel the shift in her powers as they teemed completely out of control. Reaching out through our connection she had her blocks up. Dammit. I watched as she levitated into the air, levitating rocks to orbit around her to use as weapons. Her flames had changed to white, the sky black and lightning struck leaving gaping black holes in the ground. I had no idea she could wield so much power. Shaking my head to clear that thought I ran to where she was suspended in the air. If she did not stop she was going to kill us both. And half the coast. My chest ached thinking about losing her already. That was not happening. Levitating to just below her I gripped her wrist.

"Maylee stop. Gain control before you kill yourself! Please!" Her eyes flashed as she realized my voice was pleading. "Think about all the people counting on you." Closing my eyes momentarily I knew she would either stop or send herself over completely with my words. "Think about us. Look at me Maylee. I love you. Please." I heard her intake a breath as if she had fallen several feet. Slowly as she breathed the sky turned back to blue. The rocks hit the ground causing a slight tremble. Maylee's flames had reverted back to orange before turning off like they had been siphoned away. I caught her as she collapsed the moment her feet hit the ground.

"I'm so sorry." Tears poured down her face as the realization of what happened set in. I wrapped my arms around her burying my head into the crook of her neck. Slowly I set her on the ground holding her on my lap. My own heart was between stopping and breaking out of my chest.

"It's okay now. It's okay. I'm right here. I'm not going anywhere." I could feel how tired she was. Drained. Unsure of the time passing she eventually picked her head up to look up at me. Unlike before her eyes showed doubt and fear. "Are you okay?" Nodding her response I rested my forehead against hers still catching my breath. "Don't ever do that again." I told her wrapping my arms around her tightly again. She was still trembling from her adrenaline coming down.

"I won't. I promise." Her voice sounded small. Unsure. Scared. Looking around we stood up at the same time. I could sense Maylee was light headed pulling her to my side by her waist. "Dante"

"What is it?" Still crying she pulled back to look me in the eyes.

"I don't want to do this anymore. Not if that happens. I can't deal with that. It was so overwhelming. I just. I just can't. I'm so sorry." Sighing heavily I tightened my grip around her. Holy hell. If she would have told me sooner. But unfortunately they do need us to win.

"Maylee. I know it scared you. And I know how you feel. Trust me. But in all seriousness. We can't even begin to win this war without you on our side." Shaking her head she attempted to pull away from me. My grip on her shoulder tightened down turning her back to face me as she shook her head.

"No. You are just as powerful as I am. And you know more than I ever will. Please Dante. Just let me leave." I feel as if she has sank a dagger into my chest.

"Damn you. Damn you for suddenly changing your mind Maylee." Pulling back we stared at each other.

"What are you talking about?" Confused she asked through her tears. Shaking my head I looked up at her rubbing my chest like it made any difference.

"I wish you would have decided that before we ever made it to the island. We could have ran and they would never have found us. None of them." Her eyebrows rose before narrowing on me.

"You would have ran with me even though you didn't know me?" I nodded.

"In a heartbeat." Fighting my thoughts I looked around. Remnants of our skirmish were everywhere. We needed to leave.

"Is now still a good time? Because I think we should go while we can."

"You're right. But you need a minute to relax. Stay here and I'll ready the dragons." Leaning against a large boulder she waited. Walking to the alcove I called for them.

"They are ten minutes away." Shadow communicated back to me as he flew over as a falcon.

"Okay. Thanks." Landing only a few feet away he walked up beside me as I walked back to where I left Maylee waiting.

"What happened?" Stopping I ran my hand over my hair glancing to the cliffs.

"She almost died. She lost control of her powers. I almost lost her today Shadow. I want to run away with her. Can you help us?" Snorting he shook his head.

"I can. Yes. However. You should talk to Izabella before you make any irrational decisions."

"Irrational? She almost died Shadow! Please? Just help us stay away for a while." Sighing he tossed his head in agreement. Turning I walked back to where I left Maylee sitting. She stood as I walked her direction.

"I called for them. It may be a few minutes." She nodded as I walked up meeting me part way. Attempting a smile as I cupped her face in my hands. She laid her hands over mine reassuringly.

"I'll be fine. Really."

"Alright. At least this time I was not on the receiving end." She chuckled in spite of everything as we began walking down the beach where the dragons had just landed. We climbed aboard taking off to begin our flight to Russia.

"Why Russia?" She asked looking over questioningly as I shrugged.

"I've always wanted to visit. And they have a lower drinking age." I told her grinning wide. She laughed.

"Yeah. I could use a drink about now." I nodded looking her over as we flew over the sea.

"How do you feel?" She turned her neck rolling her shoulders before answering.

"Do you really want to know the answer to that?" I nod that I do want to know. Sighing she looked away before answering. "A headache from hell. Exhausted. Other than that. I think I'm okay." I could feel she was thinking about what had happened. From losing control of her powers to not knowing how I was able to stop her. Hell I did not think I could. I thought we were going to die.

"Dante" Her voice was strained as she spoke for the first time in over an hour.

"Something wrong?" She shook her head.

"No. I just wanted to ask you something. I know you don't like to talk about your past." Hell. Here we go already. She barely manages to stop from killing us and immediately we are back to my past. "Look. I know it must have been terrible. But maybe it's not as bad as you think. I've known you long enough now that I don't think you would do something to hurt anyone unless you had no choice."

"Soon Maylee. I will tell you soon. I promise." I promise her quietly as she nods she heard me.

"Okay." After that we were both silent though I could feel her mind was racing.

Three hours later we landed in Russia. We had to be somewhere near St. Petersburg. It was a perfect location placing us close to water with plenty of trees to shield us from the weather. We made camp in a clearing in the woods we landed near. Maylee gathered wood for a fire while I pitched the tent. I watched her walk into the woods glancing back to where I was gathering rocks for the fire break. We started the campfire sitting silently a few feet apart on a large log near the campfire I had found for us. The fire was burning brightly since night was fast approaching. The silence stretched between us tight as a drum. As I stirred the fire Maylee made some tea drinking it quickly.

"Are you going to be silent all night? Or are you pissed off at me for something?" Looking over sharply I shook my head frowning.

"I'm not pissed off Maylee. I just don't know what to say right now." I set the poker aside locking my hands together resting my chin watching the flames dance.

"If it's because I mentioned your past" Leaning over I grabbed the back of her head tangling my hand into her hair kissing her hard. After a moment I drew back slowly our foreheads touching.

"Stop. Please." Shaking my head I could feel her concern. "I don't want to lose you when you find out what I used to be. What I did for them." Smiling a little she cupped my face in her hands kissing my lips gently. I wanted to tell her everything. But she had to let me in too.

"Just tell me." I shook my head sliding away from her completely. "Dante"

"Not yet." Taking her hand I looked at her evenly. "When you come to terms with what you want I will tell you." Nodding we remained silent. The sunset was beautiful fading away fast as it did not take long for night to fall.

"We should turn in for the night." I told Maylee after it had been dark for half an hour. She looked up from the fire as it was the first time I had spoke since earlier.

"Yeah. We should." I dumped a bucket of water over the fire to extinguish it. As we retreated into our tent to sleep I realized it was not the best idea for us to sleep in the same bed. Maylee walked into the tent first lying on the air mattress curling up under the blanket. Looking at her I turned stepping out walking away from the tent.

Sleep would have been great. But I did not sleep well. I repeatedly dreamed about what had happened that morning on the Irish coast. Where I had almost lost her. Dammit. Sighing I sat up looking around the clearing as Shadow in wolf form whined I had moved.

"Sleep Dante. You are both safe. I promise."

"I know. Just having a hard time sleeping is all."

"Do you need to talk?"

"No. I need sleep."

"Settle back down and sleep." Sometimes he was too damn rational. All the same I laid back down on my blankets before he curled around me protectively. I felt something. No someone was touching my shoulder. Jumping awake I grabbed for the throat only to see Maylee kneeling beside me.

"Dammit." Releasing her I leaned back rubbing my temples. "And you let her do that knowing how I react when

I'm woke up?" Shadow didn't even respond as Maylee sat back on her heels.

"I didn't know. If I would have than I wouldn't have done it."

"I know you didn't. Shadow did. He should have warned you." She stood walking back to the tent.

"Talk to her." Shadow insisted. Inhaling a deep breath I held it for a moment before releasing it walking into the tent kneeling beside her to make us even.

"I thought you made it clear you didn't want to talk to me." Standing she turned to walk out. Before she made it I grabbed her elbow turning her to face me. Alive. She was still here. Closing my eyes for a moment I had to slow my mind and heart.

"That is not what I said Maylee. I knew you had a lot going through your mind last night. It was for the best for both of us. I wanted to give you a chance to figure things out. I'm not mad at you for anything." My grip on her arm was tighter than intended loosening it. Maylee nodded stepping closer making us only inches apart.

"I had dreams last night. About what happened in Ireland." Nervously she pushed her hair back looking up at me. "And about you." Dreams? No. messages sent to her from someone. "It wasn't bad." Her voice hitched reaching for me as I turned to walk away. "Dante stop. It was not bad."

"You are going to force me to tell you. Aren't you?" I asked her feeling bitterness in my own voice. I did not want to be angry with her. For fuck sake she damn near died yesterday.

"No. I'm not. I was just going to tell you" She stopped shaking her head at me. "Forget it. Clearly you already have your mind made up." Walking away she grabbed her bag from the tent walking the trail out of the clearing.

"She has called for her dragon." Looking up at him I nodded walking down the trail breaking to a run once I heard a dragon land. She was walking up to him as I ran to her clamping a hand down on her shoulder to stop her.

"Maylee. Don't even think about it. You know you're supposed to stay with me while we are traveling." I felt her muscles tense throwing my hand off turning to Marlo tying her bag on. Grabbing her arm hard I spun her to face me not allowing her to move. Her eyes flashed angrily. If she had not completely drained herself yesterday she would have sent me flying.

"Dante. Let. Go. Now." Shaking my head I gripped her shoulders gently.

"Damn you. Stop this. Please Maylee. You just told me you wanted to run away from this. If you leave right now they will find you. And you will have no choice but to go back. Is that what you want?" Tears tracked down her face. I could feel her fear. But I could also feel she wanted to stay away from me.

"No. I don't want to go back. Are you sure you can keep us hidden?"

"Yes. I know I can." Sighing I wanted to pull her to me and hold her tight. Her body language told me to not touch her. "But you can't call for Izabella for anything if we do this. She is a friend to both of us I know."

"She will report what I'm doing to the council and they will drag me back. Whether I want to fight or not."

"Yes. They will. And they will send their best hunter to retrieve you."

"You know who it is."

"Unfortunately I do. It's Kamran." Nodding with understanding she closed the space between us. Which surprised me with the feeling she was emulating she laid her arms over my

340

shoulders resting her head on my chest. Closing my eyes I wrapped my arms around her holding tight.

"What do we do now?"

"You are both going back to Ireland before I kick both of your asses." Izabella stood before both of us with her arms crossed her face set in a way I knew she was pissed. Maylee tensed in my arms before pulling away.

"How the hell did you find us? I placed every spell and sigil I knew on us to hide." Looking to me pointedly she stayed where she stood.

"You did. But I know Maylee's raw form as well. Her vibes are very unique. You would never have been able to hide her for long. Not from me kid." I felt Maylee's emotions explode. Gritting my teeth I glared at Izabella.

"Izabella please. I can't do it." Frowning she walked up in front of Maylee her expression softening as I had pulled her behind me protectively as she stepped closer.

"You cannot do what Maylee?" Even her voice softened as she stopped in front of me.

"I can't learn all this. My powers. I can't seem to control them. I almost killed myself in Ireland. Please. Don't make me go back." Izabella stared at me as I shook my head.

"I was going to take her away." Nodding she looked back to me.

"You let him because you allowed your fear to lead you."

"No. I'm done Izabella. You can't force me to learn everything." Nodding Izabella glanced to me as I released Maylee. Immediately she stepped closer to my side instead wrapping my arm around her holding my hand. Izabella noticed the gesture tilting her head silently asking if I was okay. I shook my head. No. I was not okay. Nodding she understood before responding.

"I will give you both a few days to relax. When I come back you will be ready to come back with me. Understood?" Maylee shook her head detaching herself from my side.

"No! I don't want to." I grabbed her shoulder as she started moving forward. I knew if she challenged Izabella angrily enough she would drag her back thrown over her shoulder. Izabella frowned looking at me tilting her head.

"Her powers scared her that badly?"

"I thought I was going to lose her. Yes. She was that scared." Sighing she stepped back pinching the bridge of her nose before rubbing the back of her neck nodding.

"Okay. I propose this. I will allow you two have a few days here. I will check in on you to make sure you have not bailed on me. If you still feel this way in another two or three days I will allow you both to leave. If not you will come back with me to Ireland for further training." Maylee and I both nodded. Crossing her arms over her chest she shivered slightly nodding in agreement.

"Okay. I'll agree to that. Dante?" Maylee asked turning slightly.

"Yeah. I agree too." Nodding she shimmered out leaving us standing in the middle of the clearing. Physically I could feel that Maylee was shaking. Taking her hand I pulled her to me wrapping my arms around her holding her to me tightly.

"I don't want to go back." Rubbing her back I nodded when she looked up at me.

"I know." Stepping back she laid her hands over mine on her shoulders.

"Dante. No. I'm not going back." Rubbing my face I tried to ease the tension I felt. The fear Maylee was radiating from what had happened the day before. The doubt she had about her own emotions when it came to us together. If she had felt

342

nothing I could never have stopped her. If she felt nothing she would not reach for me when she needed comfort.

"They may not give you a choice." Maylee crossed her arms angrily pulling away from me.

"Why do you say that?" Looking around I knew it would only be a matter of time before the council sent Kamran to find her even if Izabella had been here. They would send him to drive the point home. That they were giving her no choice but to return.

"For them to leave you alone one of two things would have to happen. Either you would have to agree or have your powers stripped. Either way you have to go back." Uncrossing her arms she shook her head miserably.

"What if we just ran? Just go away and make sure they never find us." Closing my eyes I shook my head. If only we could.

"I wish we could Maylee. But we can't. Not now. Not because I don't want to. But they will not stop until they have you or somehow the other side will find you and use you against them." Acknowledging what I told her she walked into the woods to be alone. I saw Danny appear walking with her. Dammit. If my damn spells and sigils had been stronger I could have kept them away.

"No. You could not have." Shadow stated walking up to where I sat on the log from the fire the night before.

"Because I am not strong enough."

"No. The council will force her hand. One way or another. You must convince her to go on her own. The council is not above torture my friend. They will hurt her to make her fight for them."

"Like hell they will."

"Than make her see" His head swung back to the trail where Maylee had walked with Danny. *"Kamran is here."* Standing I walked to the trail.

343

"No. Izabella told us we had time."

"He will kill her Dante. Go!"

Maylee

I walked what looked like a trail further into the woods away from Dante. I needed time to think.

"Maylee. What is wrong?" Danny asked as he walked with his shoulder against mine.

"They will force me return." Using his teeth he gripped my shirt stopping me before pulling me back to him.

"Maylee. You have to go back. Not because any of them told you or because you owe them. You owe it to yourself to reach your full potential. To learn your limits and to know when you reach them to stop before you overextend again. What they did to you two was a mistake. They should never have tested you before they knew the extent of your powers. So for now. Relax as Izabella told you. And return to learn to control your powers."

"What if I still refuse?"

"The way I see it there are a few options. And a few the others did not see or just did not tell you. It is possible for the council to demand you come back. They will send a hunter to find you and drag you in literally if they have to. And I hate to tell you but I will agree with Dante. They will most likely send Kamran. He knows your energy and he is ruthless when it comes to hunting. Or another option they may consider is to have him hunt you but kill you." My chest tightened as I knew he was telling me as it was.

"I will give it a few days first." Nodding his head he disappeared into the wind. Tilting my head I saw something out of the corner of my eye drawing Starburst turning to look. In between a few larger trees was Kamran. "What do you want?"

My voice sounding much angrier than intended. He flinched at my tone before stepping in front of me.

"I was sent to find you." Running steps told me Dante was coming up beside me.

"Well. Here I am. Now what?" Kamran ran his eyes over me smirking.

"Izabella told me she had already found you and gave you an ultimatum. Good thing she found you first." Scowling at his tone I crossed my arms over my chest angrily.

"Why? Did they send you to kill me?" Glancing to Dante his face drained of all color as did Kamran's.

"No. This time they only wanted me to find you. Next time I am not sure what they will ask. So please Maylee. When Izabella comes back. Leave with her. I do not want to be sent after you again." With that he shimmered out. Once he was gone I collapsed to my knees out of breath. It was true. They had sent him to kill me. Only he issued a warning. I felt Dante's hand on my shoulder as he knelt beside me.

"Sounds like they are not giving you a choice. We will have to return when Izabella comes back." Shaking my head I looked up at him.

"No!" My voice screamed. "I refuse! They can kill me!" Angry Dante sat back staring at me in shock.

"For someone who fights as well as you do. You sure gave up quickly." Looking around before back to me as he stood up. "I love you Maylee. But I will not watch you destroy yourself to stay away from them." With that he walked back to camp leaving me kneeling on the ground. Danny reappeared walking up to where I sat nudging me to stand.

"Maylee. You need to stop this. This is turning into something it does not need to." Wiping my tears away I stood in front of him.

346

"What do you mean?" Snorting as he looked behind him Shadow walked up beside him.

"What have you done to him? He is at camp raging. Maylee. What is going on?"

"Shadow. I'm sorry. I just can't do this. I can't. The council expects so much from me. And so does everyone else." Pawing the ground nervously he glanced back to camp for a moment.

"You were excited about all this when I met you. And I know that it scared you when your powers went too far. But if you walk away right now you will be doing more than that. You will outright kill him. This is bigger than you." Pivoting around he walked back to camp.

"He's right Maylee. Now besides what happened on the coast what changed your mind?" Thinking back I remembered how skeptical I had been when Izabella found us. Realizing I had real powers and Izabella teaching me how to use them.

"That was it." I admitted shaking my head. Turning to Danny I frowned. "I lost my fight. But thinking back just now I'm angry again. I want to go back and hurt them for doing what they did to us." Tossing his head he nickered pulling me to his chest.

"It's back now." Nodding I rubbed my face realizing what an ass I had made of myself to everyone. "You should apologize to him." Nodding once again I thanked him walking to camp. Dante was sitting on the log by the campfire muttering angrily. Without a word I walked up to where he was sitting kneeling in front of him taking his hands. I couldn't even bring myself to look at him knowing I had made him so angry.

"I'm sorry. For everything. For what I said. And for making you so angry. I wasn't thinking straight." Taking a hand from mine he lifted my chin to look at him. He smirked a little as a tear made its way down my face.

"Welcome back." Choking out I could barely speak.

"Shadow and Danny both told me what an ass I was being. Hard to believe it was them that made me see. Especially Shadow. His truth was hardest for me." Glancing to Shadow Dante nodded.

"What did he tell you?"

"What is going on is bigger than me. That if I truly tried to leave I would have basically killed you." Scoffing he shook his head.

"Harsh. But effective. He is good at that. And I am glad that he managed to break through to you." Nodding I attempted to stand only to be pulled back. "Why was he able to break through to you on that alone?" Taking in a sharp breath I realized what he was asking. And even though I knew the answer. I could not bring myself to admit it.

"Because I don't want to be the reason anyone dies." Frowning he released my hand. That was not the answer he wanted from me.

"Okay." With that he stood walking into the woods. Shadow looked to me tilting his head.

"What did you do now?"

"I don't know." Sitting on the log he shifted into a panther sitting beside me.

"I think you do." Sitting upright I stared at him.

"Yes. I do. But I am not ready to tell him." Shaking his head he trotted into the woods after his master. "I am absolutely fucking this up." I said under my breath.

"I would not say that Maylee." Jumping I looked up to Izabella.

"I thought you said you were giving us a few days to relax."

"I did. Dante called for me. He told me it was an emergency." Shrugging I had no idea what he was talking about.

"He went into the woods." Pointing her to where he walked. She frowned instead sitting beside me.

"Maylee. You know how he feels about you."

"Yes." Taking my wrist she checked my hand.

"You are afraid." My body began to shake.

"Yes." Sighing she released my wrist.

"Of what? Of Dante?" Shaking my head I stood looking around nervously.

"No. Not of him." Frowning she stood making me stop to look at her.

"Than what the hell is wrong with you?"

"I don't know." Still frowning she shook her head.

"You really do not know what it is." She said more to herself. "I will talk to him. Just stay here. Please." Nodding she strode into the woods after Dante. Dammit. I knew what he wanted. And I knew Izabella wanted to scold me for not telling him. Sighing I grabbed my gear from inside the tent calling for Marlo as quietly as possible. Landing with a crash only feet away I strode to him tying my gear on as quickly as I could manage knowing both Izabella and Dante would be sprinting to stop me. Looking around I did not see either of them mounting up. I felt someone grab my wrist hard as I was about to adjust my seat.

"No. You are not leaving like this Maylee. I refuse to let you." Feeling tears in my eyes I ripped my wrist away from him shifting into place.

"I can't be around you like this Dante. I'm sorry. For everything." Without even looking at him I signaled Marlo to take off. I could hear Dante yelling as I flew higher and further away. As I flew my chest began to ache to the point I was in tears from the pain. Biting the inside of my mouth I pulled my dagger out pulling the sleeve of my shirt up slicing my right arm until the pain eased. Only a few miles later my chest ached to the point I could hardly breathe. Gritting my teeth I bore down on the pain until I could not.

"Izabella. Please. I need your help." Hunched over I felt someone grab me from behind to keep me on my dragon.

"You really do not choose ideal times for me to help you."

"I'm sorry. Really I am." She nodded keeping hold of me.

"Signal him to land. Now."

"No" I heard her growl behind me.

"Land him now. Or I will let go." Irritably I signaled Marlo to land. There was no way I made it anywhere besides Iceland. Hell probably not even the United Kingdom. As soon as we landed Izabella pulled me off roughly by the back of my shirt forcing me to sit down. "I just finished talking to him and he calls me again to tell me you took off. I had just talked him down. Now. You refused to tell me before you took off. What the hell is wrong with you?"

"He's pissed at me Izabella. That was why I left. Why I'm on my own. He yelled at me to not leave. But I couldn't stand to be around him when he wanted me to make up my mind." She sighed pulling my hands away from my face as I shook my head miserably.

"You know how you feel about him. You just refuse to admit it. And if you do not admit it soon to yourself and to him. The pain you feel in your chest will worsen. Each time you are upset with each other, arguing, separated. It will grow worse and it will never go away. Now why"

"I don't want to get hurt again. And come on Izabella. You cannot sit there and tell me you did not recruit me to die in this war. I am not stupid. How long had the others on the island been training when you finally decided to recruit my sister and I? You know I will never learn everything I need in the time allotment. And now when I am supposedly training with the council they turn on us. They tried to kill us." Izabella looked at me thoughtfully before sighing. I looked up at her as she leaned forward towards me.

"Okay. I sense your anger and confusion. But"

"No. No but. Why did you bother to recruit me if you knew I would die? Why would you allow Dante to fall in love with me knowing I was going to die?" My chest ached worse as I spoke his name. Watching my breathing Izabella waited for me to calm.

"The decision was not mine to make. If it had been up to me you would have been here much sooner. It was the council who decided"

"The same council that just tried to kill us?" Scoffing she laid a hand on my shoulder.

"They were testing you. Not trying to kill you." Yanking away I scowled angrily.

"If I had not opened a chasm that swallowed a soldier Dante would have been ran through with a god damn sword." Izabella smirked crossing her arms over her chest.

"Why would you save him if you have no feelings for him?"

"Do not change the fucking subject Izabella."

"But I am Maylee." She growled at me. Startled at the fact she took the opportunity to cut in. "The council decides when we were allowed to recruit certain power holders. You were purposely left for last due to who you are. And yes. This circles back to your lost memories. And I know you do not want to know about them. That is fine. But you need to know why Dante was so drawn to you from the first day." Shaking my head I turned away from her picking up my gear bag.

"No. I do not want to be with him knowing I am going to die. Just keep me separated from him."

"No. You will go back to the council for further training. And just because you want to stay away from him you will be

351

training with him." She stared me down as we both scowled. "That is final."

"Than I will keep running. I will use Marlo and Danny and never stop." Tears threatened to leave my eyes with my anger. Instead of staying angry her expression softened gripping my shoulders staring into my eyes.

"Maylee. Stop. I understand your anger. I do. What we are asking of you is not fair. Especially when you do not understand. But you are not being fair to Dante. He was able to heal you when I failed. You know you have a connection to him. Especially since you slept with him." I felt my face heat. She was not wrong. My chest tightened again as I shook my head.

"I should not have. Not when I need to stay away from him."

"Maylee" She pressed my pressure point hard enough I fell to my knees. Angrily she pushed me back stepping onto my shoulder with her boot. "My patience is gone with you right now." Attempting to throw her foot off she planted it into my collar bone.

"Okay. I'm listening. Let me up."

"I am taking you back to Ireland. You will train with the council. And you are going to tell me right now." Izabella emphasized her point digging her heel into my collar bone painfully. "You will stay with that boy because you are not going to die in this war. He does not deserve the pain you have caused him today. Now. Since I have you in a place you cannot escape. Tell me. When I let you up. What are you going to do?" I wrapped my hands around her ankle attempting to move her foot from my shoulder. Instead of removing it she dug her heel in again. Gritting my teeth it hurt that time.

"Let me up Izabella."

"Not until you tell me what you are doing when I let you up."

"I will tell you whatever you want until you leave. Than I am running again." I heard her sigh before digging her heel in again. "Ow. Stop. Please."

"No" She said simply crossing her arms once again. "You know. I think you might require someone else to convince you."

"Like who? Dante? I'm sure you told him I'm here by now." Smirking she shook her head.

"No. Someone much more convincing." I heard screeching before a falcon landed beside me turning to Shadow in a flash. Danny appeared at his side.

"Oh for fuck sake. Not both of you too."

"Izabella. Why do you have her pinned to the ground?" Shadow asked walking closer.

"She needs a wake up call. She was running away."

"I told you why! You recruited me to fighting in a war I am supposed to die in!" She dug her heel in again causing me to go silent. In a flash Shadow was a dog laying beside me as tears leaked from my eyes.

"Maylee. Look at me." Shadow told me gently. "Calm yourself. Immediately. Izabella let her up." Izabella scoffed removing her heel allowing me to sit up. Danny rested his nose on my shoulder.

"Take a breath Maylee. You are fine." Taking a deep breath I nodded.

"Okay. Okay. Message received. You both want me to go back too."

"Yes." Both Shadow and Danny replied. "You also owe Dante an apology Maylee." Shadow told me factly. Scoffing I shook my head before standing.

"No. I owe him more than that." Izabella smirked.

"You are too right. You need to tell him you feel the same about him as he does for you. If that was not the case you would never have saved him from that soldier." Sighing I nodded in agreement.

"I know. I know that I love him. It is just hard to admit." The constriction in my chest lifted instantly. She patted my shoulder smiling a little.

"I know how hard that was for you. Admitting it to yourself was very difficult. Now you have to tell him."

"I know. Every time he's near me I just want to be next to him. He's the only one I have ever been around who could drive me insane but also keep me calm." She nodded.

"There. Now that is admitting it." Nodding I stood walking away a few feet feeling nauseous. More because I realized what an ass I had just been trying to run away.

"He refused to tell me his past until I admitted to him how I felt."

"Seems pretty fair. He went through hell Maylee. He knows after you find out you will not see him the same."

"Shadow told me to be easy on him. That most of the time it wasn't his fault."

"That is fairly true. I saved him a few times. Two times he doesn't know about."

"But I have secrets as well Izabella. You don't even know mine." Confused she frowned stepping closer.

"What do you mean Maylee?" Sniffing a couple times I pulled up the sleeve of my right arm. "Dammit. Maylee. Why the hell did you do that?"

"I would rather be in physical pain than emotional or mental. It's something I have done for a long time." Grabbing my arm she healed the cuts that had been bleeding and the scars that had been there.

"Does Dante know you do that? How did he not see this while you were in his apartment? Or how had I not before now?" I shook my head avoiding her look.

"No. I had not done it in months. That was the first time for a while. I've been using makeup when I'm in training so you did not know."

"Why now?"

"I felt like I couldn't face my emotions. They were too strong to understand. And I hate myself for hurting him." Sighing she sat beside me taking my hand causing me to look at her.

"Why do you hate yourself to the point of pain?"

"Because I have caused nothing but pain since I have had these powers. I've lost family because of them. I'm not supposed to contact my friends. I feel like I have no where to go. No one to talk to. Why do you think I pushed myself so hard? I figured I might actually be able to do something right. Do something for the good and maybe I would deserve a break from all the bad. But as I found out. The good was too much and I ran away. I don't deserve anything good." Izabella squeezed my hand.

"I have never met two people who deserved each other more than the two of you. You have both been through hell. Different yes. He was physically abused by his father to the point it became emotional. You have been emotionally and physically abused." Pausing she looked into my eyes making it feel as if she was searching my soul. "Your mother never treated you well. And your father prefers your sister. You were ignored. You use that as your mechanism. That is why you have such a high guard. Interesting." Shaking my head as if she had me in a trance I was slightly thrown off.

"What do you mean?"

355

"You turned to your grandparents for any kind of emotional support. They were the only ones who showed you how love works. You have trust issues. Someone you loved dearly hurt you. Physically and emotionally."

"You make it sound as if I was neglected. My parents gave me everything." She smirked slightly at those words.

"What you needed. Never something you wanted."

"Of course they did." She nodded as if she did not really believe me but stood signaling we were walking. "Look. We discussed my trust issues on the way to the island. Remember?" She nodded looking distant.

"I do Maylee. And I heard your sister take those digs at you for acting the way you did towards Dante on the ship. So I do understand why you have kept your distance. But he has already proven himself to you. A few times over. Now it is your turn." Nodding I understood what she was saying.

"Alright. He's on his way. Isn't he?"

"No. I told him to stay where he was until I could find you."

"You found me over an hour ago."

"Yes."

"So he's on his way here."

"No."

"You just said"

"I did not tell him I found you. If I had he would already be here and I would never have found out from you why you ran off. Or how you felt about him." Huffing heavily I shook my head resting my hands on my hips.

"I'm not ready to tell him. I just admitted to myself and to you. I just. I just can't. Not yet."

"Maylee. You are have to tell him. He has already told me he thought about returning home just so they would end him.

He knows if he steps foot on that place they will kill him. Or worse seeing as he refused to lead them when they told him to."

"You're telling me if I don't tell him how I feel he will return home to be killed? So it would be my fault if he decided that." Pinching the bridge of my nose I was stressed out. Walking to Marlo Izabella untied my bags throwing them at me.

"Go for a run. Let me know when you are back. I am returning to Russia to calm him down." Nodding I changed as she shimmered out.

Considering it was warm and humid in these woods. I must have landed in the United Kingdom. It seemed as if I had ran for hours when I made it back to where Marlo had remained while I was gone. Breathing hard I removed my ear buds abruptly hearing two people talking heatedly. Walking closer to the voices I recognized them both as I sighed heavily shaking my head.

"Why the hell would you tell her that! It would not be her fault!" Dante yelled. I felt my chest throb when he did.

"The hell it would not be kid. I did not bust my ass for the last five years keeping you alive just for you to go back to get yourself killed!" Izabella sounded just as angry with him as she had been with me.

"What I do is none of your damn business! You should never have saved me to begin with!" Looking around the tree I watched them arguing.

"Really? What was I supposed to do? Stand by and watch some kid killed by his own father because he could never do what his father expected from him? I was not going to watch an innocent kid slaughtered." The difference of when she was angry with me versus with him was now her face was red. Whoa. Izabella was legitimately angry. She must have been calm angry when she was arguing with me.

"I told you I was not innocent Izabella. I killed that kid at the cave!" What? He looked so hurt by the fact.

"That was an accident Dante. I was there. I saw the whole thing. You were going to spare him. When you turned he ran into you. There was nothing you could do. You never killed anyone after that." Damn. No wonder he did not think I would see him the same.

There was a long stretch of silence making me jump realizing that one or both knew I was there. Quickly I turned walking back to Marlo. It was obvious from what I had overheard that he still cared about me. That he was angry with Izabella for suggesting it would be my fault he left.

Tears slid down my face burning my eyes as anger coursed through me again. So instead of staying with Marlo I ran. I could hear someone yelling for me as I ran since I had removed my ear buds. Suddenly someone wrapped their arms around my midsection pulling me to a stop sideways almost falling. Breathing hard I tried to catch my breath as I wiped the tears from my eyes. Arms around my shoulders pulled me against them holding me close. Just from the smell of who I was against I knew it was Dante.

"I'm sorry. I don't want you to leave. I don't want you to go back to them. I will tell you anything you want me to." He held me tight burying his head into my shoulder. Shaking his head he pulled back until our foreheads touched.

"I know you don't want me to leave. I did not plan on leaving. Not now. Not after I have met you and spent time with you. Okay? I'm not angry about that. Or that you want to know about my past. You have the right to know those things. But I also have a right to know what I feel for you is the same you have for me before I do that." Nodding against him I slowly nudged closer until our noses touched initiating kissing him. The connection was instant and burning as we both wanted the other. It was as if we were fighting for which of us was receiving the deeper kiss. After a few moments we slowed drifting apart his hands on my face looking at me with relief smiling a little.

"Was that your answer?" I smirked.

"Part of it." Sighing he pulled me against his side as we began walking.

"So what is the other part?"

"I'm not sure I'm ready to admit that yet." Stopping he turned me to face him.

"Maylee. Look at me." Shaking my head I felt tears in my eyes.

"I can't. Not knowing how disappointed you are that I can not seem to admit how I feel to you when I just came to terms with it myself." I heard him chuckle startling me to look up at him. Smiling at me he gave a nod.

"Do I look disappointed?"

"But I" He shook his head.

"What? You overheard me and Izabella arguing. I knew you were close. Than I heard running. I ran after you. I do not want you to think the argument was over you." Closing my eyes I knew it had been.

"So you only followed me because you didn't want me to think the argument was about me? Dante. I know it was. I heard most of the argument. And Izabella was pissed at me for running by the way."

"I figured she was when she came back to let me know where you were." He told me quietly. "But she knows we cannot allow you to take off like that. The other side would have captured you. You would not have just been running away. That was why Izabella was so angry."

"Dammit." I knew he was right. "Look. I'm not used to any of this. I'm not used to being corralled into one spot. I hate not traveling. I have told Izabella as much." He made his own exasperated sound.

"You are so damn difficult sometimes. I mean seriously. Traveling for you without any of us accompanying you is dangerous."

"Would you two shut the hell up." Izabella walked in between us shoving me away from Dante glaring at me.

"What?" Dante and I looked at each other confused as to why she was suddenly so angry again.

"We just discussed what before I told you to go for your run. Now knock it off or" I laughed shaking my head.

"Or what? What could you possibly do that hasn't been done to me already? Take me away from everything I know? We did that already. For a month without the ability to communicate back home. Torture me? Well. The enemy managed that three weeks ago attacking me on the trails. How about you throw me in jail or prison. Just do it. I'm fucking done with this." Dante grabbed my arm pulling me to face him before I could walk any further.

"Hey, its okay." I didn't even realize I had began crying until he wrapped his arms around me and I began to sob. "I know how hard this has been for you."

"It's been easier since I've been with you."

"I agree. It has been." Finally I pulled back looking up at him again. It was the truth. Doing everything on the island had been easier in the last few weeks. I felt like I could breathe and relax with him at my side.

"It's time for me to say what I should have told you days ago." He frowned.

"Tell me what?" Shaking my head I smirked.

"You know what." He smiled holding me against him tightly.

"I have no idea."

"I love you Dante. I know I should have told you sooner." The tension that had been in my chest the last two weeks finally melted away. I felt him relax as well as he smiled wider.

"I love you too Maylee."

"Now that you two have finally acknowledged the fact. You have to return to Ireland." We pulled apart quickly as both of us were angry about that.

"Why should we return? They attacked us!" She shook her head.

"No. That was Kamran's sister Aliyah testing you both before you began training. She did not realize Maylee had as much power as she does."

"Are you serious? A damned test? Without warning us? That was smart. Maylee could have" Stopping before he said it I still knew what he was going to say.

"Killed myself." He looked to me sharply.

"You could have."

"I know." I replied quietly. "They could have at least introduced themselves before they decided to test us."

"I am not going to disagree. Their technique was off on you two. They did not realize you two fought so well together since you had never actually trained together."

"No. But we communicate telepathically. That was how we fought together so well." Izabella smirked at the two of us.

"And the fact that you two fight in a similar style. Uncommon for two people who have never trained together."

"Great. So now we go back?"

"Yes. Tomorrow morning. I want you both rested up when you return. No hurry. Take your time. And Dante" He looked up at her wearily. "You know what you need to do now." Giving a small nod Izabella shimmered out.

"What you need to do now?"

"Yeah. That is her code for I have to spill my past to you."

"I had almost forgotten that."

"Wish I could." Barely audible but I had heard him. Whether out loud or in his head I was not sure. Leaning against him his eyes had glazed over.

"You don't have to tell me if you don't want to. I don't need to know. Not if it causes you that much pain." Shaking his head he led me to a log to sit on.

"We should build our campfire before I start."

"It's only" Checking my phone it was already five in the evening in this time zone. "Alright."

It did not take long for us to gather the wood we would need to keep our fire rolling for those few hours. We also set the tent up although I was not sure we would need it. The weather was beautiful and the sky was clear.

"Are you sure you want to tell me everything?" I asked after we had sat down. He nodded releasing my hand rubbing the back of his neck.

"I'm going to tell you. Just don't think too badly of me. Please." Looking weary it was as if he was begging me.

"I'll try not to. If nothing else I might just be quiet for a few days. That's usually how I process things." He nodded taking a deep breath like he was plunging into the deep abyss.

"My father first started teaching me to sword fight when I was ten." Pausing he took a steadying breath. "Even though my mother begged him to not teach me. To not involve me in what he did. He wouldn't listen to any kind of reason from her. Soon after that he taught me about secret symbols. The symbols used in magik. Mostly dark and protective symbols. Potions I did not learn until I was twelve. That was not easy." I laid a hand on his arm reassuringly. He did not know I had overheard the part of the conversation he thought would cause me to see him badly. Laying his hand over mine he nodded taking another deep breath.

"My sword training increased each year I turned older. My father hired someone to instruct me. I never learned his name but I knew for certain that he was very harsh. He was hired when I turned fourteen. I also learned to fight from horseback. He was actually the one who brought Shadow to me. Shadow was only a couple month old foal who had lost his mother. I helped raise him. The man allowed me keep him." Shadow had been telling the truth. Only at this I could see why Dante was the way he was. He stared at me for a moment before he continued.

"My father brought home some rocks from the mountains of a foreign country he had visited away on 'business'. He told me what to do with each one. I tried each one individually. They worked. He took all but one back making me work with that one for three months straight. I had to repeat the process with each one. He went as far as to send me to Syracuse for training. I did well there. Until I was sixteen. When you go to their training you ascend or receive your full powers. Once I ascended the master sent me home. And my father treated me worse than ever. When I returned he was ruthless to say the least. During training one day I received a nice slash down my leg here." He stopped drawing a line from his quadricep muscle to the inside of his knee on the right side. I had never noticed it when we had been together.

"It was a draw. I didn't win. Neither did my father. My father sent me on my first mission knowing I would fail to teach me humility I guess. I had to retrieve some rock or gem from a cave that was heavily protected. My father gave me some men

363

to help out if needed. I used a spell to enter the cave. The spell rebounded killing all the men leaving me standing alone. I don't know how or why. So I returned without the gem and had lost all my men along with it."

"He beat me within an inch of my life. Afterward he made me heal myself. He said that he had wasted his time with me and would rather put the effort into my brother who was so much better than I would ever be. After I was fully healed he pushed and shoved me until we were outside. He made me fight with my sword. My defensive powers kicked in when my knees hit the ground from exhaustion. My invisible shield went up not allowing him near me.

"I caught my breath and started yelling at him about how much I hated everything he was making me do. I still had the shield around me so I stood up and took off with Shadow. I stayed in the woods for over a week. Unfortunately I knew I had to go back. Walking Shadow up the driveway I put him away in the stable.

"When I stepped out to walk to the house my father grabbed me by the throat pinning me against the stable wall. He was furious that I had left the way I did and had another mission for me."

Dante stopped talking looking at me. I was looking into the woods trying to imagine everything he was telling me. I suddenly noticed he had stopped jerking my head toward him.

"I'm listening. I just can't imagine" Nodding he knew what I was trying to say. "I'm good. Keep going. Please." His nostrils flared as he breathed out hard nodding squeezing my hand.

"My father had another mission for me. I had to recruit another sorcerer like myself. He released me and I collapsed onto the ground gasping for air. He dropped everything onto me telling me to leave right away. I did. And found the kid I was looking for. He threw a few fireballs at me. We battled back and forth. Half an hour later I left with minor injuries. He had escaped." He looked away looking sick even now just thinking about it.

"My father found out he had escaped and was furious. I was watching my sister ride her horse the day he found out. He beat me within an inch of my life before sending me on another mission. I had to retrieve rare gems from a cave the same sorcerer was guarding. He told me to kill him if I had to and not return until I had the gems. I left quickly. I met Izabella along the way that day. When I arrived at the cave the kid smirked knowing I couldn't defeat him with my powers. We fought with weapons instead. I was going to let him go. We had both paused the fight. I turned when I heard something snap. He began to walk forward when I turned running into my sword. It killed him." Pausing he shook his head looking angry that it had happened.

"It made me sick. He had warned me about the people I worked for. I knew he was right, but I didn't have a choice. My father and one of his lieutenants had followed me to where I was after it was all done. They laughed saying that I would get used to it. Get used to killing others for them. That I wouldn't get sick if I did it more. After that they constantly sent me on missions. I would return successful but I never had to duel to the death again.

"Just before my nineteenth birthday he was sent on his own mission. He had been gone for several months, a dark figure showed up at our door telling my mother he had been killed following his duties. At least that was what they told my mom. She cried for a week straight. My sister Gabrielle helped her through it. That wasn't what really happened though. He had been home when he died. I had been with him. He was alive one moment. Next I know I'm in the house and he was dead. Both my mom and sister begged me to not follow in his footsteps. I promised them both I would change and work against them instead.

"My brother however refused saying that he would avenge our father's death. He promised to train harder and when he was ready would lead the attack on the council and their armies. We had my father's funeral. A month later I left hiding from my father's superiors. I did not want them to find me. I visited his grave one more time before I left to find someone from the council. I figured I could help." Some child hood. Damn. Mine had nothing on his.

"You said you knew what they were up to. That is why you ran." He nodded.

"Yes. My telepathic powers began to develop around the time of my father's funeral. While some of his colleagues were there I used my new power. All they could think about was using me against another person that the council had to win an upcoming war. I was supposedly so powerful and had gone on so many missions successfully. I did not want anything to do with them. As soon as the service was over I was gone. I did not give them the chance."

I thought it over silently. He watched me carefully. I really just needed to clear my mind after all that information. Summoning Danny I stood meeting him. Dante stood beside me watching me looking worried.

"I will be back in a minute." Danny came trotting out of the nearest trail. I swung up walking onto the trail he had just come off of. Dante looked like he wanted to say something but decided to let me leave. I did not go far. I just needed time to think. I told Danny about Dante's past. He was alert but seemed almost relieved.

"I overheard him before he admitted he killed someone just now." Danny tilted his head back at me.

"You realize he was not given a choice. I saw the two of you talking. He deeply regrets what he has done. He will not do it again. Why do you think he hated using his powers?" Considering what he said I nodded knowing he was correct.

"Good point." It was pitch black when I finally returned to camp where the fire was blazing. Dante looked up as he saw us approaching.

"Are you okay?" He asked worriedly walking up when I slid down.

"I'm fine. I trust you. Especially after everything that has happened lately. I'm sorry you had it so rough." I realized that I felt bad for what he had been through. Turning to look at him he was impassive.

"I escaped. And we are together. It will be us against them Maylee." He acted as if a weight had been removed from his shoulders. Holding a hand out I took it allowing him to lead me to the log sitting in front of the fire. As we sat there I rested my head against his shoulder almost falling asleep watching the flames dance.

"What would happen if you went home right now?" Instantly he tensed looking down at me worriedly.

"You can't possibly be serious." I shrugged.

"You have a mother and sister there right? I'm sure I have heard Izabella mention them." Standing he walked away a few steps fighting something in his head.

"Yes. And my brother. Younger brother." Frowning I could only imagine what he was thinking right now.

"What do they think about all of this?" He shot a very dark glance that said it all.

"Like I said. My brother is all for Theasis. He was brainwashed properly. My father kept my sister totally out of it. He didn't want his only daughter involved."

"So what would happen if we showed up?" An angry look was on his face but the anger was not directed at me.

"My own brother would try to kill me if I walked back into the house." Standing I walked over in front of him.

"We need to go. I would go to the house. Not you." He grabbed my shoulders hard.

"Absolutely not. I cannot go back there. And I will not allow you to go alone." I scowled crossing my arms stepping out of his grip.

"I can take care of myself. You do not have to protect me. I think I have shown you that." We had a stare down.

"No. And that is final."

"Maybe for you. But I could leave without you." He looked away fighting an inner battle.

"I know you would." He stared into my eyes as his voice was barely audible. "But please don't. I don't want to be the one responsible for your death. The council would kill me not to mention Izabella for allowing you to leave." He was pleading with me. Sighing I softened a little.

"Fine. I won't. But eventually you have to return."

"I know. And I will want you at my side. But this is not that time. Alright?" After promising I would not try to go to his house on my own we turned in for the night lying down on the mattress in the tent. Dante wrapped his arms around my midsection tightly resting his head on my shoulder.

"I love you Maylee." I smiled laying my hands over his.

"I love you too. We need sleep." I felt him nod against the side of my face relaxing into his embrace.

Just before dawn I woke watching Dante sleep to be sure he was still asleep. Slowly I untangled myself from him even as comfortable as I was. Silently I left the tent calling for Danny to help me leave for Texas. He blatantly refused making me alternate to Marlo who made more noise when he landed taking off the moment I was on signaling him to go right away.

Dante

The ground outside shook violently causing me to sit up. For a moment I listened for what it had been. It was the sound of one of the dragons taking off Maylee was not in the tent.

"Maylee!" I scrambled to untangle myself from the blankets hurrying out of the tent. Danny was standing just outside the campsite. No! Everything was gone. "Dammit!"

"Go after her!" I heard from Danny.

"I am. I don't have to be told twice. What was she thinking?" He tossed his head taking a step closer as I shook my head at her actions.

"She did it to protect you. She would rather take the risk upon herself than to have you walk in there and be killed." Shaking my head again I called for Dillon.

"Danny just keep watch of her. Don't let her get hurt." With that he disappeared into the air. I jumped on Dillon after dressing at top speed packing quickly taking to the air. I had to catch her. If they caught her it would be the end for us. Keeping watch of anywhere she could have landed on my way. Great. Home. How much I had hated it there. The way my father had treated me. I didn't tell her half of what happened. Not really.

She could only have had maybe half an hour jump as I flew over the ocean. Remembering what the dragon trainers had told us I knew she would not have made it to Texas without resting.

"Shadow" He perched on my shoulder as a hawk tilting his head. "Find her" Nodding he flew ahead of us into the clouds

370

where I lost sight of him. Dillon was wearing down as I saw a coast looming ahead.

"She landed in Virginia. I see her. I will fly back and take you to her." Shadow appeared in front of Dillon screeching. Signaling Dillon he tilted to follow Shadow. I thought I saw something in a clearing in the forest. Turning Dillon around we landed a little further away in case it was not someone friendly. I carefully walked through the forest into the clearing making sure to keep my senses wide open for an attack. "She is near here. That is another descendant." Nodding I heard him I observed the dragon. This one had blue spikes and ridges. I did not remember one like that.

"Friendly or non friendly?" In a flash Shadow was in dog form sniffing the air.

"Smells familiar. From the ship." Perplexed I nodded staying hidden. I waited until I could see the face of the person I was about to deal with. He stood up looking around feeling my presence. It was Nathan Kinsly. I stepped out into the open with my hands up.

"It's Dante. Take it easy." I walked toward him lowering my arms. He eyed me carefully before sheathing his sword looking no more thrilled at my appearance as I was to be here.

"What are you doing here?" He asked pointedly. I raised my eyebrows at his tone. If he was scouting for the council I could understand some hostility. If not and he was running I needed to know.

"Well. I could ask you the same thing." Nodding he saw things my way so I continued. "I'm looking for Maylee. Have you seen her?" He nodded again pointing to the east side of the clearing.

"How did you two get separated?" He asked curiously as I took a deep breath relieved she was here.

"Don't ask." I responded shaking my head walking in the direction he had pointed. I could already see her as she was seated on a tree stump meditating with Danny standing at her side. Slowly. Quietly. I walked up to her other side waiting for her to finish.

"You found me already." She stated without even opening her eyes.

"I could not allow you to go alone." Her eyes snapped open standing quickly in front of me anger flashing. I stepped back quickly knowing she needed space.

"I'm not alone as you can see. I found Nathan on my way here."

"And why was he here?" She turned away from me walking back toward the camp. I hated when she did that. I caught up to her in steps staying at her side.

"On a scouting mission." Pausing she looked over at me with raised eyebrows. "Don't worry I messaged Izabella to confirm it." She was actually being haughty with me. Seriously?

"Why did you take off like that?" She just kept walking as her expression never changed. "Maylee!" I said sharply as I reached grabbing her arm above the elbow stopping her. She stopped without trying to throw my hand off turning to me looking at the ground. That was what she did when she knew she had been wrong. Or when she felt insecure about something. I had noticed her doing this a lot once she woke from her coma. And Izabella had told me why. Which was why I had been so patient with her. Why I stopped myself from exploding the day she struck me. I knew she had bad experiences with men. I was not about to continue that for her. That was not me.

"You know why." She replied quietly causing me to worry more about her.

"I told you what would happen if they caught you!" My voice rising as I said it. "Honestly? I don't want them to win. When they do everything will be destroyed. At least if we win all we have to do is rebuild. Please Maylee. I am begging you. Do not do this. Do not go to my home." Looking up at me with half a grin on her face almost as if challenging me.

"You worry too much." God! She is so difficult sometimes. I shook my head at her.

"I don't want you to get hurt." I told her growing frustrated. Now she fully smiled standing up straight.

"I know that."

"Why are you so damn stubborn?" She turned walking all the way back to camp where Nathan was stirring the fire when we arrived.

"Must have been a good conversation. I didn't hear screaming or see anything explode." The sad part was he was being sincere. It made me chuckle. Maylee did too.

"Yeah. I was not blown away or scorched."

"I could change that." She said good naturedly holding a fireball in her hand but I signaled her.

"No. I'm good." Laughing again she walked to the west side of the woods. "Where are you going?" Stopping she half turned back to me.

"To the river to clean up. Why? Writing a book?" She asked with the same attitude as earlier. I managed to maintain my calm by some miracle.

"No. I don't want you to take off again." Raising her eyebrows at me she kept walking. I heard Nathan let out a deep breath.

"Damn. She is a firecracker." Sitting on a tree stump near him I watched her until I couldn't see her anymore. I was half tempted to follow her. Feeling watched myself I looked over to Nathan.

"You have no idea." I told him more annoyed by her actions. "What?" I asked as he shook his head after shooting me a look.

"Anyone can see you two are meant for each other. I barely recognized her when she walked into my camp. She's changed. Not to mention we all thought she was dead. Have you asked her out yet?" I thought about what he said mulling it over for a moment.

"She knows. And she feels the same. She's just having a hard time with everything. And she has changed as have her powers. All I know is that I don't want to be near her when she is angry lashing out with those powers." He smirked looking to where she had walked out of view.

"Are you two actually together now?"

"Yes. We are together now." We both looked up as Maylee came running back standing in case someone was chasing her. There was nothing. She had noticed us standing looking over her shoulder too.

"It's okay guys. You can chill. Just a letter." Holding it up for us to see. "It's from Izabella to both of us." She ripped it open reading it all the way through before handing it to me looking angry. It read like this:

***

Maylee,

You and Dante are to return to Ireland immediately! Whatever you are currently doing drop it. You both need to return ASAP for further training. Do not let anyone know you are alive just yet, it could be a disaster. I will meet you there in two days to talk further.

Izabella

When I handed it back to her I thought she was going to rip it up.

"She told us we had to go back Maylee." She nodded stiffly. I knew she was remembering she had nearly killed herself there. Speaking of which. It is nearly ninety degrees out here and she's wearing a long sleeve shirt? I found that strange. But, I have also saw shorts with sleeveless shirts in zero too. I shook it out of my mind as she stepped closer.

"But first we go to your home. I want to see what is happening before we return." I cannot say that I was surprised by this.

"Izabella told us to drop what we were doing to return to Ireland." Glaring at me her hands rested on her hips.

"I know what she told us. In case you haven't noticed I don't always listen." Rolling my eyes I knew that to be true.

"No kidding. Fine. We can go on one condition. We go during the day. They will not suspect anyone during the day, and maybe I'll be able to see my mom and sister too." She nodded stiffly turning to walk away. That's when I noticed something in her hand other than the paper.

"Maylee. Come back for a second." She stopped rigidly. I could tell she knew I had seen something I was not supposed to. Walking around her so we could be face to face I held out my hand. She refused to even look at me as I tried to figure out what the problem seemed to be. "What's in your hand? Let me see it." Glaring she held it out opening it palm up. Blood? "I thought you walked down to the river to clean up?" Nathan walked over seeing the blood frowning as he looked between us. Maylee would not look at me as I asked.

"I did. I just cut that one." She told me quietly looking the opposite direction. The blood began dripping onto the ground. From the corner of my eye I saw Nathan tense stepping back.

"Let me see your arm so I can heal it." Finally she looked up yanking her hand back from me as I almost had it.

"No!" Turning she walked away. I sent up a wall to stop her. Walking into it she turned to me furious. "Cut it out Dante! It's not funny!" Heat started to radiate off of her in waves. Nathan quickly retreated knowing what was coming. It would have been amusing if the situation had not been so serious.

"I'm not being funny Maylee. What happened to your arm?" I demanded walking up to her as she had no where to go with the barrier. "Let me see. I can heal it." I told her calmly but her eyes were electrically charged now. Like lightning was flashing across them. Suddenly I flew backwards away from her landing ten feet away. I stood slowly watching her knowing she could not actually leave. Instead she walked towards me like she was about to start a fist fight. As she walked she pulled up her sleeves holding her arm up for me to see.

"This! This is why I'm bleeding! Are you happy now?!" I was in shock as I stared at her arm.

"Maylee! What have you been doing?" She had slashes up and down her forearm. Some were still fresh leaking blood. Most were thin white scars from months ago or longer.

"You told me your secret. Now you know mine." She told me darkly. Tears began streaming down her face as I gripped her right arm examining it closer.

"How long have you been cutting?" She shrugged unable to look at me once again.

"Years. At first it was a way to escape my emotional pain. Than it became constant. Like an addicting drug. Once you start and use it for a while you're hooked. It's hard to quit." Her other arm was not touched as I inspected some of the cuts she had made.

"I thought you were right handed?" She finally looked at me for the first time in what seemed like hours.

"I am. But I cut left handed. Izabella healed the worst of them when she found me." I thought back to when we were on the island where she was out in my apartment for days. Why had I not noticed then?

"Why now?" I asked her. Taking a deep breath she looked at me evenly.

"Because I'm stressed out. The pressure is getting to me." I looked into her eyes reading her mind finding that she was telling the truth.

"Okay. Give it here." She looked at me taking a step away.

"What?"

"Your arm." I received the same look.

"Why?" She asked shortly keeping her arm against her chest protectively.

"So I can heal the cuts you made. Please?" Relenting she finally held it out looking at me wearily. The cuts healed instantly. She looked her arms over before up to me.

"Why did you feel the need to heal them?"

"To make sure you didn't bleed out. Some of those were pretty deep." She gave me an exasperated look of yeah right continuing to examine her now healed arm.

"You do realize the only way that would have happened is if I had cut the other way." When I glanced to her she looked slightly startled as I was glaring.

"Have you?" She folded her arms across her chest holding her elbows as we walked back to the center of camp.

"No. I thought about it a time or two. But I never did it."
I nodded as we sat near the fire in camp. Nathan was adding a couple logs to his fire.

"How long have you been out scouting?" He looked up at us as if he was expecting Maylee to explode.

"About a week I think. I kinda lost track of time. I was told if I stayed away too long they would come looking for me."

"Who would come looking for you?" Maylee asked tensing. I knew why she was tensing so badly. She was thinking about Kamran who was investigating her attack only a few weeks ago. Who had also been sent to find her when the council thought she was attempting to run away. Luckily Izabella had found us first. I knew if anyone could talk sense into her it was Izabella. It had devastated me to say the least that she had wanted out with as much power as she had. At the same time I understood where she was coming from. Nathan shrugged at her question stirring the fire again.

"They didn't really specify who. Just that they would come looking for me." Maylee gave a nod before rubbing her hands on her knees looking around nervously.

"Why don't the two of us go to Texas like you wanted. It's still daylight." Looking at my phone it read only noon. "In fact it's only noon right now. If we go now we can still make it to Ireland tonight."

"Alright." Standing quickly she grabbed her bag striding to the edge of camp whistling. Her horse Danny appeared within seconds walking up to her calmly nuzzling her shoulder. Looking to the trees I knew Shadow was up there as a dark grey owl swooping down in a flash of light was my horse. Maylee smirked when she saw him transform swinging onto her horse waiting for me to start traveling. I knew it would not take long to from where we were now. Chuckling I shook my head walking up to where she sat on Danny waiting for me to follow suit.

"Maylee. We're in Virginia. We will have to fly again before we ride. Unless you want Izabella to show up and beat both our asses for not following orders." She frowned glancing around before rolling her eyes dismounting.

"You're right. Dragons it is." Taking her bag she slung it over her shoulder walking up in front of me stopping. "I'm sorry. I should have" Pausing she shook her head.

"I understand." Tensing she looked up at me.

"Dante. No. I don't think" Taking her face in my hands I kissed her gently.

"I understand Maylee. I spoke to Izabella about your missing memories. What you have been through. And I understand why it took you so long to come to terms with your feelings." She showed some surprise before closing her eyes.

"And yet you still want to stay with me." I smiled at her moving her hair off her shoulder.

"Like I said before. I would never give you up." Gripping my wrist in her hand she held my hand to her cheek.

"We need to keep moving." Nodding in agreement she released my hand as we mounted the dragons flying to Texas.

As we rode I thought about everything Maylee had been through in the last few days. Hell the last few weeks. When we had flown to Russia I had expected her to make a decision about where she stood on us as a couple. With everything else that had been going on she had kept pushing it away. It was difficult to see her breaking down the way she did. And I knew I should not have added to it. But I wanted to know where she stood and whether to truly stay with her. I was only staying if she wanted me to.

Izabella had told me so many times that Maylee and I were meant to be. She would remind me of the vision I had saw. There was also the fact that when were around each other there was tension. At different times the tension was different. But after Maylee finally admitting what she felt I realized that that had been the exact reason the tension was there. Because she was afraid of a relationship after her last one before we came to the island.

Now we were a damned good team when we worked together. Even as we traveled to my home I did not feel as uneasy as I had before.

Maylee

I finally showed Dante my secret. He was shocked that I had been able to cut myself. He healed the fresh cuts looking at me as if I might do it again. No, I thought. I am not anymore. I need to stop hurting myself. I had insisted that we visit his house before leaving for Ireland knowing it was completely against his better judgment. And all the reasons why. I just felt like he needed to go back to see his mom and sister. They needed to know he was okay.

As we were about to leave Nathan's camp Dante reminded me we were only in Virginia. That meant we would have to fly into Texas but land far enough away we would go unnoticed. Once we landed in Texas we rode on horseback. Not uncommon around there so we did not draw too much attention. Although I had to wear my cloak so it felt weird when people would whip their heads around for a better look. I felt like the grim reaper on horseback without the scythe.

Within two hours of riding we turned walking down a dirt road passing a cemetery. With a jolt I realized it was the one from my dream. I was feeling heavy evil waves from all around all at once. We turned into a long winding driveway that was more like a wide trail. The woods began to clear revealing the house that was now coming into view. It was a plain two story with white siding and blue trim. Across from the house was a huge stable. Not barn. Stable.

I wanted to look around inside but I knew that was out of the question.

"Dante!" I heard the scream of a young girl's voice. I whipped around to see where it had issued from. The girl looked to be around thirteen with long black hair running at him fast. He swung off of Shadow hugging her tight when she ran into him. "I have missed you so much! Where have you been? What have you been doing?" Her questions came fast and curiously. Looking around before he held her at arms length.

"I missed you too Gabby. I will tell you. But first. Where is mom?" He asked his voice concerned as he glanced around. Gabby looked at the ground.

"She's sick again. You can come into the house. Matt's not here. Neither is anyone else. It's just us." She walked to the house leading him. He stopped her with a tap on her shoulder.

"Wait" Looking back he signaled for me to follow. "Come on. It's safe." I looked at him apprehensively. Of course he could not see my face it was covered by my hood. I shook my head pointing to the house indicating he go on. Walking back to where I stood he held a hand out to me. "Come on." I took his hand as his sister looked at him like what the hell? He looked back to her with a smile before asking.

"Where is Matt?"

"Off on one of their missions. I really wish he would renounce them like you did. No matter what I say I cannot convince him." He let go of my hand taking her by the shoulders.

"It's okay. You tried. Just don't think about it too much. Okay?" She looked back at him tears running down her face as she hugged him again.

"Please don't leave again! It's been awful here. Mom's been sick and Matt's either gone or really nasty to us." The poor girl sobbed against him. At first he shook his head as he held her looking lost on what else to do. After a moment Dante looked like he was going to explode in anger.

"Dammit" He said quietly. I could tell by his face that this killed him to hear. That he would stay to protect them if he could. "I'm sorry Gabby. I just can't stay. I'm trying to stop them. Please understand." She nodded sniffling a couple times wiping her face with her shirt.

"I know you are. I just wish you could stay and be with us. Who is that?" Starring at me he stood up right glancing back to where I stood.

"A very good friend of mine. Come on. Let's go in the house. I want to see mom. Than we have to leave." He walked with one arm around his sister's shoulders holding my hand with the other. I didn't remember him taking it.

I was on edge. There was so much evil energy emulating from this place. At the door I stopped. Dante let my hand go before he turned around to see what I was doing. I looked around the entire room before shutting the door behind me. As I had I realized that maybe I should wait outside until he was done.

"Should I wait outside for you?" I asked him as I turned around from the door. He shook his head frowning at me almost like I should have known to ask such a question.

"No. I want you to meet her." I rolled my eyes at him even though he could not see.

"She can't see my face. Or do you want me to pull down my hood long enough for her to see how ugly I am?" He shot me a dirty look. I could almost hear a growl.

"You are not ugly. Don't even go there. Yes. Only long enough for her to see you." He held out his hand to me again. Taking a deep breath I entwined my hand with his. Pulling me along beside him down the hallway with his sister leading the way.

We walked into a rather large room. In the bed sitting up was their mother. I could see where Dante and Gabrielle had inherited their eyes, and facial expressions. She looked up when Gabby walked in. Her face lit up as she seen her son walk in behind her daughter.

"You are alive. Come here son." She sounded amazed she was actually seeing him. He releasing my hand walking over tightly embracing her. I did not think she was going to let go of him. When she finally did he looked her over seriously.

"Did Matt do this?" She gave a look moms give when you should know better. A sharp almost reprimanding look.

"He may be on the wrong side Dante. But he would not intentionally make me sick or hurt us in any way. You should know better than to think such things." She looked up at me curiously. "Who is your friend?" I had stopped in the doorway watching them. Standing from the bed he walked over taking my hand pulling me over to his mom's bedside.

"No. You should not introduce me. What will she think of your travel partner as a girl?" He smirked at me as I stood in front of her bed already glaring at him from under my hood.

"I want you to meet her. And you are much more than my travel partner Maylee. And I cannot wait for the day I can tell her." Sighing as I stood there I knew I was not winning.

"I can not tell you her name because of everything happening. She's with the council. I ran into her almost literally on my way there." His mom's eyebrows had shot straight up when he said "her name" just like I knew. I tugged my hand from his grip.

"Can I take this off now?" I whispered to him. He nodded. Pulling back my hood my hair had fallen out of its band surrounding my face. His mom's face registered shock as she looked at me. I looked to him confused by her reaction.

"Is there something wrong?" He chuckled at me.

"No. Nothing is wrong." He said looking at me strangely. Well. Not so much strangely as it was a look I had received a few times. But usually only when we were alone together. Knowing. He knew that she would like me. Jerk. I cocked an eyebrow at him as he looked away. Looking back to his mom she smiled at me.

"I've just never seen anyone with those colored eyes before. I can see why my son likes you." My eyes widened taking a step back. How could she possibly have known he liked me? Well probably just by the way he's been looking at me since we've been in this room.

"I don't think I'm the only one out there with the color." I was speechless and Dante was enjoying the fact. She nodded at him approving of me. I just looked over to him glaring slightly more as I pulled my hood back up covering my face again.

Even after I had my hood back on she would look at me and smile looking back to her son.

"So you two are traveling together?"

"Yes. We are for now. We've been to a few different places. There were some really beautiful countries. I wish the two of you could come with us." I felt like I was being watched looking around to see it was Gabby who was starring at me. I read her thoughts as she stared.

'*What if Matt finds out they have been here? He will somehow.*' She was just scared as I looked back at her.

"He will not find out. We will make sure of it." Her jaw dropped looking at me in complete shock.

"How did you" Dante had heard me stepping over looking at his sister.

"She has the same powers that I have. And more. I agree. We'll cast a spell over the house so he does not suspect that we were even here." I was worried about his sister. She did not want anyone hurt. I placed my hand on Dante's shoulder causing him to glance back stepping closer.

"Would you like to come with us? We could teach you a lot about the world and magik if you want?" She looked to her brother as if asking him.

"No. I would love to. But my place is right here. Someone in this family has to stay normal." She smiled a little. I had to admire her courage. Gabby reminded me a lot of my sister. Mature for her age.

At that moment I decided that she would need a way to protect herself. And her mother if the time came. I blocked out Dante who was reading my thoughts as I walked out of the room. I could feel the energy coming off of it and followed where it was issuing from. I entered what looked like a workroom. A silver letter opener caught my attention. That was it. I picked it up carrying it back to the room handing it to Gabby. She looked at me oddly.

"You will know when to use it. When that time comes. All you have to do is speak it's name and say reveal. It will be useful when nothing else is." Dante knew what it was cringing as I handed the opener to her. I pulled my hood back so he could see my face. "She will need it. I feel better knowing she has it and knows what it is. At least she would not be defenseless." He raised his eyebrows looking apprehensive.

"You're sure about this?" I looked straight back at him unblinking.

"Yes" He let out a slow deep breath before turning walking to his sister.

"It will be your sword Gabby. But please. Call me before you use it. I will be here as fast as I can." He took her by the shoulders standing before her. "Okay?" She nodded slowly understanding that this was only growing worse.

"Okay, I will keep it close at all times." He glanced back at me as I pulled my hood back up over my face. "We have to go. We have been summoned. I will see you again as soon as possible." She hugged him tight before letting go crying silently as she held the letter opener. Her tears fell onto it as she stared at it. Finally she spoke giving it a name I could not hear.

It lengthened to a hand and a half sword. Pure silver with scrolling on the hilt. No gems, no black worked into it, no gold. I nodded in approval. Dante took a hold of it looking it over. After a few moments he handed it back to her.

"Take care of it. If you need me call or write." She looked at him in alarm.

"How do I call you?" He smirked

"Just call my phone." The sword retracted back into a letter opener as we turned to leave.

Once we were out of the house I cast a spell to keep Matt from knowing we were there. A second one to protect them from anything that might harm them. Dante looked at me in disbelief shaking his head.

"Thank you. Now we better go." Nodding we mounted the horses walking up the long winding driveway to return to where we had left the dragons. Not far ahead I could hear the sound of a running horse coming towards us. An evil vibe told me it was Matt. Sure enough riding at a full tilt run on a big red horse was a teenager around sixteen years old. His face filled with shock before rage on sight of his older brother.

My hand jumped to my hilt instantly. Dante signaled me to wait. Matt came to a halt in front of us pointing at Dante.

"You! What are you doing here?! I told you to never come back!" Full of rage he drew his sword on his brother, and I was overcome by pain. Matt's sword was a dark blade like the one that had almost killed me. My ribs felt like they had been laced open again. Dante looked over at me as I was bent over my horse's shoulder.

"What's wrong?" I looked to Matt as he kept running towards us.

"His blade, it's a dark blade. Just seeing it is making my ribs hurt again." I could barely breathe. Dante had taken his attention away from his brother. Matt was looking at me quizzically.

"Who is that brother? Your secret weapon against us?" He laughed. "Looks pretty weak to me." He raised his sword about to swipe Dante with it but I screamed in rage drawing my own meeting his blade mid air over Dante's head causing sparks to fly.

The pain was gone as our blades met. Dante ducked out from under the blades. Matt swung back again allowing us time to dismount. Once I slid down from Danny Dante held his arm out to stop me.

"No. This is my fight." He turned standing in front of me protectively. I tapped my blade on his shoulder. He glanced back when he saw my sword.

"Allow me. I've been itching to fight for a while." Matt looked me up and down sizing me up for the fight. I stayed covered with my cloak as he started forward. My blade met his for the second time. As time allowed the fight intensified. Matt could barely keep up. With a couple of well placed blows and added quickness I disarmed him. Dante stepped forward to retrieve his sword but I held my hand up stopping him.

"No. I will deal with him." I walked over to where the sword had landed picking it up carefully to not touch the blade itself. He was defeated. His face told the whole story as he was positively furious. I had him backed against a tree so that he could not run from us with no other weapons. I pointed the tip of my sword at his chest. "What are they planning?" I asked using my best interrogative voice. Matt glared at me.

"I don't know. They don't tell me those plans." I dropped his sword four feet away from him to antagonize him.

"Liar!" I spat in disgust. He eyed his sword. I bet he was quick too. It did not take me long to figure out I was better off binding him rather than holding him at sword point. "You are bound to this tree until you answer me." As I spoke I did not remember being taught that one. Matt became wide eyed looking slightly afraid.

"You're a witch! Let me go now!" He bellowed at me. I laughed looking over to Dante. I raised my sword up to Matt's throat.

"I am not a witch." I said slowly in a dangerously low voice. "I am a sorceress. There is a difference. I will not release you until you answer my question." He panicked looking to his older brother.

"Make her let me go!" Dante shook his head smiling crookedly.

"You're on your own here little brother. I learned the hard way. I'm not stopping her."

"Thank you." I told him curtly turning back to Matt. I had began to notice how much he looked like Dante. Only he was meaner, younger, and darker complected probably from travel. He looked up at me furious.

"I can stop you! I know magik too." He struggled against my binding spell spouting some words. My spell did not budge.

"Just answer and I will release you! I don't want to hurt you." My temper flared with his stupidity. Calling on my fire element heat to rolled off of me in waves. I opened my eyes finding I was engulfed in flames.

"You're going to get it now Matt. Just answer her. It would be a lot easier." Dante told him sounding most amused. Matt's eyes were wide with fear and panic.

"Don't burn me! Please! I can't tell you what they are doing or they will kill me!" I turned off my flames as at least he had given an answer.

"At least that was an answer. If you cannot tell me that. You do have the answer to my second question. Where is Annabelle Elder?" He looked over to his brother quizzically.

"She is leading the foreign descendants against council headquarters. They will be invading the coast of Ireland in three hours." I looked to Dante panic stricken.

"Time to go!" He nodded in agreement. We mounted the horses running them as fast as they could go all the way back to the dragons. Once we were much farther away I would unbind Matt but Dante had heard me.

"Leave him! They will find him soon enough." I thought back to books I had read. Wasn't there a way to figure out who cast it?

"Won't they know who did it?"

"No." The horses were slowing on their own as we neared the dragons. Mounting up we signaled them to leave.

"We need to warn Nathan." Looking over he nodded he heard me.

"We have to make it quick. I will send Izabella a letter to warn her."

Once the dragons landed we managed running dismounts into Nathan's camp. Nathan stood quickly walking to us as we bent over trying to catch our breath.

"What happened?" He asked concerned looking from one to another waiting for one of us to answer. Dante held a hand up signaling to give us a minute before answering.

"We ran into my brother on our way back." He told him darkly Nathan looked confused.

"I didn't know you had a brother." Dante nodded. "Are you guys okay?"

"Fine" I managed after catching my breath standing straight. "Although. I think I really freaked him out with my flames." Dante nodded in agreement standing up straight as well.

"You should not have done that. And you should have used my sword, not yours to fight him. They will find out you're alive."

"Are you seriously reprimanding me right now?" I could feel the heat radiating around me. By the look on Nathan's face it was safe to say I was engulfed in flames. "They will find out no matter what or when. They are readying an attack against the council and we're here arguing about whether they know I'm alive or not!" I was nearly screaming. Nathan had hid behind a large tree in case something else happened. Dante shook his head at me. He wasn't looking for a fight.

"We need to be more careful next time. Hopefully there will not be a next time." Taking a deep breath I turned the flames off. Nathan wandered back out to where we were standing. I stepped toward Dante before looking to Nathan.

"We are going to need everyone we have. If I know my sister, her force will be strong." Nathan turned packing up what was left of his camp to relay the message to the island. I turned back to Dante. "I need that spell for my sword." Drawing out star burst I thought about a plain ordinary sword. Closing my eyes Dante and I linked telepathically relaying the spell to me. It glowed golden before revealing a plain sword. There were no markings, or anything special about it. I sheathed it walking to Marlo to check that everything was clear for enemies.

Nathan was finishing tying his gear onto his dragon when I looked over to him. I could feel Dante walking up behind me his hands resting on my hips.

"Are you sure you're okay? When you sensed that dark blade I thought you were having a relapse." I tilted my head so I could see him from the corner of my eye.

"I'm fine." He gripped my hips hard turning me to face him.

"Maylee. Look at me." One hand came off my hip to lift my chin looking into his eyes.

"What?" I asked as he gave me one of those don't start looks.

"Be careful. Please?" He was looking deeply into my eyes. I could tell he was worried.

"As long as I fight a one on one with my witch of a sister. I'll be fine. Come on. No one can hurt me when my guard is up." He knew it was true but still looked apprehensive.

"You still have your dagger?" I scowled for a second.

"Yeah. Why?" He looked calm for the first time in hours.

"Just making sure. Let's go." He released me walking towards Dillon. I bent down reaching into my boot checking for good measure. Yes my dagger was there.

"Dante" He stopped just before climbing aboard Dillon turning to see what I wanted.

"What?" He asked in a normal voice. It was unnerving that he did not act the slightest nervous. While I was scared beyond my own mind. I had battled one on one, even two on twenty. But this was different. I could tell. The feeling that was setting in is that we may or may not live through this. My mind was torn in two. Almost running I was against him wrapping my arms around him holding him tightly. His hand came up holding the back of my head burying his into my shoulder.

"It will be okay. We both have enough training for this. I know you are more than capable of kicking their asses." Pulling back he smiled at me. "Be careful. Watch your back." Nodding at his advice he pulled me close again touching our foreheads.

"I have never been this nervous about a fight. This just feels different. Something about it is unnerving me." He nodded bringing my chin up we kissed. It seemed more electric than usual as we were as close to each other as we could be. Finally he pulled back both of us were breathless as we looked at each other. "I wish things could have been different." Confusion crossed his face as he held my face in his hands.

"What are you talking about?" I took his hands off of my face.

"I'm going to die before this is over Dante. It's always some foretold bullshit with anything like this. It's completely cliché but it is almost always true. You should find someone else to be with." He sighed holding my face again smirking.

"I know what the prophecy says. Neither of us will die. I love you Maylee." Smiling he kissed me again keeping our foreheads touching.

"I love you Dante." His smile could not have been any larger. He chuckled before looking around.

"I think we better go. We have a battle to win." Smiling I nodded.

"Yeah we should." We quickly mounted our dragons taking off for the coast of Ireland.

Izabella

Huffing as I walked through the beach sand to the cliff wall looming ahead up to where the door would open. It took a lot to rile my anger as much as the council has the last few weeks. Today they decided to cross the line. Far far over the line. The stone door in the cliff wall opened as I approached sensing my powers. As I walked the hallway the torches were already lit as I stopped in front of the double doors that were where the council deliberated. Without a second thought I kicked the door open. All six members jumped violently as I stopped in front of their table.

"YOU HAVE TO BE FUCKING JOKING!" Aliyah stood from her chair looking exasperated.

"Izabella. To what do we owe this unexpected visit? And rage? I do not believe I have saw this side of you in"

"Cut the bullshit Aliyah. I know what you lot did." The five other members looked to her as she stood smirking back at me.

"I believe I do not know what you are"

"You sent your brother to kill Maylee." The others members made sounds of shock before watching the two of us like a tennis match.

"She is a liability. Dante has more than enough power to be our champion. We do not need her. In case you did not notice Kam did not kill her. He was reprimanded upon return for failing his mission." My rage bristled barely contained.

"Maylee is not a liability. She has to be taught to control her powers when she becomes emotional. What you did to her when they arrived was unfair. You saw what she is capable of. She is as strong as the three of us. Train her. Give her a chance to show you what she is truly capable of." Aliyah shook her head.

"No. When she returns I will kill her myself. As I told you. Maylee is a liability and will be eliminated." Chris and Keira made sounds of protest.

"Aliyah" Keira spoke up shaking her head dismally. "I am with Izabella on this. Maylee is full of raw power. I know Izabella has taught her control on Ettoupaviog. Her intentions are pure. Maylee wants to help. I vote that we allow Maylee time to train here." There was a murmur of agreement among the five members. Angrily Aliyah slammed her fist on the table growling in her throat.

"Fine. But I will push her to her limits."

"You pushed her to her limit with your damn test. If Dante had not stopped her she would have died and taken him with her. Along with your headquarters." Aliyah smiled wide standing straight.

"Yes. I was not expecting her to hold the power she does. But that does not change the fact she is a liability." My teeth ground in anger. The only reason Aliyah wanted Maylee eliminated was she knew Maylee had the power to choose to not follow orders. I finally shook my head smirking.

"I think I have you figured out Aliyah. You tell us in your opinion Maylee is a liability. She is not a liability. Her powers match ours so that you do not have the ability to control her. Even if you applied a rein to her. Which is why Kamran refused to kill her. He knows what she is."

"Kamran wants nothing more than to fuck her. I gave the order to keep her in his sights after her assessment. I ordered him to cast a spell on her to seek him out. Instead Shadow helped her escape Kamran."

"Shadow knows what Maylee is to Dante. His memory was not erased as theirs were. If you want Dante to be your champion instead of Maylee. You will kill him. They are twin flames Aliyah. Not soul mates. Twin flames. One cannot live on if the other dies. And they have bonded already. Just in the last two weeks. That was how Dante stopped her yesterday. Through their bond. Now. Since the rest of the council has decided to allow her to train here I will be visiting to ensure you do not attempt to eliminate her in training." The others murmured looking at each other.

"Fine. I will grant her immunity while she is in training. Bring her back by sunset. Or she will be punished for leaving without permission. Along with Dante. And since we are on the subject." Aliyah turned walking down to where I stood.

"You will not injure or maim him for a reaction from Maylee. Not only would she react. I would be here within minutes insuring you are removed from the council immediately for crimes against our own." Aliyah smiled wide stopping in front of me with her back to the five other members.

"Do not worry Izabella. I will be fair to her. We need to speak about your other charge. Away from them." She indicated with a look over her shoulder. They all stood leaving the room so that we were alone.

"I swear if you hurt him because you are hell bent on killing her"

"Enough Izabella." She growled cutting me off. "If we were going to kill him it would have been a few days ago when Theo told him he was on their kill list knowing he was actually working for us. He failed his mission. We should have killed him for it. The full council decided he was to live. I agreed knowing he may replace Maylee as the one we need to win this war. Even if he refuses to use his powers. I have ways of changing that."

"You set him up to fail. He was terrified you would show up the night he returned to kill him."

"A Farraro terrified of being killed for failing their mission. Very unlike his family. Weak of mind." Shaking her head she glanced to the door. "I will be fair when they return. However"

"I know. By tonight. You said as much. I will go" The doors opened as a lady from the back rooms ran in with a paper in hand.

"They are attacking here tonight." She handed Aliyah the paper. Wide eyed she nodded handing it back looking to me determinedly.

"Get them here. Now Izabella." Nodding I walked out of the conference room to the dark hall. Once on the beach I shimmered back to the United Kingdom where I left them when Maylee had tried to run away. They were gone. Dammit. They knew how to test my patience.

Acknowledgements

I would like to take this opportunity to thank my family for supporting my dream of publishing my books. Since I was a child I wanted to be an author. After graduating high school in 2006 I began the process of creating this storyline. The first draft was handwritten in lined notebooks while I attended college. Never would I have dreamed that this would become a reality in time. Thank you for your support.

About the Author

I grew up in the Mid Michigan area riding horses and working on cars with my dad. Up until my early twenties I actively showed horses. I took a decade long hiatus until my daughter was three riding her ponies in lead line classes. The past couple years we have taken another break to enjoy life on our three acre farm with our dogs one blue merle mini Aussie Merlin and Chocolate Labrador Pitbull mix Fudge. A flock of chickens, black pony Mariah and lastly my bay paint Bugatti. On my weekends off my daughter and I enjoy traveling and kayaking.